PRAISE FOR THE NOVELS OF JOHN W. CAMPBELL
AWARD–WINNING AUTHOR AMY THOMSON . . .

Through Alien Eyes

"*Through Alien Eyes* updates Robert Heinlein's *Stranger in a Strange Land* with a gentler and more modern message."
—*The Denver Post*

"A solid, convincing story of human paranoia and the potential disaster it could cause when we finally meet an intelligence that doesn't look, or think, the same way we do."
—*Science Fiction Chronicle*

"An unusually thoughtful novel of first contact."
—*Publishers Weekly*

"A suspenseful plot and stellar characterization distinguish a tale ultimately concerned with environmental, political, and moral issues."
—*Booklist*

"A thoughtful view of human nature filtered through the perceptions of a pair of engaging and well-meaning, though sometimes unpredictable, aliens."
—*Library Journal*

The Color of Distance

"A long and loving evocation of a complex alien ecology."
—*The Washington Post Book World*

"Fast-paced, suspenseful science fiction presenting intelligent sentient life, different enough from our own to be fascinating and defined enough to be believable . . . terrific."
—*VOYA*

continued . . .

"An energetic and entertaining first-contact novel, complete with charming, strange, dangerous aliens and two intelligent, competent, imperfect heroines, one human, one not."
—Vonda N. McIntyre, author of *Nautilus*

"Intriguing."   —*Locus*

Virtual Girl

"Definitely not your usual girl-grows-up story. An entertaining and observant look at human beings from a computer's point of view. A diverting and highly promising first novel."   —*Locus*

"A promising debut novel with a decidedly different point of view."   —*Science Fiction Chronicle*

"A very good book in many ways and a superior first novel. Absorbing and suspenseful. It's worth your time and money to introduce yourself to Maggie. An engaging and believable character."   —*Aboriginal Science Fiction*

"A coming-of-age novel for the cyberpunk era . . . with a depth of compassion not found in most."   —*The Denver Post*

"An excellent first novel. Grabs your attention and doesn't let go."   —*Kliatt*

"Steeped in tradition with a '90s sensibility, state-of-the-art technology, and a complexity of characterization reminiscent of Shelley. Thomson's robot isn't a generic automaton. She's real."   —*Minneapolis Star Tribune*

Storyteller

AMY THOMSON

ACE BOOKS, NEW YORK

An Ace Book
Published by The Berkley Publishing Group,
a division of Penguin Group (USA) Inc.,
375 Hudson Street, New York, New York 10014.

First edition: December 2003

Library of Congress Cataloging-in-Publication Data

Thomson, Amy.
　Storyteller / Amy Thomson.—1st ed.
　　p. cm.
　ISBN 0-441-01094-6
　1. Storytelling—Fiction. 2. Parent and child—Fiction. I. Title.

PS3570.H64648S76 2003
813'.54—dc22

2003057926

To my daughter, Katherine Chán Yuán Vick, who not only taught me to think outside the box, but also how to put the box on my head and wear it like a hat.

And to my wonderful husband, Edd Vick, who also looks pretty good wearing a box as a hat.

ACKNOWLEDGMENTS

Writing a large book while raising a small child is nearly impossible without good child care. I want to thank the following people who looked after Katie while I wrote:

Tanya King, Teresa Glenn, and the staff of the José Martí Child Development Center.

And many thanks to my husband, Edd Vick, who is not only the world's greatest dad (just ask our daughter!), but also listened to me maunder on endlessly about Thalassa and the harsels, and proofread far beyond the call of marital duty.

And to the members of my writers group, Sound on Paper: Leslie and Chris Lightfoot, Roberta Tower, Laura Staley, Kara Dalkey, and Edd Vick, for their thorough and detailed critiques.

I also wanted to thank the following people for their help in getting the fiddly little details right:

Loren MacGregor for double-checking my Greek.

Jihane Billacois for double-checking my Arabic.

The Seattle Public Library Quick Information Line for providing near-instantaneous responses to all kinds of unusual questions. Not only were they fast, they answered even the strangest questions without laughing once.

Kelly Sandy, Sid Stillwaugh, Mickey Moss, Howard Mojfield, and Tom Kendrick from the National Oceanic and Atmospheric Administration for advice and reassurance on ocean tides on Thalassa.

My brothers Joseph and Michael Thomson, for all sorts of strange oceanic and nautical details. Any mistakes of language, grammar, and fact are my fault entirely.

The following people provided inspiration:

Jean Olivier Héron for his wonderful print, *Comment Naissant les Bateaux, planche 2: Le Coter (sloop).* This print gave me the initial idea for the harsels. Readers wishing to view this picture and more of Héron's work may seek it out at:<http://www.jeanolivierheron.com/>.

Kim Graham, a sculptor of truly extraordinary talent, for helping me sculpt a harsel. Actually creating a creature that had only existed in my mind was an incredible experience. Wow!

And Bill McKinzie and Captain Eric Kellen. Thanks for the lovely cruise!

Geoff Taylor's marvelous book *Whale Sharks: The Giants of Ningaloo Reef* lived next to my desk while I was writing this book. It provided much useful information about large plankton feeders. I confess that occasionally I took it out when I was bored just to look at the wonderful pictures.

Other books that were inspirational, evocative, or just plain useful were:

Corsica: Portrait of a Granite Island and *The Dream Hunters of Corsica*, both by Dorothy Carrington.

The Pillars of Hercules by Paul Theroux.

My Family and Other Animals by Gerald Durrell.

Patrick O'Brian's amazing Aubrey / Maturin series (of course!).

Ted Brewer Explains Sailboat Design and *Understanding Boat Design, 4th Edition* also by Ted Brewer.

And finally to my mother Muriel Thomson and to Lindblad Expeditions and their wonderful ship, the *Lindblad Explorer*. During my childhood they took me to islands ranging from Attu to Zanzibar and fostered a lifelong love of islands and island ecologies that has cropped up in almost every one of my books.

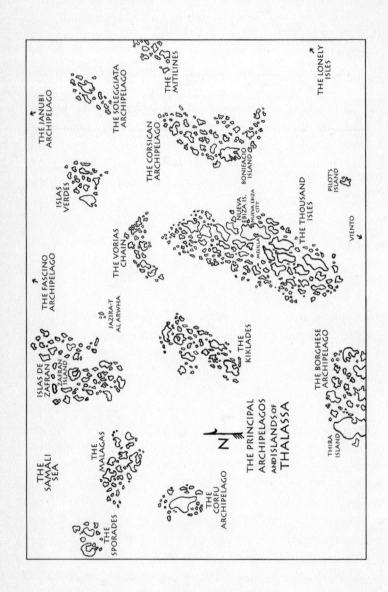

CHAPTER 1

SAMAD SAW A CROWD FORMING. CURIOUS, he pushed his way through the press of people to see what was going on. A storyteller, wrapped in her Guild's traditional brightly colored shawl, was rattling her drum to signal the beginning of a performance. The teller was an old woman with iron-gray hair. Her skin was weathered to the color of oiled leather, and a deep web of wrinkles radiated out from the corners of her olive-green eyes. It had been a long time since Samad had heard a story, and he longed to stay and listen. This storyteller looked like she knew a lot of good tales.

A merchant, richly dressed in a tunic of off-world shimmercloth decorated with several rows of expensive metal buttons, glared down at Samad. The man pointedly shifted his fat, jingling purse and comm unit to the other side of his belt. The merchant's haughty gesture reminded Samad that he had nothing to give the storyteller in return for her story.

Longing weighed like a cold stone in his empty belly as he looked around for a way to slip quietly out of the crowd.

Just then, the storyteller caught his eye. An ironic and surprisingly mischievous smile creased her leather-brown face, deepening the web of wrinkles round her eyes. Samad found himself smiling back. She winked at him, then looked away. A wave of misery washed over Samad. He was caught between offending the storyteller and incurring a debt he could not pay. He would have to slip away as soon as the story began. If he didn't hear her tale all the way through, he wouldn't have to give her a gift.

The storyteller set aside her drum and drew herself up, waiting until the murmuring audience quieted. Then she began to speak in a rich voice that lent the rough local Arabic a dignified, almost majestic feel.

"This is a story about the Pilot, and how she came to our world. Most of you know some of the Pilot's story. We don't know how many of the legends are true; but the Pilots Union records show that a Jump pilot was stranded in this system nearly five hundred years ago, a decade before Thalassa's first pioneers arrived.

"Although the Pilot was never found, the first pioneers found herds of livestock and young orchards of Terran fruit trees on dozens of islands, as well as caches of preserved fruit, vegetables, and meat.

"The pioneers also discovered a space shuttle and the remains of human habitation on Pilot's Island in the Summer Sea. The Pilot's body was never found. Perhaps she died; perhaps she never existed at all. The legends we have about the Pilot may or may not be true, but generations of our people have kept her alive by telling her stories."

The storyteller paused to sip from a worn plastic cup. Then she leaned forward, as though about to impart a secret to her audience.

"Imagine a cramped, battered old freighter that had hauled goods around the Ring of Worlds for many decades. It was almost five hundred years ago, during the time of the Second Expansion. This ancient freighter's Jump pilot had been pushing ships through Jump Space for nearly forty years. She was long overdue for burnout. Back then, there were so few people with the Talent for Jumping that every pilot was kept flying right up to the edge of burnout and sometimes beyond. Since she was considered a likely candidate for burnout, this pilot was only allowed solo, low-priority shipping runs to the outer colonies. She didn't mind. She could still Jump, and that was what mattered to her. Her home world, her family, her friends were all mere shadows in comparison to her desire to experience the ecstasy and mystery of Jump Space one more time.

"But during the last couple of Jumps, the Pilot's Talent had begun flickering in and out. Her course lay through an uninhabited system where she would drop off some survey probes to investigate a possible colony planet, and then on to Epsilon Eridani, where she could get a complete checkup.

"As she approached the system, the Pilot started to push the ship back into real space. Suddenly her talent faltered and then winked out completely. For one terrifying moment, she was caught in the shift between Jump Space and real space. A red-hot needle of fire lanced through her brain as the freighter lurched and juddered, slamming back into real space as though dropped from a great height.

"The Pilot slumped against the worn cushions of her Jump chair and shut her eyes. There was only an aching void where her Talent had been.

"Pain flared again in the Pilot's head as she opened her eyes. Her console was alive with flashing red warning lights. She sat up, fighting the pain, and began dealing with all the systems that had gone haywire during the rough transition to real space. When the last warning light had changed to a safe, serene blue, and the ship was safely on a new course, the Pilot staggered to the autodoc. She entered her symptoms and then set the sensor net on her head. The net tightened, and she winced at the familiar prickling sensation as the sensors dug into her skin, seeking neurons to probe. She felt a sudden warmth and tingling over various parts of her skull as the sensors mapped her brain.

"The autodoc hummed for several minutes, then spat out a diagnosis that confirmed her fears. Her Talent was gone. She would never Jump again. She was trapped in this empty system. She thumbed approval for her treatment, and the autodoc hissed as it sprayed a dose of painkillers and sedatives into her arm. She stumbled to her bunk, fell in, and was asleep almost instantly.

"She slept for a long time, and woke slowly, feeling wooly and a bit vague. A faint twinge in her head was the only remnant of the previous night's agony. Then she remembered what had happened. Her piloting Talent had burned out, and she was marooned here. It would be a couple of months before she was missed, and more months, possibly years, before a pilot could be scheduled to search for her.

"She would have to survive for a year or more on this cramped freighter, living on recycled ship rations. And even if she were rescued, she would be Talentless and planetbound. Washed up. She had lived for those ecstatic moments in Jump Space. Now she would never feel that sweet, timeless joy again.

"A tide of grief threatened to overwhelm the Pilot. She paced the length of the crew quarters, no more than a dozen strides long, fighting the despair that threatened to overwhelm her. She still had to deploy the survey probes. Only when the probes were safely away could she think about the next step.

"It would be five long weeks before the Pilot's ship reached orbit around the planet to be surveyed. Once the initial course corrections were entered, there was little to do besides basic maintenance and housekeeping. To keep busy, she inventoried the freighter's hold. The ship's cargo included a wide array of tools, housing kits, and even an agricultural tissue bank, complete with incubators, all scheduled for delivery to a colony world farther out on her aborted run. There was plenty of equipment useful for surviving on the surface of a habitable world, if the planet proved habitable.

"Even the busywork was not enough to keep her mind off of her fate. Several times she set a sharp knife to her wrists and thought about opening her veins, but she still had a mission to complete. And there were better ways for a pilot to die. Besides, she didn't have the nerve to do it.

"The Pilot felt a heavy relief when the ship finally reached orbit, and she could begin launching the probes. Soon her mission would be completed, and then she could think about an end to her pain.

"It took only a day to deploy the survey probes, but her mission plan required her to make sure they were operational and to log their preliminary reports. She looked down at the blue, cloud-swathed world turning below her and wondered if it was as beautiful as it appeared from space.

"The preliminary survey data revealed a living world filled with promise. The air was breathable and the climate temperate. Though there were no continent-sized landmasses, the planet's vast ocean was dotted with millions of islands, green with vegetation.

"Someday humans would come here, and they would make this world their home. The Pilot was bitterly pleased that the loss of her Talent had not been wasted on a barren, inhospitable planet. She logged the preliminary report and methodically began shutting down the ship.

"A few hours later, the old freighter was dark, quiet, and beginning to grow cold. The Pilot paused to reread the note she had placed on her console, then took one final look around at the ship that had carried her so far. At least it would survive this trip, even if she would not.

"The Pilot climbed into the waiting shuttle and buckled herself into the pilot's seat. She flicked through the startup procedures and felt the gratifying rumble of the powerful engines. With deft touches on the attitude-control buttons, the Pilot guided the shuttle gently away from the ship.

"For a long moment, the Pilot admired the planet below her. There were islands below the shuttle now, scattered flecks of green and brown on the deep blue ocean, veiled by white whorls of cloud. She pointed the shuttle straight down at the blue, blue ocean below her and punched the ignition on the main engines.

"The shuttle's acceleration shoved the Pilot back into her seat. She smiled grimly and watched the planet grow nearer in the forward view port until its blue and white island-flecked immensity filled her vision. This world was beautiful, so beautiful that it brought tears to her eyes. She felt a sudden twinge of regret that she'd never live to explore it.

"The navigational computer began bleating warnings about an incorrect atmospheric insertion. She turned off the sound and ignored the flashing lights as the ship dove toward the planet. Suddenly, the words *Safety Override* appeared on the computer screen. The controls froze up and refused to respond. With a loud roar, the attitude jets cut in, pushing the nose of the shuttle up and away from the gleaming blue ocean.

"The Pilot swore and yanked on the steering yoke, but it didn't respond. She tried to shut off the navcomp, but the controls were completely dead. The craft shuddered as it hit the atmosphere, slowing even further. She watched helplessly as the shuttle steered itself onto a safe glide path and splashed down in the ocean, bobbing like a cork on the choppy sea.

"The Pilot sat in her chair and swore until anger, frustration, and grief overwhelmed her. Then she finally wept.

"Gradually, the Pilot became conscious of an eerie sense of presence in her mind, as though someone was staring over her shoulder. It was so strong that she looked behind her to see if there was someone else in the shuttle. She felt the mental presence respond with ringing chimes that somehow evoked curiosity and amusement. A sudden wave of terror passed over her. Was she going crazy?

"Opening the hatch, the Pilot surveyed the vast expanse of dark-blue ocean. Crazy or not, it didn't matter. It was time to finish things. If she couldn't die one way, she would die another. She crawled out onto the hull of the wildly rocking shuttle, clinging to the handholds designed for zero-g work.

"A wave broke against the side of the shuttle, drenching her. The water was cold enough to make her gasp for breath. *Good,* she thought grimly, *I'll die even faster.* The Pilot crawled to the tail of the shuttle and pulled herself upright. She looked down at the deep blue, choppy sea, and then jumped in. The cold water numbed her and dragged at her baggy coveralls as it closed over her head. The trapped air inside her clothes pulled her back up to the surface. The powerful swell shoved and dragged at her until she was dizzy and disoriented.

"The sense of a mental presence felt even stronger now. It rang in her mind like bells chiming in an underwater cathedral. The presence's feeling of curiosity had a dissonant thread of concern running through it as it watched her.

"A cold, choppy wave slapped the Pilot as she drew breath. She choked on the salty water. Her body struggled reflexively against the cold, dark ocean as she slipped beneath the rise of another swell. Underwater, with no choppy swell to fight against, it was easier to let go and sink through the cold water toward death.

"Something bumped her legs. Fear shot through her. Her eyes snapped open, but all she could see was a dark shadow rising beneath her. The huge presence suddenly seemed as omnipresent as the ocean itself, radiating calmness and reassurance. Then something rough-skinned and massive lifted the Pilot out of the icy water.

"Her body took a huge, grateful breath of air while her mind struggled to grasp what had happened. She was lying on the broad back of a very large sea creature. Its purplish gray skin was as rough as sandpaper.

"Behind her she heard a billowing rustle. She looked up. An iridescent purple and pink sail had unfurled from the creature's back. She stared at the sail for a long moment, too chilled and stupid with shock to take it in. Then she crawled behind the towering sail to get out of the chilly, relentless wind.

"Once out of the wind, she felt warmer almost immediately. The brilliant sun warmed her dark, quick-drying uniform. Gradually, her shivers began to ease.

"Coming slowly back to herself, she examined what she could see of the creature. The exposed area of the creature's back was almost five meters long and some three meters across at its widest point, and there seemed to be far more of the creature underwater.

"The mast was thicker than her thigh at its base and towered nearly eight meters over her head. It was jointed like a wing, with long, flat ribs running across the towering, translucent sail. The sail shaded from deep purple near the mast to pale pink at its trailing edges. The gleaming, improbable sail's beauty lifted her exhausted spirits.

"She felt the presence in her mind glow in response to her admiration. Sudden realization dawned in her shocked and sodden brain. The strange presence in her mind came from the creature.

" 'What are you?' she whispered, awestruck.

"A complex song resounded in her mind. It began with the harsh, laughing cry of some kind of sea bird. The song also held within it the endless surge and swell of the ocean, and the stretched tension of wind against a living sail, combined with a sense of ancient time. Like Jump Space, it was too big for her to take in. It seemed to fill the aching void in her mind where her Talent had been. She closed her eyes and let the song resonate in her bones. There was a surge of pleasure from the huge creature at her response.

" 'I'll call you a harsel,' she decided. The word held in it the cry of the birds and a hint of the sail. The rest remained as inexpressible as the vastness of the sea or the depths of Jump Space.

"A deep, resonant gong sounded in the Pilot's mind. She sensed acceptance and approval.

"Then the harsel urged her to move. Tentatively, she headed toward what she supposed was the creature's nose until she was in front of the mast. Another deep peal sounded, and the huge creature turned, cutting a smooth, tight curve in the water. The sail fluttered as they turned into the wind, then bellied out into the place where she'd been standing. The creature had wanted her to get out of the way of the moving sail.

"She realized that she had no idea where the creature was taking her. 'Where are we going?' she asked it.

"She felt the harsel query her. Her gaze fell on the white shape of the shuttle, which was surprisingly far away now. They had sailed farther than she had thought. She felt a sudden surge of fear. She didn't want to lose the shuttle, her only link to the orbiting freighter.

" 'The shuttle. Please take me back there.'

"The harsel gonged acknowledgment, and turned back toward her shuttle.

"The Pilot sheltered against the towering sail, letting the brilliant sun warm her as they sailed toward the shuttle. Her uniform was still damp and chilly, and she realized that she was hungry and thirsty. Apparently this was not her day to die.

"The harsel tolled its approval of her decision. It wanted to know more about her. She could feel the surge of its curiosity, all the questions it longed to ask of her, competing with the creature's resolve to wait until she was fed and rested. The Pilot smiled and rested a tired hand on the harsel's broad, rough-skinned back. 'Thank you. I will answer your questions later. I promise.'

"She felt the harsel's surge of pleasure. It arched itself higher in the water and tightened its sail, speeding up until the water foamed at its sides and spray began to fly.

" 'Careful!' the Pilot exclaimed, when a clot of cold spray drenched her again.

"The harsel contritely slowed down, continuing on to the shuttle at a more sedate pace.

"The huge alien sidled carefully up to the rolling, pitching shuttle. The Pilot grabbed one of the shuttle's handholds and let the rise of the swell lift her off the harsel's back. She scrambled up the side of the shuttle into the warm, familiar shelter of the small spacecraft.

"Inside the shuttle, the Pilot could feel the harsel's presence in her mind, regarding her with a mixture of curiosity, fascination, and amusement. She reached out to it, grateful for the company, and it responded with an inward pulse of welcome. The Pilot felt the knot of pain inside her ease. She was no longer alone.

"Bracing herself against the buoyant shuttle's wild rocking, she put on a warm, dry coverall and opened a self-heating ration pack. The hot food drove the last of the chill from her bones. When she was finished eating, she settled herself in the pilot's chair to think things over. All that seawater seemed to have blunted her death wish. But if she wasn't going to die right away, what should she do next?

"She needed to return to the freighter and bring back supplies for a more permanent settlement. But her suicidal plunge and the subsequent override had left her without enough fuel to reach the freighter. So she would need to set up the shuttle's emergency fuel distiller. But distilling volatile shuttle fuel would be too dangerous on this bobbing cork of a shuttle. She needed solid ground. And that meant finding an island.

"Calling up the preliminary survey maps on the computer, the Pilot began searching for a suitable island.

"As she did this, the harsel focused on her with sudden, intense interest. The Pilot smiled and let the harsel watch through her eyes as she zoomed the survey map through several successively wider views, until a full view of the planet's surface was visible. Suddenly the harsel's understanding rang jubilantly through the Pilot's mind. The harsel was wildly excited at this new view of its world.

"The Pilot pointed out the closest island on the map and explained her need to reach dry land. The harsel disagreed. It guided the Pilot's attention to another island a little farther away. After a long and confusing interchange involving a lot of incomprehensible underwater landmarks, she realized that this island had a better harbor.

" 'All right,' she said. 'How long will it take to get there?'

"There was another long, confusing series of mental images that seemed to be about duration.

" 'I don't understand,' she replied with a sense of bewilderment.

"The harsel sent her a mental picture of the shuttle following a harsel.

" 'Yes,' she replied. 'How far?'

"The harsel radiated confusion. The Pilot closed her eyes and visualized sunrise and then sunset, one full day. 'How many sunrises and sunsets?' she asked inwardly.

"The harsel gonged understanding, a sound the Pilot heard both in her mind and faintly through her ears.

"Two full days flared and died in her mind's eye. Two days' travel, at the harsel's rate of speed. It was more than 400 kilometers by the map. She didn't have enough fuel to go more than a third of the distance. Could she persuade the harsel to tow her?

"In a flurry of images, the Pilot suggested the idea to the harsel. It pondered the idea for a while, trying to understand what she was asking. The harsel swam around the shuttle, gauging its size.

"Then it sent her the strangest picture of all. The harsel wanted her to put the shuttle inside of it.

"Her blank confusion amused the harsel. When its laughter ceased ringing in her mind, it told her to go outside and look. The harsel surfaced next to the shuttle. The Pilot gaped in amazement as its back split open, releasing a flood of seawater. Empty of water, the harsel rose higher in the water, revealing its entire length. Now she could see that the huge creature was shaped like a large, wide-bodied fish. It was more than twenty meters long and far wider than she had expected.

" 'May I look inside?' she asked.

"The harsel assented. She climbed out of the shuttle and leaped onto the creature's broad back. The opening ran from the back of its sail to the base of its tail. Peering inside the huge chamber, the Pilot was even more amazed. The chamber was enormous, with wide, flat ribs curving up to a ceiling six meters high.

"Gathering her courage, the Pilot lowered herself into the vast space. Once inside, she could hear the one-two-three beat of the harsel's heart, sounding like a ponderous, stuttering drum. The vaulted chamber of its hold was lined with tough, rubbery skin. Cold seawater sloshed around her ankles, and barnacles crunched under the soles of her shoes as she paced off the length of the space. Small, brightly colored fish darted in to snatch up the crushed shellfish. There was the marine smell of very fresh fish, with an odd, spicy hint of cinnamon and the clean scent of citrus. With its wings fully retracted, the shuttle would fit inside with a little room to spare.

" 'It won't hurt you?' the Pilot asked.

" 'NO.' The harsel replied, using its first human word. Then it sent an image of the shuttle moving inside very slowly.

" 'But we must be careful,' the pilot told the harsel.

" 'YES. CAREFUL.'

"The Pilot was relieved that the huge alien was learning her language. The creature's bell-like mind speech was beyond her.

"She climbed out of the harsel's vast hold and stood watching as the harsel submerged, then came up in front of the shuttle. It opened its back very wide. The Pilot retracted the shuttle's wings as far as they could go. Steering with quick squirts of the booster engines, she eased the shuttle slowly into the harsel's gaping hold. It slid inside with only a couple of barnacle-scraping bumps. The walls of the small spacecraft creaked a bit as the harsel closed its ballast chamber, but no harm was done. The wind caught the harsel's sail, and they were on their way.

"The Pilot spent much of the two-day trip riding on the harsel's broad back. She communed with the huge creature, learning its ways and working out the basics of a common mental language. The Pilot fascinated the harsel. It bombarded her with endless questions about life on land and in space.

"Oddly enough, space travel and zero gravity made more sense to the harsel than life on land. It found walking extremely funny. And the concept of falling seemed utterly unbelievable to a creature that had lived its entire life in the embrace of the ocean.

"When her mind grew tired of stretching itself around the harsel's alien thoughts, the Pilot stood on the shuttle with a portable lantern and cleaned off the barnacles, weeds, and burrowing parasites from the vaulted roof of the harsel's hold.

"The harsel responded with intense pleasure, as though a long-endured itch was finally being scratched. The brightly colored fish gorged themselves on the falling barnacles and the bloody remains of the crushed parasites. Soon the little fish began following the Pilot, swimming around her legs like a flock of hungry cats.

"It was just after noon on the second day when they reached the island. The shuttle floated out of the harsel even more easily than it went in. The Pilot beached the shuttle, climbed out, and became the first human to set foot on Thalassa.

"She found a nice spot overlooking the little cove where she had first landed and began setting up a campsite. The harsel's presence rode along in her mind as she worked, utterly fascinated by dry land. Their mental bond had grown stronger during the trip, and she welcomed the great fish's company.

"The next morning, after setting up the fuel distiller to

begin refueling the shuttle, the Pilot climbed to the island's central peak. The far side of the peak ended in a sheer cliff, overlooking a boulder-strewn gravel field far below. She looked at the bottom of the cliff, far below her. One step out into nothing, and she could accomplish what she had come to this world to do. The harsel could not stop her. But—

"To her surprise, she found that she wanted to live. Part of her still yearned for Jump Space, but the harsel's mind-song had turned it into a bittersweet ache rather than a longing for oblivion.

"She turned around and looked back the way she had come, the green, green island, full of wonders she had yet to explore. Her gaze went wider, out over the dark blue, shining sea. In the distance she could see other islands, and she knew from the survey maps that there were millions more scattered over the blue ocean. There was whole new world to explore.

"The Pilot started back down the hill. She had a great deal of work to do in order to build a life here.

"But that's a tale for another day," the storyteller concluded. "I will be telling the next story in the Pilot's Cycle tomorrow, at two o'clock and four o'clock, here in the Market."

The story over, Samad came back to himself with a rush of horror. He had been drawn into hearing the whole tale, and now he was obligated to pay the teller. With a growing sense of shame, he watched the rest of the audience drop money, buttons, and other small gifts into the storyteller's bowl. His pockets were empty. The rich merchant who had scowled at him earlier tossed a heavy ten-centino coin into her bowl. The coin landed with a metallic clatter, knocking a scatter of beautifully carved wood and bone buttons out of the bowl. Samad saw several people in the audience frown. The storyteller looked up at the man. Compared with her quiet dignity, the wealthy merchant seemed cheap and over-dressed.

"My family is descended from the Pilot," the merchant declared in a haughty, carrying voice. "It's good to hear someone tell her story. You must come and tell stories to my children some evening."

"Perhaps," the storyteller allowed in a noncommittal tone of voice.

"Then I will expect you tomorrow night around eight," the merchant told her.

"Sadly, ser, I am engaged both tonight and tomorrow night at Voula's Taverna. But you could bring your family to hear me later this afternoon. The presence of a prominent family such as yours will encourage others to take an interest in our illustrious pioneer ancestors."

The merchant seemed to swell with pride. "Then I will bring them to listen."

"Thank you, ser," the storyteller said, bowing low. "I shall look forward to your presence."

Samad thought he saw a grimace flicker over the storyteller's features as she bowed, but she wore a dignified smile when she stood up to thank the audience for their gifts.

The story had seemed like such a rich banquet while it was being told. Now he was a poor beggar again, unable to pay for what he had just been given. He was desperately tired of living off other people's charity and scavenging food from richer people's garbage. There was nothing in his pockets but lint. He couldn't even afford buttons for his tattered shirt. It was held together with ties of frayed string.

His empty stomach grumbled as he walked past a pile of golden loaves marked with the distinctive crown-and-flower pattern of Perez's Bakery. Tonight, the other bakers would give away their stale loaves. But by then the storyteller would be eating a hot meal at the taverna. He'd tasted

Voula's cooking before. Even cold from the trash, her food was good. The storyteller wouldn't be interested in a loaf of stale, dry bread.

Perez never gave any of his loaves away. He chased off anyone who begged for bread, never giving so much as a crumb to those in need. Samad wished that someone would punish Perez for his miserly ways. He looked again at the mound of golden, crusty loaves, and temptation overwhelmed him.

Ignoring his protesting conscience, Samad bent as though he was removing a stone from his shoe. He watched the baker from the corner of his eye, waiting until the man's full attention was on a customer. Then he slipped a half loaf up his sleeve and walked casually on without a backward glance. Just as he thought he'd gotten away with it, a hand fell on his shoulder. It was Perez's apprentice, a gangling, pimply faced teenager.

"I saw you take that loaf!" the apprentice accused.

Samad twisted out of the boy's grip, tucked the loaf more firmly up his sleeve, and ran. He vaulted over a bin of old electronic parts, ducked between two booths, and pelted down the next aisle followed by angry shouts and the sound of heavy feet pounding behind him. Then Samad plunged into a crowd of plump housewives listening to a honey seller reciting recipes. The women scattered like startled hens as he charged through them.

Despite his clever dodges, the pounding feet of the baker's boy drew closer. Samad darted beneath the belly of a rangy draft mule. The startled mule lurched forward, upsetting a basket of ripe plums and jostling a clay jar of oil off the back of the wagon. It broke open on the paving stones with a heavy thunk. His pursuer's relentless running feet splashed into the widening puddle of oil. There was a sudden cry and a wet splat as the baker's boy skidded on the plums and fell against the legs of a trestle table loaded with produce. A multicolored avalanche of fruit and vegetables cascaded onto Samad's pursuer. The ripe, sweet scent of crushed and bruised fruit spread through the air.

As the vegetable seller harangued the apprentice in a voluble blend of Arabic, Spanish, and Greek, Samad slipped down an alley formed by the backs of two rows of stalls. He emerged, whistling innocently, into the main square where the storyteller had set up. Pulling the somewhat battered loaf from his sleeve, he presented it to her with a flourish.

"This is for you, Sera Storyteller," Samad said, addressing her formally. "It's payment for the story you told."

The wrinkles around the storyteller's eyes creased as she smiled at Samad.

"Thank you—" she began.

Then, a hand gripped Samad's arm.

"I got you, you grimy little thief!"

It was the spotty-faced baker's boy, fruit-stained and oily but triumphant.

Samad struggled, but this time the boy's grip was too tight to shake.

The storyteller stood. "What's going on here?"

"He stole a loaf of bread from my master's stall. I nearly killed myself, chasing after him. Now I'm taking him to the Guardia."

"No!" Samad shouted, struggling even harder against the apprentice's iron grip.

"Easy now!" The storyteller told the baker's boy. "You're hurting him."

"Calm down now, and let me settle this," the storyteller told Samad. "I'll see you're treated fairly."

Samad stopped struggling and looked anxiously from the apprentice to the old woman.

"How much was the bread?" the storyteller asked the baker's boy.

"It was a quarter-centino loaf," the apprentice replied, "I saw him slip it up his sleeve."

"Like this one?" she asked holding up the loaf Samad had given her. Just then, Perez the baker bustled up, looking angry.

"Yes, that's our bread, Sera," Perez confirmed. "We're the only ones in Melilla with that design on the top. So you caught the thief then, Ghazi? Good work!"

The storyteller stood. "My name is Teller. I'm a Senior Master in the Storytellers' Guild. I'm afraid this is my fault, ser," the storyteller told the baker. "I sent the boy to get the bread for me. He must have stolen the loaf so that he could keep the money."

Samad started to protest, but the storyteller silenced him with a look.

"Allow me to make reparations," she continued. "Here's a centino for the loaf, and this for your trouble, Ser Perez," she said, holding up a brassy ten-centino coin. "If you would like, I will tell stories by your stall tomorrow. It will draw a crowd that will buy up all your bread. You can go home early tomorrow with a bulging purse and no leftovers."

Samad expected Perez to argue, but the baker nodded. "We will be honored by your presence, Sera Teller." He paused, then inquired, "But what about the boy? He shouldn't go unpunished."

Samad glanced anxiously from the storyteller to the baker's boy. The storyteller knelt down to talk to Samad.

"Do you pledge your honor to abide by whatever punishment I set, young man?"

"A beggar's honor?" the apprentice sneered. "How much is that worth?"

Samad stiffened in offense, but Teller laid a quelling hand on his shoulder.

"It's worth everything in the world, if the beggar is an honorable man," the old woman said quietly.

The storyteller turned back to Samad. "Do you promise to abide by my punishment?"

"Will you hurt me, sera?" Samad asked.

The storyteller smiled. "A wise question. Do you deserve to be hurt?"

Samad considered this solemnly. "Well . . . maybe a beating."

He saw the storyteller's lips purse in disapproval.

"But not the Guardia." He was terrified that they would send him back to the grim foster home he had run away from. He would rather die than go back there.

"I won't hurt you, Samad," the storyteller said. "Do you trust me enough to honorably submit to my punishment?"

"By my honor, I will, sera. I swear by my name, Abd al-Samad," he said solemnly. The storyteller's eyebrows lifted when she heard his name. "Most people just call me Samad," he added.

"Very well then, Abd al-Samad. I swear by my honor, and by my membership in the Guild of Storytellers, that you will come to no lasting harm through my punishment of you."

She turned to the baker and his apprentice. "Are you satisfied Ser Perez?"

Perez nodded grudgingly. His apprentice looked like he was about to say something, but a sharp glance from the baker silenced the boy.

"Thank you. I will see you tomorrow," she said, bowing gracefully to the baker.

"We look forward to your stories," the baker said. "Come on, Ghazi, let's get back to the stall."

The baker and his apprentice made their way through the gathering crowd.

The storyteller rolled up her mat, slung her pack on her back, and picked up her staff.

"Well then, Samad, let's go find a quiet place to talk this over."

She led him to a sunny plaza near the Street of the Collimators. It was a quiet place. The distant whine of machines created a drowsy undertone to the steady trickle of the fountain in the square. In the distance, Samad could hear the plaintive chant of the muezzin in the local mosque, calling the faithful to prayer. Teller sat on the wide lip of the fountain, leaning against a large concrete urn planted with the native red-leafed tsekoulou plants. She gestured to Samad to join her. When they were settled, she took out the loaf of bread, a cheap glazed saucer, and a bottle of oil. She broke the loaf in two and held out half to him.

"Here, you look hungry," she said. "Eat."

"Sera, I can't eat this! It was my payment to you for your story." He looked down, face darkening with embarrassment as he remembered her paying the baker twelve centinos for a half-centino loaf of bread. "I mean . . ." He glanced up at her. "It was *supposed* to be my payment for the story. But it cost you so much!" He looked down again, eyes welling with tears. "I'm sorry, Sera Teller. I shouldn't have done it."

"There are other ways to pay for a story besides stealing," she reproved gently. "For example, you can always pay for a story with another story."

"But I don't know any stories, sera."

"Of course you do, Samad. There's one story you know better than anyone else."

He looked up at her, hazel eyes wide with surprise. "There is?" he asked.

"Yes, there is. And it's a story I want to hear. Tell me, Samad, how did you come to be here, stealing bread to pay for stories? Where are your parents?"

"My mother's dead," he began. "And I never met my father, but my mother said he was a Jump pilot." He looked up at her defiantly, as though daring her to call him a liar.

"What do you remember about your mother?" Teller asked.

Samad shrugged. "She was a Jump pilot, too, but she lost her Talent and couldn't do it anymore. We lived in Nueva Ebiza, near the spaceport. She sang to me when I was little. We'd go to the park, sometimes." He looked down at the ground, remembering. "When I got older, she started going out a lot. And she'd come back all strange. She'd stare off into space and laugh at nothing." He met Teller's gaze without flinching. "It was drugs, usually sa'adat. I hid the stuff when I could, but she would just go out and buy more. There was a small fortune of the stuff hidden all over the apartment when she died."

"How did she die?" Teller asked.

Samad shrugged. "I found her in bed. I thought she was sleeping, but she wouldn't wake up. She was so cold." He looked away, lost in that terrible memory for a moment. "They said it was an overdose."

"How old were you when this happened?" Teller asked.

"I'd just turned six," he told her.

"What happened after your mother died?" Teller gently prompted him.

"When I couldn't get her to wake up, I went and got a neighbor. My mother used to pay the woman to look after me when she went out. The neighbor called the Guardia. They took me away and put me in a foster home in the Janubi Archipelago. I didn't like it there. It was cold all of the time, and we were beaten if we didn't get our chores done. So I ran away. I hid on a big cargo-sailer, and then a fishing boat, and wound up here in Melilla." He looked at her, his hazel eyes wide and frightened but still determined. "I won't go back there," he told her. "Don't try to make me." He watched her intently, ready to run.

Teller shook her head. "I won't make you go back, Samad. So tell me, how do you survive? It gets pretty cold and rainy here in the winter."

"There's an innkeeper who lets me sleep in the stable if I keep his courtyard swept clean."

"And food?" she asked. "What do you eat?"

"There's a baker who gives me stale loaves that haven't sold. And there's plenty of food in the garbage at the end of the day. I do all right," he said defiantly. "I've been in Melilla more than a year now."

"I can see that you manage pretty well," Teller told him. "That's a long time to be on your own. You must be pretty tough. Thank you for telling me your story, Samad. It's a good one. I enjoyed listening to it."

Samad felt naked and ashamed at having revealed so much of his past. But telling the storyteller had made him feel a little lighter somehow. His stomach growled. All that running and dodging and being afraid had made him very hungry.

"Enough talk," the storyteller said. "Now let's eat!"

Teller poured the oil into her saucer, carefully not watching Samad. The boy looked ready to run away if she blinked. This ragged, scrawny boy had been through so much. She understood why he was so stiff-necked and proud now. All Samad had was his honor. She glanced sidelong at the boy, wondering how old he was. At least eight, but he acted older. She wondered how long he'd been in that grim-sounding foster home and how long he'd managed to slip through the cracks. Things like this weren't supposed to happen to children on Thalassa.

She set the saucer of olive oil on the bench between them. "Please, eat a little something with me," she invited, handing him half of the loaf. "I'm starved, and it would be rude for me not to share my food with a guest. All I have to offer right now is bread and oil, but the bread is fresh, and the oil is good."

Despite his hunger, Samad politely waited for her to take the first bite. But hunger overtook the boy as soon as he started to eat. He ate all of his half of the loaf and looked longingly at Teller's.

"Here," Teller said, "I'm not as hungry as I thought I was. Would you please help me finish this loaf? It's too good to go to waste."

Samad hesitated, glancing warily at her before accepting the rest of the bread. Teller refilled the oil dish, hiding a private smile at the boy's appetite. She had to do something about Samad. He needed a good home before stealing became a habit.

At last the loaf was gone, except for crumbs. Samad relaxed, lulled by a full stomach and the warm sun.

"Well, Samad, I promised the baker that I would punish you."

Instantly Samad was as wary as a startled zibok.

"Now remember, you promised by your name that you would abide by the punishment I set you."

"And you promised you wouldn't hurt me," Samad warned.

"So I did. Your punishment shall be to act as my guide while I'm here in Melilla. Will you accept this punishment, Abd al-Samad?"

Samad's face lit with a dazzling smile. "You want me to

be your guide!" he exclaimed in wonderment. Then, recovering his dignity, he continued, "By my name, and by my honor, I will accept this punishment. Where would you like to go first, honored sera?"

CHAPTER 2

WHEN TELLER BID SAMAD GOOD NIGHT AT the door to her inn, she wondered whether she would ever see the wary boy again. But when she looked out her window the next morning, she saw Samad waiting for her in a doorway across the street. She dressed and hurried outside to invite him in for breakfast.

Samad hesitated, his eyes flicking to the door of the inn and back to her. He was hungry but too wary to go inside the inn.

"I tell you what, I'll get breakfast to go, and we'll make it a picnic," Teller suggested. "I don't suppose you know of any good places for that?"

"Yes, sera. There's a nice spot where we can watch the boats in the harbor."

Samad showed her a sheltered niche between two buildings where the sun shone, but the chilly spring wind could not find them. It was the kind of place that a street child would know about, safely hidden from the eyes of passersby, but with a panoramic view of the harbor. When Teller handed Samad his meal, he hesitated, pride warring with hunger. That bothersome pride gave her a handle to manage him with.

"Please eat, Samad. It's going to be a long day, and I don't have time to wait while you get food out of the trash." She watched as his dislike of accepting charity warred with his shame at being seen rummaging for thrown-away food.

"Yes, Sera Teller," he replied and bit into the hot, fragrant meat roll she had given him.

Teller looked away and down past the steep sweep of tiled roofs and whitewashed stone walls while the hungry boy tore into his food. From this vantage point the boats in the harbor looked like toys. The sky was a pale, clear blue. Off to the east, it was still clear, and the morning sun was bright enough to bask in. Thetis, the smaller of the two moons, had set, leaving Amphitrite hanging in the western sky like a pale ghost, veiled and then revealed by the scudding clouds blowing in from the southwest.

A front was blowing in. The weather report posted at the inn predicted another gale moving through the archipelago. She didn't want Samad to sleep outside in that kind of raw weather. If only she could get him to trust her enough to share her room. Once she won his trust, perhaps then she could coax him to come with her. Then she could try to find him a decent home.

She glanced at Samad. His meat roll was already nearly gone. Teller hid her smile by biting into her own meat roll. At least the boy was going to be easy to feed.

"I promised Ser Perez that we would tell stories by his stall today," Teller said when Samad had finished all the available food. "Before we go, I want you to wash your face

and run this brush through your hair. We are going to present you as a reformed character, so you need to look nice."

"But sera!" Samad protested, "that miserable miser
doesn't deserve it!"

The wrinkles fanning out around the corners of Teller's
eyes deepened as she smiled. "You're right, Samad. He
doesn't deserve it, but you do."

Samad stared at her in surprise.

"Samad, the better you look, the worse Perez looks."

Samad pondered her words.

"Why does it matter?" he asked.

"Because I hope to teach Perez a lesson. I asked around.
Every other baker in town gives bread to the poor, but not
Perez. I hope to change his mind today."

"What are you going to do?" Samad asked.

"Just what I promised. Tell stories by his stall." Her
smile grew predatory, the creases on either side of her mouth
deepening. "I didn't say what *kind* of stories, though."

Samad's eyes danced with laughter as understanding
came. He tidied up the food wrappers, then washed his face
and hands in a nearby fountain. He allowed Teller to comb
out the tangles in his black hair, arranging his wild black
curls into a deceptive semblance of tameness. Thus fortified,
they set off for Perez's stall.

Word of yesterday's encounter had spread. There was a
crowd waiting when they showed up, eager to glean any
new gossip. Teller smiled. They wouldn't be disappointed.

"Greetings, Ser Perez," Teller said. "Thank you for providing me with this opportunity to tell stories."

She spread her mat and painstakingly settled her Guild
shawl around her, allowing the audience's anticipation to
build. When the time was right, she set out her bowl and
began rattling her drum. The crowd drew in around her,

ready for her stories. She set down her drum, waited a moment, and began.

"Once upon a time, there was a baker whose bread was as fine and light as the clouds in a summer sky. The baker's grandfather had done the Sea King a favor, and in return, the Sea King had given his family the gift of making exceptional bread. This baker charged twice what the other bakers did and still sold out by the middle of the day. He was rich and prosperous. His family dressed in fine clothes and lived in a big, well-furnished house.

"One day, when the rich baker had nothing but the stale heel of a loaf left over from yesterday's lunch, a little orphan girl came into his shop. Her clothes were worn and ragged, and her face was pinched with hunger.

" 'Could I have just the heel of a loaf, Master Baker?' she pleaded. 'I've no parents, and I'm cold and hungry.'

"The baker shook his head. He didn't want to gain a reputation for giving bread to every hungry beggar who needed a free meal.

" 'There's nothing left, little girl,' he lied. 'Maybe you could try the baker across the street.' The rich baker didn't like the baker across the street because he gave his bread away to anyone who claimed to be poor or hungry.

"So the girl went to the baker across the street. He was a young man who had recently inherited his childless master's big house and bakery. He lived alone in the big house except for his master's old dog. The big house made him feel small and lonely. The little girl's plight touched his own loneliness. He gave her a loaf of bread, still warm from the oven.

" 'If you need a place to stay, there is room in my house. I would be grateful for the company,' he told the little girl.

" 'Thank you, I can sweep the bakery for you if you like.' And so the little girl went to live in the kind baker's attic.

"The next day, an old woman bent with age came to the stingy baker's store as he was cleaning up at the end of the day. All that remained was a loaf that was singed at one end.

" 'Please, kind sir, might I beg a loaf of bread from you?' she asked him. 'I have nothing to eat. Even a burned loaf is better than nothing when you are starving.'

" 'Be off with you,' the stingy baker said officiously. 'I have nothing to give you.'

"So the old woman went to the kind baker across the street and asked him for bread.

" 'This will fill your stomach until better days come,' the kind baker told the old woman as he gave her two loaves of bread. 'And there is room in my house if you need a place to stay. You could help look after the orphan girl who lives with me.'

" 'Thank you, my dear, that is very kind of you,' the old woman said. 'I'm lonely as well as old.' And so the old lady came to live with him, too.

"The next day a poor mother carrying a baby stopped to beg at the stingy baker's stall. All that he had left was a lumpy, lopsided loaf that was too misshapen for him to sell.

" 'My baby is hungry, and I have no food for him. Perhaps you have a loaf you can't sell. We'd be grateful for anything at all.

" 'Go away, I have nothing for you today,' the stingy baker said haughtily. 'All *my* loaves are perfect.'

"The mother shifted her baby higher on her shoulder and walked across the street to the kind baker's shop, where she asked him for bread.

" 'Of course,' he said, tickling her baby till it laughed. He gave her three loaves of bread. 'There's room in my house for you and the baby, if you would like it. And your little one will cheer up the old lady who lives with me.'

"And so the mother and her baby went to live with the baker.

"On the fourth day, the stingy baker sold every loaf he had baked. All he had left at the end of the day were the crumbs at the bottom of his bread baskets. A little sparrow fluttered onto one of the shelves and began picking at the crumbs.

" 'Be off with you, before you soil my nice shelves,' the stingy baker said, shaking a broom at the tiny bird. It flew off to the kind baker's shop.

"The kind baker gave the bird four handfuls of bread crumbs.

" 'Come live with me,' he told the little bird. 'There's an empty birdhouse under the eaves, and your singing will cheer up the children who live in my house.'

"And so the little bird went to live under the eaves of the kind baker's roof.

"That night, when the stingy baker went to check his tubs of dough, he discovered that the dough wouldn't rise. The next morning he had no bread to sell. The shelves in his shop were bare for the first time in decades.

"Meanwhile, the kind baker came home to find that the women had fixed him a tasty fish stew. He ate so much that he fell sound asleep. When he awoke, the air was filled with the wonderful sweet smell of fresh-baked bread. The shelves of his store were piled high with cooling loaves, light as clouds. There were huge baskets of intricately braided rolls and long, crusty baguettes, and sweet pastries studded with raisins and currants.

"There was a knock on the door. He opened it. Three green-skinned sea sprites stood there, richly dressed in pearls and coral.

" 'The King of the Sea smelled your bread and sent us to buy some,' they told him.

" 'Please, take as much as you need,' the kind baker said, amazed by the miraculous appearance of the lovely bread on his shelves.

"The sea sprites each took a loaf of bread. They gave the baker a fish-skin pouch filled with pieces of rare black gem-coral. It was a princely sum for three loaves of bread.

"To celebrate his good fortune, the kind baker gave the rest of the bread to the poor. He sold one piece of the black coral, and used the money to buy the finest flour; the freshest yeast; butter as yellow as daffodils; and eggs still warm from the hens' nests. *Tonight I will bake the most beautiful bread I've ever made,* the kindly baker said to himself as he returned from the market with his supplies.

"Meanwhile, the rich baker's bread still refused to rise. He bought new yeast, changed the flour, and tried adding more sugar and less salt. Nothing seemed to help. The dough lay in the baker's tubs, heavy and lifeless as mud. When dawn came, the rich baker was sitting outside on his stoop despairing over his unrisen dough. The miserly baker saw the richly dressed sea sprites go into the other baker's shop. A few minutes later, they emerged with loaves of bread. Through the shop window, he saw the poor baker staring in amazement at the contents of the pouch the sea sprites had given him.

"*That baker has stolen my luck! He never used to make bread that good,* the rich baker said to himself. *I'll stay up tonight and find out his secret.*

"So the rich baker watched through the window that night. He saw the baker come in, begin work, and then yawn, sit down on a stool in the corner, and fall soundly asleep. The old lady, the mother, and the orphan child tiptoed into the bakery. The sparrow fluttered down from the rafters, settling on the floor in front of the mother. Then the bird changed into a beautiful young woman, graceful as a strand of seaweed waving in the current. She greeted the others warmly, and then set to work. The mother put her baby to sleep in a basket in a warm corner, and began sifting flour. The old woman saw to the proofing of the yeast. The young girl brought firewood for the stove, while the beautiful sparrow woman lit the fire in the oven.

"When the flour was sifted, the mother began to mix and knead masses of white, springy dough. The girl placed her hands on the tubs of kneaded dough. The dough rose under her touch until it was as light as a cloud. Then the grandmother took the risen dough, punched it down, and shaped it into loaves. After the little girl oversaw its second rising, they put the pale loaves into the oven to bake. The rich baker watched enviously as the three women rolled out pastry light as air, and filled pies with rich fruit filling. A wonderful smell of baking filled the air.

"When the baking was done, the young woman turned into a sparrow once more and summoned a huge flock of birds. The birds fluttered their wings, creating a breeze that carried the smell of baking out to sea. The old woman, the mother, and the girl swept up the bakery and tiptoed out. A few minutes later, the kind baker awoke. He stared in wonder at the baked goods surrounding him. The rich baker watched as the sea sprites came and bought two loaves each, paying for them with two small sacks of moon-bright pearls.

" 'So the fool doesn't even know what's happening,' the rich baker said to himself. 'Maybe I can get the King of the Sea to come buy my bread!'

"When the kind baker left to sell the jewels that the sea sprites had given him, the rich baker fell in beside him.

" 'Congratulations, my friend, on your good fortune!' the selfish baker said.

"The generous baker thanked him. 'I only wish I knew

what was happening. Every evening I eat a big dinner, and then I get so sleepy that I fall asleep right after I start work. Every morning when I wake up, my shelves are piled high with the most beautiful baked goods. I wish I could stay awake long enough to find out what is going on,' he said. 'I'd like to thank whoever is doing this.'

"Well then, the answer is simple. Skip dinner tonight and see if you stay awake.'

" 'But I wouldn't want to offend the women who fix dinner for me,' the baker told him. 'They're so kind!'

" 'Slip your meal under the table to the dog. Then pretend to go to sleep, and watch to see who's doing your baking for you.'

"And so the kind baker did as the stingy baker suggested, giving the dog his meal and pretending to fall asleep in the corner of the bakery. Then the three women and the sparrow came in. His eyes widened as the bird transformed into a beautiful young woman. The baker watched through heavy-lidded eyes as the bird woman knelt to tend the fire. He was so fascinated by her beauty that he barely noticed the miracles made of dough that the others were creating. He looked at the sparrow woman, flushed and rosy from the fire's heat and realized that he had fallen in love with her. He watched quietly until the last loaves were out of the oven, and then he stood and took the sparrow woman by the hand.

" 'Please! Don't fly away just yet. I wanted to thank you for all you've done.'

" 'We wanted to repay your kindness to us,' the beautiful young woman told him.' She was blushing, but she did not take back her hand.

" 'I know when I was kind to the others,' the baker said. 'But what have I done for you?'

" 'I was the sparrow you gave bread crumbs to,' she told him. 'I am the Sea King's eldest daughter. My father gave me the guise of a sparrow so that I could carry stories back to him of what went on in the world above the water. I saw your kindness to the poor and began to watch you.' She turned her head away shyly but still did not let go of his hand.

" 'You're the Sea King's daughter?' the baker said in wonder.

" 'Yes, I am,' she replied.

" 'That must be why you're as beautiful as the sea itself,' he told her softly. 'I'm in your debt for all that you have done for me.'

" 'Perhaps she would accept a kiss as payment,' the old woman suggested.

"The Sea King's daughter blushed crimson with embarrassment, but still her hand remained in his. She looked up at him and smiled.

" 'Gladly,' said the baker, and stepped forward.

"Just then there was a knock on the door. The beautiful maiden's eyes widened. 'My father's servants!' she said. With a whir and a rustle of feathers she was a small brown bird again. She flew out the window and was gone.

"The grandmother laid a hand on the baker's arm. 'You love her, don't you?'

"The baker nodded. 'Of course.'

" 'When my son's servants seek to pay you for the bread they have come to buy, you must refuse whatever they offer you, and demand the Sea King's eldest daughter's hand in marriage.'

"Then the three women vanished, leaving behind a spotless bakery filled with fresh-baked bread.

"There was another knock on the door and the baker opened it. The three sea sprites were standing there, garbed in pearls and gems.

" 'We have come to buy your bread,' one of them said.

" 'Come in, come in,' said the baker.

"The three sea sprites came in, choosing three loaves apiece. Their leader tried to give the baker three heavy pouches filled with gold.

" 'No,' the baker said. 'It's not enough.'

"The sea sprite pulled out another three sacks, and held those out as well.

" 'No,' the baker said. 'I wish to marry the Sea King's eldest daughter.'

"The sea sprites' leader stiffened in anger. His bright red ruff stood out from his head like a huge collar. His huge azure eyes flashed like lightning on a stormy sea. 'You would dare ask such a thing?' he demanded in a harsh and angry voice.

"The baker trembled with fear but stood his ground. 'Yes, I do.'

"The sea sprites threatened and blustered and warned, but the baker refused to change his mind.

" 'Well then, you will answer to the king for your insolence!' They threw a jeweled net over him and carried him off in a swirl of wind and water.

"When the whirling maelstrom surrounding the baker and his captors vanished, they were in a vast vaulted chamber made from a single giant shell. The walls and roof of the cavern were studded with beautiful glowing jewels. Brightly colored fish swam in and out of the line of windows that spiraled across the ceiling. The Sea King was seated on a throne carved from a single pearl, and waited on by dozens of courtiers and attendants. One of the sea sprites swam forward and whispered in the ear of a courtier, who whispered in the ear of another more exalted courtier. That grand personage came forward and conferred with the Sea King.

" 'Bring the man forward!' the Sea King ordered.

"The baker was untangled from the net and led before the king.

" 'You asked for my eldest daughter's hand in marriage, in return for a few loaves of bread?' the king asked.

" 'Y-yes, Your Majesty. If she will have me, that is.'

" 'Bring my daughter to me!' the king ordered.

"Amid a flurry of whispers and bows and apologies, the courtiers scattered like a school of startled minnows.

"When the courtiers were all gone, a small, brightly colored fish swam up to the king. In the wink of an eye the fish was gone, and the Sea King's daughter stood before her father, clad in royal raiment.

"She bowed gracefully. 'Greetings, Father. I see you have met the man I wish to marry.'

" 'But daughter, this man is only a common baker.'

" 'A baker, yes,' his daughter agreed. 'But far from common.' And she told her father of his generosity and kindness.

"As she spoke, three small fish swam in through the window, and hovered, watching the proceedings. When the princess had finished her story, the fish transformed into the old woman, the mother, and the orphan, now garbed as magnificently as the princess.

"The grandmother stood forward. 'My son, I was the old woman the baker took in. I agree with my granddaughter; he is a kind and well-spoken young man.'

"The mother stepped up onto the dais and greeted the Sea King with a formal kiss. Her baby gave a crow of delight and wriggled out of her arms, to swim onto the king's lap.

" 'Husband, this man fed and sheltered our baby and me, when he thought us no better than beggars. I feel he is worthy of our daughter's hand.'

"The little girl curtsied to the Sea King. 'Father, he was nice to me, and I like him. I think they should get married.'

" 'I seem to be outnumbered here,' the king told the baker. 'Are you sure you want to belong to a family with so many pushy females?'

" 'Nothing would give me greater delight.'

" 'If you feel the same after living with us for a year and a day, then you may marry my daughter,' the Sea King said.

" 'Father, there is another matter we would speak to you about,' the princess said. 'One of our gifts is being abused.' And she told him of the wealthy, proud baker, who had refused to give them so much as a bread crumb.

" 'I have lifted your blessing from him temporarily,' the Queen of the Sea informed her husband. 'But you must pass final judgment on this man.'

" 'Your Majesty,' the baker said. 'I have been this man's neighbor for many years. May I speak on his behalf?'

" 'Go ahead,' the Sea King allowed.

" 'He has a family: daughters, sons, and a wife. If you withdraw your blessing from him, what will become of them? Perhaps you could give him one last chance. Have your emissaries tell him that he must give a generous tithe of his bread to the poor or lose your gift permanently. It would be a shame to have to take back so fine a gift, once bestowed.'

"The Sea King looked thoughtful. 'That is a generous and wise suggestion, young man. I see my daughter has bestowed her love wisely. So it shall be!'

"And so, after a year and a day, the generous baker married the Sea King's eldest daughter. And the Sea King came to value his advice so much that he made his son-in-law the Vizier for Matters Above the Sea. As for the stingy baker, he started giving his bread away. And he discovered that the more he gave, the more bread seemed to come out of his ovens. And as far as I know, they are all prospering still."

·   ·   ·

Muted chuckles and a spattering of applause passed over the audience when the tale was done. Teller glanced at Perez to see what effect her story had on him. The baker was looking embarrassed and a little angry. She decided that it was time to change the pace. When her bowl had been filled with gifts, Teller told two funny stories before returning to the theme of generosity, until the baker began to look uncomfortable again. She didn't want to make Perez angry, only prick his conscience into doing the right thing.

It was easy to affect a crowd of people with a story. Once you got part of an audience on your side, most of the others usually followed. Influencing a single person was much harder. But she seemed to have Perez where she wanted him, on the uneasy edge of self-examination. She began telling more gentle stories now: "The Three Oranges," "The Lovers of San Vitale," "The Virgin's Robe." They were tales of understanding, forgiveness, and repentance. Glancing over at the baker, Teller saw his face had become thoughtful and sad.

By noon, Perez's shelves were nearly bare. Teller decided it was time to bring the storytelling session to a close. As the audience filed past to fill her bowl again, she saw a girl dressed in threadbare clothes creep timidly up to the baker's stall and ask for something. The baker hesitated, glancing at Teller. Then he smiled at the girl and handed her a round brown loaf. The girl thanked him with a curtsy and darted away again, shy as a wild bird. Perez smiled after her.

Like all Thalassans, Perez had been raised on stories. Stories had made him laugh and cry, and stories had taught him the proper road for a person to walk. A lifetime of stories had made it possible for the storyteller's tales to remind him of the importance of giving. Teller smiled to herself as she bent to roll up her mat.

Perez came up to Teller and Samad as the crowd dispersed.

"Thank you, Guildmaster, for telling your stories by my stall today."

"You did well then?"

Perez nodded. "I normally have twice this much bread left at the end of the day, and here it's only noon! I think I'll give what's left away, and spend the afternoon with my family."

"I did well, too," Teller said. "Would you mind if I came by tomorrow and told some more stories?"

"I would be honored," he said. He held out two loaves of bread wrapped in a beautifully embroidered cotton cloth. "This is my gift for the stories. I baked the bread, and my daughter embroidered the towel."

"Then I am doubly thanked," she told him.

Perez turned to Samad. "This is for you," he said, holding out a small, paper-wrapped parcel. "Without you, Sera Teller would never have come by today."

"Thank you, ser," Samad said. His voice was stiff with pride, but he managed to be gracious.

"Go ahead, open it!" Perez urged.

Inside was a set of eight beautifully carved greenwood buttons, each in the shape of a different fish, each kind clearly recognizable.

"They're beautiful," Samad said quietly, running his fingers over the carefully carved wood. "Thank you, Ser Perez."

The baker shrugged, embarrassed by the fineness of his gift. *"De nada,"* he demurred in Spanish. "My brother carves, now and then."

They had done well today, Teller thought as they walked off. She was pleased by Perez's apparent change of heart and by his invitation to tell stories there again tomorrow. It was a good spot. And a repeat visit might help set Perez's change more firmly in his heart.

•   •   •

Samad watched Teller warily as she ate. He had finished his meal several minutes before, and it lay solid and comfortable in his stomach. Though he'd already spent two full days with Teller, being warm and fed was still a novel sensation. He liked it, and that worried him. Sooner or later, the bill was going to come due on all this kindness, and he only hoped he'd be able to pay it. He watched Teller lift her fork from her plate to her mouth. Occasionally her gaze flickered over him, but mostly she kept to herself. He liked her silence, but he worried about what lay behind it.

A gale had blown in from the Sea of Storms. Samad looked out the window at the silver sheets of rain driven by the wind. He wondered where he was going to sleep tonight. He had been so busy with Teller over the last couple of days that he hadn't swept the stable yard for the innkeeper who let him sleep in his hayloft. He knew of a sheltered doorway south of the market. It was close to the Street of the Smiths, so he ran the risk of being rousted by the Guardia, but it was deep enough to be out of the storm.

"Samad," Teller said, interrupting his worries. "It's a wild night out there. You'd be welcome to curl up in a corner of my room."

Samad tensed. Was he finally being expected to pay for all the meals that Teller had fed him?

"I'll be all right, sera," he insisted. Fear had turned the food in his belly into a stone.

"As you wish, Samad. But if you change your mind later on, you'll be welcome to as much of the floor as you need."

Samad left as soon as he could after that. Despite his worries, he tried to walk out into the wind and rain as though he was headed for a warm hearth and a roof over his head.

Teller watched the door close behind Samad, and sighed. His speedy exit had told her how afraid he still was. Had she pushed things too far with her offer? Would he come back tomorrow? What if something happened to him out there?

She shook her head. Samad had given his oath to serve her, and he was a resourceful and cautious child. She would have to trust to the boy's prowess and his sense of honor. Teller paid her tab with a few small coins and a handful of buttons, and headed upstairs. She lay awake for a long time, listening to the rattle of rain and then sleet against her windows and thinking about Samad, out there somewhere in that wild, wet night.

The next morning she woke early. Peering out of the window through a steady, settled spring drizzle, she saw Samad huddled in a doorway across the street. He looked cold, wet, and miserable. She dressed as quickly as she could and hurried downstairs, a towel over her arm. She found a private parlor room with a fire in the hearth, and laid the towel down over the back of a chair to warm, then dashed out to get Samad.

The child's lips were blue with cold and he offered no resistance to her as she led him into the warm parlor and sat him before the fire. Voula, the innkeeper, glanced in, assessed the situation, and returned with more towels and a pot of hot cocoa. Teller smiled gratefully at her. Voula merely shrugged.

"I'll be back with breakfast in a bit," she said. "Get that cocoa into him as soon as you can. It'll do the most good."

Ignoring the unwashed funk rising from his drying clothes, Teller toweled Samad's wet hair and plied him with hot cocoa and food until his shivering subsided. All of a sudden he sat up, looking alert and wary again. The food and warmth had done their work. Samad was himself again.

"Finish your breakfast, Samad, we have a long day ahead of us." Teller told him, relieved and saddened by the boy's fear. He had chosen to honor his oath by returning. But she had not yet earned his trust.

"Yes, sera," he said obediently. He had polished off a huge fritatta rich with cheese and vegetables, and was starting to slow down halfway through a double portion of bacon. Perhaps, she thought with an inward smile, he was finally starting to get enough to eat. Certainly his skin was less waxen and pale, and his skinny frame seemed fractionally less skeletal. If he kept eating like that, he wasn't going to be able to squeeze into those ragged clothes he was wearing. She would have to do something about that.

Samad fought the relaxation and sleepiness brought on by a full stomach and the luxurious warmth of the fire. It had been a cold and miserable night. Two different members of the Guardia had thrown him out of the doorways he had sheltered in. Samad had wound up huddled behind a collection of garbage bins in an alley. His hiding place was out of the raw wind but exposed to the rain. When dawn came, Samad had huddled in a doorway across from the inn, waiting for Teller.

Samad glanced furtively up at Teller. She had buried her long, bony nose in a big mug of hot, spiced tea. Her watchful, intent gaze met his over the rim of the cup.

"Where would you like to go today, sera?"

"It's too wet and too early for stories yet, Samad. I want to have a leisurely breakfast and just wander for a couple of hours."

Samad watched Teller carefully as they wandered through Melilla. The meal and the fire had warmed him thoroughly, but there was still a spot between his shoulders that remembered the biting chill of last night's storm. It would be good to sleep somewhere warm, but would it be safe? Could he trust Teller to be what she seemed, a cynical, funny old woman with a core of solid kindness, or would she metamorphose into a nightmare in the dark silence of her room?

So far, the storyteller had treated him fairly. She hadn't forced him to do anything he didn't want to do. And she hadn't turned him over to the authorities. He dreaded being sent back to that bleak, punishing warehouse for unwanted children. He was hungry, cold, and lonely, but he was free.

But some part of him wanted to trust Teller, wanted to believe that he could stay in her room and be safe and warm and dry. It had been two years since his mother had died, and he hadn't met an adult he trusted since then. He remembered Teller drying his hair in front of the fire. The memory touched a forgotten place where there was warmth and safety and someone to protect him. It was something he hadn't known for a very long time, not since the drugs had turned his mother into a vague, affectionate stranger.

Teller had taken him to that safe, warm place once. He watched her warily now. Could he trust her to take him there again?

Teller seemed to take no notice of his watchfulness. She wandered the streets, chatting with strangers, listening to whatever they had to say. But sometimes Samad would catch her turning away, as though she had been watching him.

The rain let up about midmorning. They set up beside Perez's stall for a brief storytelling session. But though Perez was glad to see them again, the cold and the damp hurried people through their shopping, and their audiences were scant and easily distracted.

"Some days are like that," Teller said, when Samad tried to console her. "Let's get some lunch, and then I want to buy some clothes."

By evening, Samad was no closer to a decision about sleeping in Teller's room. It was growing late, and by the time Teller had finished telling stories at the inn, a light drizzle was falling. Samad was exhausted, and he didn't want to face another cold, rainy night outside. But could he trust her?

Teller rose from her seat near the hearth. "I'm tired, Samad. My offer of last night still stands. You can stay in my room, and I promise that you will sleep safe and warm. No one will bother you. Are you coming?"

He was on his feet and halfway up the stairs behind Teller before he realized that he had decided without thinking about it, propelled by a cold feeling between his shoulder blades and the lonely place inside him. He hesitated for a moment, thinking it over, and then continued up the stairs to Teller's room, frightened but determined. He simply couldn't face another cold, wet night alone. Not now, not when he felt so warm and fed and comfortable.

Teller's room was low-ceilinged and cozy. A low bank of coals smoldered in the hearth at one end, filling the room with the smoky, wet-dog scent of burning peat. Teller stirred up the fire, coaxing up the blaze with some small branches from the bundle of kindling and adding a couple more chunks of peat to drive the chill out of the room. The revived fire cast a gentle glow on Teller's bony, ironic face. She smiled reminiscently.

"You know, I once had an off-worlder ask me why we didn't just install hydrogen furnaces instead of burning peat. I told him that we've wood and peat enough, and the time to appreciate a good fire. I think of that man every time I tend a fire. So rich in ideas, so poor in time."

She hung the poker up, and looked at him. "I'll be down the hall in the bathroom, changing. Make up a bed wherever you like. There's blankets and linen in the closet if you need them."

With that she left him alone. He stood in the middle of

the room for a moment, unsure what to do next. It would be better to sleep close to the door, in case he had to make a speedy retreat. But if he had any sense, he'd be sleeping out in the rain. He peered out the window. It wasn't a bad drop, if he had to run. He unlocked the window, hoping he wouldn't have to run for it. Having made sure of his escape route, he took off his pack and spread his blanket near the hearth.

Samad was curled up near the fire, pretending to be asleep, when Teller came in. He tensed as her footsteps approached, paused, and then padded quietly away. There was the rustle of bed sheets and the creak of the bed frame as she crawled into bed.

"Good night, Samad. Sleep well," Teller called as she turned out the lamp.

He slept poorly at first, starting awake at every sound, but there was the great, warm, luxurious presence of the fire at his back, and the reassuring sound of Teller's light, steady snore. It was so wonderful to be warm and dry! At last he relaxed and fell deeply asleep. It was midmorning when he woke.

He remembered where he was and sat up abruptly. Teller was seated on the bed, sewing a button on a shirt she had bought yesterday in the market.

"Good morning, Samad. You slept in."

"Forgive me, sera," he said. He should have woken before her.

Teller shook her head. "There wasn't anything that needed doing, and you needed the sleep. Here," she said, holding out the shirt she was working on. "I was putting on the buttons that Perez gave you. I hope you don't mind."

He took the shirt. It was made of thick, soft blue wool with thin white stripes. The crispness of the fabric betrayed its newness. He fingered the beautiful buttons that Teller had put on for him. Cutting those buttons off in order to buy something would be like selling his own fingers.

"No sera, I . . . It's too much."

"Take it, Samad. You've earned it. With your help I've made more than twice as much money as I usually do. Go ahead, try it on," she urged.

Hesitantly, he slid the shirt over his head. He stood stiffly, looking down at the shirt. It fell in rich blue folds to midthigh and felt as warm as last night's fire. Finally, he let himself take the fabric between his fingers, feeling its softness and warmth.

"It's beautiful," he whispered. He couldn't remember when he'd had a shirt that was entirely new. It must have been when his mother was alive, but back then, he'd taken such things for granted. He blinked back a sudden prickle of tears.

"It looks good on you, Samad. And there's room for you to grow into it." She held out her hands for the shirt. "Let me sew on that last button."

"I can do it, sera."

"No, Samad. I'll finish it out in the hallway while you try these on." She held out a pair of sturdy black wool pants.

"But, sera—" he began, but one look at her determined face told him that it was useless. He shrugged, embarrassed, but secretly pleased as well. "Thank you, sera." He said, meeting her eyes. She smiled back at him, and that was a gift he prized far more than the shirt.

Samad listened to Teller bring the second story in the Pilot's Cycle alive. Her eyes shone as she told of the Pilot's early years, her struggles to build a base and grow enough food to feed herself. Then she talked of the Pilot's travels with her harsel companion. Normally, this was one of Samad's favorite stories. He loved to imagine seeing the vast empty world of Thalassa for the first time. He tried to imagine what it had been like before fields, fences, and orderly orchards clothed the islands, when the only sails on the horizon were wild harsel. Normally he listened, enthralled, but today, he fingered his fine new clothes and worried.

In the week and a half since Teller had allowed him to guide her, he had grown used to hot meals and warm, dry places to sleep. He had come to like Teller, and even to trust her, and that scared him. He had grown used to being with Teller, and he didn't want to lose her.

But traveling storytellers never stayed long in any one place. Someday soon she was going to leave, and then he would have to go back to dinners scavenged out of the trash and the cold, lonely life of the streets.

He stroked the cuff of his shirt. At least he had warm clothing. But even that was a problem. His new clothes, with their beautiful, hand-carved buttons, would attract thieves. Once Teller was gone, he would remove the buttons and sell them. He could get enough to live on for a week or more. He could rub dirt into his fine new clothes and sew patches on them so they would look ragged. Then he wouldn't have to fear their being stolen.

Sudden tears welled in his eyes at the thought of intentionally spoiling Teller's gift to him. He wiped them on his sleeve, then glanced up quickly at Teller to make sure she hadn't seen him. She was caught up in the details of her story. Good. He didn't want her to see him crying. Samad inhaled sharply and tried to focus on her story. He should enjoy Teller's stories while they lasted. It would be a long time before another storyteller would let him listen for free.

Teller watched Samad brooding beside the fire. His new clothes had delighted him at first, but in the last few days he had grown withdrawn and uncommunicative. Had she somehow wounded that sensitive pride of his?

"Samad, what's bothering you?" she asked him.

"Nothing," Samad said, not taking his eyes off of the fire.

Teller sat beside him. She thought she glimpsed tear tracks on his face when he glanced up at her.

"It looks like something to me," Teller said. "Have I hurt your feelings somehow?"

Samad shook his head, not looking at her.

"Has someone else hurt you?"

He shook his head again.

"Are you worried about something?"

Samad sat still for a long moment, and then grudgingly nodded.

"What are you worried about?"

He shrugged his shoulders. Teller repressed a sigh of frustration. Pulling out information from Samad one tiny bit at a time was like uprooting couverta weed. She waited, repressing her impatience, while Samad stuttered through several false starts.

"You're going," he finally managed.

"And you'll miss me?"

He drew his shoulders up as though afraid of a blow, and nodded again.

"You know," Teller offered, "you could come with me."

Samad's head came up and he stared at her, owl-eyed with amazement. It was all Teller could do to keep from laughing at his expression.

"I could?"

She nodded. "But Samad, I want you to think about this. I travel rough, and I travel hard. I'll be going south through the mountains to Nueva Ebiza on this trip. There's still snow up in the high passes. It will be very cold. And you must promise to do exactly what I say."

"Yes, sera. I will," he told her seriously. "And you gave me these warm clothes. I won't be cold."

"We'll have to get you a warm coat and some good shoes as well," Teller said. "We'll be leaving in two days' time. Can you be ready by then?"

Samad nodded. He was ready now. He would happily walk barefoot on hot coals all the way to Nueva Ebiza if it meant that he could be with Teller.

"Then it's settled." She held out her hand, and Samad took it.

"Thank you, sera," he said. "You won't regret this."

Teller smiled at the boy's solemnity. "Of course not, Samad."

Samad stared into the dying fire, listening to Teller's light snore. He was too excited to sleep. Teller was taking him with her! He wasn't going to have to go back to being alone! He lay there thinking of how to show Teller that he would be worth keeping. He would start by tending the fire and learning how to put up the tent. Maybe he could carry her pack for her, too. He would get up early and make breakfast for her. He remembered making breakfast for his mother.

Samad rolled over restlessly, turning away from the painful memories of his mother and her death. Perhaps, just perhaps, if he was really, really good, maybe she might let him stay forever. It would be fun, traveling with Teller.

He turned back over. There was no point in getting his hopes up yet. He'd been hopeful before and disappointed before. But Teller traveled all over Thalassa, just like the Pilot. He might even get to visit some of the places where the Pilot had been! He pulled the blanket up over his head and let himself dream of all the places they would see.

•   •   •

Teller watched Samad sleeping. They'd been on the road for two days now, and she was astonished at how much drive and energy there was in Samad's small frame. He had started the fire, pitched the tent, and washed and dried her socks. He'd even tried to fix her breakfast. Though the meal was fairly dubious by her standards, it wasn't bad for an eight-year-old boy who'd never cooked over an open fire before. Samad woke up before her and never went to bed until she was in her sleeping bag. And he walked all day long through the chilly rain and the mud without a word of complaint.

Teller had deliberately picked the shorter, harder mountain road to Nueva Ebiza. She wanted to test Samad, to get some idea of what he was made of. She also wanted to make life with her seem difficult and unpleasant. Hopefully, by the time they got to Nueva Ebiza he would be ready to settle down with a new family.

The morning after Samad had agreed to come with her, she'd sent the boy off on an errand and called the central Guild House in Nueva Ebiza. She told them about Samad and asked them to find him a home. Shortly before leaving Melilla, she'd received a report about several interested families. She'd selected the Karelli family. It was large and loving, with several adopted children and two biological children. The Karellis had been hoping to adopt a boy of Samad's age. They'd adopted several children whose lives had been even worse than his. She felt confident that the Karellis had the experience to be good parents for Samad.

Teller smoothed away a black curl from Samad's forehead and sighed. She would miss the boy. His company had leavened her loneliness. She hoped the glowing reports about Samad's new family were true. If the Karelli family was as wonderful as the Guild said they were, perhaps she would feel better about leaving Samad in their care.

Teller yawned. Samad wasn't the only one who was work-

ing hard on this trip. She was pushing her own limits. Usually she took a less strenuous route, going from town to
town, staying at inns for the night. But she was glad to have
done this. It had been a long time since she had struck out
across the countryside. Over the years she had become a
creature of towns and villages, and that saddened her.

She stood up and stretched her tired, sore muscles,
banked the fire, and settled into her sleeping bag for a good
night's rest. They would be crossing the pass tomorrow. If
they made good time, there was a small inn where they
could stay for a night or two.

Samad glanced up at the innkeeper with a shy smile of thanks
as he topped up Samad's mug of mulled cider. After three
days of slogging through the rain with Teller, the warmth and
hospitality of this country tavern was very welcome. This was
their second night here. On the first night, they had
squelched in through the door, sucked down a hot dinner, and
steeped the chill from their bones in the steaming water of
the bathhouse. Then they had climbed wearily up the steps to
the low-ceilinged room in the attic and fallen into bed.

The innkeeper had waved away Teller's money, asking
her to stay another night and tell stories in the bar. To
Samad's relief, she had agreed. They spent that morning
washing the mud out of their clothes and gear. In the afternoon, they visited a small country schoolhouse where Teller
told stories to the children.

It was strange, being in a school again. While he was at
the foster home, he had made it halfway through second
year. He could read and even write a little, but he rarely had
access to books, and even less access to electronic texts.
There was a library in Melilla, but he had stopped going
there when the librarian began asking him where he lived
and who his parents were.

Looking at the cheerful, well-scrubbed children sitting in a circle around Teller, he felt lonely and left out. He had watched and envied the children playing in the schoolyard in Melilla, but going to school would have drawn the attention of the authorities. Today he was with Teller, which made everything all right, except he was still an outsider. It would be nice to belong somewhere.

As Teller told stories, Samad looked longingly at the brightly colored books on the shelves. Maybe when they got to Nueva Ebiza, he would ask Teller if they could visit a library.

When the storytelling session was over, the teacher came up to him.

"This is from us, to thank you for coming today, Samad," she said, handing him a slim red volume. It was a beautifully illustrated collection of stories.

"Thank you," he said, "Thank you very much!" His hands caressed the binding, eager to investigate its contents.

On the ride home, he opened the book and tried to read. It was a hard book, but there were pictures for him to look at when the reading got too difficult.

"Do you like books?" Teller asked him.

He looked up from the page he was deciphering and nodded shyly.

"Would you read a little bit out loud to me?" she asked.

He shrugged, ashamed at how badly he read.

"Just a page or two, Samad," Teller coaxed.

Hesitantly, Samad began to read out loud, stumbling over the hard words. Teller listened intently, eyes shut. After several paragraphs, he stumbled to a halt, too self-conscious to continue.

"I'm not very good," he mumbled, embarrassed by all his mistakes.

"I thought you did very well, Samad. I wasn't sure you could read at all. How much schooling have you had?"

"Not much," he confessed. "I was just starting school when my mother died. I was in second year when I ran away."

"Then you did extremely well, Samad."

He shrugged and looked away, embarrassed by her praise.

"Would you like me to work with you on your reading?" she asked.

He looked up at Teller, surprise and hope in his eyes. "Yes please, sera. I would like that very much." He glanced down at the wooden railing on the wagon, afraid that his excitement would show. Could this mean that she meant to keep him with her permanently?

"Well then, when we get back to the inn, we'll spend a little while going over your book. I'll help you with the unfamiliar words."

"Thank you, sera," he said, happiness swelling inside his chest like a bright yellow balloon.

The last of the other patrons filed out the door, leaving Teller and Samad alone in the common room. Out here in the highlands, people went to bed early. But the storytelling session had been a success. The room had been full and the audience attentive. The crowd had drunk and eaten its fill, much to the delight of the innkeeper. He had invited them to stay an extra night, but Teller had politely declined. The longer her trip with Samad, the harder the parting would be. She frowned into the fire. Tomorrow they would walk down to the next town and catch the train into Nueva Ebiza. The Guild had arranged for them to stay with the family who wanted to adopt Samad. It was time to prepare him for that introduction.

"Let's go upstairs," she offered. "I think there's time for one more story, just for the two of us, before we go to bed."

Samad brightened noticeably at this. Teller topped up his cider and her ale, and they went upstairs, mugs in hand.

While Samad built up the fire, Teller mentally rehearsed her story. She had been working on it since before they left Melilla, shaping it and adjusting it as she gained greater insight into Samad's character. Still, it was going to be a difficult story to tell. She wanted this story to gently nudge Samad into accepting the possibility of a new home, with new parents. She felt a little sad, thinking about Samad leaving her. But it wouldn't be fair to ask a boy as young as Samad to follow her all over Thalassa. And she had her own work to do.

The fire was crackling nicely, and Samad was waiting. It was time to begin.

"Once upon a time," Teller began, "there was a little kitten who'd lost its mother. It survived on scraps of food it found in garbage cans and sheltered wherever it could find a corner out of the rain. The kitten managed like this for quite a while, but fall turned to winter, and the weather grew rainy and very cold. One day the kitten, made daring by cold and starvation, crept into the back room of a fish seller's shop and stole a fish. The owner of the store saw the hungry kitten take the fish and chased after her.

"The kitten fled, the fish clenched in her teeth. She scrambled away, slipping on the slick cobblestones. But just as the shopkeeper was about to catch the kitten, a dog rushed out from an alley, tripping the kitten's pursuer.

" 'Follow me!' the dog called out. 'This way!'

"The kitten followed the dog. He led her into an alley and through a gap in a fence into a backyard. From there they scrambled down a culvert, under a hedge, and into the warm, fragrant darkness of a stable.

" 'We should be safe here,' the dog said. The kitten, suddenly alone with a dog several times her size, arched her back and retreated, her hissing muffled by the fish in her mouth.

" 'It's all right,' the dog reassured her. 'I won't hurt you. You don't need to be afraid.' He moved away from the kitten. 'Go ahead and eat.'

"After a couple of quick, nervous licks to wash off the worst of the dirt from the culvert, the hungry kitten tore into the fish. She slowed down when she'd eaten about two-thirds of the fish. A dozen bites later, her stomach bulging, she stopped and looked up at the dog.

" 'You can have the rest, if you'd like,' she offered.

"The dog, who had been watching from a safe distance, stepped up, nosed the remains of the fish, then gulped it down in two bites.

" 'Thank you,' the dog said. 'Would you like to stay here for the night? It's warm, dry, and safe. You could sleep in the hayloft.'

"It would be nice to be warm and dry for once, the kitten thought. And the dog had saved her from the fish stall man.

" 'Thank you,' the kitten said. She washed herself off thoroughly, then burrowed into the hay beside the dog. She slept deeply for the first time since she lost her mother.

"The dog continued to look after the kitten, helping dig food out of trash bins and scaring off other animals trying to steal her food. In return, the kitten caught mice for them to eat and crawled through tight spaces for food the dog couldn't reach. In a short time, they became close friends.

"But the dog could see that the kitten, though she seemed happy, needed a home and people to belong to.

"The dog continued to ponder the problem of finding a home for his friend without finding an answer.

"Then one day, as they were patrolling the market, an old woman saw them. She knelt down and held out a bit of the sausage roll that she was eating. The kitten came as close as she dared, and the old woman tossed the morsel of sausage to it. The kitten ate the sausage, and then looked at the dog and back at the old woman.

" 'Do you want me to give your friend some as well?' the old woman asked. 'Here then.' And she tossed a bite of sausage to the dog, who snapped it up eagerly. The old woman smiled at the two animals, picked up her bags, and walked off.

"The two animals cautiously followed the old woman home. She lived in a neat little brick cottage surrounded by a big garden.

" 'It's a nice place,' the dog said.

" 'I'll bet there's all kinds of bugs and mice to chase in the garden,' the kitten agreed longingly.

"The garden was so pretty and the house so charming that the two animals began to pass by every day. Whenever they encountered the old woman, she would pet them and give them something to eat.

" 'If only the old woman would take in my friend,' the dog thought, 'then she would be happy and safe. But how can I make this happen?'

"A few days later, the kitten caught three plump mice, which she proudly presented to the dog.

" 'Why don't you save one and give it to the old woman who feeds us?' the dog suggested.

" 'That's a good idea,' the kitten said, and she carried the mouse to the old woman's house. The old woman was out working in her garden, and the kitten laid the dead mouse at her feet.

" 'What a clever little cat you are!' the old woman praised her. 'If you'll wait a minute, I'll bring you some milk.'

"The kitten looked up at her and mewed plaintively, her tail straight up in the air.

"The old woman went inside and came out with a saucer of milk, which she set on the front stoop. The kitten lapped it up eagerly. When the saucer was clean, the old woman reached out and scratched the kitten's ears. Soon the little cat was sitting in the old woman's lap, purring loudly.

"You're such a sweet little cat. Why don't you come and live with me?

"Hearing her words, the dog felt a rush of sadness. He was glad that the kitten had found a home, but he would miss her company a great deal. With a heavy sigh, he got up to go.

"But the little cat saw the dog get up. She leaped from the woman's lap and trotted over to the dog. She sat down and looked from the dog to the old lady and back again.

"The old woman laughed. 'Yes, your friend is welcome to stay with me as well.'

"The little kitten trotted to the doorway and looked back at the dog.

" 'Well, come on. We've got a home now,' the kitten said.

"And so the two friends found a home with the old woman. And they were very happy together. And as far as I know, they're living there still."

Teller looked at Samad. He was sitting by the fire, his eyelids heavy with sleep, but he was still awake, and smiling.

"I liked it," he said. "It was a good story."

"Thank you Samad. It was the first time I've ever told it to anyone."

"Then you honor me, sera," Samad said.

Teller smiled. "Thank you Samad. Come on, it's time for bed. We've got a long trip in front of us tomorrow."

Teller banked the fire and tucked Samad in. Then she climbed into her bed and switched off the light, leaving only the faint red glow from the banked fire. The story's ending had surprised her. She had originally planned to end the story by having the dog leave the kitten safe in her new home, but some mischievous djinni in her subconscious had insisted on including the dog in her happy ending. She rolled over, bunching the pillow under her head.

Well, the story was told. Hopefully its message about finding a new home had reached Samad. Tomorrow they would get to Nueva Ebiza and check in with the Guild. She wanted to get Samad a haircut and take him to a doctor as well. The child was probably way behind on his vaccinations. And maybe they could have dinner at Carlucci's.

Given all they had to do tomorrow, it would be best to stay at the Guild House. Then the day after that, they would go stay with Samad's new family and begin the process of transferring his affection to them. Teller sighed. Samad would only be hers for one more day. She knew how the dog felt, watching the kitten in the old woman's lap. The happy ending in this story would be Samad's, not hers.

The next few weeks were going to be painful. She would be relieved when it was all over and she could get on with missing Samad. She hoped his new family would love his spirit and his sense of adventure as much as she did. God, how she was going to miss him!

Samad lay back and stared up at the red-lit ceiling, feeling incredibly happy. Teller had made up a story just for him! It was a good story, too. Maybe someday he and Teller would find a home, just like the kitten and the dog had. But he wasn't in any hurry to settle down. He liked traveling. Even being cold, wet, and tired had been fun because he was with Teller. But if Teller wanted to settle down, he'd be willing to settle down with her.

He yawned and turned over in bed. It didn't really matter where he was, as long as he got to be with Teller.

CHAPTER 3

TELLER FROWNED DOWN AT THE ADDRESS
written on the scrap of paper in her hand, and then up at the
broad-beamed white house in front of them. There were
worn spots on the lawn and a brightly colored toy ornithopter lay canted on one side under a wooly-leaved aka
shrub. The house was well kept up and freshly painted. In
the distance, Teller could hear the bells of the cathedral
chiming ten o'clock.

As she studied the house, two children came running
around the corner of the yard, shrieking in play. The first
child, a girl of about ten, scooped up the ornithopter and
ran around the bush, while the second, a boy of six, ran after
her. She threw the toy, which flapped and fluttered through
the air until it struck the white fence that enclosed the yard.
As the little boy ran to pick it up, he saw Teller and Samad
standing at the gate.

"Does the Karelli family live here?" Teller asked the little boy.

The boy nodded. "Are you the storyteller lady?"

"Yes, I am."

"I'll go get my mama." And he ran inside yelling, "Mama! Mama!"

The girl, a freckled redhead, opened the gate. "You'll have to excuse my brother's manners, he's too young to know any better. Please come in. Our parents are looking forward to meeting you."

As they came up the walk, the front door opened, framing a small woman with black hair and a warm smile.

"Are you Teller?" she asked.

"I'm Teller Bernardia, and this is my friend, Samad."

Suddenly shy, Samad bobbed his head at Sera Karelli.

"Welcome to our house. I am Athena Karelli. You've already met my daughter Alonsa and my son Nikolas. I'll show you your rooms and introduce you to the rest of the family."

Teller watched the Karellis closely as they made her and Samad welcome in their home. The children seemed loved and secure. As soon as they were settled, Samad ran off with little Nikolas and his twelve-year-old brother Amin, eager to play with other children after all this time among adults.

"He's a good child," Teller said wistfully. "I hope you like him as much as I do."

"It's clear that you love him very much," Athena replied.

"But he deserves a stable home life with a family who loves him. I'm on the road for most of the year. It wouldn't be fair to drag him around with me."

"But you'll miss him," Athena added. "And who wouldn't?"

"His mother," Teller said angrily. "She let drugs come

between her and Samad. And the foster home he ran from was too busy punishing him for his mother's sins to see what a gem they had." She shook her head and smiled apologetically at Athena. "I'm sorry. It makes me angry to see a child treated this badly on a beautiful world like ours."

"I understand," Sera Kerelli said. "A couple of our adopted children have terrible pasts, too. It's easy to be angry with the parents when you see the damage they've done to their children. But—" She shrugged. "Without them, we would not be the family we are. I try to understand the parents as well as the children." She smiled again, an ironic grimace with pain and anger at its heart. "And sometimes I wake up at two o'clock in the morning wanting to strangle their birth parents for what they've done to my child."

Teller nodded. "That's it exactly."

It was fun staying with the Karellis, Samad thought. He'd never seen a family like theirs. Most of the kids were adopted. Some of them had had pretty rough lives before the Karellis took them in. If his foster home had been like this, he'd never have run away. But then he'd never have met Teller.

Before he'd met Teller, he'd dreamed of living with a family like the Karellis. But he couldn't imagine living with them now. Much as he liked the family, they were sedentary as oysters. Living with them would bore him to tears now that he had traveled with Teller. Besides, the Karellis had each other. They were complete. Teller was alone. She needed him, and he needed Teller. Samad liked the Karellis, but he was quietly glad he wasn't one of them.

It was little Nikolas who let the bull out of the pen. Samad had just told him Teller's bedtime story about the kitten. Nikolas looked up at him, his blue eyes heavy-lidded with sleep, and said, "I'm glad you're going to be my brother. You tell good stories."

Samad's breath caught. "What did you say?" he demanded.

His tone of voice woke Niko up. "N-nothing," he faltered. "I wasn't supposed to say anything about it. It was supposed to be a surprise."

"What surprise?"

"My parents want to adopt you. That's why you're staying with us. You won't tell on me, will you?"

"No!" Samad whispered. Fighting back tears, Samad ran from the room. How could Teller do this to him! Didn't she see how much they needed each other?

He headed for Teller's room, intending to confront her with what Nikolas had said, but Teller wasn't there. Her storyteller's shawl and staff were gone, too. He felt another surge of panic, afraid that Teller had abandoned him with the Karellis. Then he recalled that she said she was going to a Guild meeting. Samad looked in the closet. Her travel-stained pack was still there, along with most of her clothes. Relief washed over him. She would be coming back.

Samad lay in bed, waiting for Teller's return. Despite his worries, he was so tired that he was half asleep when he heard her familiar tread outside his door. Sudden fear jolted him fully awake. Maybe she really didn't want him after all. When she came in to check on him, he pretended to be asleep.

He heard her murmur, "Oh Samad," and sigh sadly, and then she quietly tiptoed out of the room. He waited a few minutes and then got up to follow her. She wasn't in her room. He heard voices downstairs and crept toward the sound. Halfway down the darkened staircase, he saw her seated at the kitchen table with Ser and Sera Karelli. He crouched down in the shadows and watched them talk.

"Are you sure you want to go through with this?" Sera Karelli asked.

Teller shook her head and nervously smoothed her hair back into its bun. "I have to, Athena," she said and sighed. "I love Samad too much to subject him to the kind of life I lead. He'd be traveling most of the year, sleeping in strange places, eating strange food, and learning only what I can teach him. He'd have no family, not much of a home, and almost no friends his own age. I'd hesitate to ask another adult to share a life like mine, much less a child. And I'm too set in my ways to settle down."

"When are you going to talk to Samad about this?" Ser Karelli asked.

Teller shrugged and looked away, her face pained. She looked very old all of a sudden. "I don't know."

"You're going to have to talk to him," Sera Karelli insisted.

"I know, I know," Teller replied, "but I don't know what to say." She shook her head. "My whole life depends on talking, on telling stories, but I don't know how to talk to him about this." She was silent, head hanging, thinking.

"Maybe if he stayed with you for a couple of weeks while I went away, he'd decide on his own that he wanted to live with you," Teller suggested.

The Karellis looked at each other and then down at the table. They looked awkward and uncomfortable.

Sera Karelli's eyes met Teller's. "You know Samad best. Is that what he'd want you to do?"

Teller shrugged. "If I told him now that I wanted him to live with you, he'd get angry and dig in his heels. But if the notion came to him on his own, then maybe it would work."

"But what if Samad decides he doesn't want us to adopt him?" Ser Karelli asked Teller.

"I don't know," Teller said. "I guess I'd have to find another family." She sighed heavily again. "I hope he decides to stay with you. You're such wonderful people. I know you'd love Samad and take good care of him." She rubbed her eyes. "It's late. Let's talk more about this tomorrow."

"Good night Teller," Samad heard Sera Karelli say as he slipped back up the stairs to his room, his head and heart heavy with what he had just heard.

He climbed into bed and tried to make plans, but his mind was too muddled to think about the future. Finally, he slipped into a sleep troubled by uncertain dreams of people leaving him behind, while he grew smaller and smaller, until he was a tiny baby unable to do more than sit there and scream in enraged protest.

He spent most of the next two days in a state of shock, fragments of the overheard conversation between Teller and the Karellis cycling over and over through his mind.

A few nights later, Teller sat down beside him and gently explained that she had to leave town on business for a couple of weeks. Would he mind staying with the Karellis while she was gone?

Faced with Teller's departure, Samad discovered a sudden resolve. Whenever Teller left, wherever it was that she was going, he was going, too. He would show her that he could keep up with her, that he didn't mind cold or rain or no money. Besides, she *needed* someone to look after her. Hadn't he been helpful on the trip here? Hadn't he helped her make more money when she was telling stories in Melilla?

But if he protested now, she wouldn't let him go. So, hesitantly, he agreed to let her go, making her promise to come back soon.

In the end, it was easy. Teller left two days later, just after breakfast. After saying good-bye, Samad retired to his room, saying he wanted to read. Once alone, he swiftly crammed a few remaining items into his waiting knapsack. Then he climbed out his window and dropped to the ground. He slipped out the back gate into the alley. From there it was just a few steps to the street and freedom.

Samad ran down the street in the direction Teller had gone. He soon spotted her. Teller's head was bowed, and she walked as though her pack weighed a couple of hundred kilos. This time of day, the streets were quiet, and it was easy to follow her from a distance. Samad walked on the other side of the street, keeping trees and bushes and parked jitneys between him and the storyteller as much as possible. But Teller only looked back once. Fortunately, he was hiding behind a small truck, and she didn't see him.

Teller walked past the bustle of Nueva Ebiza's main port to a long, low, empty dock in a quiet part of the harbor. Samad watched as Teller walked to the end of the long pier and sat down. Taking off her shoes, she put her feet in the water and sat looking out at the harbor. Samad managed to sneak out to a big equipment locker halfway out the dock. He peered out from behind the locker, wondering what would happen next.

Teller pulled her feet out of the water after about five minutes. She dried her feet on an old towel and warmed them under her skirt for a while before putting her socks and shoes back on. She sat there, patiently waiting for about ten minutes. Suddenly, Teller sat up and looked intently at a spot in the water about twenty meters from the end of the pier. Samad felt a prickly sensation as though someone was watching him. He looked behind him, but no one was there.

Then the patch of water began to boil and surge. Something broad and darkly purple emerged. The water exploded into a brilliant halo of spray as a tall, triangular sail unfurled with a wet, billowing sound. Samad gaped in amazement. It was a harsel, the biggest one he had ever seen.

Like every child on Thalassa, Samad had dreamed of becoming a har captain. He had watched in rapt delight whenever one of the mysterious great fish sailed into Melilla's harbor. Like the other children, he had followed the harsels' captains as they walked through the town. He had clustered shyly with the other kids at the entrance to the pier as the harsels were loaded and unloaded.

But the huge creature gliding toward Teller dwarfed every harsel he had ever seen. Its translucent pink and lavender sail looked like a slice of the dawn sky. Samad watched openmouthed as the harsel glided to a stop at Teller's feet. The towering sail furled as neatly as a seabird's wing into a long hollow on its back. Water rushed from its cavernous hold as it opened its back to admit the storyteller.

Samad glanced back, expecting a crowd of watchers, but the quiet pier remained deserted. The gawkers and idlers were over at the main port.

"Hello, Abeha," Teller said out loud as she stepped onto the creature's broad back. "That wasn't a very subtle appearance, was it?"

Samad felt a faint pressure in his mind. He had felt similar flickers of presence when the harsels docked at Melilla but had dismissed it as imagination. Now he realized that it was the harsel mind-speaking to Teller. Samad strained his inward ear, but he couldn't make out any words, only a deep feeling of love and concern emanating from the harsel to Teller.

What was going on? Why hadn't Teller mentioned the harsel? Where were they going, and why? How could he follow Teller now? The great beast would surely notice him if he tried to sneak aboard, and then it would alert Teller. Panic swept through Samad at the thought of being left behind. What was he going to do?

Just then, Teller emerged from the gaping hold of the

harsel. Samad ducked behind the equipment locker as she strode up the dock, her brow furrowed in thought. She was so preoccupied with her own thoughts that she didn't notice Samad, though he could have touched her as she strode past. He watched Teller head for the distant offices of the port.

Then Samad felt the harsel's presence focus on him. He shrank against the locker. The harsel radiated reassurance.

"Wh-what do you want?" Samad asked, frightened despite the harsel's attempt to calm him.

"IT'S ALL RIGHT. COME CLOSER," the harsel said in his head. "I JUST WANT TO LOOK AT YOU."

Fighting his fear, Samad crept to the end of the dock. The harsel rolled on his side. One great eye, the size of a saucer, emerged from the water and focused on him. This close, Samad could smell the huge creature. It was a pleasantly marine smell tinged with lemon and a hint of some elusive spice. Samad's heart pounded with excitement. He had never dared to come so close to one of the huge creatures before.

"MY NAME IS ABEHA. SIT DOWN. PUT YOUR FEET IN THE WATER. DON'T WORRY. I WON'T BITE." The harsel's deep, bell-toned voice felt faint and distant, but Samad could sense an undertone of gentle amusement in the creature's mental voice.

Trembling, Samad took off his shoes and socks, pulled up his new wool pants, and put his feet in the chilly water. "Like this?" he asked out loud.

"YES. THAT'S MUCH BETTER," the harsel said, his mental voice suddenly sharper and easier to understand. "I CAN HEAR YOU CLEARLY NOW." The giant eye regarded him closely. "WHO ARE YOU, AND WHAT DO YOU WANT WITH TELLER?"

Slowly at first, Samad told the harsel how he had met Teller. By the time he got to Teller's plan to leave him with

the Karellis, he was talking to the harsel as though the giant
fish were an old and trusted friend. Then he finished the tale
and felt suddenly afraid. What would the harsel do now?

"TAKE A DEEP BREATH. CLOSE YOUR EYES. RELAX. LET
ME LOOK INSIDE YOU," the harsel coaxed.

Samad hesitated, afraid of letting the harsel probe deeper.
But he had to convince the harsel that he needed Teller and
Teller needed him. He pushed aside his fear, closed his eyes,
and opened his mind to the giant creature. Despite its great
size, the harsel's presence was gentle and deft. Suddenly the
harsel's examination was over. Samad swayed forward as
though a support had given way. He clutched at a bollard to
steady himself.

"ALL RIGHT. YOU CAN COME WITH US. BUT YOU MUST DO
EXACTLY THIS." And in Samad's mind the harsel's plan appeared wordless and entire. Immediately, he grabbed his
shoes and ran up the pier toward the warehouses.

As the boy ran off, Abeha rolled ponderously upright
again. If Samad proved to be all he seemed, he might be the
solution to their problems. The harsel reached mentally
shoreward, reassuring himself that he had seen what he had
thought he'd seen, but already the running boy was too far
for the harsel to feel more than a faint sense of urgency and
hope, fading as fast as an underwater sunset. If his plan
worked, there would be time to learn more about the boy.
The harsel submerged, waiting for Teller's return.

Samad pelted down the dock and into the maze of warehouses, following Abeha's mental image of the harbor,
learned, no doubt, from Teller herself. He found the right
warehouse and crept cautiously inside. There, high up in the
scaffolding among the small boats in dry dock, was the
harsel's crew pod. He clambered up the wooden scaffolding
to the crew pod, punched in the entry code, and climbed in,
shutting the door behind him. Guided by the harsel's men-

tal map, Samad felt his way through the pitch-black pod until he reached the forward storage bay and climbed inside. Then the harsel's instructions and guidance left him, and he was alone in the dark.

Samad settled himself inside a large coil of rope and pulled a tarp over himself. A few minutes later, he heard the distant rumble of the lifting crane. Muffled voices shouted directions in the familiar Nueva Ebizan polyglot of Spanish, Arabic, and Greek. There was a series of loud clunks and clanks as the pod was lifted out of its cradle. Samad clung to the shifting coil of rope as the pod was eased out of the storage bay.

The pod was lowered onto something. With a shuddering jar and the deep, throaty rumble of a powerful engine, the crew pod began moving again, now on some sort of carrier. Samad settled more deeply into the cushioning coil of rope and hung on as the carrier bumped and lurched along.

The rumble of the carrier stopped. A few minutes later, the pod was lifted into the air. He heard Teller's anxious voice shouting orders, and wondered if he could trust Abeha. What would Teller do when she discovered he was aboard?

The pod descended. Samad felt and heard the crew pushing the pod into place. Underneath the muffled voices shouting orders and the creaks and thumps as the crew pod was eased into place, Samad heard another sound, a sort of steady three-beat rumble, like a huge, waltzing engine. Samad wondered what it was.

"THAT'S THE SOUND OF MY HEARTS BEATING," the harsel informed him. Samad jumped at the sudden presence of the harsel in his mind. He felt the harsel's amusement, like a cascade of ringing bells, and then a quiet chord of reassurance.

There was a loud clanking of tackle, and the pod seemed to settle. Then the walls of the crew pod creaked, and the waltzing rumble of the harsel's hearts grew louder. A fan started to throb somewhere in the pod, and Samad smelled the marine scent of the harsel.

"I'VE JUST CLAMPED THE WALLS OF MY HOLD ONTO THE CREW POD," Abeha informed him. "TELLER WILL BE COMING ABOARD IN A FEW MINUTES. SHE'LL RESTOCK HER STORES, AND THEN WE'LL SET SAIL." There was a note of impatient yearning in the harsel's mind speech. Abeha was eager to be at sea with Teller.

Covered by the tarp, Samad listened as Teller moved around the cabin, opening and shutting doors. His heart pounded each time he heard her go past the door.

Samad felt a faint pressure in his mind as the harsel spoke to Teller. Again he strained, but he couldn't make out their words. There was no way he could tell whether Abeha had told Teller of his presence. He could only sit there in the darkness, trusting that the harsel would keep his secret.

Then he felt the harsel move. There was a distant billowing and a muffled thump. Briefly, the beat of the harsel's hearts grew faster and louder. Water burbled smoothly along the great creature's sides, and the deck tilted gently to one side as the wind filled the harsel's sail. Samad could feel a slow, swaying rise and fall as Abeha sailed out into the harbor.

"WE'RE ON OUR WAY!" the harsel announced, its mental voice like a peal of bells.

Samad relaxed. After days of panic, worry, and fear, he was with Teller. But now that he had achieved his goal, new questions surfaced. Why had Teller never mentioned Abeha? Why was Teller traveling as an itinerant storyteller when she was a prosperous har captain? Why was she trudging through the rain and snow, looking for places to tell stories, when she surely had a fancy house somewhere and metal in the bank? He puzzled over the mystery without finding any solution that made sense. At last, lulled by the gentle rocking sway of the harsel, he fell asleep, his questions unanswered.

CHAPTER 4

TELLER CLOSED THE FOOD LOCKER, A PUZ-
zled frown on her face. Food was disappearing. She pored
over her stores log, shaking her head in dismay. It wasn't really a big problem, she had more than enough for the four-
day trip, but it *bothered* her. Perhaps one of the stevedores
could have pocketed the braefish and the canned peaches,
but the four jars of Amariah's cinnamon crab apples had
been in a locked cabinet.

The obvious explanation was some kind of stowaway, but
Abeha would never have allowed a stranger on board. For a
terrifying moment, Teller wondered if her memory was giving way. But noting what she used in her stores log was an
old habit, and she would have to be deeply senile before she
would forget to do it.

No, there must be another explanation. The jars must
have been taken when they were in port. But why take food

from a locked crew pod when there were so many easier places to get it?

Teller slapped the logbook back on its shelf irritably. This was a peculiar voyage all around. She kept hearing strange bumps and thuds. At first she had suspected that something was loose, but the sea wasn't running high, and the sound was irregular, vanishing almost as soon as she noticed it. Abeha also seemed strangely preoccupied, which made her miss Samad even more. She continually caught herself wondering how the boy was doing.

Well, he was with the Karellis now. She would just have to get used to missing him. She slammed the locker shut and climbed out of the crew pod to sit on the harsel's broad back. There was no point in fretting over it. Sooner or later the answer to the mystery of the missing stores would present itself. Or not. She had plenty of food for the four-day trip to Ischia. She gave herself up to the sun and the wind and the broad blue sea.

Teller was just settling into sleep when she heard a door click quietly open.

"*Lights on!*" she shouted, and the lights blinked on to reveal Samad standing frozen in front of the door to the head. He stood there a moment and then dove into the forward storage bay. The door swung shut behind him as the harsel breasted a swell.

Teller opened the door to the storage bay. Samad was hiding under a pile of canvas that had been unfolded and used for bedding. A bucket neatly filled with empty jars and cans was wedged into one corner. She recognized Amariah's handwriting on one of the empty jars of crab apples.

"Samad! What are you doing here!" she demanded. "And how in hell did you get on board?"

"I wanted to come with you!" he told her. "I won't be a burden, I promise!"

Teller sighed. "Come on out, Samad," she said wearily.

"You promise not to make me go back to the Karellis or Melilla?" he demanded.

"Samad, you can come out like a grown-up, or I can drag you out like a small child. Those are your choices right now."

Samad cautiously emerged from behind the pile of canvas and stepped out into the cabin. To give herself time to think, Teller made them both hot chocolate.

She set the two mugs on the galley table and sat down across from him.

"How did you get on board, Samad?" she asked.

Samad shook his head and looked down at the table. The shine in his eyes threatened to overflow and become tears. "I can't tell you that," he replied.

"Oh for pity's sake, Samad, it was Abeha, wasn't it?"

Samad shook his head again. "I can't tell you," he repeated.

Teller looked up at the ceiling. "Hey, Abeha, did you let this kid on board?" she shouted.

There was a long, pregnant silence.

"YES," the harsel replied in a tiny voice.

The huge harsel sounded so shamefaced and abashed that Teller laughed out loud. Samad smiled, too, which surprised her more than it should have. He must be able to mind-speak with the harsel. How else could he have talked his way aboard?

"Why did you do that?" Teller said, speaking inwardly now, to exclude Samad.

"HE WANTED TO COME." The big fish still sounded ashamed.

"You've never done anything like this before. Why now?"

"BECAUSE YOU NEED HIM AS MUCH AS HE NEEDS YOU," the harsel replied.

"What!"

"IT'S TRUE," Abeha insisted. "EVER SINCE YOU GOT ON BOARD, YOU'VE BEEN MOPING BECAUSE YOU MISSED HIM."

"Of course I missed Samad," Teller replied. "He's a good kid, and I'm fond of him. But he belongs with a real family who can love him and provide a stable home."

"OH?" the harsel said, his mental voice dissonant with sarcasm and irony.

"Yes, he does," Teller replied.

"BUT THAT'S NOT WHAT SAMAD WANTS. HE WANTS TO BE WITH YOU," the harsel pointed out.

"Abeha, children often want things that aren't good for them," Teller explained.

"BUT YOU ARE good for him," Abeha insisted. "I'VE LOOKED INSIDE HIM, AND I KNOW."

"And I'm a human, and I know what's best for a human child, Abeha. I say he goes back to Nueva Ebiza."

"NO!"

"Yes!" Teller shouted out loud.

"NO!"

"Yes, Abeha! Turn around now! We're going back to Nueva Ebiza," Teller said, moderating her voice with an effort. She couldn't afford to lose her temper.

"MIGHT I REMIND YOU THAT I'M BIGGER THAN YOU ARE?" Abeha pointed out in a mild and reasonable tone of voice.

Teller noticed Samad's lips twitching as he fought back a smile. Abeha was letting him hear his side of the conversation. It wasn't funny, dammit. Why the hell was Abeha letting Samad hear what he was saying to her?

"BECAUSE THIS CONVERSATION CONCERNS HIM," Abeha replied. "WHEN WE'RE TALKING ABOUT SOMETHING THAT DOESN'T CONCERN HIM, I WON'T OPEN MY MIND TO HIM."

"Abeha, we need to take Samad back to the Karellis; they must be worried sick about him," Teller insisted, speaking out loud to include Samad.

"No! I won't go back!" Samad insisted. "Besides, the Karellis know where I am. I left them a note."

Teller squatted down so that she and Samad were on eye level, and she placed both hands on his shoulders. "Samad, I love you, I really do. But right now, you need a family and a consistent place to live. I travel too much, and I'm too old and sour to be a good parent."

"No you're not," Samad said. "And I like to travel."

"Samad, the Karellis love you, and they can provide you with a real home. I live inside a big fish. It's dark, it's cramped, it's wet, and it's smelly."

"I BEG YOUR PARDON?" Abeha interrupted. "I THOUGHT YOU LIKED IT."

"But I don't want to live with the Karellis! I want to live with you," Samad protested.

"And what about school, traveling around with me?" Teller asked.

"You can teach me. You know everything," Samad said. The infinite confidence in his gaze was terrifying.

The harsel's sarcastic laughter jangled like out-of-tune golden bells.

"Abeha, that's enough out of you!" Teller said. "You aren't helping one bit! Now please come about, and let's go back to Nueva Ebiza."

"No!" "NO" Samad and Abeha spoke in unison.

"I'M NOT TAKING SAMAD BACK TO NUEVA EBIZA. HE'S STAYING WITH US!" the harsel informed her.

"Goddammit, Abeha! Don't start playing games with me!" Teller snapped.

"I'M NOT PLAYING GAMES," the harsel said. "I MEAN IT. I WON'T TAKE YOU BACK TO NUEVA EBIZA. SAMAD STAYS

WITH US. HE NEEDS YOU, AND YOU NEED HIM. AND I NEED
BOTH OF YOU."

"What's that supposed to mean?" Teller said. "I don't
need a damned keeper, Abeha, and looking after you is *my*
job."

"I WORRY ABOUT YOU. I ALWAYS HAVE. YOU NEED SOME-
ONE TO LOOK AFTER YOU WHEN YOU'RE ASHORE," Abeha
insisted. "THAT'S WHY I NEED SAMAD. IF HE'S WITH YOU, I
WON'T WORRY."

"I'm old enough to take care of myself," Teller replied.

"I KNOW THAT, BUT I STILL WANT TO KNOW THAT SOME-
ONE IS LOOKING AFTER YOU WHEN YOU'RE ON SHORE."

"Why now? After all the years we've been together?"

"BECAUSE SAMAD CAN DO IT. AND I CAN TALK TO HIM.
THE ONLY OTHER HUMANS WHO CAN DO THAT ARE AL-
READY HAR CAPTAINS. AND I TRUST HIM. BESIDES, HE'S
GOOD FOR YOU. YOU NEED HIM, BUT YOU'RE TOO STIFF-
NECKED TO ADMIT IT."

"Abeha, I know you worry," Teller soothed, speaking inwardly so that Samad couldn't hear. "But I've taken care of
myself through good times and bad. You know I need my
freedom. Please, let's turn around and take Samad back."

"NO. HE STAYS."

The argument continued for the rest of the night and
into the next morning. Teller tried threats, pleas, placation,
and reason. None of it worked. The harsel remained stub-
bornly insistent that Samad stay with them. At some point,
Samad set soup and sandwiches in front of Teller. She ate
mechanically, her mind intent on her argument with Abeha.
Around four in the morning, Teller noticed Samad curled
up asleep on the galley bench. She covered him with the
blanket from her bunk and went back to arguing with
Abeha.

By dawn, Teller was getting too sleepy to argue, but she hung on grimly until midmorning before giving in.

"All right, all right, Samad can stay. But it isn't going to be easy on either of us," Teller warned the harsel.

"NO, I SUPPOSE NOT," the harsel said. He tried to sound grave and regretful, but the undertones of his mental voice rang with joy. "YOU'RE GOING TO HAVE TO WAIT A WHILE TO TELL SAMAD, THOUGH. HE'S STILL SLEEPING."

Teller smiled down at Samad and smoothed the blanket over him. She poured herself a cup of last night's coffee, grabbed some bread and cheese to eat, and shrugged on her jacket. Then she tiptoed out of the cabin and climbed up the metal rungs set into the back of the pod. Abeha opened his hold to let Teller climb out onto his broad back. She leaned against Abeha's tall dorsal fin, admiring the familiar curve of the giant fish's sail as it gleamed iridescently in the morning sun.

It was a perfect day for blue-water sailing. The sun was bright, and a strong breeze was blowing. The waves were studded with whitecaps, and an occasional whisk of spray landed on her jacket. Sea birds curvetted against the waves, soaring high against the glorious, cloud-studded blue sky. Off on the horizon she could see the green-clad volcanic peaks of the Kiklades Archipelago ranging off to the west. She inhaled deeply through flared nostrils, smelling the wild, fresh scent of wind-carried spray, then exhaled, letting go of all her fears and hesitations about adopting Samad.

I'm a parent, she said to herself. "A parent," she repeated out loud. *It's been a hell of a long time since I was a mother,* she thought. Now that she had stopped worrying about the possible complications, it felt good. She was no longer alone.

"WHAT ABOUT ME?" The harsel asked, but there were undertones of humor in its question.

"Well, you got me into this. I guess that makes you his father," Teller told Abeha.

"GEE, AND I'D SO LOOKED FORWARD TO BEING A MOTHER," Abeha remarked.

Teller became suddenly silent, reminded of their old argument. "You're much too young to be a mother," she said at last, trying to keep her mental voice light, and failing.

There was a very long silence in which Teller could hear her heartbeat and Abeha's, beating in very different rhythms.

"YOU'LL HAVE TO TEACH ME HOW TO BE A GOOD PARENT," the harsel offered at last.

"You'll be fine, Abeha," Teller reassured the harsel. "I'm the one who should be worried. It's been a long time since I've been a mother. I've probably forgotten how it's done."

After that, there wasn't anything more to say. Teller sat on the harsel's broad back, feeling a bit light-headed with tiredness, but very happy. She watched the scudding clouds bunch up against the slopes of the distant island peaks, imagining the future she would share with Samad.

Samad woke from a dream in which he was trapped in the bow of a sailboat with hungry manaos circling patiently below, waiting for him to fall in. Still groggy, he tried to roll over and encountered a hard, unyielding surface. A surge of fear raced through him; he was trapped. Then he felt Abeha's reassuring presence, and Samad remembered where he was. He recalled Teller's frowning, angry face as she and Abeha argued over his fate last night.

If Teller had really wanted him, then she wouldn't have tried to leave him with the Karellis, and she wouldn't have argued so fiercely with Abeha about whether he could stay. Teller had lied to him, then abandoned him to the care of strangers. After last night, Samad wasn't sure that he wanted to stay with Teller. But without Teller, what was he going to do? He didn't want to go back to the Karellis. They were nice people, but they weren't *his* family.

At least he wasn't stuck in Melilla anymore. Spring was here, and summer was on the way. He would find somewhere else to live, someplace where people were kinder and the weather was warmer. He didn't need Teller. He could manage on his own. He could and he would. Despite his resolve, Samad blinked back tears in the safe darkness.

Then he heard the walls creak as the harsel relaxed its grip on the crew pod. Teller's feet thudded on the rungs of the ladder as she climbed down from the harsel's back. Samad swiftly knuckled the tears from his eyes and sat up, bracing himself for whatever she had to say to him.

Teller opened the door. "Lights on!" she commanded, and the lights brightened gradually, giving his eyes time to adjust. Teller was clad in a worn yellow raincoat, and her hair was wet.

"I'll get you a towel," he volunteered, rolling off of the bench and pulling a clean towel off the rack.

"It's okay, Samad—" Teller began, but he had already tossed her the towel.

Teller caught it. "Thank you." She hung her wet coat in the shower stall and began drying her hair.

"Are you hungry?" he asked, trying to delay their inevitable conversation.

"I'm fine, Samad," she said, wrapping her damp hair in the towel. "Sit down." He sat back down at the little galley table. Teller sat across from him. She took a deep breath. "Abeha and I talked things over last night, and we would like you to stay with us."

"You don't really want me," Samad told her.

"That's not true!" Teller replied.

"Then why did you try to leave me with the Karellis?" he demanded.

"Because I believed it would be best for you," she confessed. "I was wrong." She looked down at the table and then back up at him. "I'm sorry, Samad. I've treated you very badly."

Shaken by Teller's unexpected apology, Samad looked away.

"It won't happen again. I promise," Teller said.

The silence stretched for a long while, neither one certain what to say to the other. Then Teller put a hand on Samad's arm.

"What were you going do on your own?"

Samad looked down at the table and shrugged. "I don't know yet. Find someplace better than Melilla, I guess."

"Then stay with me, Samad. You'll be well-fed and clothed. You'll get to travel all over Thalassa. You'll be safer than if you lived on the streets. We won't always get along, but I won't let anyone hurt you."

"You won't try to give me away to someone else?" Samad asked her bluntly, his hazel eyes meeting hers.

Teller looked down, her face darkening with shame. "No," she said. "Never again. I promise you that. And you're free to leave whenever you want."

Samad sighed and looked up at her. "I need to think about it," he said.

Teller nodded. "I understand, Samad." She looked very tired.

"Can I get up on Abeha's back? I haven't been outside since we left Nueva Ebiza." He desperately needed some time alone to think things over.

"Of course. Take my coat. Stay in the hollow where the sail goes until you get your balance. Abeha will be keeping an eye on you, but the water's chilly, and it'll take some time for him to come about and pick you up if you fall in."

"Don't worry, I'll be careful," Samad reassured her. Then

he opened the door to the crew pod and escaped onto Abeha's broad back, into the blue and gold glory of the afternoon, burdened by the weight of his decision.

Teller retrieved her blanket from under the galley table, climbed wearily into her bunk, and closed her eyes. She was so tired that even her worries about Samad couldn't keep her awake.

When she awoke, Samad was quietly trying to make dinner. She got out of bed and helped him get things started. While Samad kept an eye on the galley, Teller opened up the spare bunk. The bunk's unused hinges protested loudly as she unfolded it.

Teller surveyed the dusty, lumpy mattress with a frown. It had been a long time since anyone had slept on that bunk.

"Looks like I need a new mattress," Teller remarked as she thumped it to drive off the dust and even out the lumps. Then she pulled the extra bedding out of the storage locker and made the bed.

The timer dinged. Dinner was ready. Samad dished up the bean stew, while Teller sliced thick hunks of bread and cheese to go with it. The two of them ate in silence. The silence continued as Teller washed the dishes and then settled in with a book.

"Teller, tell me a story," Samad asked.

The silence between them had grown so intense that Teller jumped at the sound of Samad's voice.

"Okay," Teller said. "You get ready for bed, and I'll think about what story to tell you."

Samad brushed his teeth and changed into the lightweight pair of pants that he used for pajamas. Teller watched him. What could she say to repair the damage that her clumsy interference had caused? She shook her head. There was only one thing she could say, and that was the truth.

The top bunk creaked as Samad climbed into it. Teller made a mental note to oil the hinges tomorrow.

"Are you ready for a story?" Teller asked.

Samad nodded. Teller leaned against the edge of Samad's bunk.

"Well then," she began. "Once upon a time, there was a grumpy old woman who thought she had everything she needed. She traveled all over the world telling stories. Her best friend was an enormous harsel with a sail the color of a dawn sky. Her life was busy, and she thought she was happy.

"Then one day, she met a young boy who had just gotten himself into trouble. He was thin, he was ragged, and he had no mother or father. She decided to try to help the boy. So she listened to him, fed him, and clothed him. Because she believed that her own life wasn't good enough for him, she found a family willing to adopt the boy. Then, her duty done, she turned back to her life again. Or so she thought.

"But even her harsel's company could not fill the empty place in her heart that the boy had left behind. She would not admit it to herself, but leaving the boy with strangers, even kind strangers, had been a mistake. She missed him more than she would let herself know. Deep down, at the center of her loneliness, was the belief that the child could not love someone as old and set in her ways as she was.

"But the boy was wiser than the old woman in the ways of the heart. He would not let go of her. He followed the woman to the harbor where her harsel waited for her, and the harsel, seeing how much the boy loved her, helped him sneak on board.

"The old woman was surprised and angry when she first found the boy, but now she is happy that the boy is here, and hopes that this story will end with the boy deciding to stay, and that they will live together happily ever after."

In the hanging moment between the end of the story and

Samad's response, Teller wondered why she always had to put things in a story. If only she could tell the truth straight on. . . .

"Teller," Samad said, touching her arm lightly. "It's all right. I want to stay."

In her mind's ear, Abeha pealed wordless chords of jubilation. Teller clasped Samad's hand. Then they slid awkwardly into a hug. She blinked back the sting of tears.

"Thank you, Samad. I'm glad you're staying."

She released Samad, sniffed a few tears away, and smiled. She smoothed the covers over him.

"Get some sleep," she told him. "We've got a lot to do tomorrow."

Samad nodded sleepily. "Good night, Teller."

"Good night, Samad."

She lowered the lights and moved quietly around the cabin, settling things for the night, then climbed into the bottom bunk. First thing tomorrow, she would turn on the comm and call the Karellis to tell them what had happened. When they got to port, she would have to find out how to legally adopt the boy.

"Hey, Abeha," she said inwardly. "We're parents."

"I KNOW," the harsel replied. "I'M LOOKING FORWARD TO IT."

CHAPTER 5

AFTER A COUPLE OF MONTHS, SAMAD SET-
tled into a comfortable routine with Teller. He quickly
learned to maintain the crew pod and its environmental systems. Crew pods were not merely passive cabins for crew
and cargo. They were exquisitely molded to the shape of
their harsel's hold and covered with several inches of resilient foam padding. The crew pod's life support system enabled them to remain submerged indefinitely, so that the
harsel could ride out a bad storm beneath the waves.

In addition to maintaining the crew pod, there was the
harsel to look after. Every month or so, they pulled out the
crew pod, donned diving gear, and removed the parasites,
barnacles, and seaweed that accumulated on the harsel's
sides and hold. The first time Teller cooked up the parasites
and seaweed from Abeha's hold, Samad was appalled. But
once he got up the nerve to taste it, the parasite stew turned
out to be delicious.

"Doesn't Abeha mind?" Samad asked Teller.

"WHY SHOULD I?" the harsel inquired.

"Because we're eating things that ate your flesh," Samad told him. "They grew on you. Doesn't that bother you?"

"OF COURSE NOT. THOSE PARASITES *ITCH*. and they damage the skin of my hold."

"What did you do before humans came?" Samad asked.

"THERE'S A WHOLE COMMUNITY OF CREATURES LIVING ON AND INSIDE US. THERE ARE CREATURES THAT GRAZE ON THE SEAWEED; OTHERS THAT EAT BARNACLES; AND STILL OTHERS THAT EAT FLESH BURROWERS. BUT HUMANS DO A MORE COMPLETE JOB OF REMOVING PARASITES. I REMEMBER THE FIRST TIME THAT TELLER CLEANED MY HOLD. IT WAS BLISS!" The harsel sang a shimmering cascade of pure pleasure. "WE DIDN'T LIVE AS LONG BEFORE THE HUMANS CAME," Abeha added. "NOW THAT THE HAR CAPTAINS ARE RUNNING FLOATING HOSPITALS FOR THE HARSELS, EVEN WILD HARSELS CAN GET THEIR HOLDS CLEANED. HARSELS LIVE LONGER, HEALTHIER LIVES NOW. AND WE PRODUCE MORE AND HEALTHIER OFFSPRING SINCE WE STARTED PARTNERING WITH HUMANS."

Teller looked suddenly haunted. Something in Abeha's last remark had upset her. Samad gave her a questioning look, but Teller turned away. Abeha claimed to not remember the incident when Samad asked the harsel about it. Samad sighed. He loved Teller, but he wished that she were not so mysterious.

On shore, things were much as they had been before, though Teller was more open with him about her plans. They stopped at ports with harsel facilities as often as possible, so that Abeha's crew pod could be removed. But when the island they were visiting had no facilities, they left the crew pod in place and went ashore in the inflatable dinghy stored just outside the pod's airlock.

Abeha sailed with the other harsels while Teller and Samad visited the island. They traveled from town to town or household to household, telling stories and gathering gossip. Depending on the size and population of the island, they would be gone anywhere from a couple of days to a couple of weeks. Then they would rendezvous with the harsel and sail off to the next island.

All in all, it was a glorious summer, full of sun and sea and the excitement of new places and new people. Samad learned basic seamanship. By summer's end, he could read a chart, navigate by the two moons and the stars, and knew a fair amount of basic sailing.

In addition to learning seamanship, he also heard more stories than he ever knew existed in the world. Each new story only fueled his enthusiasm for more. He had memorized the entire Pilot Cycle, from the Pilot's first landing through her long sojourn alone on the planet. Then there were the stories of early years of the colony, where she appeared from nowhere to help those in need. And finally there were stories about her mysterious disappearance. Several islands claimed to host the Pilot's grave site, but several other stories claimed that the Pilot had ridden off on the back of her harsel and was never seen again.

Teller also helped Samad improve his reading skills. They downloaded books from every library they could find, and nearly every island had at least one small library. Teller also visited bookstalls in all the big port towns. She was continually trading storytelling sessions for new downloads. She even bought hardcopy books, which they read and then donated to libraries in outlying islands.

Teller downloaded a lot of textbooks, and she kept Samad busy learning their contents. Teller taught him math and geography, history, science, and Arabic and Castilian grammar. She also insisted on teaching him Greek. He liked most everything but the math and the grammar, but by the end of their first year together, he could speak flowery formal Arabic and genteel Castellano as well as the gutter argot he had grown up with. He could also carry on simple Greek conversations and do basic arithmetic.

But Samad could not see how Teller managed to live off of the money they made. True, they lived cheaply. Teller was resourceful at finding free lodging and food wherever they went. The small change and little gifts gathered after her stories would have been nearly adequate if she had performed regularly. But she was always stopping to help others. Sometimes it was a beggar in the streets. Other times she spent the morning listening to someone lost and alone pour out their troubles. Or she would spend a week or two helping out where someone was ill. Sometimes she did the chores, and other times she looked after the patient. She always refused payment for doing this. If there was a flood or a disaster, she would load the crew pod's normally empty storage holds with relief supplies and carry them where they were needed. When Samad asked why she helped so much, Teller replied that it was what the Pilot would have done, if she'd been alive.

And then there was Abeha, the biggest harsel he'd ever seen or heard of. None of the other storytellers were partnered with a harsel. Most people simply assumed that Teller was a retired har captain who had joined the Guild as a hobby in her declining years. But the Senior Guild members treated Teller with too much respect for her to be a mere hobbyist. There was nothing retired about Teller or Abeha, either. They took what they did very seriously. Samad had no idea what, exactly, they *were* doing; but it was a good deal more than telling stories.

Nor was Teller just a har captain, either. Except for emergencies, the only "cargo" she hauled was hardcopy books for various libraries, and those barely filled a single storage locker. And she never accepted payment for the books or their transportation.

A harsel the size of Abeha could haul half again as much cargo as any ordinary harsel. Teller could be wealthy if she chose. But Abeha's crew pod was worn and shabby, where the other har captains' were new and well-appointed. Teller's clothes were sturdy and well made, but they had seen long use. But despite her aging crew pod and old clothes, the other har captains treated Teller and Abeha with a respect approaching awe. And like the Guild, it was always the oldest and wisest captains that treated them with the most respect.

Clearly there was something different about Teller. But Samad couldn't figure out what it was. The har captains treated her with respect because their harsels did. The storytellers treated her with respect because she was an important member of the Guild. But the few people who actually seemed to know why she was so important were as close-mouthed as Filitosan menhirs. When he asked Abeha about it, the harsel told him to go ask Teller. And when he asked Teller, she smiled and said that she was just an old woman, and not important at all.

There was a secret at the heart of Teller's life, and not knowing it bothered Samad. But when he probed Teller about details of her past, she always found some way to put him off. If he persisted, she simply became silent.

So instead of prying at Teller's secret, he watched and waited for a clue that would reveal it. He hoped that some-day Teller would trust him enough to tell him what made her so different.

Summer ended, and fall began. They sailed south, into the tropics. The warm azure water was the realm of the sea sprites. Their scaly green heads bobbed up out of the water to watch them as they sailed past. On the sandy white beaches, sleek green sea sprites suckled their young. Often they would ride Abeha's bow wave, crisscrossing in front of the harsel with a joyous grace. Then one of the sea sprites leaped over a meter out of the water to snatch a heavily laden fisher bird from the air. With a snap of its wide-jawed head, the sea sprite shook the bird out of its skin. The bird's feathered skin floated on the surface like a bloody rag, while the sea sprite devoured the rest of the bird in three quick bites. Then it dove beneath the azure water and vanished.

"BEFORE THE HUMANS CAME, THE SEA SPRITES WERE ALL WE HAD FOR COMPANY," Abeha said as Samad watched the floating feathers recede behind them on the empty sea. "WE DIDN'T KNOW HOW LONELY WE WERE."

"Do you remember that far back, Abeha?" Samad asked. "I didn't realize you were that old."

"HARSELS HAVE LONG MEMORIES. WE CARRY OUR AN-CESTORS WITH US." And Abeha sang a fragment of a memory song. "THAT SONG CONTAINS THE MEMORIES OF ONE WHO DIED MANY GENERATIONS AGO. ALL OF US HOLD SOME OF OUR MOTHER'S AND GRANDMOTHER'S MEMORIES INSIDE OF US."

"Do you know anything about the Pilot's harsel?"

"I CARRY THOSE MEMORIES," Abeha said.

"He must have been a wonderful harsel," Samad said with a sigh. "I wish I'd known him."

"I'M TOLD THAT HE WAS VERY NICE," Abeha said. There was a faint chime of amusement in his voice.

"But he couldn't have been as wonderful as you are," Samad assured him.

Abeha's golden laughter pealed through Samad's head. "I'M SURE THE PILOT THOUGHT HER HARSEL WAS JUST AS WONDERFUL."

All too soon it was time for Abeha to join the other

harsels in their migration to the icy southern reaches of the Great South Sea. During the long days of the Southern Hemisphere's summer, the nutrient-rich waters became a rich broth of plankton. In four months' time Abeha would return, sleek with rich feeding and full of news of the other harsels.

During Abeha's absence, Teller and Samad joined a traveling school sailing around the Vorias Archipelago on an old schooner named the *Oriu*. The *Oriu* traveled in a circular route through the islands, spending a couple of days at each stop, tutoring local children on the courses they received over the satellite network. In addition to Teller, who taught Thalassan history through storytelling, the *Oriu* carried teachers proficient in several languages, as well as reading, writing, science, and math.

In return for storytelling sessions and seminars on Thalassan history, the other teachers tutored Samad during the runs between islands.

As the ward of one of the teachers, he was expected to be a model for the other students. The teachers were constantly pushing him to learn more and more, almost competing with each other over how much they could teach him. Since Teller would lose face if he looked stupid, he studied hard. But there were days he was tempted to jump overboard and swim to the nearest island.

At last Abeha's tall sail appeared on the horizon. Samad watched impatiently as the harsel came closer. Finally, he could bear it no longer. Snatching off his shirt, Samad leaped over the railing and swam out to meet Abeha.

"Abeha! It's so good to see you!" he said as the harsel gently lifted him onto its broad nose. "Did you miss me?"

"OF COURSE SAMAD. AND, FORTUNATELY, SO DID THE BIG MANAO THAT WAS TRAILING YOU."

"What manao?" Samad exclaimed, looking back at where

he'd been swimming. The big predators weren't common in these waters, but occasional attacks did happen. Then he caught the undercurrent of amusement in Abeha's mind speech. "Abeha!" he shouted, "You're teasing!"

"YES, BUT YOU SHOULD STILL BE CAREFUL, SAMAD. TELLER WOULD NEVER FORGIVE ME IF SOMETHING HAPPENED TO YOU. HOW IS SHE?"

"She's fine," Samad said. "But it's been nothing but school, school, school ever since you left. My brain is full!"

Abeha's laughter chimed in his head, washing over Samad in a wave of pleasure. "THERE'S STILL A LITTLE EMPTY SPACE!"

Samad's heart leaped at the sound of the harsel's laughter. "Oh Abeha! I'm so glad you're back!" He leaned against the harsel's mast, feeling it shift and thrum as Abeha pulled alongside of the schooner. Teller dove over the side and climbed onto the harsel's back.

"Hello, Abeha. Did the migration go well?"

"JUST LIKE ALWAYS," he assured her. "AND YOU? HOW IS THE TEACHING GOING?"

The two of them talked as casually as if Abeha had only been gone for a day, but Teller's face had lost that tense look that had become more and more pronounced the longer that Abeha was away. It was time that he left them alone. Samad swam back to the schooner. When he looked back, Teller was seated against the mast, eyes closed, a peaceful smile on her face. One hand rested gently on the harsel's back. Samad smiled, happy beyond words at the harsel's return.

But Abeha's arrival did not mean that Samad got a break from his studies. As a farewell present, the teachers gave them a surplus satellite receiver. Samad had to spend hours listening to the satellite teachers drone on and on. If he complained, Teller suggested that they settle down somewhere so that he could attend a regular school. Samad always backed down. The Satellite School might be incredibly boring, but at least he was with Abeha.

The spring term ended as they were sailing northeast toward the Mitiline Archipelago. But even though formal school was out for the summer, Teller continued to grill him on his math and test his linguistic fluency by speaking to him in different languages. At least with Teller, the lessons could take place up in the warm sunshine on Abeha's back.

After visiting the Mitilines, they sailed south through the Corsican Archipelago to Filicudi. From there they looped west along the coast of Marsala and then north again past the tropical isles of Abir, Sursur, and Altair Abayyid, where the muezzin's call echoed across the warm, still sea and tiny flying fish skimmed ahead of Abeha like skipped stones. When they passed to windward of an island, the scent of greenery and spices wafted far out over the sea. At night the water glowed with eerie blue phosphorescence. Samad would sit on Abeha's nose and watch the phosphorescence churning in his bow wave.

They stopped at Jazira-t al-Arwah, the Island of Souls, where most of Thalassa's major religions had their seminaries. They were greeted by a respectful delegation of representatives from each of the religions represented on the island. They were shown to spare but comfortable quarters. They had a surprisingly lavish feast of bastilla, chicken roasted with lemons, and flaky roast fish for the meat eaters. For the vegetarians in attendance, there was a rich vegetable tagine, couscous made with vegetable broth, rich, creamy kugel, and a plate of byesar served with a pillowy-soft pile of hot pita bread. For dessert there was rich baklava and rugela. When the feast was over, Teller and Samad thanked their hosts and belched appropriately. Then Teller left to confer with their hosts, while Samad headed back to their room and fell asleep.

For the next week, Samad only saw Teller in the mornings, over breakfast. The rest of the day he spent exploring the island, going wherever entrance was permitted. Samad passed many classrooms full of earnest students studying various holy texts. He wandered through courtyards of rabbis and imams quietly discussing fine points of Jewish and Islamic law. Once he tiptoed into a silent sanctuary full of black-robed Jesuit priests meditating under the watchful eye of a saffron-robed Buddhist nun.

The island was full of murmurs and music, bells, choirs, cantors, and muezzins, all praising the divine in their various ways. Even the patterns of light and shade in the breezy limestone-pillared arbors and courtyards seemed imbued with special significance. When he tired of the civilized courts of religion, he explored the wilder parts of the dry, rocky island. But even here, the fragrant scrub was crisscrossed with paths that led to small retreats and hermitages, where mystics prayed and meditated. The island was as full of devotion as a sponge is full of water. It felt as if you squeezed the air, blessedness would rain down like holy water. Even the lizards stared off into space as though contemplating the divine.

They stayed there for more than a week. Teller seemed to absorb more of the island's serenity and peace with each day they stayed there. Samad was pleased at the change but was a little relieved when they carried their bags down the long, white stone stairway to the pier where Abeha was waiting. After so long amid the white limestone chapels and courtyards, the water seemed even more intensely blue than he remembered. Clouds of pure white fairy gulls flicked past on long, narrow, swept-back wings as they rounded the point with its lighthouse and small whitewashed chapel and emerged into the choppier, darker blue waters of the strait beyond.

Samad looked back at the rocky green-and-white island they had left behind. It was a fascinating place, but he had felt very much like an outsider. None of the religions had called to him. He wondered if it was the same for Teller. She had never spoken of any deep, spiritual beliefs.

"What is your religion?" he asked Teller.

Teller turned away from the island and looked out at the white-capped azure water of the strait and the islands beyond it. In the distance, a fleet of harsels tacked one after the other. Their sails bloomed like flowers as they swung onto a new course. The sea wind stirred her gray hair.

She smiled mysteriously and gestured at the sea, the islands, and the wide blue sky arching above them.

"Thalassa is my religion, Samad."

Samad looked at the wind-tossed blue sea and the distant line of harsels. "I think it's mine, too," he confided.

Over the course of this year's travels, they had shuttled through a confusion of seasons: summer in the tropics, then spring and summer again in the north, and finally, on the cusp of the Northern Hemisphere's fall, they sailed back into the warm tropics again. Now they moved into spring again as they sailed deeper into the Southern Hemisphere. They were heading for the island of Thira in the Borghese Archipelago, on the northern edge of the Great South Sea. Teller would teach there while Abeha headed south with the other harsels.

As the weather cooled, Samad pulled out the warm clothes that Teller had gotten him so long ago in Melilla. He tried them on and was amazed to see his legs protruding from the pants. His fine blue shirt that Teller had sewed Perez's buttons onto was tight across his shoulders.

Teller looked up and smiled. "You've grown a lot, Samad," Teller remarked. "And filled out, too."

"But these clothes were special," Samad mourned. "You gave them to me, remember? And Perez gave me the buttons."

"Like it was yesterday, Samad. I'm afraid if I blink my eyes, you'll be all grown up." Teller tousled his hair affectionately, but there was a hint of sadness in her eyes.

Samad shrugged. "It'll take a little longer than that, Teller. I promise."

"I'll buy you a new shirt at the next port, and you can sew those buttons onto it."

Samad looked down at the shirt, stroking the soft, well-worn fabric. "I was going to sell these buttons after you left, Teller. It was going to break my heart to do it, but I had to live." He looked up at her. "I was so afraid of being alone again."

Teller gave him a hug. He felt Abeha's warm presence enfolding him as well. "Well, you're not alone now."

"I've got you and Abeha. I'll never be lonely again."

A shadow passed over Teller's face, and, though the words were hidden from him, he could tell that Abeha was speaking privately to her. Teller smiled fondly at him and gave him another quick hug. "No, Samad, you're too easy to love," she said gently. "Does that sweater we picked up in Filicudi still fit?" she asked, changing the subject.

By now Samad knew better than to ask what was the matter. The shadow had passed for now. Samad struggled out of his outgrown shirt. He wished he knew what made Teller so sad, but neither Teller nor Abeha would even admit that there was anything wrong.

Abeha left them at Thira to join the harsels' southern migration.

"I'll miss you, Abeha," Samad said when the time for farewells arrived.

"AND I'LL MISS YOU, TOO, SAMAD," Abeha replied sadly, his words tolling like a funeral bell. "STUDY HARD."

"Only if you'll come back as soon as you can! I don't want to be stuck in school forever!"

The harsel's laughter pealed down the scale in Samad's mind. "DON'T WORRY, SAMAD, I PROMISE I'LL COME BACK," the harsel said, answering the unspoken fear behind Samad's thoughts. Samad ran forward to the harsel's mast, the only part of the great creature he could truly embrace. He laid his cheek against the rough skin for a moment, letting his inward love and gratitude say all that words could not. As his ear pressed against the mast, he could hear the gentle luff of the sail. Under that steady vibration, he could hear Abeha's hearts beating.

"Good-bye, Abeha," he said, releasing his hold.

"GOOD-BYE," the harsel returned with a surge of love and sadness. "TAKE CARE OF TELLER FOR ME."

"I'll take care of her for both of us," Samad reassured him.

"I KNOW," Abeha replied with a warm chord of gratitude.

Samad stepped to the wharf, feeling Abeha's massive, gentle presence recede from his mind as he left the harsel's back. He began loading their baggage onto a cart, giving Teller the time to say farewell in private.

Abeha turned his sail to catch the wind and coasted away. They stood watching the harsel until he rounded the breakwater.

"Well," Teller said. "I guess we'd better get going."

Samad nodded. The crew pod was already on its way to storage. All that remained was to load their things onto the wagon that would carry them to their quarters. He turned toward land, his belly feeling like a stone. They were going to be staying in one place for four months. It seemed like forever. He leaned into the cart, pushing it up the pier. He could hardly wait for Abeha to return so that he could spend another year just like the last one.

School was not as bad as he had anticipated. All of the studying he had done over the last two years had paid off. Even though he had missed several years of school, he was able to keep up with his age mates in class in every subject except math. To his surprise, he was at the top of the class in history and reading.

He had dreaded coming into the term so late, but a number of other har captains' kids joined the class at about the same time. Their awe of Abeha made them treat Samad with deep respect. And Teller was the focus of much interest from the rest of the student body. Storytellers were regarded as persons of mystery and glamour, and Teller was no exception.

Soon Samad was the center of a circle of admirers, all eager to know more about Teller and Abeha. It was fun at first, but gradually Samad realized that most of the kids were more interested in the storyteller and her harsel than in him. And living with Teller had gotten him into the habit of reticence.

His circle of friends dwindled down to two. First was Ettore, the quiet, dark-haired son of a har captain. Samad had sat next to him at lunch one day. They had started talking about harsels and just kept talking.

A couple of weeks later, as Samad and Ettore were walking home from school, they came upon a group of boys clustered around a girl. Samad had noticed her at school because she had always seemed to be alone. The boys were jeering, and the circle of bullies was slowly tightening. The girl's face was pale but defiant. She looked ready to fight them all, no matter what it cost her. Almost without glancing at each other, Samad and Ettore decided to intervene.

"Hey!" Ettore called out. "Leave her alone!"

"Yeah? What are you going to do about it?" replied a large, lumpy boy, whose face seemed made to wear a sneer.

Samad had been the victim of bullies himself, when he had been poor, ragged, and alone. Mostly, he had run. Today, Samad decided to stay.

"We're going to stop you," Samad told him.

"Oh, and who are you?" the boy demanded. His eyes flicked sideways, and Samad, following the bully's glance, saw another boy about to pounce on Ettore.

"Behind you, Ettore!" Samad called. Samad ducked, punching the first bully in the stomach, hard. His hand sank deep into the boy's belly, and the boy bent over, wheezing. Then Samad pivoted in time to block a rabbit punch from someone else.

Ettore, warned by Samad, dodged the first blow and only took a glancing blow from the second. He started to fight back. Behind Ettore, Samad saw a red and brown blur. The girl had joined the fight. She fought with a desperate ferocity that spoke of many such battles. Then someone connected with a jab to Samad's nose.

"Hey! What are you boys doing?"

It was a man, coming out of a house. The bullies melted away.

The man started to lecture them. The girl stepped forward, curtsying politely. "I'm sorry sir. It was my fault. They were protecting me. Do you have any ice? My brother here's got a nosebleed."

Samad touched his nose, and his fingers came away red.

The man's manner changed. "You should take better care of your sister," the man advised Samad. "I'll get some ice," he said and vanished into the house, returning a few minutes later with a newspaper cone full of crushed ice.

The girl thanked him politely; oblivious of her own

swelling lip and the reddening bruise on one cheek. Ettore spoke up then, reassuring the man that everything was all right, and that they'd see the girl home safely.

The man scolded them once or twice more, then retreated into his house.

"Thank you," the girl said. She held out the dripping cone of ice. "Put this on the back of your neck. You should pinch your nose like this; it'll help stop the bleeding," she said, pinching her nose to show them how.

Samad did as she said, and the bleeding slowed almost immediately.

"I'm Ettore. Who're you?" Ettore was clearly impressed.

"My name is Agnese."

"I'm Sabad." Samad said, his nose still clogged with blood. "Are you okay?"

Agnese nodded. "Thank you for rescuing me. Usually I can take care of myself, but today there were just too many of them."

Samad shrugged, Ettore looked down at his feet. Neither knew what to say next.

"But you really shouldn't be seen with me," she cautioned. "My mother's . . ." she hesitated. "My mother lets men visit. For money. If you're seen with me, your parents aren't going to like it," she told them. "I don't want you to get into trouble."

"Oh," Samad said. He remembered his own mother, and the shadow her drug addiction cast over his life. "I see." He thought about Teller, and the Pilot, how they always helped out whoever needed it. He looked at Agnese. She was tense, bracing herself for another rejection. Ettore was looking at him, waiting to see what Samad was going to do.

"I don't care what your mother does," he said. "But could you try to pick some bullies who don't hit so hard next time?"

"Yeah," Ettore added. "And maybe not so many, either."

"Can we see you home?" Samad offered.

Agnese hesitated. "Just as far as Via Santo. I'll be all right after that."

Samad and Ettore started walking to and from school with Agnese. After so long as a street child, it felt good to be able to help someone else. And it gave him a way to sail out from under Teller's shadow. It took several more fights, but eventually the bullies found easier prey.

Then a delegation of concerned mothers came to see Teller. Teller listened politely and then turned to Samad to ask him what happened. As truthfully as possible, he told her how he met Agnese.

Teller listened with her usual intentness, but Samad could see a slight tightening of the corners of her eyes that only happened when she was hiding her anger. He met Teller's gaze defiantly. Let her punish him. He was not ashamed of his friend.

"Could you name some of the young men who were harassing Agnese?" Teller asked him.

"Adriano Vicente, Cosmo Akilina, Cesar Gonsales, and Victor Bonsalves," he replied. Sera Akilina and Sera Bonsalves were part of the delegation that had come to warn Teller about Samad's friendship with the daughter of a whore.

"You're sure that's all of them, then, Samad?"

He nodded. "Some other kids were watching, but they were the leaders."

"I see," Teller said. "Thank you, Samad." She laid an affectionate hand on his shoulder, and he felt the knot of tension in his stomach relax.

She turned to the other women, and Samad saw a flash of anger in her eyes. She drew herself up in the small, narrow chair she was sitting in. Her presence suddenly filled the shabby living room of the teachers' residence where they were staying. Their visitors drew together like a clutch of nervous hens.

"I'm proud of what Samad did. He saw a wrong and stepped in to stop it. When your sons stop bullying girls because of their mother's reputation, I'll speak to my son about not defending those girls. Until then . . ." Teller stood straight as a young reed despite her iron-gray hair. "Thank you for coming."

Samad listened, amazed. Teller had called him her son! He ducked his head and smiled, not wanting to embarrass her with his joy.

"Thank you," he told her, when the delegation of women had left.

"For what?" she asked. "You did something that was good and brave and kind. I'm the one who should thank you. Now, tell me about Agnese and her mother."

"I don't know her mother very well. She's beautiful, and seems a little sad. Agnese said that her father was a fisherman whose boat was lost in a storm. They had nothing after her father died. Her mother had no choice but to . . ." He hesitated. "Do what she does," he finished lamely. He couldn't bring himself to call Agnese's sad, dignified mother a whore, no matter what she did to keep a roof over their heads.

"Doesn't she have any family?" Teller wondered.

"Agnese never mentioned anyone. I think her grandparents are all dead. Or . . ." He shrugged. "Maybe they don't get along."

"Thank you, Samad. That was well told. Let me see if I can find some way to help Agnese and her mother."

"Really?" Samad said, his eyes shining.

"Really," Teller replied, ruffling his hair. "Give me a few days to think about this, and I'll see what I can do. And Samad?"

"Yes?"

"Better not say anything to Agnese or her mother until I find some way to help them. I don't want to offer them false hope."

Nothing happened for several weeks, and then one day Agnese came to school in a new dress.

"Samad! Guess what happened! My great-aunt Lucia has left us four thousand dinario!"

"Four thousand dinario!" Samad repeated. "Agnese, that's wonderful! I'm so happy for you. What will you and your mother do with that money?"

Agnese looked briefly downcast. "Mama wants to go to Tiranesi and open a shop. We'll be leaving as soon as the term is over. I'm happy to be going, but I'll miss you, Samad."

"I'll miss you, too," Samad told her. "But with all the traveling we do, we'll surely see you again. We'll look for you if we're ever on Tiranesi."

"But what about Ettore? Will I ever see him again?"

Samad shrugged. "Who knows? His father's a har captain. Perhaps someday they'll go to Tiranesi, too."

That night, when he reached the teachers' residence, he told Teller about the good fortune that had befallen Agnese and her mother.

"So you don't need to figure out a way to help them after all."

"I'm glad they found their own way out of their troubles," Teller said with a pleased smile. "It's usually better that way."

Teller accompanied Samad and Ettore when they went to the harbor to bid farewell to Agnese and her mother. Agnese and her mother were leaving on one of the little wooden ferries that plied the waters between islands. Agnese cried when she said good-bye, but her mother looked defiantly cheerful as she stood on the wharf, with their worldly possessions packed into one battered canvas suitcase.

"Your grandson was kind to Agnese," she told Teller. "He's been well-raised."

Teller shook her iron-gray head, feeling suddenly old. "He's my son, and whatever kindness he showed your daughter came from his heart no prompting from me. I'm proud of him, though. Your Agnese's a good girl. She's got a lot of courage."

Agnese's mother glanced at Teller warily, then, realizing that there was no insult intended, smiled with a tentative pride. "I'm proud of her. The times we've been through have been hard." She drew herself up. "But that's going to change, thanks to our good fortune."

Teller nodded. "I'm glad. Please write us when you get settled, so we can visit when we're on Tiranesi. We'll be here for another two months at least, and they'll forward my mail after that."

"I will," Agnese's mother promised.

Samad stepped forward and awkwardly shook Agnese's hand. Ettore shook her hand as well, then stopped, looked her in the eyes for a long, searching moment, and leaned forward to kiss her on the cheek.

Agnese turned bright pink and covered her cheek with her hand.

"Good-bye Ettore," she said. "Thank you."

"Come along, Agnese," her mother said. "It's time to go."

Agnese and her mother picked up their suitcase and started up the gangplank. Agnese turned back to wave at Samad and Ettore, but her mother walked onto the ship without a backward glance, her back straight, her head held high. Teller was impressed by the woman's dignity, and sorry that she hadn't gotten to know Agnese's mother better.

Teller followed Samad and Ettore up the wharf. All Agnese and her mother had needed was enough money for a fresh start. The hard part had been finding a way to get that money to them in a way that preserved their dignity. Watching Agnese's mother walk proudly up the gangplank on her way to a new life made it all worthwhile.

"Hey boys!" she called to them. "I'll race you to the ice cream shop!" And she ran after Samad and Ettore, her heart light as a wind-blown pennant.

With Agnese gone, Samad spent more time than ever with Ettore. The two became inseparable companions, often sleeping over at one another's houses. Through Ettore, he met the other har captains' children wintering over on Thira. Over the course of the school term, they had recovered from their initial awe of Abeha. With that out of the way, Samad discovered that he liked most of them very much. Like him, they loved to travel, and they had lots of stories about the places they had gone and the things they had seen. He looked forward to seeing them again as they all headed north.

About two weeks after the summer term ended, the wind shifted, blowing cold out of the south. That wind brought the first harsels back on their northerly migration. Akuale, Ettore's father's harsel, was among the first to return. He sailed in with three or four others on a fresh fall day, a breeze sending clouds and fleecy whitecaps scudding from horizon to horizon. Ettore and Samad were at the lighthouse on the point, watching for the returning harsels. As soon as he realized that the pale gray sail on the horizon was Akuale, Ettore ran to tell his father. Samad remained behind, watching the sea until night fell, but there was no sign of Abeha.

After Akuale's return, Samad spent most of the day down on the docks, helping Ettore and his family prepare for their long trading journey. Whenever a harsel's sail appeared on the horizon, Samad stopped and looked to see if it was Abeha's. After a week of careful stowing and sorting, Ettore's family was ready to sail. Samad stood for a long time on the dock, watching as their sail dwindled in the distance. He missed Ettore's company even more as he sat on a rock near the South Point lighthouse, scanning the horizon for Abeha. When waiting became too tedious, he would return to the harbor and help one of his other friends' families load up their harsels and leave.

After three weeks with no sign of Abeha, Samad noticed that Teller was getting anxious. She started asking the other harsels for news of Abeha. None of them seemed to have any news. The few that had something seemed strangely reticent. Samad walked with her, trying not to show how much her concern was affecting him. By the fourth week, Teller stationed herself by the lighthouse on the point, looking out to sea, watching the other harsels leave, their crew pods laden with trade goods.

Teller sat on the rocks out by the lighthouse, chin on her hands, watching the last of the har captains leave port. Abeha had always been one of the first harsels to return from the south. The other harsels' lack of news only increased her concern.

"Look!" Samad said, pointing off to the south. "Is that a sail?"

Teller sat up, peering intently at the blur on the horizon. "Maybe. The binoculars, Samad?"

She looked through the binoculars for a long time, her

body tense with concentration. It was a sail, and it was heading for Thira.

"Is it him?" Samad demanded anxiously.

"I'm not sure. It's still too far away."

She stared through the binoculars until her eyes swam. Samad was staring intently out at the horizon, one hand gripping the seam of her shirt. Then the approaching harsel turned slightly, and something in the way it moved and the new silhouette of the distant sail caused a sudden thud of certainty in her gut. She felt almost giddy with relief.

"It's him!" Teller announced, handing Samad the binoculars. "It's Abeha!"

Samad peered intently through the glasses for a long moment, then broke into a pleased grin.

"Finally! Shall I go tell the harbormaster that you'll be needing your crew pod?" he asked her.

Teller nodded. Samad handed her the binoculars and sprinted back up the point. At the rate he was going, he'd be too winded to tell the harbormaster anything when he got there. She smiled, happy that this long period of tense waiting was finally over.

Teller put the binoculars in their case. Then she took off her shoes and rolled her pants up to her knees. Clambering down to the water's edge, she stuck her feet into the chilly autumnal sea.

"Abeha?" she called inwardly.

"I'M BACK," came the reply, faint but clear.

"It took you long enough," Teller said. "I was getting worried."

"I WAS HUNGRY," Abeha replied, sounding peevish and defensive.

"You know what will happen if you eat too much," Teller warned.

"I KNOW," Abeha replied, his voice in Teller's head was

growing stronger as he drew nearer. Teller could sense an undercurrent of guilt in the harsel's voice.

"I need you too much to lose you, Abeha," Teller confessed.

"I KNOW," Abeha replied, sounding more resigned than angry now. "I KNOW."

"I'm glad you're back," Teller offered. "I missed you."

"I MISSED YOU, TOO," Abeha replied, love and longing ringing in his voice. He turned in a long, sweeping curve that made Teller's heart soar. She was so relieved to see him. Just then, a wind-driven wave slapped at her legs, soaking her pants.

"GO IN BEFORE YOU FREEZE," Abeha scolded her, "I'LL BE THERE AS SOON AS I CAN."

"All right," Teller said, joy rising like a spiraling seabird within her. "I'll see you soon."

She clambered up the rocks, slipped her shoes onto her still-wet feet, and ran to the harbor as quickly as a girl.

CHAPTER 6

SAMAD SAT ON ABEHA'S BROAD BACK, CLAD
in foul-weather gear against the blowing spray of the gray
and stormy sea. Abeha's sail was reefed as small as the
harsel's powerful web of muscles could contract it. Despite
the reef in his sail, Abeha was heeled over sharply as he raced
through the storm-tossed water, waves crashing over his
broad back.

Samad sat astride the harsel's dorsal ridge, his lifeline
clipped to a padded ring buckled around the base of the
harsel's mast, feeling the surge and sway as the great fish
sped through the gale. He shared Abeha's exultation in the
wild sea and the driving wind. It was good to be at sea
again, freed temporarily from the drudgery of school. Abeha
rejoiced with him; his singing resounded in Samad's head
like an avalanche of church bells.

A school of sea sprites rode the great fish's bow wave,
their bodies flashing with bright colors like streaming rain-

bows. They crossed back and forth in front of the speeding harsel, leaping from the water as though propelled by sheer joy. Off to one side a long-winged ma-o-ha bird skimmed across the face of a wave, a winged mote of calm amid the vast, raging sea. With a subtle shift of its wings, the bird lifted away from the water and skimmed past them, silent as a ghost. Samad's heart soared like the bird, racing with joy at Abeha's return.

"I'm so happy you're back, Abeha. I missed you so much," Samad said when the bird was lost in the driving spray.

"I'M HAPPY TO HAVE YOU BACK WITH ME," Abeha told him. But Samad could feel a deep sadness underneath the harsel's words.

"Something's bothering you, Abeha," Samad said. "What's the matter?"

"THERE IS SOMETHING I MUST DO THAT WILL MAKE TELLER UNHAPPY," Abeha told him.

"What is it?" Samad asked.

"I CAN'T TELL YOU YET, SAMAD," the harsel replied. "I MUST TALK WITH TELLER FIRST. WHAT I HAVE TO SAY WILL NOT BE EASY FOR HER TO ACCEPT. I NEED YOU TO BE READY TO HELP HER."

"Please tell her soon, Abeha," Samad urged. "I don't like keeping secrets from Teller."

"DON'T WORRY, SAMAD," the harsel reassured him. "I WILL SPEAK TO HER AS SOON AS I CAN."

Abeha fell abruptly into a listening silence. "THAT WAS TELLER. SHE SAYS THAT LUNCH IS READY," the harsel relayed.

"You'll be okay?" Samad asked.

"I'LL BE FINE," the harsel told him. "GO AND EAT."

Teller paced the length of the harsel's dorsal ridge. Yester-day's glorious gale had blown itself out. Today was gray and

foggy and eerily still. Abeha had furled his sail and drifted
in a doze. Samad was still asleep in his bunk. For the moment, Teller was alone with her thoughts, and she was glad
of it. Something was going on. There was a strange sorrow
underlying Abeha's thoughts. After an initial burst of high
spirits, Samad had become quiet and watchful, as though he
was waiting for something to happen.

She paced back and forth across the harsel's back,
mulling over the little clues that led nowhere until she realized that Abeha was awake and watching her think.

"Good morning," she said. "Did you sleep well?"

"NO, SOMEONE'S BEEN PACING UP AND DOWN ON MY
BACK," the harsel replied. But there was very little levity in
the harsel's presence.

"What's going on, Abeha?"

"I'M GOING TO CHANGE, TELLER. I HAVE TO."

"No! You can't, Abeha. I love you. I *need* you!"

"I MUST," Abeha insisted. "IT'S LONG PAST MY TIME TO
DO SO."

"*No!*" Teller cried.

"I KNOW HOW MUCH YOU NEED ME, BUT YOU HAVE TO
LET ME GO," the harsel said.

"*No!*" Teller shouted again. Her voice sounded small and
weak amid the blanketing fog and the wide, calm ocean. She
turned as if to flee, but there was nowhere to run. She fell to
her knees on Abeha's broad back. "No. Don't do this to me,
Abeha!" Teller pleaded in a desperate whisper. "Please!"

Just then, Samad emerged from the harsel's hold. His
hair was still rumpled from sleep; there was a worried look
on his face. His jacket gaped open, and Teller could see that
he was still in his pajamas. Teller stood up.

"What's the matter?" Samad asked. "Abeha said you
needed me."

"IT'S TIME FOR ME TO MATE," Abeha told him.

Puzzled, Samad looked at Teller. "I don't understand, Abeha's mated before hasn't he?"

"MANY, MANY TIMES," Abeha agreed.

"So why is this time different?" he asked.

"I HAVE CHOSEN TO BECOME FEMALE," Abeha explained.

"What?" Samad said, blinking in surprise. "How can you do that?"

"IT'S A QUESTION OF BODY FAT, SAMAD," the harsel explained. "ONCE MY BODY FAT REACHES A CERTAIN LEVEL, I BECOME FEMALE, AND MY EGGS BEGIN TO DEVELOP. I'M RIGHT AT THE THRESHOLD NOW. I ONLY NEED TO FEED HEAVILY FOR ANOTHER WEEK OR TWO, AND THEN THE CHANGE WILL START. BUT I WANTED TELLER TO KNOW BEFORE IT HAPPENED."

Samad looked at Teller. To his surprise there were tears in her eyes.

"All right, so Abeha becomes a girl, and lays eggs instead of—well—instead of being a boy. Why are you so upset?"

Teller got up and took Samad's hands. "Females mate only once, Samad. They die giving birth to their young."

"No!" Samad shouted. "Abeha! You can't do this to us!"

"I MUST, SAMAD," Abeha said. "WITHOUT THIS SACRIFICE, THERE WOULD BE NO HARSELS."

"B-but why now? Can't you wait a few years?"

"I HAVE WAITED A LONG TIME ALREADY, FOR TELLER'S SAKE. BUT I CAN'T PUT IT OFF ANY LONGER."

"Why not?" Samad demanded.

"EVERY SIX YEARS, THE TWO MOONS ALIGN TO CREATE A SERIES OF VERY EXTREME TIDES. DURING THESE TIDES, THE HARSELS CONGREGATE IN BAYS WHERE THE CONDITIONS ARE RIGHT FOR MATING. BECAUSE I'VE WAITED SO LONG, I'VE GROWN SO BIG THAT THERE'S ONLY ONE MATING BAY THAT I CAN STILL SAFELY ENTER. IF I DON'T MATE THERE THIS YEAR, I'LL GROW TOO LARGE TO ENTER THAT

BAY AS WELL. THIS IS MY LAST CHANCE FOR A FEMALE MATING."

"Couldn't you just decide to live?" Samad asked.

"IF I DON'T MATE AS FEMALE, I'LL BECOME AN OUTCAST AMONG MY OWN PEOPLE," the harsel said. "MY NAME WILL BE FORGOTTEN, AND MY MEMORIES LOST. IT WILL BE A LIVING DEATH."

"You'll still have us. Me and Teller," Samad offered. "We'll still love you."

"I KNOW YOU DO," the harsel said gently. "I WOULD WAIT IF I COULD, BUT I AM A HARSEL. I MUST SERVE MY PEOPLE BY BEARING YOUNG."

"But you'll *die!*" Samad cried.

"I HAVE LIVED MUCH LONGER THAN MOST HARSELS, SAMAD. I HAVE LOVED MY LIFE, BUT NOW IT IS TIME FOR ME TO PASS ALONG MY LINEAGE. IT GRIEVES ME TO CAUSE YOU PAIN, BUT I *MUST* DO THIS." Abeha enfolded Teller and Samad in his warm, loving presence. Samad could feel the intensity of the harsel's grim resolve and the depth of his sorrow.

"I love you, Abeha!" Samad told him. "I don't want to lose you!"

"I KNOW, SAMAD," the harsel said, speaking only to him. "BUT YOU ARE YOUNG AND CAN FACE THIS GRIEF. TELLER HAS KNOWN ME MOST OF HER LIFE. OUR LIVES ARE DEEPLY INTERTWINED. LOSING ME WILL SHATTER HER. SHE WILL NEED YOU. AND I NEED TO KNOW THAT YOU WILL BE THERE TO HELP HER."

"No! I can't! It's too much!" Samad shouted, and he fled down into Abeha's hold.

Things were tense aboard the harsel for the next few days. Teller wandered, mute with grief. Abeha was silent as well, a hurt, determined silence. Samad, caught between them, could only watch, helpless, as Teller and Abeha struggled with their anger and their need for each other. How could Abeha expect him to heal Teller? He was too young, too inexperienced. He could, and did, make sure that Teller ate, but there was nothing he could say or do that would cheer her up. How could he, when he was nearly as devastated as Teller?

It was a sad relief to finally make landfall at Kyrenia.

"I'm going to go make arrangements, Samad. Can you please see that the crew pod is safely stowed, and then come find me at the inn? We're staying at the Sea Sprite again."

Samad nodded. He suspected that Teller wanted to be alone. And, much as he loved her, he needed some solitude himself.

"SAMAD?" Abeha asked when Teller was gone.

"What is it?" Samad said resentfully. The emotional weight of the harsel's troubled presence had rubbed all the surfaces of his mind raw.

"I'M SORRY, SAMAD. I NEVER REALIZED HOW HARD THIS WOULD BE FOR YOU," Abeha apologized. "WHEN I MET YOU, I HOPED THAT YOU WOULD TAKE TELLER'S MIND OFF OF ME, GIVE HER SOMETHING TO LOOK FORWARD TO, AF-TER I—"

"You mean you *planned* all this? You *expected* me to pick up all the pieces for you?" Samad demanded.

"I'VE HELD OFF FROM COMPLETING MY FINAL MATING BECAUSE I WAS AFRAID THAT MY DEATH WOULD BE TELLER'S AS WELL. THEN YOU CAME ALONG. YOU WERE PERFECT, JUST WHAT TELLER NEEDED."

"And so you just thought you'd use me, is that it?" Samad shot back. "You never bothered to try to find out how I'd feel about all of this, did you? Damn it, this isn't just Teller's life anymore! It's mine, too!"

Samad picked up his pack, swung it onto his shoulder, and fled, leaving the crew pod just as it was. His sense of anger and betrayal was like a raw wound. The harsel's pleas grew faint and then died away to nothing as he strode away from the harbor. He kept going until he was halfway up a high, rounded hill overlooking the small harbor town. He paused for breath and looked back at the town, enclosed by the placid, grassy hills and the wide, oblivious ocean. He was wholly alone at last.

Samad climbed the rest of the way up the hill and lay back in the long, wiry grass. He watched the clouds slowly billow and glide across the endless azure sky, thinking as little as possible. It felt good up here. There were no impossible demands, no quiet despair. He was tempted to just shoulder his backpack and head into the hills. To run away from the whole mess, leaving Teller and the harsel to settle things on their own.

He could leave if he wanted to. He was old enough now to sign on somewhere as an apprentice. He could settle down and learn enough to make a comfortable living. He could live like an oyster, sedentary and safe in his own shell.

He sat up and looked down at the town of Kyrenia, nestled between the sea and the hills. It seemed so tiny from here, a cluster of maybe a hundred buildings, edged by the docks. Fishing boats were spread like scattered grain on the dark blue surface of the sea. He could see the inn where they were staying.

They had stayed at the Sea Sprite last summer, on their way to Thira. He remembered the fireplace in the inn's main room. Embedded in the black basalt stones lining the fireplace were thousands of tiny chips of shiny volcanic glass that threw back the light of the fire like a million tiny embers. The mantelpiece was made of a single twisted log of opalescent petrified wood, polished to a gemlike gleam. Teller had rested her palm lovingly on it and smiled as though she were encountering an old friend.

Teller. What was he going to do about Teller? Teller and Abeha had taken him in when he was a shabby, half-starved child. And now they needed him. He couldn't leave Teller to face Abeha's death alone. Besides, the life he shared with Teller and Abeha was the only life he could imagine living. He couldn't leave them now.

He shouldered his backpack and followed the afternoon sun down the hill into town.

Going back was not easy. Abeha had vanished, crew pod and all, when he returned. Samad shrugged. The harsel could manage with the pod in place for the few days they would be on Kyrenia. There would be hurt feelings to soothe when the harsel returned for them, but he would deal with that when the time came.

The real problem was Teller. She sat hunched and silent over her dinner, toying with her food without really eating. The stories she told were dark and depressing, and her audience began to dwindle. When the last of her audience had crept away, she found a quiet corner and started drinking.

Over the next few days, Samad watched Teller with growing feelings of helplessness and fear. Nothing he did seemed to help ease her pain. After a couple of days, Teller gave up even trying to tell stories. She paid her tab in cash and sat in the corner of the bar, dark and self-absorbed, drinking with a steady, wordless determination that terrified Samad. When Teller's evident pain got to be too much to bear, and he couldn't stand her drinking anymore, he went upstairs and read or tried to sleep. His conscience yammered at him to do something, but Teller was too wrapped in grief to respond to his attempts.

After a week, they rejoined Abeha, but Teller's depression continued. Abeha became increasingly frantic with worry. Samad, caught in the middle, was tempted to tie

himself to an anchor and jump overboard. He began to long
for port, where he could spend a little time alone.

Then, late one night, as they were cruising between islands, Teller sat up in bed. Samad, who had become increasingly sensitive to changes in Teller's mood, woke almost
immediately. He felt Abeha's listening presence focus on
them both.

"What is it?" he asked.

"I can't sleep," Teller said. "I've had a Pilot story running
through my head for the last couple of hours. Would you
like to hear it?"

Samad blinked the sleep out of his eyes and propped
himself up on his elbows. Teller wouldn't venture a story
this late at night if it weren't important. Besides, this was
the first time she'd spoken of anything besides an immediate task for a couple of weeks.

Samad fought back a yawn. "Yes, I would, Teller," he
said, trying to shake off the clinging grip of sleep.

"All right then," Teller began. "Most people believe that
the Pilot was simply lost at sea or died in obscurity somewhere. But the true story can be found if you know where to
look and what stories to believe. The Pilot quietly merged
into the colony. Eventually, she met and married a quiet,
gentle man full of long silences. He loved her and shared her
secrets and love of solitude. Together they settled a big tract
of land on Bonifacio Island and raised a family. Their grown
children settled the land around them, starting families of
their own. It was a good, full life.

"Then the Tauran influenza struck. Bonifacio was hit
early and hard. In less than a week, half the island was sick.
The Pilot's husband and her youngest granddaughter were
the first people in the area to come down with it. Two days
later, everyone in that part of the island was ill, including
the doctor and her nurses. Comm calls for help went unan-

swered by emergency personnel who were too sick to reply. By then three of the Pilot's four children were sick, and all her grandchildren were stricken as well. People in outlying settlements had to manage alone. The Pilot, who had helped so many people, had no one to help her as her family sweated and gasped their lives away. She was filling in the grave that held her second son's family when one of the colony's four medical 'thopters finally brought help.

"By the time the emergency medical teams got to Bonifacio, almost a quarter of the four hundred fifty souls on the island had died. A third more were still severely ill, and the rest were either recovering or exhausted. Even with help from the medics, another thirty-five people died. Bonifacio was an island of grief. Every family on the island had lost someone to the plague. The Pilot's life was one of many shattered during the epidemic.

"The medics were able to save the Pilot's youngest daughter and two of her children. They had been up in the hills with the sheep when the epidemic broke out. Her daughter's isolation had saved their lives. They didn't get sick until after help had arrived. Her eldest grandchild survived. He was taken in and raised as part of her daughter's family. The Pilot's husband; three of her children; and eight of her grandchildren died in the epidemic.

"The Pilot wandered, lost in the dark shadow of despair. Her remaining daughter tried desperately to bring the Pilot out of her grief, but nothing worked. One day her daughter woke to find the Pilot's bed empty. A note left all her possessions to her daughter and her grandchildren."

Teller looked down. Samad had fallen asleep. His eyelids were dark crescents framed by black lashes. She watched the boy sleep, her face unreadable. At last she shook herself and headed for the door, shedding her clothes as she went.

Naked, she stepped out into the harsel's hold, dimly lit by a few small spotlights. Moving as silently as possible, she climbed to the top of the pod. Where the walls of Abeha's hull came to a peak, there was a small gap, just big enough to crawl through. She crawled along the space, moving toward the front of Abeha's hold. The harsel's thickened layer of fat made it a tighter fit than usual, but Teller squirmed her way to the front of the pod and climbed down a recessed access ladder to the forward end of Abeha's ballast chamber.

There, where Abeha's great ribs met like the prow of a boat, there was a small, triangular space. It was a dark little cave of flesh, resonant with the great fish's heartbeats. Teller sat, sheltered beneath the harsel's ribs like a baby in its mother's womb. She closed her eyes and gave herself over to grieving. She keened in a bare, shredded whisper for her family, and for the many other beloved people, human and har, that death had taken from her over the long years. Fat, hot tears forced their way out between tight-shut lids. At last, wrung out by grief, she rested her head against the massive wall of the harsel's hold.

"But that was not the end of the story either," Teller whispered into Abeha's listening darkness. "The Pilot walked down to the sea, to a hidden cove where she stored her crew pod. Wading out into the water, she summoned her harsel. He came for her at sunset, ghosting silently into the little cove as gracefully as a bird. The great fish took her away from humans and all their heartache. The Pilot lost herself among the harsels' alien songs, out on the endless, infinite sea."

The story over, Teller sat there in silence, listening to the ponderous, comforting waltz of Abeha's hearts, her thoughts held in silent sympathy by the harsel.

"Their lives blew out like candle flames," Teller remembered. "Gone, just like that." She pinched her fingers together in the darkness, as though snuffing out a candle. "I should have been grateful that Barbara lived, but every day, and all through the night, all I could think of was what I'd lost." Teller closed her eyes in remembered pain. "I was becoming a living ghost. You took me away and helped me remember what living was like. If you hadn't done that . . ." She shook her head.

"I CAN'T DO IT AGAIN," Abeha whispered in her mind. "YOU HAVE TO LET ME GO."

"I know," Teller admitted, "but you're the only one who remembers. What will I do without you?"

"LET THE BOY HELP," Abeha advised her. "SAMAD LOVES YOU. HE NEEDS YOU."

"He's helped already, Abeha. I would have drunk a lot more at Kyrenia, but he was always there, watching. Even when he was up in our room, I knew he was worried about me," Teller said. "But I'm afraid of what will happen without you. What if I forget everything?

"OTHER HARSELS WILL HOLD MY MEMORIES," Abeha reassured her. "YOU CAN REMEMBER WITH THEM."

"But they won't be you!" Teller protested.

"PERHAPS NOT, BUT OUR MEMORIES WILL LIVE ON IN THEM."

Teller shook her head. "Nothing will replace you, Abeha," she said, laying her hand on one wall of the harsel's hold.

"I KNOW, TELLER, AND I'M SORRY."

"Oh Abeha, we've lived such a good life together,"

"YES WE HAVE," Abeha agreed. "AND MY PEOPLE ARE GRATEFUL FOR WHAT YOU HAVE BROUGHT TO US. YOU OPENED OUR EYES TO THE REST OF THE UNIVERSE, AND YOU BROUGHT OTHER HUMANS TO SHARE OUR WORLD WITH US."

Teller smiled and shook her head. "They brought themselves."

"WITH YOUR HELP," Abeha reminded her. "WITHOUT YOU, WE MIGHT NEVER HAVE FORGED THE COMPACT."

"The Compact isn't enough," Teller said. "Humans are greedy and forgetful. Given a chance, my people would destroy the very things that make this world so unique and precious."

"WHICH IS WHY YOU MUST LIVE ON AFTER I DIE. MY CHILDREN WILL NEED YOU."

"Everyone dies, Abeha. My response to rejuve is incredibly rare. I'm one of the oldest humans in the universe. But even I won't live forever." Teller thought of the long, empty years stretching ahead after Abeha's death. "I'm not sure I want to live without you, Abeha. I'll be so alone!"

"YOU HAVE SAMAD. HE NEEDS YOU, TELLER."

"It isn't enough, Abeha."

"IT WILL HAVE TO BE. IN HONOR OF ALL WE'VE SHARED, YOU MUST TRY TO STAY ALIVE. THALASSA STILL NEEDS ITS PILOT."

"I'll try Abeha. I promise I'll try."

"THANK YOU, TELLER," Abeha said. "YOUR PROMISE FREES MY HEART."

The two of them spent the rest of the night in a bittersweet communion, remembering their long, intertwined lives. When the pale, watery dawn came, Teller dressed and went up onto Abeha's broad back, and the two of them watched the sun come up, sharing the view through each other's eyes.

CHAPTER 7

THEY SPENT THE NEXT COUPLE OF MONTHS sailing slowly northeast toward the mating grounds. Abeha fed greedily, fueling the development of her eggs, and storing up fat to feed her offspring after they hatched. As her fat reserves grew, Abeha rode higher in the water. Her leeway increased, and she began to roll and wallow in high seas.

The harsel's approaching mating and eventual death made every day seem precious to Samad. He sometimes found himself doing everything as slowly and deliberately as possible, in an attempt to stretch out their remaining time together.

They sailed among the wild harsels, far from the usual lanes of shipping traffic. The harsels, hearing of Abeha's decision to become female, sought her out, to honor her and share memories of her life. A great fleet of wild harsels usually surrounded them. The sea resounded with their singing. At night their mindsongs rang through Samad's dreams.

The wild harsels were extremely curious about Abeha's humans. During calm weather, Samad was often invited to ride on the wild harsels' backs. At first, Samad had difficulty understanding the wild har. He was used to Abeha's almost human use of words. The wild harsels communicated in images and sensations; only a few of them were able to use words. They were fascinated by life on land and longed to know everything about it.

When he was with the wild har, Samad found himself having incredibly vivid memories of the oddest things. Sometimes the memories were long and involved. He remembered a trip through the countryside with Teller, seeing every flower, smelling the scents of dust and crushed grass as though he had never experienced them before. Sometimes the memories were only extremely vivid sense impressions: the taste of bread still hot from the oven, or the smell of hay and manure in a barn. The wild harsels drew these memories from Samad's mind like a magician pulling silk scarves from the empty air.

It should have been scary, but the harsels never retrieved unpleasant, personal, or frightening memories. Often Samad would spend what felt like ten minutes involved a pleasant daydream, only to discover that he had been sitting there for a couple of hours.

He spent several afternoons sharing his memories with a harsel named Haiea. Then Haiea wove a memory song from Samad's favorite memories. It wasn't until the song was done that Samad realized that they were the focus of intense concentration by nearly a hundred harsels.

"YOU SHOULD BE HONORED," Abeha told Samad when he came aboard after Haiea's concert. "HAIEA IS ONE OF THE FINEST MINDSINGERS OF HIS GENERATION. THIS IS THE

FIRST TIME HE'S COMPOSED A MEMORY SONG ABOUT HU-
MANS."

"I thought it was wonderful," Samad said. "But I didn't
realize that it was a performance."

"THE SONG IS A MASTERPIECE." Abeha told him. "CEN-
TURIES FROM NOW, HARSELS WILL BE SINGING THOSE MEM-
ORIES OF YOURS."

Samad looked back at Haiea's sail, receding into the distance. "How can I thank him?" he asked Abeha.

Abeha's laughter rang through his mind. "HAIEA CRE-
ATES MINDSONGS BECAUSE THEY BRING HIM JOY, NOT FOR
THANKS. HE SINGS WHETHER NO ONE IS LISTENING OR
EVERYONE IS LISTENING. BESIDES, HE KNOWS HOW YOU
FELT ABOUT THE SONG. HE LISTENED TO YOU AS YOU WERE
LISTENING TO HIM."

If the harsel fleet passed an island with a suitable harbor,
they would stop while Teller and Samad donned diving gear
to clean the harsels' bottoms and holds. After working on
the harsels, Samad and Teller rowed ashore to explore the islands. They cooked their evening meal over a driftwood fire
while the sun set and the stars came out. If the weather was
clear and warm, they would sleep there on the beach under
the moons and stars.

Once, while exploring one of the deserted out-islands, they
discovered a gnarled grove of ancient mango trees. Though
they were covered with vines and epiphytes and scarred by
storms, the trees still boasted a heavy crop of ripe fruit.

Teller climbed up and bounced up and down on a thick
tree limb, sending a shower of ripe mangos thudding down
onto the leaf litter below.

"It's not every day that you get to eat fruit from a tree
that the Pilot planted," she remarked when Samad handed
her a relatively unbruised mango.

"The Pilot planted these trees?" he said, looking around at the massive, gnarled trunks of the venerable trees.

Teller nodded. "It's a Verified site. I'll show you on the chart."

Samad wandered from tree to tree, eating the sweet, sticky mango. When he glanced back, Teller had finished her mango and was probing a cluster of stones, half-buried in the thick humus of the forest floor. He came over to help her shift the stones. Then she picked up a stick and began stirring the dirt, disturbing a swarm of many-legged bugs. Samad stepped back to avoid the scattering insects, but he clearly heard the metallic clink that made Teller pause. She scrabbled in the dirt and came up with a small metal ring. She brushed the clinging dirt away from the ring and then examined it closely.

"Here," she said, handing the ring to Samad. "It's a pull ring from one of the Pilot's ration tins."

"How do you know it was the Pilot's?" Samad asked.

"The colonists' survival rations had different pull rings. It's one of the ways archeologists identify a real Pilot site like this one."

Samad gazed at the silvery ring for a long time before handing it back to Teller.

She waved it away. "I want you to have it, Samad. I know how much the Pilot means to you."

"Really?" Samad said, eyes wide with awe.

The wrinkles around Teller's eyes deepened as she smiled. "Really."

Samad strung the little metal ring on a leather thong and wore it around his neck, a precious relic of the Pilot. He gathered a dozen fairly fresh mango seeds from beneath the ancient trees.

"What are those for, Samad?" Teller asked him.

"I thought I'd plant them on some other island where there aren't any mangoes." he explained to Teller. "If someone gets shipwrecked or settles there, they'll have mangos to eat."

"I'm sure the Pilot would approve," she told him. "Those seeds probably won't breed true, but they come from good trees that have survived everything that Thalassa can throw at them. Who knows, maybe one of them will grow up into a new variety."

For the most part, Teller seemed to be coping by doing her best to pretend that nothing had changed. But it was hard for her to keep up the pretense when surrounded by a fleet of harsels intent on eulogizing Abeha before her death. Occasionally it would all get to be too much, and Teller would need to get away from Abeha and her escorts.

Then Teller would unship the sturdy dory that she kept for longer voyages over the open ocean, step its mast, fuel its hydrogen engine, and head for human civilization.

At Abeha's insistence, Samad always accompanied Teller on these trips. She accepted Samad's company with grudging grace. Leaving the harsel fleet behind, she sailed the seaworthy little boat with unerring accuracy to some tiny island village. Once she got there, she headed for the nearest taverna, where she sat and drank in moody silence.

Watching Teller drink, he remembered his mother, lost in a glassy-eyed drug dream, and wondered if Teller would kill herself with her drinking the way his mother had killed herself with drugs. Frightened, he pushed the thought away, but it always returned to haunt him.

Teller would wake late the next morning, groggy and ill. She wandered through the market, waiting until the bar opened and she could drink. Sometimes, she tried to tell stories. But her dark mood soured the tales in her mouth. Her jests became sardonic and biting, and her listeners slipped away.

When drinking failed to ease her pain, Teller would take off into the back country. She drove herself hard, sleeping in the open wherever night took her, until at last sheer exhaustion did what drink could not.

After several of these grueling hikes, Samad began to stay behind at the inn. He knew that Abeha wouldn't like his letting Teller go off by herself, but he simply couldn't keep up with her. And Samad knew that one of the reasons Teller drove herself so hard was to wear him out so that she could finally be completely alone. She needed her solitude.

And Samad needed it, too. Being caught between Teller and Abeha was hard. He needed a chance to relax and be a kid again. So while Teller wandered, Samad poked about whatever village they had landed at, playing with other kids or telling them the stories he had learned from Teller.

His storytelling was rough and ragged at first, but under the brutal tutelage of other children's attention, Samad learned to hold an audience with a well-timed pause or a sudden change of pace. Soon he began collecting a few carved buttons and some pieces of candy. Emboldened, he began making up stories himself, embroidering new adventures onto the worn hem of the Pilot Cycle.

One day he was sitting amid a circle of admiring children, telling a rousing story about the Pilot, kidnapped by a gang of off-world pirates, when a shadow fell across his back. Samad, caught up in his story, tried to ignore the shadow, but it was stealing his audience's attention. Finally, unwillingly, he turned and looked behind him.

A man stood there, cloaked in the brilliant, hand-woven short cape worn by male storytellers. He was short and stocky, with a round, firm belly and the wiry strength of

someone who had grown up herding sheep in rough country. Though his face seemed more suited to laughter, his
current expression was stern and angry. With a commanding flick of his head, the stranger dispersed the half-dozen
children in Samad's audience.

When the other children were gone, the stranger hun-
kered down beside Samad.

"What were you doing?" the man inquired.

Samad shrugged and looked down. "It was just a story I
made up," he mumbled.

"About the Pilot, yes?"

Grudgingly, Samad nodded.

The stranger picked up Samad's cap and examined the
contents. There were three or four pieces of candy and a couple of buttons. "Telling stories for gifts, were you?" he observed. "You're not a member of the Storytellers' Guild, I
suppose."

"I'm with Teller," Samad said. "She's a Guild member."

"But *you* are not."

Samad shook his head, hot with anger and shame.

"Where is Teller?"

Samad shrugged. "Out walking the hills somewhere. I
don't know when she'll be back." It was a lie; Teller was
somewhere in town, buying supplies or maybe loading
them into the boat, but Samad wanted to talk to Teller first,
to find out just how much trouble he'd gotten her into.

"I see," the man said. "I'll talk with Teller when she returns. In the meantime, no more stories. I'll be watching."

"And who are you to tell me no?" Samad demanded. He
was shocked and angry that Teller's name had not carried
the day.

"My name is Florio Hakiapulos. I'm the Guild represen-
tative for this archipelago. It is forbidden to tell stories for
money without a Guild license, or to add stories to an offi-

cial story cycle without Guild approval. You've done both. I'm surprised Teller hasn't explained this to you. She could get into real trouble with the Guild."

"Teller doesn't know I'm doing this," Samad said, leaping to her defense. "I was bored. So I started telling stories. Teller always asks for gifts, so I did, too."

"I see." The storyteller stood, looking thoughtful. "Please tell Teller to talk to me when she returns." He turned to leave, then paused and turned back with a sudden, sunny smile.

"I'm sorry I had to stop you. It was a good story." He walked off, whistling a tune to himself.

Samad watched the man walk away, his heart roiling with emotions. He didn't know whether to be flattered or frightened. He had gotten Teller in trouble, but Ser Hakiapulos had liked his story.

At least the lie he had told had bought them a little time to figure out what to do next. Samad ran back to the boat. If Teller wasn't on the boat, then he'd search for her in the market, and then the tavernas.

Teller was in the dory, loading the contents of a basket into their small solar-powered refrigerator.

"Hey, Samad," she called as he hurried down the dock. "You're just in time to help me stow the last couple of baskets. You ready to sail?"

"We can't go yet, sera," Samad said. "There's a man from the Guild. Ser Hakiapulos is his name. He wants to talk to you before we go."

"Florio? Florio Hakiapulos?" Teller inquired. "A storyteller? About so tall? Dark? Stocky?"

Samad nodded.

Teller's haggard face split open into a sudden smile. "Florio's here?" she said, clearly delighted by the news. "Well, let's put this away and go find him!" She reached for one of the two remaining baskets.

"Wait, Teller!" He paused, groping for words amid his own inner turmoil. "There's trouble. I—I—"

"What is it, Samad?" Teller asked, sitting down on a bollard so that they were eye to eye.

Samad felt even worse at this sign of concern and affection from Teller. He flushed darkly and looked away.

"Samad, please tell me what's wrong."

"I was telling stories," he told her. "For money. It was just for other kids, sera. I'm sorry. I didn't know I wasn't supposed to. And now he wants to talk to you." He stopped, afraid of what she would do. "I'm very sorry I got you in trouble, sera," he added.

The delight drained from Teller's face. She looked sad and tired. "I'm the one who's at fault here, Samad," Teller told him. "I've been too preoccupied with my own problems. If I'd been paying attention, I would have known what you were doing and talked to you about it." She stood up with a sigh. "Well, let's go get this straightened out," she said. "I expect Florio will be at one of the tavernas."

But he wasn't at any of the tavernas. After two hours of fruitless searching, they found him sitting on a gear locker beside their boat, waiting with all the patience of a river-smoothed boulder. He stood as they approached.

"Teller!" he called, holding his arms wide in welcome, his face wreathed in a broad smile.

"Florio!" Teller ran down the dock, into his arms. To Samad's amazement the two of them kissed like long-parted lovers.

"Well, Florio, it appears that we've been chasing each other all over town," Teller told him when they were done. There was a broad, almost goofy grin on her face.

"It's the story of our lives, I'm afraid," he replied with fond regret.

"Your son is handsome, I can see your face in his. Where is his father?" Florio asked her.

Samad blinked, startled but flattered that someone would think he was actually Teller's son.

The wrinkles around Teller's eyes creased in amusement. "I don't know. I never met him."

"What?" Florio said, looking startled.

"Samad was living on the streets of Melilla when we met," Teller explained. "He was such a good guide that I adopted him. He's been looking after me for nearly two years now. His mother was a pilot, and probably his father as well."

"Ah." Florio said, as if that explained something. "He's a good kid. You chose well."

Teller shook her head with a rueful smile. "He chose me. I was just lucky. So . . ." she said, stepping back from Florio's embrace. "I understand he's been telling stories behind my back."

"Good ones, too," Florio acknowledged, smiling at Samad. "Better start training him, Teller. We need new storytellers."

"Don't teach grandma to suck eggs," she chided with a laugh. "Remember who trained *you.*" Samad had never seen Teller look so young and coquettish.

"*Mahleesta dhaskala,*" Florio replied in Greek. *Yes, my teacher.* His tone was gently chiding and sarcastic.

Samad looked from Teller to Florio, confused, wary, and more than a little angry at being excluded from their shared intimacy.

"Did you really think I had a child? At my age?"

"I've grown to expect surprises from you, Teller," Florio replied.

"Just how old are you?" Samad interrupted.

"Old enough," Teller replied lightly.

"But still young enough," Florio teased, waggling his eyebrows in an outrageously flirtatious fashion.

"Oh Florio!" Teller scolded with a giggle. "Stop! You're making me feel like a giddy young forty-year-old!"

Florio laughed. "No, teacher. *You* make *me* feel young."

"Samad," Teller said, laying her head against Florio's shoulder. "Florio and I need some time together. We'll be taking a room at the taverna where he's staying tonight."

"Wait a minute—" Samad began. But the two of them were already walking off, holding hands like two teenagers in love.

Samad followed after them, feeling confused, crestfallen, and left out. Once they reached the taverna, Teller booked a room for Samad and arranged for his meals. Then Florio and Teller headed upstairs, entwined in each other's arms. Samad ate lunch alone, then went upstairs to read and wait for Teller to reappear. Dinner came and went, and Teller still had not emerged from Florio's room. He paused in front of Florio's door, about to knock, when he heard Teller murmur something in a low, intimate voice. Florio laughed at whatever she had said, and the bed creaked as someone shifted position on the mattress. Samad turned away, his face hot with shame and anger, and he went back to his room.

Teller finally emerged late the next morning. She came down the stairs into the public room of the taverna with a spring in her step and a smile on her face. She hadn't looked this happy since the day Abeha had returned from the southern migration.

"Ready to go, Samad?" Teller asked.

Wordlessly Samad nodded. He shut his book and fell in beside her, stunned at how much more cheerful Teller was today, and hurt that Florio had been the one to cheer her up.

When they reached the boat, Samad went forward to cast off the bow rope, while Teller pushed off from the pier and started the dory's small hydrogen engine, powering out into the harbor. When they were out from under the lee of the land, Teller turned off the engine and raised the mainsail. The sunlit water of the harbor purled and chuckled under the brightly painted bow as the boat gathered speed in the light breeze. The wind freshened as they headed out to sea. Teller lifted her face to the sun, took a deep breath of the cool morning air, and laughed from sheer pleasure.

Teller's cheerful mood only angered Samad further. As they approached the mouth of the harbor, he saw a distant figure standing on the breakwater. It was Florio. As they passed the point, Florio lifted his bright storyteller's cape, letting the wind unfurl it like a flag. Teller let her own Guild shawl stream out in the breeze in reply. Florio waved once, then stood watching as they sailed out of the harbor.

Samad shook a stray lock of hair out of his face, frowned, and turned away. Florio looked like he was barely half her age. And a former student. How could she do such a thing? Didn't she care what people thought? How could she go off and leave him all alone like that, just to spend the night with Florio?

"Hey, Samad!" He looked up, startled. The island had receded into a smudge on the horizon, and the sun was high in the sky. Teller was looking at him, hands on her hips.

He glared up at her. "What!" he demanded.

"It's nearly time for lunch. I've got spanakopita or lamb stew. Which one do you want to eat?"

"I don't care," he snapped. "I'm not hungry." He turned away again, gazing moodily at the boat's wake.

Teller sat beside him. "You're mad at me for going off with Florio, aren't you?"

Samad just shrugged.

"Look," Teller began, "I'm sorry if I upset you. It's just that Florio and I—"

"He's half your age!" Samad interrupted. He turned to look at her, his face blazing with anger. "Are you going to fuck *me* next?"

Teller slapped him.

They stared at each other for a moment, too shocked and angry to speak. Samad stormed off to the bow of the boat and stared out at the open ocean. He fought back tears of anger, his shoulders high, braced for whatever Teller was going to say next. But there was only silence. Finally, he glanced back at Teller. She was seated in the stern, watching him, her face drawn and sad. She looked old again, and Samad felt a twinge of guilt.

"Samad," Teller began. "I'm sorry I hit you. I lost my temper."

Samad looked back out at the horizon for a moment. He shrugged, then nodded, accepting the apology.

Teller came forward, checked the trim of the sails and the rudder, then sat down next to him, putting a tentative hand on his shoulder.

"You're my son, Samad. Florio isn't. Yes, he was my student once. It was a long time ago, and he likes to tease me about it sometimes. But we didn't become lovers until long after he'd stopped being my student and became my friend. Anyway, my love life isn't really any of your business, Samad."

Samad felt the embers of his anger flare up again.

"Right," he said tightly. "You just left me to cool my heels in a rented room without telling me when I'd see you again. I promised Abeha that I'd look after you, but how can I do that when you run off and leave me all alone?" Samad looked away, embarrassed by the frightened quaver in his voice.

"Samad, I said I was sorry, and I meant it," Teller replied. "I shouldn't have left you alone. It was selfish of me. But—" she sighed and smoothed back her gray hair. "Look, Samad, I know you take your promise to Abeha seriously, but Abeha's not human. He—" Her pause was painful, *"She* doesn't understand how hard a promise like that is to keep."

"But what if you don't come back?" Samad demanded. He swiped at his eyes, angry at his sudden surge of tears.

"I've always come back before," Teller told him, enfolding him in a hug. "And I'll keep coming back. You're my son, Samad. For as long as I live, you'll *be* my son. I hope that, for as long as you live, I'll be your mother. I love you. But there are just some things that I need another adult for."

"Like sex?" Samad said dryly.

"That, and more than that. Especially now that Abeha's—" she paused.

"Dying," Samad completed.

"Abeha's not dying yet, Samad. But she only has a year or so left. It will be hard to watch what's going to happen to her. Florio . . ." She paused, "Florio's one of my best and closest friends. I'm going to need his help. He comforts me in ways you can't."

Samad stared down at the neatly coiled bowline. He felt hurt and inadequate. "I'm sorry I'm not enough help."

"Oh, Samad. I know how much you want to help, but this—" she shook her head. "You help me more than you realize, Samad. But sometimes I need a different kind of help. I've asked too much from you, lately. You should be relying on me, not the other way around."

She paused, gathering her words. "I didn't behave well, back there," she acknowledged. "I hurt you, and I'm sorry. I was in pain and not thinking clearly."

Embarrassed by Teller's blunt honesty, Samad shrugged and looked away.

"I'll try to do better, Samad. But in order to do that, I'm going to need to spend some time with Florio. And you're going to have to let him help me. Understand?"

Samad didn't know what to say, so he just nodded.

Just then the wind shifted, and they had to attend to the boat. When the sails were retrimmed, Teller served out the spanakopita, and they ate in silence.

"Samad, do you want to begin training as a storyteller?" she asked when the meal was over and he started to clear away the dishes.

"Me?" Samad said. The last remnants of his bad mood evaporated. "A storyteller? Really?"

"You're a bit young for it, but I think you're good enough, and Florio agrees with me."

"He does?"

Teller nodded. "Florio likes you, Samad, and he knows good storytelling when he hears it. Only, no more making up Pilot stories, okay? And until you're a Journeyman, I'll have to be there when you're telling stories."

Samad nodded. "All right," he agreed.

"Well then, I'll be your teacher, if you'll be my apprentice. Deal?" Teller held out her hand.

"Deal!" he confirmed, shaking her hand.

"All right, apprentice. Sit down, and I'll give you your first lesson."

Abeha was pleased by the improvement in Teller's mood when they returned in the dory. The harsel was eating ravenously, fueling the ripening eggs developing under the tough skin of her hold, and thickening the layers of fat that would feed her young in the months before they emerged. The company of other harsels was always welcome, but she had missed Teller.

Abeha was relieved to be dying before Teller. Their lives

were intertwined in a way that even most partnered harsels would have found difficult to understand. Living without Teller would be like losing her rudder fins; she would lose all sense of direction and purpose. Abeha knew that Teller felt the same keen sense of loss. That was why she needed Samad to look after Teller while she was away from her.

But in the last few days, several senior har captains and their harsels had joined the fleet. Abeha was glad to have their company. They understood Teller's grief, though they were helpless to alleviate it. Harsels usually outlived their captains. Often one harsel would be captained by several generations of the same family. Or a harsel would partner with a human for a time, and when the har captain retired or died, he rejoined the wild harsels, returning to his own kind with a greater understanding of the short-lived, land-dwelling creatures that shared their world.

Even though Teller found the har captains' solicitousness maddening, her frustration blunted the edge of her grief. And now that Samad was her apprentice, Teller had another distraction from Abeha's approaching death. And Abeha herself found Samad's quick, bright, inquisitive presence a welcome relief from the endless elegiac parade of harsels. Glad and honored as she was by their company, their mournful remembrances were starting to get on her nerves. Harsel females were treated like honored ghosts by the other hars. At least Samad and Teller treated her like she was still alive. She would be dead soon enough as it was, and the thought of living on through her children was shallow comfort sometimes.

Teller listened to Samad recounting "The Tale of the Three Oranges." The boy was an eager student, but he questioned everything, and answering his questions took a lot of thought. Florio had probably hoped that teaching Samad would keep her too busy to fret over the loss of Abeha. He was right, too, Teller thought with an ironic lift of one eyebrow. It was oddly comforting to find herself the subject of Florio's manipulation.

But all this concern and distraction would not delay Abeha's death. Teller simply refused to think past the moment of Abeha's death. Living without Abeha was, quite simply, unimaginable. She would deal with the harsel's death when it happened. Until then, Teller tried to live each day as normally as possible, despite the deathwatch of mournful harsels and somber har captains that surrounded them.

And so time passed, blue sky over blue water by day, and dark water under dark sky at night. Each day was as precious and distinct as a jewel. Teller turned her face away from the oncoming shadow, while those around her— Abeha, Samad, Florio, the har captains, and the harsels—all watched and worried.

Then one day, a large, moist blister appeared on the inside of Abeha's hold. Samad pointed it out to Teller, who gently ran a finger over it.

"MY EGGS ARE RIPENING," Abeha told them. "THE CREW POD MUST COME OUT. I THOUGHT I HAD MORE TIME."

"How soon?" Teller asked, focusing on Abeha's immediate needs and trying not to think about what they implied.

"ONE DAY, MAYBE TWO. BY THE THIRD DAY, THERE'LL BE DAMAGE."

Teller nodded. "We don't have a lot of choices for a harbor. We're about a day's sail from the Jazayir al Hudr Archipelago. The island of Jerba al-Haddis has a good sheltered harbor, as I recall, but the currents are very strong this time of year. Reaching the island will be tricky. But it's our best choice. We'll head there with a couple of har captains to escort us in case we have to pull the pod early. The pod's only barely seaworthy on her own. We'll need a tow."

"AT LEAST THE FEEDING WILL BE RICH ON THE WAY."

Teller smiled. "You're turning into a pig," she remarked.

"THE MORE I EAT, THE LONGER I'LL LIVE," Abeha replied.

Teller's face grew grim. Her wall of denial was crumbling under the weight of too much truth. She needed to get away from those horrible bulging blisters for a while. "I'm going to go lie down," she said. "Let me know if there are any problems."

Samad watched her step into the crew pod. "Abeha, what are we going to do without the pod?"

"YOU'LL HAVE TO RIDE WITH ONE OF THE OTHER CAP-TAINS," Abeha explained, "OR BUY A LARGER BOAT. THE DORY'S A WEATHERLY CRAFT, BUT IT'S NOT BIG ENOUGH FOR LONG CRUISES."

"I see," Samad said. "No wonder Teller's upset. Should I go in or leave her alone?"

"I THINK ALONE IS BETTER RIGHT NOW," Abeha said.

Samad stood silently inside Abeha's hold, listening to her hearts beating.

"Once your eggs ripen, can we come into your hold?" he asked her.

"NO, SAMAD, I'M AFRAID NOT."

Samad nodded, feeling a deep canyon of loss opening inside him. "I'll miss this. I'll miss you."

"I KNOW," Abeha said, "AND I'LL MISS YOU, TOO. IT'LL BE LONELY WITHOUT YOU LIVING INSIDE ME. BUT YOU'LL STILL BE ABLE TO RIDE ON MY BACK."

Samad gently touched the blister on the wall of Abeha's hold.

"Does it hurt?" he asked.

"NO, SAMAD, I'M FINE."

"I wish things were different, that you could have babies and live."

"SO DO I, SAMAD. BUT THINGS ARE THE WAY THEY ARE."

Samad could feel Abeha's sorrow. This was the first of many losses for her. He leaned carefully against the wall of her hold, letting his grief mingle with the harsel's.

"I love you, Abeha."

"I KNOW, SAMAD. I LOVE YOU, TOO."

The blisters inside Abeha's hold grew larger and more numerous as they approached the Jazayir al-Hudr Archipelago. As the next day's dawn broke, they saw the mountaintops of Jerba al-Haddis in the distance.

By noon they had reached the windward side of the island. But the current was strong, and the wind was against them. It would take days to reach the leeward side, and the harbor they were seeking.

"We'll have to find another island." Teller declared. "Abeha, how are you doing?"

"THE POD MUST COME OUT SOON. TONIGHT, IF POSSIBLE, TOMORROW MORNING AT THE LATEST."

Teller called up the relevant charts on her display tablet. "Let's head for here." Her finger tapped a C-shaped island with no name, only a designation number. The tablet zoomed in on the island, and Teller peered at it. "The chart says that the water is deep, and there's a good anchorage there. With luck and a favorable wind, we'll reach it by midafternoon."

But the winds and currents continued to be contrary, and late afternoon found them only halfway to their new goal. Teller consulted her charts again and found a tiny cluster of islands only a few kilometers ahead.

"We'll shelter between these two islands. The moons are both near full; we'll be able to float the pod out after sunset if we have to."

"GOOD," said Abeha. "THE SOONER THE BETTER. THOSE BLISTERS ARE READY TO BURST."

The sun was nearly touching the horizon as they reached the channel between the two islands. They were sheltered from the wind and the current, but the water was still very choppy.

Teller stood on Abeha's back and frowned down at the rough sea.

"It's going to be tricky, getting the pod out without bumping the sides in this swell."

"SOME OF THE BLISTERS HAVE ALREADY BURST, TELLER. WE HAVE TO DO IT NOW."

"We'll fasten tow ropes to the pod," Teller told Abeha. "You submerge. I'll go in and release the anchor lines, and the harsels will steady the pod as we ease it out."

"YOU COULD GET HURT IF THE POD SHIFTS WHEN YOU'RE IN THERE," Abeha cautioned.

"I'll be careful."

The sun was sinking as they set the tow ropes. Abeha folded her sail, opened her hold, and sank beneath the waves.

"ALL RIGHT, TELLER." Abeha said. "BE CAREFUL."

Teller nodded, then put on her mask and breathing gear, while Samad watched anxiously from the back of another harsel. It was growing dark by now, and he watched the boiling patch of water that marked the spot where Abeha had sunk beneath the choppy waves. Samad found himself holding his breath in sympathy with Teller. The minutes passed, and the tension mounted. No one said a word.

"Maybe we should—" one of the har captains began, breaking the seal of silence.

Just then, Teller's head broke the surface. She spat out the mouthpiece of her breather. "Pull!" she shouted. "Pull now!"

The two harsels took up the slack with a couple of strokes of their massive tails. They shifted out of the eye of the wind, each on a separate tack, letting the wind and their sails do the work of pulling the crew pod out of Abeha's hold under her direction. A few minutes later, the pod bobbed to the surface, followed by Abeha.

"Abeha? How are you? Did the pod hurt your eggs?" Teller shouted as she swam toward the harsel.

"I'M FINE. I FELT A BUMP OR TWO AS IT WAS PULLED OUT, BUT IT DIDN'T DO MUCH DAMAGE," Abeha informed Teller and Samad.

Samad passed on the message to the other har captains, who nodded and smiled in relief. Teller swam over to the harsel that carried Samad and pulled herself onto its broad back.

"You were down for so long!" Samad fretted as he handed her a towel. "I was afraid something had happened to you."

Teller put a cold hand on Samad's shoulder. "I'm sorry. It took longer than I expected." She shivered. "Let's go below. I'm freezing."

They spent the night in the crew pod of one of their escorts, a har captain named Demitrios, partnered with a harsel named Hookau. Samad and Teller slept on fold-down bunks in the large forward storage compartment of the crew pod. Demetrios traded in spices, and the hold had the musty, pungent, and exotic scent of his usual cargo.

Sleeping inside a strange harsel was difficult. Samad kept waking as his dreaming mind reached for Abeha and found a stranger instead. When Samad finally managed to stay asleep, he dreamed of an endless search through room after room, looking for someone that he desperately needed to find. He woke early, feeling stiff and unrested. Teller looked just as tired as he felt.

"Let's get some breakfast and get going, we have a busy day ahead of us," Teller told him. "We're going to peel the skin off of the inside of Abeha's hold and make sure that her eggs are okay."

"Why do we need to do that?" Samad asked her.

"Normally, the dead skin is eaten away by the community of scavengers and cleaners living inside a harsel's hold. But our crew pod takes up so much space that Abeha's hold doesn't have enough scavengers to do the job," Teller informed him as their host set breakfast on the table. "If the skin isn't peeled away, Abeha's eggs won't ripen properly. It's a delicate, messy job. Are you up for it, Samad?"

He nodded. He would do anything to help Abeha.

"Isidro and I will help, too," their host offered.

"*Efaristo,* Demitrios," Teller thanked him. "We appreciate it."

"Sera, we are honored to be able to help you and Abeha."

Teller looked down for a moment, then glanced up again. "It is a kindness we are honored to accept."

"Well, then, eat up, eat up. Especially you, little one," Demetrios said, ruffling Samad's black curls. "*Na fao.* You look too thin."

Samad glanced at the metal mirror on the locker door opposite the table. His reflection shocked him. His face looked as thin and careworn as it had when he lived on the streets of Melilla. Abeha's transition had been hard on all of them, and there were still many more months to go before the end.

He took another mouthful and munched dutifully away, though the food had turned tasteless in his mouth at the thought of Abeha's death. He couldn't imagine the great harsel dead. She was too huge, too fully alive to ever die. How could he fill the hole left in his soul when she was gone? He swallowed and pushed his plate away, his breakfast turned to stone in his stomach.

"*Efaristo,* Demitrios," he thanked his host. "It was delicious, but I'm full now."

After breakfast, Teller rowed over to their crew pod and

clambered aboard, emerging with an armload of diving gear, while Samad busied himself with the dishes.

"Now that the lining of her hold is peeling away, Abeha needs to keep the eggs submerged," she said when she returned. "We'll be working underwater, in dive gear. That water's cold; you'll need your wetsuit," Teller said, handing it to him, along with a swim mask, gloves, fins, and a scraper.

"You need to be careful with that scraper," Teller advised. "You don't want to push too hard and damage her eggs."

Samad nodded solemnly and began pulling on his dive suit. The insulating skin of the suit clung to itself as he tugged it on. He wondered, as he always did, where Teller had found the suit. Off-world dive suits like these were rare on Thalassa, especially small ones in his size. She claimed to have found it used in a shop in Nueva Ebiza, but he'd never seen a suit like it on sale anywhere.

Samad could feel a slight pressure in his mind as Hookau spoke inwardly to Demetrios.

"Isidro is on his way over with the boat," Demetrios told them. "Abeha's ready as well."

A few minutes later, Samad heard the whining growl of Isidro's skiff. They climbed out onto Hookau's back to meet him. It was a misty, dead calm morning.

"Good weather for it today, eh?" Isidro observed as they climbed into his skiff. "Too bad it wasn't calm like this yesterday."

Teller nodded, and they sped off to where Abeha waited for them. As they drew near, Samad could make out her ballast chamber gaping open just below the surface. Isidro dropped anchor a little distance away. When the skiff was safely anchored, they dove over the side. Silver trails of bubbles trickled out of Teller's rebreather as she led them into the darkness of Abeha's immense hold.

Samad sucked a hissing breath through his rebreather and exhaled, sending a stream of bubbles rising to the surface like silver jellyfish. He played his light over the walls of Abeha's hold and breathed out another whoosh of bubbles in surprise. The familiar space of her hold looked like it had been vandalized. Shreds of skin hung like wet laundry from the vaulted walls of the harsel's ballast chamber. Samad swallowed. There was a hollow feeling in the pit of his stomach at the sight.

"IT'S ALL RIGHT, SAMAD." Abeha reassured him. "I KNOW IT LOOKS TERRIBLE, BUT UNDERNEATH THAT UGLY DEAD SKIN ARE THOUSANDS OF HEALTHY EGGS. MY HOLD WILL BE FULL OF HEALTHY YOUNG HARLINGS. WITH SO MANY YOUNG, IT IS CERTAIN THAT THE THREAD OF MY LIFE WILL BE CARRIED ON BY MY CHILDREN."

Teller beckoned Samad over and showed him how to lift away the dead skin with the scraper. Under the skin lay a thick, protective layer of mucus. Beneath the mucus, Samad could see Abeha's eggs gleaming dimly, like big, translucent grapes. On the other side of the hold he could see the lights of Dimitrios and Isidro flickering through the water as they cleared away dead skin. Teller tapped Samad on the shoulder and pointed at a brown patch about half a meter wide. Teller mimed a blow, and he nodded understanding. It was a bad spot where the eggs had been damaged during the removal of the pod.

They worked steadily, clearing about a quarter of the harsel's hold. When they became chilled, they climbed back into the skiff, pulled anchor, and sped back to Hookau. While the others warmed themselves on Hookau's back, Demitrios went below to heat some soup. They sat with the sun heating their backs, sipping hot avgolemono, rich with chicken and thick with rice. After the soup, there was feta cheese, olives, and some thick, hard, ship's biscuits.

Isidro's appreciative belch and sigh of satiation broke the silence. Samad ducked his head at Demetrios in appreciation.

"Abeha looks amazingly good," Dimitrios observed. "I've never seen so clean a hull wall, Teller. There's a lot of eggs, and almost no parasite damage. You've taken good care of her."

Teller shrugged, but Samad could see that the compliment pleased her.

"It's particularly amazing, given Abeha's age," Isidro added. "Her previous captains have also done right by Abeha. Do you know who they were?"

Teller shook her head. "No, I don't. She's been with me most of my life though. How long have you been with Halina?" she asked. Under Teller's apparent ease, Samad thought he noticed a note of wariness.

"Halina was with my mother," Isidro said. "I grew up inside him. When mother retired, Halina asked me to continue on as his har captain. My mother misses him a lot. She still sails with us every chance she gets." He looked somber for a moment. "I can't imagine life without him."

Samad began gathering up the dishes with a loud rattle. "Is there anything else I can bring up for you?" he asked politely, determined to divert the conversation from this disastrous path. "Some more coffee or cheese?"

Dimitrios and Isidro shook their heads.

"We're fine." Teller said. "Demetrios, you did the cooking, we'll do the washing up. Samad, I'll help you carry the dishes downstairs."

They finished cleaning Abeha's hold late the next afternoon. Every scrap of dead skin had been removed. The walls of the harsel's hold gleamed in the light of their headlamps. Nearly every centimeter of her hold was covered with green eggs the size of muscat grapes. Teller had to admit that it was an impressive sight. Few wild harsels could boast of such fertility. This solid expanse of eggs was the result of years of careful maintenance. Over the centuries, Teller had meticulously removed parasites from the walls of Abeha's hold before they could cause permanent scarring.

"THANK YOU, TELLER," Abeha said. "THIS IS YOUR ACHIEVEMENT AS MUCH AS IT IS MINE."

Teller shrugged. She found it hard to take pride in this. "I'm glad that you are pleased," she managed to say.

"I KNOW," Abeha replied, acknowledging all that Teller left unsaid.

This would be Teller's and Samad's last time in the harsel's hold. Abeha would keep her hold shut tight, protecting her developing eggs, until she mated.

A couple of months after mating, Abeha's eggs would hatch. Her hold would be filled with thousands of harlings, each silvery fish as long as Teller's little finger. They would live and grow inside her hold, nourished by a gelatinous "milk" secreted by the lining of her ballast chamber. In time, the harlings would grow twenty centimeters or longer. But nourishing her young would slowly deplete Abeha's own flesh, and in the end . . .

Teller shook her head. She should focus on the present. Every last minute inside Abeha's hold was precious.

Finally, it was time to go. She motioned to Samad that they were leaving. Samad swam slowly up and out, pausing at the mouth of Abeha's hold to lay a hand on the harsel in farewell. Then it was Teller's turn. She looked back into the vast cavern of Abeha's hold, remembering all the years she had lived there.

"Oh, Abeha!" Teller cried inwardly, feeling as though the pain would tear her apart.

Abeha enfolded her in a surge of grief and love. "I WISH THINGS WERE DIFFERENT. I WISH I COULD LIVE AND SEE

MY CHILDREN GROW UP, AS HUMANS DO. I WISH WE COULD BE TOGETHER FOREVER!"

"I know," Teller said. "I wish you could, too."

Teller turned and followed her bubbles up to the surface, feeling her connection with Abeha grow more tenuous with each passing meter. Somehow she made it to the stern of the skiff that Isidro had loaned them for this final trip. Samad helped her into the boat. She stumbled to the bow and sat down, feeling like she had been torn open.

Teller looked down into the sunlit water, watching the rays of sunlight waver and diffuse in the depths. A sea flower drifted past, its bell undulating in the waves. She closed her eyes. Though she had spent months and even years parted from the harsel, Abeha's presence lingered in the back of her mind. The knowledge that Abeha was out there in the sea sustained her, even when the great fish was half a world away. Despite her promises, she doubted that she would outlive Abeha by very much. They were too closely linked to live without each other. The harsel's death would be hers as well.

She looked over at Samad, busy starting the skiff's engine. What was going to happen to him after she was gone? She needed to provide for his future.

Despite the spotty training he had received, Samad showed a real gift for storytelling. Probably the best thing she could do was to train him as well as she could. She could use her Guild connections to ensure that he would have the finest teachers when she was gone. But he needed to be worthy of those teachers. He tended to get too carried away by the stories he was telling, giving away their endings. His voice had a pleasing tone and timbre, but it was still weak. He needed to learn to project more. And there were so many other things he needed to learn. Samad was good, but he needed to be better. It was time to get serious about his training.

After a lunch that neither of them had much appetite for, they settled themselves on Hookau's broad back.

"Tell me the story of 'Nazreddin's Pot'," she commanded.

"Very well, then," Samad replied. He sat up straight, and with a mischievous grin, began.

"Once there was and twice there wasn't, a very wise mullah named Nazreddin. One day he needed to cook dinner for a number of his friends. None of his pots was big enough. So he went to a neighbor and borrowed a pot from her. The next day, he returned the pot. Inside was another, much smaller cooking pot.

" 'What is this little pot for?' the woman asked Mullah Nazreddin.

" 'Well, last night after dinner, your pot gave birth. This is its baby.'

"The neighbor was pleased but astonished. She thanked the mullah for bringing back the baby pot with its mother.

" 'It would be a shame to separate a family,' Nazreddin told her solemnly.

"A few months later, Mullah Nazreddin had to give another feast. He went to his neighbor and borrowed her big pot. The neighbor gladly loaned it to him.

" 'Do you think the pot will give birth again?' she wondered as she handed him the pot.

" 'Only Allah knows for sure,' Mullah Nazreddin replied gravely.

"Several days passed, but there was no sign of the pot. A whole week passed, and the neighbor finally went to Nazreddin's house to retrieve the pot.

"When she got there, she found the house in mourning.

" 'Who has died?' the neighbor asked Nazreddin.

" 'I'm very sorry, but your pot died two days ago,' Nazreddin told her sadly.

" 'What! How can that be? A pot cannot die!' the neighbor cried.

" 'If you believed me when I said that your pot had a baby, why don't you believe me when I tell you that your pot has died?' "

Samad remembered the story correctly and told it well, but the twinkling in his eyes and his broad smile telegraphed the punchline too far in advance.

"Now, tell it in Greek," she said. "And try not to enjoy the ending so much. You're giving it away."

They spent the rest of the day working on Samad's storytelling. Samad told the Nazreddin story in several languages, altering the inflection and the pacing, until Teller was satisfied with each version. When his voice tired, Teller lectured him briefly on how to speak without straining his voice, and then she taught him another story.

The next day they arrived at Jerba al-Haddis, a rocky coastal oasis ringed round with high yellow sandstone cliffs. There they bid a grateful farewell to Demetrios and Isidro, who were bound farther south and east, to the Spice Belt. Teller traded the dory and two gold ingots for a schooner named *Esmeralda*. Samad's eyes widened when she produced the precious metal, but he said nothing.

The *Esmeralda* was a ten-meter schooner. She was a well-built, seasoned vessel, showing signs of wear but in excellent repair despite her age. Teller and Samad moved all their usable gear from the crew pod into the schooner. She put the emptied crew pod into storage and paid down a year's rent.

"Why don't you just sell it, sera?" the harbormaster asked her. Clearly he had heard that Abeha had become female.

Teller shook her head. "Who would need such a thing? It's too big to fit most harsels. Besides, it's too old and out of date to interest another har captain. Put it up where it will be high, dry, and out of the way, and I'll be back for it in a year or so."

"As you wish, sera," the harbormaster said with a polite bow.

Teller watched anxiously as they loaded the battered old crew pod into the top bay of their dry dock. She looked up at it for several long minutes after the stevedores had stowed it and left. So much of her life had been lived inside that windowless box. Even though she knew that the worn old crew pod would never be used again, she couldn't bear to cast it off. It held too many memories.

Teller took a deep breath, closed her eyes for a moment, and then turned to leave the pod behind.

"Let's go, Samad," Teller said. "Abeha's waiting for us."

CHAPTER 8

THEY TURNED EAST AFTER JERBA AL-HADDIS.
Abeha fed ravenously the whole way. The thick layer of fat
under Abeha's skin made her back feel rubbery underfoot.
Her fat buoyed the harsel up so that she bobbed like a rubber duck in the water, her sides exposed nearly to her eyes.
Teller and Samad rode on her back whenever the weather
was fair.

As they headed east, more and more harsels joined their
fleet, until they were surrounded by a vast forest of sails,
shading from palest white, to pink, blue, and purple. They
were joined by half a dozen other females, smaller than
Abeha, but still well grown and long-lived. Harsel outriders
scouted out the richest patches of plankton, ensuring that
the females ate well.

The fleet converged on the Tabbal Archipelago on the
edge of the Samali Sea. They sailed into the broad channel
between Zâfrán and Filfil islands, and there, spread out

across the channel, were thousands of harsels. There were more harsels than Samad had ever seen before, more than he had known existed.

"So many harsels!" Samad exclaimed. "Every harsel in the world must be here.

Teller shook her head. "No, Samad. There are over a million harsels living in the oceans of Thalassa. There are maybe seven or eight thousand here. The rest are mating elsewhere. Still, this is a bigger accumulation of mating harsels than I've seen in a long time. I think they're here to do honor to Abeha."

"Are there really that many harsels?" Samad marveled.

"Thalassa is a big place, Samad. Ninety percent of it is ocean. There's room for more than anyone can imagine in these seas. Humans have barely scratched the surface of this world. And that's as it should be."

Samad looked at the vast array of harsels sailing back and forth in the channel.

The waiting harsels greeted Abeha and the other females with a clamorous rejoicing of mindsong. An escort of over a hundred already-arrived females sailed out to greet them.

"Morituri te salutamus," Teller said in a voice full of ironic pain.

"What?" Samad asked. "That isn't Italian."

Teller shook her head. "It's Latin, Samad, one of the grandmother languages for Italian, and Spanish, too. The phrase means, 'We who are about to die salute you.'"

"HUSH, THAT'S ENOUGH PAIN FOR TODAY. THIS IS A CELEBRATION, TELLER," Abeha admonished.

"I'm sorry, Abeha. I'm not in the mood for a party. We'll go anchor and get settled at Uberagua's taverna. This is for the harsels, anyway."

"THEY WOULD DO YOU HONOR AS WELL," Abeha told

her. "THEY KNOW YOUR LOSS, AND WISH TO EASE IT IF
THEY CAN."

"Thank them for me, and tell them that I will join them
later," Teller said. "I just can't do it, Abeha."

"I UNDERSTAND," Abeha replied. "SAMAD, WOULD YOU
LIKE TO STAY AND WATCH?"

"Go ahead, Samad," Teller told him when he turned to
ask her. "I'll be fine. Besides, one of us should witness this.
Maybe someday you can make a story about it. Take the *Esmeralda*'s inflatable raft, and row ashore when they're done."

Samad tucked the lightweight package of the raft under
one arm and leaped from the railing of the boat onto
Abeha's back. Teller handed across the paddles for the raft,
then she turned the *Esmeralda*'s helm, trimmed the mainsail, and sped back out of the channel.

"Where's she going?" Samad enquired.

"THE CHANNEL IS CLOSED TO HUMAN SHIPPING UNTIL
AFTER THE MATING IS OVER. SHE'S SAILING AROUND TO A
HARBOR ON THE OTHER SIDE OF ZÂFRÁN ISLAND," Abeha
informed him.

"When will the mating start?" Samad asked.

"NOT FOR SEVERAL MORE DAYS. WE'RE WAITING FOR
THE TIDES TO PEAK. AND THERE ARE STILL MORE HARSELS
COMING."

"More?" Samad remarked incredulously, "Where will they
all go?"

"THE ENTRANCE TO THE MATING BAY IS FARTHER
DOWN THE CHANNEL. THERE'S A LONG, NARROW PASSAGE
INTO THE BAY. THE BAY'S RESTRICTED ACCESS MAKES IT
PERFECT FOR MATING."

"Then this isn't where you mate?" Samad asked.

"NO, WE ARE WAITING FOR THE TWO-MOON TIDE. THAT
WILL NOT HAPPEN FOR SEVERAL MORE DAYS." Abeha told

him. "HUSH NOW, THE HARSELS ARE STARTING THEIR WEL-
COMING CEREMONY."

The fleet of females opened up an aisle in the middle of
the channel. Abeha glided majestically toward them. As
they passed down this aisle, a chorus of mindsong broke out.
The music was majestically joyous. Samad could feel
Abeha's pride at this acknowledgment and greeting. The
great harsel was at last following the path laid out for her
kind. There was joy in doing this, mixed with the knowledge of pain and death to come. But without that pain and
loss, there could be no continuity, no new harsels in the
world. Sharing the songs, Samad understood why Abeha
was doing this. He wished that Teller were here to share
what he was feeling.

"SHE HAS FELT IT BEFORE, SAMAD," Abeha told him.
"SHE UNDERSTANDS, BUT HER PAIN IS TOO GREAT."

Samad nodded.

"I KNOW HER PAIN, AND I AM TRYING TO HELP HER, BUT
TODAY I MUST BE A HARSEL, FOLLOWING A HARSEL'S PATH.
LISTEN WITH ME NOW. WE WILL WORRY ABOUT TELLER TO-
MORROW."

Samad closed his eyes and let the complex, bell-like music ring through his mind. The songs spoke of generations
of harsels sailing the wide, windy oceans. There was a sense
of ancient depths, of birth and rebirth, sadness and joy. The
harsels' music swept him out of himself and into an alien
sense of time and place.

"SAMAD. SAMAD. WAKE UP. IT'S TIME FOR YOU TO GO,"
Abeha said, interrupting the flow of the mindsong.

It took a minute for Samad to shake off the trance. When
he opened his eyes, the sun, trailed by the moons Amphitrite and Thetis, was about a handspan above the top of
the long, high ridge of land that jutted out into the channel.

On it Samad could see a dark cluster of trees, with a vineyard spread out below.

"THE TAVERNA IS UP ON THAT RIDGE," Abeha told him. "TELLER WILL BE WAITING FOR YOU."

Samad nodded, still feeling a little dazed from the mindsong. "I see it," he told Abeha.

"THE ENTRANCE TO THE MATING BAY IS AROUND THAT POINT. YOU AND TELLER WILL BE ABLE TO WATCH US ENTER THE BAY FROM UP THERE. I UNDERSTAND THAT IT'S QUITE A SIGHT."

"I'll need to hurry, if I want to get to the taverna before dark," Samad told Abeha.

"YOU GET THE RAFT READY, AND I'LL GO AS CLOSE TO SHORE AS I CAN," Abeha told him.

Samad unrolled the raft and opened the inflation valve. There was a throbbing flutter and a hiss of indrawn air as the raft inflated itself. When the raft was nearly inflated, he coupled the blades of the paddles to the oar shafts, then stood waiting as the harsel sailed in to shore.

Abeha turned into the wind. "THIS IS AS CLOSE AS I CAN COME. THERE'S A BIT OF SHELTER BEHIND THAT BIG ROCK FOR YOU TO BEACH THE RAFT."

"Thank you, Abeha," Samad said as he pushed off. "Good luck in the mating."

Abeha replied with a wordless, mental embrace, filled with love, pride, and sadness. Beneath that embrace, Samad could feel a tiny, suppressed knot of fear.

"If you need me for anything Abeha, just let me know."

"THANK YOU, SAMAD." Abeha replied. Samad felt the harsel's knot of fear relax a little, and he smiled.

Abeha unfurled her sail and came about. Samad bent his back to rowing, watching as the harsel sailed out of the shadow of the ridge into the late afternoon sunlight. Her sails gleamed in the soft, golden light. Samad blinked away a sudden stinging in his eyes that was not due to windblown spray. He would miss Abeha terribly.

The taverna was hot, crowded, and smoky. Samad pushed his way through knots of loud, laughing, off-world tourists and somber groups of har captains. He found Teller sitting alone in a dark corner with a half-empty bottle of retsina. Judging from the determined way Teller was drinking, she was clearly beginning a massive drunk. Samad sat down beside her. There was a burst of laughter from a group of tall, pale, glitter-clad outworlders two tables over. Teller glanced at them, her frown deepening.

"Goddamned tourists," she muttered and took another swig from her bottle of retsina.

"You planning on staying drunk the whole time?" Samad asked.

Teller nodded, shrugged, then looked away. "Best way I can think of to get through it."

"What if Abeha needs you?"

"For what?" Teller asked.

"I don't know, Teller," Samad replied, "but she's scared."

"I know," Teller replied. "So am I."

"What if she hangs up in the channel?" Samad asked. "What if something goes wrong during the mating?" *What if I need you?* he thought.

"I have faith in Abeha. She knows what she's doing." Teller looked down at the names carved into the table's worn wood surface, her hands moving caressingly over the tabletop. "Mating's a matter for harsels," Teller told Samad. "If Abeha needs help, she'll have to get it from the other harsels. Interfering, even to help, would be a major violation of the Compact. The harsels would all leave their har captains, and we'd have to get by with human-built boats." She shook her head. "That would work well enough for the big

islands, but there are thousands of small, isolated settlements on the out-islands that would be totally cut off from
the outside world." She shook her head. "So there's nothing
to do but sit and worry." Teller picked up the bottle and
took another pull. "And drink," she finished, brandishing
the bottle defiantly.

Samad fled upstairs to their room without a word.
Throwing his bags into a corner, he flopped down on the
bed, exhausted. He was fed up with Teller's drinking. Despite his efforts to stop them, tears of hurt, fear, and defeat
forced themselves out from under Samad's eyelids. He
turned over, letting the tears flow onto the pillow, crying
silently in the dim, lonely, rented room.

Samad woke to fingers of morning light gilding the wall
beside him. Teller lay in the other bed, snoring loudly.
Samad got up, combed his fingers through his unkempt,
curly hair, and went downstairs to see if he could find some
breakfast. He felt grumpy and out of sorts, as hungover
from stress as Teller would be from last night's drunk.

Alazne Uberagua was up and bustling quietly about the
nearly deserted early morning dining room. She nodded
wordlessly at Samad as he sat down. She set a tiny cup of
thick black coffee in front of him, along with a large glass of
fresh orange juice, and four small pastries, each no more
than a bite or two, to hold him until his real breakfast came.
It was the custom of the tavernas in the Samâl wa Sarq group
of archipelagos, and welcome today.

"*Kahlee mehra,* Samad!" a cheerful voice called across the
dining room. "Good morning!"

Samad looked up. To his dismay he realized Florio was
standing at the entrance to the dining room. "*Yasas,*" he
mumbled grudgingly, "Hello."

Florio came over to his table. "So Teller's here already, is
she?"

Samad nodded, concentrating on his sweet rolls, hoping that Florio would take the hint and go away.

"How is Abeha doing?"

Samad shrugged, still not looking up.

"And Teller, is she all right?"

Samad shrugged again.

"Look, Samad. I'm sorry about stealing Teller from you for an evening. It was awkwardly done, and I regret it, but I care about Teller, too. I'm here to do what I can for her, and for you, too, if you'll let me."

Samad stared stonily at his cooling coffee, trying not to let his anger show. Florio sighed and stood up. "You shouldn't have to do this all by yourself, Samad. I love her, too. Let me know if I can help," he said, and walked back to his table, shoulders slumped. Samad looked up as he walked away. He remembered Teller drinking her pain away last night, and how overwhelmed he felt by it.

"Hey," Samad called out to Florio's retreating back. "Wait. I—I'm sorry."

Florio turned back to Samad. "It's forgotten," he told Samad, with a wave of his hand. "May I join you for breakfast?"

Samad nodded, and Florio sat down across from Samad and waited for him to speak. The landlady set a plate of pastries and a cup of coffee down in front of Florio.

"She drank a lot last night," Samad told him when the innkeeper had gone back into the kitchen. He looked across at the empty corner where Teller had sat last night. "It—" He shrugged. "It scares me when she does that," he admitted.

"You know there isn't much you can do," Florio told him, his brown eyes intent on Samad's face.

Samad shrugged. "But I'm supposed to take care of her. I promised Abeha—"

Florio put a hand on Samad's arm. "Samad. It's not your fault, and you shouldn't blame yourself. You can't fix this. Only Teller can."

"But how can I stop her?" Samad persisted.

Florio sighed. "Teller's certainly taught you how to be stubborn. I tell you what. Let's take her on a hike into the hills today. If we wear her out, she'll be too tired to drink."

"I don't know—" Samad began.

"Me, either," Florio confessed, "but have you got a better idea?"

"No, but she's tough as ironwood," Samad said, remembering how hard it had been to keep up with her on her long, grueling hikes. "I don't think we'll wear her out."

"At least we'll get her out of this damned bar," Florio pointed out. "These off-world tourists would drive even a stone mad!"

Samad grinned. "You should have seen them last night. All dressed up like a whore's breakfast. I never saw so much glitter and so few clothes on one person before."

Florio roared with laughter, his head thrown back and his eyes mere slits in his face.

"A whore's breakfast!" the storyteller exclaimed when he got his breath back. "Thank you, Samad. Now every time I see one of those overdressed off-world tarts, I'll be fighting back a smile. If I'm not careful, they'll think I'm flirting with them. It's bound to lead to trouble!"

Samad laughed with Florio and felt the tightness in his chest ease. He was suddenly grateful for the storyteller's company. He wasn't going to have to go through this all by himself.

Teller finally emerged around noon, morose and hungover. Samad and Florio fed her breakfast and whisked her out of the inn before she was awake enough to protest. They walked through vineyards, orchards, and groves of olives and native agrito trees, whose fruit was a popular local condiment.

Once past the cultivated hills, they walked up and over the spine of the ridge and down into the next valley, where they were entirely surrounded by rolling hills covered with golden grass. Ahead was a small range of mountains; the tallest had a tiny cap of snow on its peak. The land was empty, except for an occasional herd of sheep off in the distance. Evening found them out on the hills. They sheltered in a small shepherd's hut built of stone, with a little cluster of citrus trees in a small yard ringed with sharp stones to fend off grazing animals. The trees were watered by a trickling stream that cascaded from a crevice at the base of a massive, curving rock that formed one wall and part of the roof of the little hut.

Florio pulled out a loaf of bread, some cheese, olives, and a slightly wilted salad. They harvested a few ripe oranges from the trees and ate a decent, if rough, meal.

Sitting in front of a small fire of branches from the woodpile, Teller leaned back against the yellow stone wall of the hut and sighed.

"Thanks for getting me out of that inn. I think if I'd spent another night there, I might have strangled one of those damned squawking tourists. And that would have not done the Uberaguas any favors. Alazne's been kind enough to put us up, when she could sell my room to an off-worlder for twenty times what I'm paying her. You know one of them actually tried to interview me yesterday about Abeha. God only knows how he knew who I was." She shook her head ruefully.

Samad touched her arm. "I'm sorry I wasn't there," he apologized. "I would have chased him away."

Teller smiled. "I doubt it. He was slipperier than toadfish slime, that one."

"I wish I'd been there too," Florio said. "I'd've liked to have heard you tell him off. You probably handed him his *huevos* on a plate."

"I only wish that were true," Teller said ruefully. "I was so surprised that I just told him to go away and poured myself another drink. It was Alazne's son Erramun who shooed him away." She grinned. "That boy's gotten big since I last saw him. He's like an oak tree with legs. His grandfather was like that, too, at his age." Her glance slid sideways to Samad, "Or so Alazne tells me," she added.

"I was glad to get out of there, too," Samad admitted. "It was Florio's idea."

Teller took Florio's hand. "Thank you, *aghapitos,*" she told him.

"It was my pleasure, *aghapitee,*" Florio said, looking warmly back at her. "You know that."

The air seemed suddenly thick and soupy to Samad. "I think I'll take a walk," he declared, standing.

He went outside and stood, waiting as his eyes adjusted to the light. From inside, he heard Teller murmuring something to Florio. There was a smoky note of warmth in her voice that Samad recognized from the first time that he'd heard her talk to Florio.

He heard Florio say something back to Teller, and she laughed her rich, rough laugh. Then there was silence.

Samad looked up. The two moons were hanging low in the western sky, two dwindling crescents. They were closer together than he ever remembered seeing them before. According to Teller, in another four days, they would be close enough that little Thetis would slowly pass behind larger Amphitrite. It would take nearly a day for the eclipse to finish. For the next few days, the tides would be extreme, very high tides followed by very low tides. It was then that the harsels would mate. Their mating bay was the largest and deepest of the few saltwater bays where the tides were low enough and the channel narrow enough to provide the necessary conditions for the harsels to mate successfully.

He heard Teller laugh again and murmur something to Florio. Samad walked down the grassy slope, lighting his way with a tiny pocket torch, away from the sound of their amorous voices. He lay down in the grass, feeling a little lonely and sorry for himself but relieved that the burden of Teller's sadness lay on someone else's shoulders for a while.

It was a beautiful night. Samad looked up at the deep, star-studded, plum-purple of the night sky, wondering what sex felt like. He couldn't imagine himself with a girl, but that would probably change as he grew up.

He was starting to drop off to sleep when he heard a series of distant rhythmical cries of passion, rising for a minute or two, and then silence. He waited another twenty minutes and then got up and wandered slowly back to the hut that lay like a dark smudge in a fold of the silent, eternal hills.

In the light from the fire, Samad could just make out Teller and Florio lying together on the far side of the fire. Teller's quiet breathy snuffle mingled with Florio's deeper, rumbling snore. Samad's bedroll was spread ready for him. He lay down and let sleep take him.

The next morning, they sat by the fire and ate a cold breakfast of oranges and stale bread smeared with honey. Golden beams of morning light speared in through the propped-open door, illuminating the stone hut's red-earth floor and the walls of yellow stone. Outside, a greenthrush caroled the same sweet four-note song over and over in the morning air.

"It's so peaceful here. I wish we didn't have to go back to the inn," Teller said, putting a couple of small coins into the tin box on the mantelpiece in payment for their lodging and the oranges.

"Me, too," Florio agreed. "But we're out of food, except for oranges."

"I could go back to the inn and get some," Samad volunteered. "Then we could stay out here another night."

"But then we'd miss the harsels' entrance into the channel," Teller protested.

"You know, you *are* a har captain. You're permitted within the restricted zone," Florio pointed out. "We could move out of the inn entirely and go stay out on the other side of the point. Then it would be just us and the harsels. Between us we've got enough camping gear to do it."

"It would be fun, Teller!" Samad said. "And no stupid off-worlders either!"

Teller shook her head, "I promised Alazne and Karmel that I'd tell stories about the harsels."

"I'll do it," Florio offered. "You've got enough on your mind, *aghapitee.* I know most of the harsel stories, and I can tell them as well as you can. You shouldn't have to deal with a bunch of off-world tourists at a time like this."

"Well . . ." Teller began, clearly wavering.

"Let's do it!" Samad urged. "I'm tired of inns, and this way the Uberaguas can make more money from the off-worlders."

"All right! All right! But if the weather turns bad, don't blame me," Teller conceded.

"Then it's settled," Florio declared. "Let's head back to the inn and check out."

And so they found themselves a campsite amid a grove of furry-barked farwa trees on the point overlooking the channel into Mohai Bay. Their camp was only half an hour's walk back to Uberagua's taverna, but it felt like they were the only ones on the whole island. If they headed out along the point, they overlooked the long, narrow channel that led to the mating bay. A short hike in the other direction, up the point and onto the shoulder of the next ridge, and the harsel's mating bay was spread out like a huge map before them, a wide expanse of water shading from pale jade green to emerald in the depths. The bay was bordered by a wide band of drowned grass, waving like hair in the incoming tide.

They ate their evening meal on the point overlooking the channel as the sun set. Close behind and a little to one side were the moons Amphitrite and Thetis. By now the two moons were little more than a handspan apart.

"That section there is called the Narrows. Do you see the pale green water there? That's shallowest point in the passage. If Abeha's going to hang up anywhere, it will be there." Teller told them. "The harsels will begin sailing in on the tidal surge, about an hour past dawn. The tide will peak about midday tomorrow, and that's when Abeha has the best chance of getting through the channel."

"Then we should make an early night of it." Florio said.

There was little talk as they tidied the campsite and prepared for bed. Samad went to bed early, leaving Florio and Teller sitting beside the last embers of their dying fire.

They got up early, ate in silence, and walked down the point to watch the harsels sail up the channel as the first rays of the sun lit the low mountains across the bay. The water was still dark, though a few whitecaps flecked the surface. Already the initial swells of the tidal bore were rolling through the channel. A chill breeze blew, and Samad was grateful for the hot cup of tea that Teller handed him.

"Look!" Florio called. "They're coming through the channel!"

Squinting, Samad could make out a column of harsels, sailing four abreast down the narrow channel.

"They look so small from up here," Samad said.

"They are small. Those are the youngest males," Teller explained, handing him the binoculars. "The harsels come through the channel in order of age, youngest to eldest. Once the males are all in the bay, then the females come through in the same order. Abeha will be the last harsel into the bay."

Florio squeezed her shoulder. Teller managed a brief, nervous smile.

"It'll be all right," Samad reassured her.

Teller shrugged. "There's nothing any of us can do if something goes wrong. It's all up to the wind, the tide, and the harsels themselves."

All morning long the harsels sailed in a steady stream through the long, narrow passage into the bay. Thetis was completely eclipsed by Amphitrite and would remain so for most of the day. Tired of watching the parade of incoming males, they hiked over to take a look at the bay. By now, it was filled with a multicolored array of sails, as the males tacked back and forth, jockeying for favored positions.

"How can they fit any more harsels in the bay?" Samad wondered.

"I always wonder that myself," Teller told him, "but somehow they manage. Still, it's a bigger mating than most."

The column of males entering the bay was now only two abreast, and they were much larger than the first entrants.

"We should head back," Teller said. "We don't want to miss the females' passage through the channel." She glanced up at the sun, now almost at the zenith. "I hope the tide will be high enough for Abeha."

"She'll be all right, *agapitee,*" Florio soothed.

They hurried back up, over, and down, and reached their previous viewpoint just as the last few males sailed through the channel. There was a pause like the gathering rise of a wave, and then, one by one, singing as they came, the female harsels began sailing down the channel.

It took nearly two hours for all the females to sail past. Samad watched the tidal bore grow smaller and smaller as the tide rose toward its peak, and tried not to worry.

"There are a lot more females than usual this year," Teller commented. "I think Abeha's decision influenced a lot of other harsels to do the same." She sighed wearily. "I hope that there's no trouble in the channel," she fretted for the hundredth time that morning.

"She'll be all right, Teller," Samad reassured her once again. Perhaps if he repeated it enough, they would both believe it.

Teller stiffened. "Look! There she is!"

Abeha was sailing around the bend in the channel. From this vantage point the great harsel appeared graceful and deceptively serene. Samad's belly and throat tightened as Abeha passed into the Narrows and reached the lighter green water that marked the shallowest point of the passage. Abeha hesitated a moment as she approached the rocky shoals. Then she adjusted her course and slid past the shallow reef as smoothly as a cloud scudding before the wind.

Teller let out a huge sigh of relief. Samad felt as though a heavy stone had been lifted from his chest.

"She made it! She's all right!" Teller exulted. She hugged Samad and Florio, and danced around in joy, shouting, "She made it! She made it! She made it!" over and over again. Florio and Samad danced with her, finally collapsing breathless on the grass.

Teller got up first and began picking up her backpack. "Come on," Teller urged. "If we hurry, we can see her coming into the bay!"

Florio and Samad hurriedly gathered up their gear and

followed Teller back up the hillside, cutting across the point that the harsels were sailing around. They reached the ridge overlooking the bay and collapsed in a breathless heap.

The view was spectacular. The wide, long, emerald-green expanse of water was packed with male harsels, all facing the entrance to the bay, watching as the last of the females made their entrance. They were singing. From this far away, the sound was clear but not overwhelming, like church bells tolling in the distance. Inside his head, Samad could hear the mindsong as an echo behind the sound of the harsels' voices. The song was majestic and sad, celebrating the sacrifice the females were making. Even at this distance, Samad's heart swelled with bittersweet sadness in response to the song.

All the females had entered the bay except for Abeha. There was an expectant pause. The singing died away. The only sound was the hiss of the grass as the wind passed through it, and the faraway carol of a greenthrush.

"Where is she?" Samad worried. "Is she all right?"

"Shh!" Teller whispered. "She's the eldest. Wait."

Then Abeha glided into the bay; her sail spread majestically, nearly a third larger than any other harsel there. She was greeted by a joyous shout of welcome from the assembled harsels. Abeha was the oldest female, and her appearance marked the formal beginning of the mating ceremony. She paused and waited until the other harsels' clamor ceased. Samad's ears rang in the sudden silence. His head felt suddenly empty and light as an old eggshell.

The other females sailed out to meet Abeha, falling majestically into line behind her in order of age. When they were all in order, Abeha began to sing. One by one, the other females joined their voices to the chorus. The males fell back, opening an aisle for the females. As the females sailed into their midst, the males began to sing back, their beautiful, layered harmonies rising and falling in call and response. Soon the ordered chorus broke up into thousands of individual songs, shimmering like sunlight on choppy water.

"They'll keep this up for hours," Teller declared. "Let's eat."

So they sat in the tall grass and ate bread, cheese, and fresh fruit. Florio brought out a small skin of wine, and they formally toasted Abeha's successful passage through the channel.

As the afternoon passed, Thetis appeared from behind Amphitrite's crescent, while the bay resounded with the harsels' songs. It was almost as if they were singing the moons apart. The songs grew in intensity and volume as the sun, trailed by the barely visible crescent moons, sank toward the horizon, and the tide ebbed. As sunset neared, the harsels were crowded together in the deepest part of the bay, singing and jockeying for position. The long, narrow channel had dwindled to a slender ribbon of water, winding between the exposed fangs of the rocky bottom. The water gleamed like blood in the westering sun. Low as the tide seemed now, it was still more than three hours from its lowest ebb.

"The males will begin to release their milt at low tide, when the water is still," Teller said. "By sunrise, the bay will be red with it. With no moons, we won't be able to see much tonight. But the harsels will be mating continuously for the next two days. We'll get to watch all day tomorrow and the day after. They'll leave at high tide of the third day. That will be the dangerous time for Abeha. The tide will be almost a meter lower, and she might hang up in the channel. I wish she'd leave early, but she's too much of a traditionalist."

Teller looked grim, and Florio took her hand. She gave

him a thin, unconvincing smile. "I know, I know, don't think of it until the mating is over. But it's hard."

"I know it is." Florio glanced up at the setting sun. "Why don't you come with me to the taverna tonight, and listen while I tell stories. You can set me straight if I tell something the wrong way."

Samad snorted. "What does it matter if a bunch of ignorant off-worlders hear the stories wrong?"

"It matters a great deal," Teller chided. "Off-worlders carry our stories to the stars. If they hear a tale told wrong, then they will tell the wrong story to the rest of the galaxy." She looked out over the bay, toward Abeha.

"There's nothing you can do for her," Florio said gently.

"Yes, I know," Teller replied. "But I'd like to be alone tonight. I trust you to tell the stories correctly, Florio. Why don't you take Samad with you? It's time he made his debut."

Samad's eyes went wide. "A-are you sure I'm ready, sera?"

Teller nodded. "You're ready, and Florio will be there to look after you."

"You'll be all right here?" Florio asked.

"Abeha's still alive, Florio," Teller said. "I'll *be* all right! I just need some time alone. Please."

"You're not coming?" Samad exclaimed in a hurt tone.

Teller shook her head. "No, Samad. It's traditional for an apprentice to tell his debut tale without his teacher present. Florio will witness your first telling for the Guild. There's just one more thing you're going to need." She drew a flat, square box out of her backpack.

She handed it to Samad. "Go ahead, open it."

He opened the box and drew out a black cape. Around the hem was a border of the same multicolored cloth that made up Teller's shawl and Florio's cape. He looked at Teller; his mouth opened and shut, but no words came out.

Teller smiled. "It's your Journeyman's cape, Samad. Wear it with honor."

"Teller!" Samad managed at last. He threw his arms around her. She hugged him back, tears sparkling in her eyes. Samad wiped his face on his sleeve when he drew back. "Thank you, Teller!" he said, sniffing.

"Congratulations, Samad," Florio said.

Teller draped the cloak around Samad's shoulders and stood back, looking at him. "Looks good on you, Samad. Now, go and earn it."

"You ready, Samad? We should leave before full dark, so we can see where we're setting the beacons."

"Give me a minute to grab my pack!" Samad said.

Samad carefully folded his good shirt and pants and put them into his backpack, along with a flashlight. He glanced over at Teller, seated in front of the low fire.

"Is there anything you need before I go, sera?"

Teller smiled, "No, Samad. I'll be fine. Go with Florio, and pay attention. There's a lot you can learn from him."

"Yes, sera," Samad replied, concerned despite her reassurance.

"And stop worrying about me, Samad. You need to focus on what you're going to be telling tonight," Teller told him. "I'll be all right. I promise."

"Yes, sera," Samad repeated as he shouldered his pack. He followed Florio up the hill, glancing back just before they rounded the flank of the slope. Teller was watching them go. He lifted his hand in farewell, and she lifted hers in return.

Samad placed the last of the trail beacons that would guide them back to camp in the darkness. Florio stood waiting for him, a short, dark cipher in the twilight. They had reached the main road that led to the taverna. The road was little more than a glorified herder's track, but it was well trodden and easy to follow, even in the gathering dusk.

"Do you really think that Teller's all right?" Samad finally ventured to ask.

"Yes, Samad, I do. I'm more worried about what will happen when Abeha dies. Teller's life is so intertwined with Abeha's." He shook his head. "Abeha was right. You are good for Teller. You're not afraid to poke her when she crawls into her shell. Most of Teller's friends are too much in awe of her to do that."

"What's so special about Teller?" Samad asked. "She gets so mysterious sometimes. I can't even worm out of her how old she is, or where she was born. I swear, it would be easier to get a stone to talk."

"It would be," Florio agreed. "I never could get her to talk much about herself either."

They walked in silence for a few minutes. Samad could see the lights of the taverna twinkling in the distance. If Florio knew any of Teller's secrets, he wasn't telling.

"So, do you think you're ready to tell a story tonight?" Florio asked.

"Do *you* think I'm really ready?"

"I wouldn't have agreed to be your Guild witness if I didn't," Florio told him.

"Does Teller really think I'm ready?"

Florio nodded his head. "She suggested it, Samad. So she must think so. But Teller sprang it on you with very little warning. Are you prepared? Do you have a story to tell?"

Samad thought this over, turning various stories over in his mind, trying to find one that would fit tonight's audience. "I'd like to tell the story of the Compact. But it's more of a historical account than a true tale."

"Yes, but it's an excellent choice for tonight. If you hadn't decided to tell it, I would have. The off-worlders need to hear it," Florio said. "Do you know it well enough to tell it?"

Samad closed his eyes and ran the story through his mind like a rosary of beads, then nodded. "Yes. Yes, I do."

"Okay," Florio said. They shared the preoccupied silence of two storytellers readying themselves for their audience.

The taverna was crowded and hot when they arrived. Conversation was loud in the public room, and there was the pungent, alien scent of some strange smoke lingering in the air. Sera Uberagua greeted them with a smile that changed to concern when she saw that Teller wasn't with them.

"Is Teller all right?" she asked.

"She needed to be alone tonight. She sent me and Samad instead," Florio told her. "Teller has said that he's ready to tell his first story tonight."

"What a shame Teller will be missing it!" Sera Uberagua declared.

"It is a tradition among storytellers that the teacher not be in the audience for an apprentice's first tale," Florio told her. "That way the apprentice focuses on the audience instead of their teacher. Teller wasn't there when I told my first story either. But we are both satisfied that Samad is ready."

"Please thank Sera Teller for honoring us with Samad's first story," Sera Uberagua said. "Can I get you anything to eat or drink?"

Samad shook his head, suddenly nervous and queasy.

"Go sit outside for a bit, Samad," Florio suggested. "I think the off-worlders' dreamsmoke is getting to you."

Samad stepped out onto the quiet patio and stood looking out at the dark, distant bay. The taverna was farther back from the bay than their campsite, and the harsels' songs sounded very faint. He closed his eyes and concentrated, trying to hear their mindsongs with his inward ear.

Footsteps interrupted his inward listening. He turned. It was Florio, carrying a tray.

"I brought you some soup and bread. Eat. It'll settle your stomach."

Samad tried the soup. Rich and warm, it undid the knot in his belly. He finished the bowl and ate a soft, sweet crusty roll. He had been hungrier than he had thought. The nervous flutter in his stomach was nearly gone, and he felt more solid and alert with the food in his stomach.

"Thanks," he said. "You were right, it did help."

Florio shrugged. "I still get a little nervous just before I go on. You get used to it, in time."

Samad nodded. They sat in silence, listening to the harsels for a few minutes.

"You ready?" Florio asked.

Samad nodded, his throat suddenly tight.

"Let's go. I'll tell a couple of fillers to warm them up, and then introduce you."

He followed Florio to the small dais that served as a stage at one end of the room. Karmel Uberagua came up.

"Since these off-world people don't know how to shut up and listen properly, I've set up the sound system." Karmel handed them each a loop of cord. "Put these around your necks," he told them.

Florio slipped the loop mike over his head, adjusted the fit, and then helped Samad with his. "After I tell the story of Nazreddin and the three har captains, I'll introduce you," he told Samad.

"I'll be ready," Samad told him. He went and sat down at a small, round table just beside the stage. Karmel gestured to a shadowy figure behind the bar, and a spotlight slowly came up. The audience quieted. Karmel stepped into the spotlight, and waited a beat until everyone's attention was focused on him.

"Tonight, esteemed sers and seras, we are honored to present to you two generations of storytellers, both trained by Teller, one of our world's most revered Master Storytellers. Our local patrons need no further explanation, but to our guests who have come from far across the sea of stars, I will tell you that here on Thalassa, storytelling is considered a fine art. Ser Florio Hakiapulos is an acknowledged master of the art. For over fifteen years he has enthralled audiences around the world. And tonight, we have a special treat; Teller's current apprentice, Abd al-Samad Bernardia, will be making his debut performance. They will tell you some of our traditional Thalassan folktales, as well as some of the history and legends surrounding the harsels, so that you will have a greater understanding of the harsels' ways. Sers and seras, I give you Master Storyteller Florio Hakiapulos, and Apprentice Storyteller Abd al-Samad Bernardia."

There was a polite patter of applause with a few cheers from the locals as Florio moved to the center stage, his storyteller's cloak dashingly draped over one shoulder. Florio seemed taller, broader, and more commanding onstage. His gaze roved over the audience, measuring it and gathering their attention. When all eyes were on him, he put his wide-brimmed hat down on the hatrack placed on the stage for that purpose, seated himself on the barstool under the spotlight, and began.

"Once there was and twice there wasn't an old man who lived over on the island of Chelm. Now this old man had a mule who loved apples above all else on this world. . . ."

Samad's attention wandered away from the familiar story of the foolish old man and his mule. He looked out over the audience, watching the off-worlders in their shiny fabrics, a fortune in precious metals winking at ears, throats, and cuffs. They seemed so gaudy and out of place in this plain room with its thick stucco walls and dark, massive timbers. He tried to imagine telling them about the Compact, and couldn't. How could they understand? They'd never lived on one of the out-islands. They had no idea how lonely it could be; how dependent most of the people of Thalassa were on the harsels and their captains. The har captains brought trade, company, and the kind of news and gossip that could only be told over a mug of foamy beer or a cup of coffee.

". . . and so the mule became mayor of Chelm, and he governed as wisely as any of the human inhabitants of that island until the end of his days."

The audience laughed and applauded, and Samad relaxed. Perhaps he could tell these strangers a story. And if he could tell a story to an audience as exotic and distracting as these people, he could tell a story to anyone.

When the applause subsided, Florio began the story of Nazreddin and the three har captains. Samad listened to the convoluted nonsense tale with a nostalgic smile. Even though he knew the tale by heart, and could tell it himself, he laughed with the rest of the audience at the sudden, wry twist that brought the tale to its end.

Then Florio was introducing him, and it was time to get up and tell his story. He checked the drape of his Apprentice cape and stepped onto the stage.

The lights were so bright that the audience was just a dim blur in the darkness. He sat down upon the stool, remembering to keep his back straight.

"This is the true story of how the Pilot and the harsel's Council of Memory created the Compact that brought humans and harsels together on Thalassa," he began.

"Four centuries ago, Thalassa was a very different place.

The colony was still in its first generation. Its human population was barely twenty thousand people, mostly refugees
from the Mediterranean basin following the explosive erup-
tion of Stromboli. Metal was scarce, there were few boats,
and the comm network was unreliable. There was almost no
interisland trade. Isolated settlements could easily be cut off
from the outside world. Life was precarious, difficult, and
lonely.

"It was here on the Isla de Zâfrán that one of the most
important events in our world's history occurred. In the
time of this story, Zâfrán had been recently settled by the
Uberagua family, ancestors of the family that owns this excellent inn. Back then, there were only a few sapling fruit
trees. The groves of olive trees and the vineyards had not
been planted. Like many of the settlers on neighboring islands, the Uberaguas herded cattle. Hoping to make more
money by selling leather instead of raw hides, they built a
tannery at the mouth of the Kurkum River, which runs into
the head of the harsels' mating bay. The tannery grew and
prospered, taking in hides from nearby settlements and
turning them into finished leather.

"But the Uberaguas had underestimated the height of
the mating tides, and the tannery was flooded, releasing
thousands of gallons of noxious tanning agents into the pure
water of the river. As the tide receded, a cloud of noxious
tanning chemicals washed over the assembled harsels. The
surviving harsels fled on the next high tide, their gills
scarred. The har females, unable to mate, beached themselves and died a slow, painful, and dishonorable death. It
was the first failed mating in two thousand years.

"In response to this disaster, the harsels convened a
Council of Memory, an assembly of senior harsels charged
with holding the memories of their people. After deliberat-

ing for several weeks about what to do, the Council sent a delegation to see what had happened to Zâfrán Bay.

"At high tide, the Council's delegation sent a young harsel up the shallow river to the site of the tannery to see what had happened. The youngster returned with the news that the humans were rebuilding the tannery. Harsels are extremely slow to anger, but the reconstruction of the tannery was an insult that they could not ignore. The delegation decided that it was time to let the humans know of their anger. They summoned every harsel in the Samali Sea to come to Zâfrán. They came by the hundreds as fast as their sails could move them.

"When enough harsels were assembled, they unleashed a torrent of angry mindsong against the twenty human settlers living on Zâfrán. At first the mindsong was like the buzzing of a fly against a windowpane, but as more harsels arrived, it grew in intensity. Soon thousands of harsels surrounded the island, with more coming every day. Even the most mind-blind humans on the island felt the harsels' anger hammering against their skulls. Infants screamed continuously, children rocked and pounded their heads against walls until they had to be physically restrained by adults who could barely think through their own agony. The settlers retreated to the central mountains, where the pain was less intense, leaving behind their livestock and gardens.

"By the time word reached the Pilot, the settlers on Zâfrán had endured ten days of this mental siege, and the harsels showed no sign of stopping. Through her harsel, the Pilot explained to the Council of Memory that the humans did not realize what they had done. She asked for and received several days' worth of peace from the harsels while she went to talk to the besieged settlers. She beached her dinghy and walked up into the hills, where they had taken shelter from the pain.

"Pale and shaken, the settlers emerged from the caves where they had been hiding. They greeted the Pilot with grateful eagerness. Their eagerness turned to dismay and anger when she explained the source of the mental assault and why the harsels were doing this.

"'But my baby died,' one mother said, 'and look at my other two children!'

"The two children, a boy and a girl, sat next to each other, rocking and unresponsive. Next to them sat another half dozen children, all under the age of six, all lost to the outer world. The Pilot recoiled in horror.

"'My husband couldn't stand the pain,' another woman said. 'He went outside and shot himself. And Edurne's little son died, too. He wouldn't eat and couldn't sleep. There was nothing we could do to help him.'

"'I-I'm sorry.' The Pilot said. 'Your suffering has been terrible, and I share the pain of your loss. But there has been suffering on both sides. Hundreds of harsels perished in great pain when the tannery flooded. The harsels insist that the tannery must not be rebuilt. I have been sent to try to settle this issue.'

"And so began a long and difficult negotiation. The settlers wanted recompense for their suffering, and for the loss of their livestock and crops, as well as for moving the tannery. The harsels, who owned nothing, had no understanding of the human's material losses. And just as the settlers were beginning to soften, a delegation from the colonial government arrived to straighten things out, and everything began all over again.

"The harsels were growing impatient; some threatened to begin the mental assault again. The settlers, furious over the damage done to their children, were adamant in their demands for restitution. The talks were breaking down. It was looking very bad for everyone involved. Then the Pilot's harsel made a suggestion.

" 'Harsels have no money, nor any pockets to keep money in, nor hands to pay money with,' the Pilot's harsel said. 'But perhaps we can create something that will help all humans and all harsels on this world. I propose a partnership between harsels and humans. Harsels will partner with humans and carry people and their things from island to island, as I transport my partner.'

" 'And perhaps the losses the settlers have incurred can be repaid from the revenues made by that partnership,' the Pilot suggested.

" 'But what about my daughter?' demanded the mother of one of the dead infants.

" 'And my husband,' demanded another settler.

" 'And our lost children who stare into space?' said another.

" 'Who among you can bring back our dead?' asked the Pilot's harsel. 'We have lost many of our own, and the offspring that would have carried on their line. There is nothing we can do for the dead, except remember them. But perhaps our healers can help the children we have harmed.'

"And so the lost children were carried out to the harsel's mindsingers. And the mindsingers sang the children back into themselves. Healing the children made all the difference. The parents, relieved that their children were well again, backed down on their demands for reparations. The harsels were so appalled by the damage they had done to the humans' children that they were eager to atone by entering into partnership with humans. Once the initial anger and misunderstandings were resolved, the rest was relatively easy.

"The tannery was moved to the other side of the island and placed well out of reach of the highest mating tides.

The colonial government placed strict controls on the effluent from the tannery.

"The initial source of irritation resolved, the Council of Memory entered into talks with the colonial government, with the Pilot and her harsel acting as translators and mediators. After several months of careful talks, they agreed upon a formal Compact. Humans were prohibited from harming or interfering with the harsels in any way. The harsels' mating bays were identified and placed under the highest degree of human protection. Harsels, in return, promised never to launch another mental attack on a human settlement. The basic rules governing a harsel-human partnership were agreed upon. A mechanism for resolving any future differences between harsels and humans was created. The Compact was ratified and signed by the colonial government, and solemnized in mindsong by the harsels. Every schoolchild on this world must know the Compact by heart. Immigrants must memorize the Compact in order to qualify for citizenship. Every adult harsel can sing the mindsong about the Compact.

"The harsels and the Pilot found and trained the first har captains. Soon a modest but growing fleet of har captains traded goods and transported people, passing along news and gossip, and connecting the out-islanders to the larger world. The profession became considered both profitable and honorable. The injured settlers of Zâfrán received full reparations. The tariffs paid to the harsels have been invested in projects to aid and assist them. Sophisticated weather forecasts are passed along to the harsels, helping them avoid storms and dangerous seas. A network of floating clinics and hospitals has improved the harsels' health, fertility, and longevity. Because of the Compact, humans have been able to settle remote islands and create a reliable trading network that supports those islands. Over the cen-

turies, harsels and humans have achieved a peaceful coexis-
tence. Together we have prospered more than either would
have separately."

Samad paused a moment before delivering the last line of
his account. "But most of all, here on Thalassa, humans are
not alone." He thought of Abeha as he said this, and his
heart swelled, and tears prickled at the backs of his eyelids.

The story over, Samad stepped away from the storyteller's
seat and bowed to his audience. Applause and even cheers
for his tale swelled and lingered, especially among the locals. He ducked his head, surprised by their response. The
audience had listened and liked his story. He felt pleased,
relieved, and overwhelmed in equal measure.

Florio stepped back onstage as the applause died. He
thanked Samad, squeezing his shoulder encouragingly.
Samad bowed again, and stepped into the welcome, anonymous offstage shadows. Now that the story was over, he felt
oddly restless and jittery.

Samad slipped out of the stuffy taverna onto the stone-
paved patio. Scattered across the patio were a dozen small
wood tables where couples sat, knees touching, faces illuminated by flickering candlelight. It was no place to be alone.

In search of greater solitude, Samad wandered down the
hill to a graveled terrace overlooking the dark water of the
bay. There was a low wall around the terrace that marked
where the hill began to slope more sharply down to the bay.
Samad stepped over the wall, onto the sparse grass and
gravel below. He settled back against the wall, alone with
the wind, the hillside, and the dark void of the bay. In the
distance, he could hear the harsels singing. Closing his eyes,
he listened inwardly to the distant chorus of mindsong.
There was a new excitement tonight. Samad felt aware of his
body in a way he never had before. The harsels' singing
reached a peak and then dissolved into the chaos of thou-

sands of males singing individual courting songs. Samad opened his eyes and sat up. The mating had begun.

He was about to get up and tell the Uberaguas, but then he heard the crunch of gravel underfoot. Two people were on the terrace. Uncertain what to do, Samad hesitated.

"At last," said a man with an off-world accent. "I've been trying to get you alone all night long."

"I'm here now," another man with a deep bass rumble of a voice replied. He sounded familiar, his accent was local, but Samad couldn't tell who it was.

Then there was the soft rustle of clothing, and the whisper of two people moving together in the darkness. Samad listened, wondering what they were doing. He peered over the wall but could only see the faint gleam of an off-worlder's shirt, nearly swallowed in the shadow of another, much larger man.

"Oh, yes," the off-worlder sighed. "There. That feels so good."

A wave of horrified realization swept over Samad. The two men were having sex. He crept softly along the low wall, afraid of what would happen if they discovered him there. He reached the shadows where the wall tapered into the hillside, and looked back. The two men shifted position slightly, and light from the distant patio illuminated them for a brief moment. His breath caught in surprise. He didn't care about the off-worlder. But the man with him was Erramun Uberagua.

Gripped by a sudden, helpless fascination, Samad watched the outworlder reach down to caress Erramun.

"Oh my," the off-worlder purred. "You're big all over."

Samad became aware of a strange tightness and heat centered in his groin that grew as he watched the two men fondle each other. Frightened by the intensity of his feelings, he fled into the darkness, running until he tripped over a stone and fell.

He lay on the grassy hillside, chest heaving, listening to the echoing throb of the harsels' mating songs in his mind. The harder he tried to rid his mind of Erramun and the off-worlder, the more vivid they seemed and the more urgent the tension and heat in his groin became. It must be the harsel's mating that made him feel like this. It couldn't be anything else. Two men having sex could not have aroused him. He wanted to be normal, like everyone else. He wanted a family, a known future, not some dark and terrifying mystery like this. As a child on the streets, other children had whispered warnings about men like the off-worlder and Erramun. He didn't want to be like that. He wouldn't be like that. He would be normal.

But if he was normal, why hadn't Florio and Teller's passion stirred him like this? He'd seen men and women in the midst of passion once or twice, and nothing had stirred within him. Why now? Why them? It must be because of the harsels' mating. The harsels' passionate mindsongs had woken something in him. It had to be. It had to. Gradually, his breathing slowed and his heart stopped hammering. He got up and went back to the taverna.

The storytelling had just ended when Samad slipped back inside. Florio caught his eye, and Samad felt a sudden rush of fear. What if Florio knew what had happened?

Florio excused himself from a crowd of admirers and came over to Samad.

"Congratulations, Journeyman," Florio said, giving him a hug. "You really earned your cloak. I'm proud of you, and Teller will be, too. It isn't easy to turn a historical account into a tale that moves an audience."

Samad shrugged. He'd been so startled by the encounter

on the terrace that he'd almost forgotten the story he had told.

"It needed better balance, more polish," Samad demurred.

"Perhaps," Florio said. "And that will come. But you told the whole thing without stumbling or missing an important detail. And more importantly, you touched their hearts. Relax, Samad, you did fine."

"Thank you, Florio," Samad told him. "The mating's started. I felt the singing change when I was outside."

"Good, I'll tell Karmel. I thought Erramun was out there keeping track of things. He's talented at hearing the harsels. I've always thought he'd make a good har captain."

Samad cast a quick, guilty glance at the door. Just then Erramun came in, his bulk filling the doorframe. Samad looked away, afraid that if he met Erramun's eyes, the big man would know that Samad had seen him. Five minutes later, Samad noticed the off-worlder on the patio, laughing and talking as though nothing had happened. Erramun treated the man with the same remote politeness that he showed toward the other off-worlders. Samad marveled at his casualness.

"Samad!"

Startled out of his reverie, Samad looked up at Florio. "What?"

"Are you ready to go?" Florio asked him. "You looked like you were on the other side of the sun just now."

"Let me get my pack."

Samad trudged quietly behind Florio on the long walk home.

"Are you all right, Samad?" Florio asked finally. "You seem quiet tonight. Are you thinking about your performance? I meant it when I said you did well."

"I'm worried about Teller, Florio," Samad lied. He didn't

know how to talk about what he'd seen and felt, out on the terrace. Florio was still too much of a stranger. And he didn't want to bother Teller. She had enough problems.

"I understand, Samad," Florio said, "but I'm pretty sure she's fine."

"Fine for now, I guess," Samad said, grateful to be distracted from the images running through his head. "But when Abeha—" He hesitated, not wanting to say it. "When Abeha dies, what then?" he finished.

"Samad, there's only so much you can worry about. There are lots of people who really care about Teller. There's the har captains, and the storytellers, and hundreds of people she's helped out, one way or another. People will be there to help Teller, and to help you, as well."

"But what if . . . what if she *dies?*"

"She's a survivor, Samad. She's lived through more than you can imagine."

"But that's what Abeha's worried about. And she knows Teller better than anyone else could!"

Florio stopped and turned to face Samad in the darkness. "Samad, if she—if the worst happens, then I promise that I will be there to take care of you. If you want me to, that is. If you don't want to stay with me, there are plenty of other people who would be honored to take you in. You have more friends than you probably realize. But," Florio continued. "I don't plan on letting Teller kill herself if I can help it."

Samad glanced sidelong at Florio, moved by his offer. But he wasn't worried about himself. He'd managed before Teller came; he could survive without her if he had to. What worried him was the promise he'd made to Abeha, that he wouldn't let Teller die.

"Thank you, Florio. I appreciate that." He sighed. "I— *we're* going to need a lot of help."

"I'll be there, Samad. I promise."

•   •   •

Teller watched Samad and Florio walk away. They paused every hundred meters to set a trail beacon to guide them back to camp in the dark. At last they passed out of sight, and she sighed in relief. Teller gathered her gear, checked it over carefully, and walked down the other side of the ridge toward the shore of the bay, laying down her own trail of beacons. Humans were barred from the bay during mating, but the harsels had quietly made a rare exception for Teller. She had received permission to be in the water during mating, as long as she told no other humans. Much as she loved them, Samad and Florio could not be told. For a while, she thought that Samad's and Florio's solicitousness was going to keep her from her swim, but then Florio had volunteered to tell stories in her place, and she had urged Samad to make his debut. Her heart contracted with guilt as she recalled Samad's look of concern as he left. But the boy was ready. Silently, she wished Samad luck and hoped that his debut would go well.

Teller made her way carefully down the hill to the arm of a point that enclosed a secluded cove. The air seemed charged by the harsels' singing. The sun had set, and it was dark by the shore, though there was still some light in the sky. Teller set her gear down by a convenient large boulder near the bank of shingle that was the shoreline during more normal tides. She took her mask and artificial gills out of the pack and then pulled a clinking string of empty wine bottles out as well. Teller undressed, neatly folding her clothes and putting them in her pack, where they would stay dry. She set a beacon on top of the rock, so that she could find it again in the dark, and tucked another of the egg-sized beacons inside her mask.

She slung the wine bottles over one shoulder, and carrying her diving gear, crossed the exposed tidal flats to the wa-

ter. The closer she came to the shore, the stronger the elec-
trical feeling of excitement became. At the edge of the water, she set her clinking burden of wine bottles down, and
set another beacon so she could find them later.

Donning her mask and unfolding the ruff of gills on her
rebreather, Teller waded into the milk-warm water. The
harsels' singing throbbed in her bones. When the water was
past her waist, Teller dove in and began swimming. She
swam with strong, assured strokes through the dark water
out of the cove and into the bay. Out in the bay, the harsels'
singing was so intense that the water felt like it was made of
music.

Suddenly the singing stopped, leaving an echoing stillness behind. The only sound Teller could hear was the pulse
and hiss of her rebreather. Into that sudden silence she heard
Abeha begin a new chant, one that Teller had heard before,
in other mating seasons. But not sung with Abeha's voice.
Here in the water it was powerful enough to dissolve her
sense of self. She let herself drift on the slack tide, awash in
the harsel's mindsong. Abeha's powerful song resounded
through the bay and echoed off of the bones of the encir-
cling hills. Her solitary voice was exultant yet sad. Teller's
listening heart swelled with pride, grief, and wonder at its
beauty.

Then the other females joined her, weaving their own
voices over and around Abeha's, creating a tapestry of sound
and emotion. Teller could just make out the females sailing
in the darkness toward the surrounding ring of males, their
pale sails gleaming faintly in the starlight.

The males raised their voices in reply, weaving their own
longing into the females' tapestry of mindsong. As the ring
of females reached the surrounding males, the chorus dissolved into thousands of individual courtships, males calling to females, and females responding.

The dissolution of the chorus woke Teller from her trance. She reached with her mind, searching for Abeha's voice in the chaotic chorus. Abeha was surrounded by amorous males vying for her attention. The males crowded each other, blocking the wind from each other's sails, tolling bell-like challenges at each other, building themselves up to a peak of arousal. At last Abeha sailed alongside a male, accepting his suit. The male lay over on his side, releasing a cloud of milt beside her. Several other smaller males shouldered close to Abeha and her chosen mate, releasing their sperm as well. Abeha opened her hold, taking in the milt, then withdrew, watching the other males vie for her favor. After fifteen or twenty minutes, she sailed forth and chose another male.

The bay was a frenzy of mating. The males' milt diffused into the water. The breeze carried the musky, low-tide smell of it to Teller. As the mating built in intensity, she could taste it on her lips, fishy and oddly astringent. Her mouth began to tingle pleasantly, and soon she could feel that tingling all over her body. She swam back to shore and retrieved her string of empty wine bottles.

Teller swam out into the bay again. When she reached a spot where the tingling on her skin was particularly strong, she uncorked the bottles, filling them with a rich broth of seawater and milt. The males' milt was reputed to be a powerful aphrodisiac, and sold for a high price. She would give the bottles to people who had helped her and Abeha.

The tingling grew stronger the longer she stayed in the water. When the tingle grew to a sense of urgency, Teller emerged from the bay and washed off in a nearby freshwater stream. The tingling ebbed to a warm, throbbing glow. It was getting late. She dressed, restowed her gear, and began the long climb up the hill. She was back in camp only a few minutes before Samad and Florio returned. Samad seemed surprisingly subdued for a newly made Journeyman Teller. She glanced at him worriedly. He saw her looking and vanished into his tent. She started after him, then thought better of it. He clearly wanted to be alone.

She took Florio's hand and led him off into the darkness, to a hollow in the hills where she had spread her blanket.

"Is Samad all right? Did his story go well?" she asked Florio when they were safely out of Samad's hearing.

"His story was fine. It's you he's worried about," Florio told her. "He's terrified that Abeha's death will kill you, too."

Teller, her body tingling and eager from her swim, was brought suddenly to earth. She looked away into the night, toward the singing darkness of the bay.

"Will her death kill you, Teller?" Florio demanded, his hands tightening on her arms.

Teller shrugged. "I don't know," she said. "I can't imagine living without Abeha. His—" She paused and corrected herself, *"Her* voice has been in my mind all the years I've lived on Thalassa. I—"

"Samad needs you," Florio said hoarsely. "And I need you."

"And the har captains need me, and the Guild needs me, and the harsels too. . . ." Teller continued. "Everyone needs me, but I'm not always going to be around to help. Sooner or later, Thalassa is going to have to manage without me."

"You know what you are to this world," Florio stated. "How can you leave us all?"

"Everyone dies, Florio," Teller pointed out. "Sooner or later, the rejuve will wear out, or I'll have an accident. I won't live forever, *aghapitos."*

"So you'll just abandon us all to our fates, then? Samad, me, the whole damned world?"

"It's not like I have a choice, Florio."

"Yes, you do!" Florio insisted.

"Dammit, Florio, you just don't understand!" she whispered, all too conscious of Samad, curled in his sleeping bag just beyond earshot. "It's not that I don't *want* to live after Abeha dies. I don't think I *can!*"

Florio took her in his arms and stroked her still-damp hair. "Tell me about it."

"Abeha holds most of my memories, most of my stories," Teller confessed. "If I'm away from her for more than a few weeks, they start to fade. I lose some of them. When I see her again, they come back, bright as ever. I don't know how much I'll lose when she dies. Maybe it'll all go, and I'll wind up a drooling idiot." She lifted her head off of his chest, looking into the darkness. "I don't want to live if I get like that, Florio. It would be cruel."

"But maybe you won't," Florio suggested. "Maybe you'll be just like the rest of us, a bit fuzzy around the edges. Have you written it all down?"

"I've always kept a journal, Florio," she told him.

"Then use that."

"But it's not the same!"

"Sh-h-h, *aghapitee.* Worry about what you *can* change," Florio whispered soothingly. "Trust the people who love you. We'll still be here, even after Abeha's gone. Let us help you. Please."

Teller smiled. Poor Florio, he wanted to help so much, and there was so little he could do. "Thank you, *aghapitos,*" she said. She laid her head against his chest, taking comfort in his warm, familiar presence. Her body's restless urgency was reasserting itself.

Florio sniffed her hair. "You've been swimming in the bay, haven't you?"

Teller turned in his arms, placed a finger on his lips, and

pulled him down onto the blanket. "I can't say anything. Don't ask."

She kissed him. She felt him responding. The heat she had repressed since her swim in the mating bay kindled into passion. Soon they were making love in the grass.

Samad lay in the tent, unable to sleep. He wished that he could talk to Teller about what he had seen and felt back at the inn. The two men together, and how it had made him feel.

Distantly, Samad could hear the sound of Teller and Florio having some kind of intense discussion. The conversation subsided into murmurs of reassurance, then silence for a while, followed by the faint, but unmistakable sounds of passion. He rolled over angrily, jamming his pillow over his ears. Sex was everywhere tonight. That must be it. Like everyone else, he was just responding to the lust broadcast by the harsels' mating. The whole thing was just a fluke. He would forget it had ever happened. He lay there, doing his best to forget until sleep took him.

The next morning dawned bright and clear. Florio's cheerful singing and the clatter of pots and pans woke Samad from a disturbing dream of arousal. Samad lay there, looking up at the sunlit roof of his tent, trying to remember his dream, but already it had evaporated in the bright morning light.

Samad threw back the covers of his sleeping bag and peered out of his tent. Florio was whipping up eggs for an omelet. There was a thick, crusty loaf of bread that Florio had brought up from the inn last night, neatly sliced; and next to it was a crock of salty butter with a knife standing hilt upward in it. A bottle of grape juice floated in a bucket of cold spring water.

"You're in a good mood," Samad remarked.

Florio beamed back. "It's a beautiful day," he agreed.

"And you got laid last night," Samad accused, feeling a rush of anger as he said it.

"This morning, too," Florio conceded cheerfully. "I'm glad we didn't wake you." His eyes flicked downhill, where Samad could hear distant splashing. "She's feeling good this morning," he pointed out. "I hope her mood lasts."

Samad gave a grudging shrug and helped himself to the grape juice without a word, unwilling to destroy their good mood with his own worries.

"Good morning!" Teller caroled, striding up from the stream, her hair still wet. "Brrr! That water's cold! Did you sleep well, Samad?"

He nodded, incredulous at her cheery mood. Teller peered into the bowl of omelet filling that stood waiting by the grill. "Braefish roe and mushrooms!" she exclaimed. "Yum! I'm hungry this morning!"

"And good sharp cheese," Florio added, as he poured the eggs into the waiting pan, carefully swirling it to get a papery thin edge. He set the pan back on the grill, and gave her a big, happy hug. Samad was so pleased to see her happy that he nearly forgave Florio for his smugness.

After breakfast, they sat on a high hill overlooking the bay. The green water was stained with the males' rusty brown milt. The females tacked slowly across the bay, with many pauses while they mated. The harsels' songs became more insistent as the tide surged back into the narrow passage, green swirls of seawater mingling with the milt-stained waters of the mating bay.

There was something hypnotic in the endless calling and circling. Samad didn't notice the ebbing of Teller's good mood until midafternoon, when hunger broke the spell of watching. By then she was slump-shouldered and with-drawn again.

Samad and Florio did what they could to lighten her mood, but nothing really helped much. The next day and the following night inched by with agonizing slowness. Teller sat and watched, hunched and miserable, while the harsels endlessly called and circled and mated.

The morning after the final night of mating dawned misty and silent. The mating was over. The harsels drifted across the brown water like mist-shrouded shadows, their sails hanging slackly in the strange, mist-softened light. It looked like they were floating in a sea of old blood. Samad shuddered at the thought.

There was a step behind him. It was Teller.

"Florio's asleep," she told him quietly.

"The mating's over, isn't it?" Samad said in a low voice.

"Yes." Teller confirmed. "They'll be leaving today. They're waiting for the high tide."

"Will Abeha make it out all right?"

Teller shrugged and looked down, pushing at a clump of grass with her toe. "I wish I could be sure, Samad. You saw what the bottom of that passage looked like at low tide. If she catches up on any of those rocks . . ." Teller closed her eyes in pain. "The eldest leaves first. That's Abeha this year. If she grounds in the Narrows, she could block all the other females inside the bay, as well as most of the larger males. They could lose the entire mating."

"Why doesn't she leave last?" Samad asked.

"She's the eldest; going first is her right. And the harsels begin to leave when the tide is at its peak. If she waits, her chances of getting out safely are much worse." Teller looked down at the eerily still bay and shook her head worriedly.

"Abeha's smart," Samad soothed. "She knows the passage. She won't hang up."

"I hope you're right, Samad," Teller said. "I hope you're right."

The two of them waited as the tide rose. The clear green seawater borne in on the incoming tide swirled in visible gyres through the reddish brown water of the mating bay. The clinging mist lightened but did not entirely burn off. Florio joined them about midmorning. A light breeze began to ruffle the surface of the water and stir the grass around their legs. As though the breeze was some kind of signal, the harsels glided silently into formation.

"It's time." Teller said, her voice tight with tension. "They're getting ready to go."

And silently as a dream, Abeha led the harsels toward the channel. Florio glanced at his watch.

"I prevailed upon the dam keeper to open the floodgates on the hydro dams upstream this morning," he confessed. "The surge should just be reaching the passage about now. It'll give Abeha an extra twenty or thirty centimeters in the Narrows."

"Florio!" Teller chided, "What if the harsels find out?"

"Who's going to tell them? I didn't tell the dam keeper why; I just promised him one of your little bottles. I won't tell, and neither will Samad. That leaves you. You won't tell the harsels, will you?" he said, looking pleadingly at her.

Teller looked at him for a second, and then smiled as though a burden had been lifted from her. "Thank you, *aghapitos,*" she said, gratefully. "I hope it helps."

"I hope she doesn't need it." Florio answered.

"We'll soon see," Teller said. "She's in the passage now."

The three of them stood watching as Abeha glided majestically down the narrow channel. Samad's breath caught in his throat as she approached the spot where the fangs of barnacled rock rose in her path. The harsels following Abeha stopped, waiting to see what would happen. Abeha lowered her sail and slowed to a stop. She approached the hidden shoals cautiously. She made one attempt to pass the rocky fangs, then suddenly backed up in the water, and approached again a dozen meters to starboard. Suddenly she rolled sideways, her dorsal ridge nearly touching the water, and gave one, two, three powerful strokes of her massive tail. She slid forward, and then stopped with a sudden lurch. Samad heard Teller's breath catch in her throat. Abeha heaved with her tail several times, and the great fish shuddered forward, righted, and then raised her sail and glided on down the channel. She had passed safely over the jagged rocks of the Narrows.

Teller's face took on a look of concentrated abstraction as she spoke inwardly to Abeha.

Then she smiled and let out her breath with a whoosh, and Samad took a breath of his own, feeling the clean, sweet air in his throat.

"She made it! She's safe! She's scraped up some, but she made it through!" Teller hugged Samad and Florio, nearly dancing in her excitement. Samad felt a dizzying sense of relief. Abeha had made it through the Narrows. She was all right. And they were finally going to leave this place. It felt as though he'd been here forever.

"Are you ready to go?" Florio asked.

"We'll need to pack up."

Florio shook his head. "Everything's all packed. I did it when you and Samad went up on the ridge to watch the harsels."

"Thank you, *aghapitos,* thank you for everything!" Teller said, hugging him.

"I thought we might have to leave quickly, if something happened to Abeha."

"It's a good thing you did. I want to take a look at where Abeha scraped herself on the rock, and make sure that she's really all right."

They scooped up their gear and started back down the trail to the inn, following what had become a well-beaten path. It was all Samad could do to keep from breaking into a run, so eager was he to be off this island. It was a beautiful place, but there were so many dark and uneasy memories here. He glanced at the taverna, over on the next ridge, and remembered that night out on the patio with a queasy sense of fear. He pushed the memory away. It was time to move on.

They hurried along, all of them eager to leave. When they reached the taverna, Teller went in to thank the Uberaguas. Samad waited outside. It was quiet. All of the tourists had gone down to the bay, armed with bottles, to capture some of the milt-stained water. With the guests gone, the old inn felt abandoned and lonely. In a day or two, this place would be just another sleepy out-island like any other, with more sheep than people, shipping their wine, olive oil, wool, and mutton off to distant ports of call three or four times a year. According to Florio, the inn was shut down between matings, and the Uberaguas went back to farming and sheepherding till the harsels returned again. The flashy, thrill-seeking off-worlders would go back to Nueva Ebiza, and from there to the stars, leaving Thalassa to its own again. Samad could hardly wait for them to leave his world alone.

Erramun Uberagua came out of one of the buildings, a huge bundle of laundry slung over one massive shoulder. He glanced over at Samad, nodded, and continued on his way, oblivious to the wave of terror that rolled over Samad. A few minutes later, Florio and Teller emerged from the inn with Alazne Uberagua, who walked with them to the gates of the estate.

"I hope we'll see you again, Teller," she said. "You'll always have a welcome with the Uberagua family."

Teller smiled. "Thank you, Alazne."

"Well then," Alazne said with the briskness of one trying to cover up sudden sorrow. "We will carry you in our hearts until then."

"As I carry your entire family in my heart," Teller replied. The two women embraced.

Alazne turned to Florio. "And you, stay out of trouble," she scolded affectionately.

"I will, *Tia* Alazne." He stepped forward and kissed her formally on both cheeks. The old woman patted his face. "You're a good boy, Florio. Visit when you can. We miss you when you're not here."

Then the old woman turned to Samad. "I wish we'd gotten to know each other better, young man. Perhaps next time?"

Samad nodded.

"And take care of Teller, eh?"

"I will," Samad replied. "Whenever she lets me."

Alazne laughed. "That's always the problem, isn't it?" She shook her head. "Ay, she's a tough one to help." She smiled and kissed Samad lightly on the forehead. *"Vaya con Dios, mijo."*

"Vaya con Dios, tia," he replied politely.

Then they were on their way. Samad glanced back to see Alazne standing there before the stark, whitewashed stone pillars of the gate, a tiny woman garbed in black, watching them leave.

"I hope I see her again," Teller said. "She's become an old woman since I last saw her." There was a lonely note in her voice. Samad glanced up at her and was surprised to discover tears in her eyes.

Florio shrugged. "The Uberaguas are a long-lived family."

"I know, but I get so tired of watching people get old."
Her voice sounded bleak and very tired.

"We all do, *aghapitee*. We all do," Florio soothed, putting
his arm around her. "Come on. Let's go see if Abeha's all
right."

CHAPTER 9

TELLER STOOD ON THE DECK OF THE ESMER-
alda, looking out at the choppy gray sea. Abeha and her escort of harsel males were feeding on a rich patch of plankton.
Abeha's tall sail made her easy to spot, even though she wal-
lowed heavily in the water, her hold full of ripening eggs.

In the two months since they had left Zâfrán Bay, Abeha
had continued to gorge herself while her fertilized eggs
ripened inside her. The harsels had headed south, to the rich
feeding grounds on the edge of the Great South Sea.

Sometime in the depths of midwinter, Abeha's eggs
would hatch. A milky substance secreted by the walls of her
hold would nourish the two-inch long hatchlings. The more
Abeha ate, the longer she could feed the mindless, hungry
harlings sheltering in her womblike hold. The longer the
hatchlings stayed in her hold, the bigger they would be, and
the better their chances for survival when they emerged.

Teller had never seen a female harsel as fat as Abeha. And

she had gained this weight despite the deep, raking gashes in her keel from the fanged rocks of the Narrows. Teller closed her eyes, remembering the blood in the water and the gallons of wound sealant that she and half a dozen other har captains had hurriedly applied to the bone-deep gashes. Abeha had been right. The next mating would have been too late. But that didn't make it any easier to accept the harsel's approaching death.

Samad stuck his head out of the deckhouse.

"The weather report on the radio's predicting a blow tonight," Samad called over the rising wind. "Should we put on more storm lashings?"

Teller nodded. The storm was no surprise. She'd seen the mackerel belly clouds closing in at dawn. The barometer had fallen steadily throughout the morning, too. It was the third serious gale in the last ten days. The winter weather was closing in. The harsels seemed to thrive amid the gales, but the *Esmeralda* couldn't handle the high winds and mountainous seas of winter in the Great South Sea.

It was time to head back to port. If Teller had been alone, she'd have stayed until the boat sank and took her with it, but she couldn't risk Samad's life.

"All right, Samad. You put on the storm lashings, and I'll reef the sail," Teller told him. "After the storm blows over, we're heading back to Viento."

"For the season?" Samad asked, looking unhappy.

"I'm afraid so, Samad. It's just getting too dangerous out here. We've already stayed out long past any other boat on record."

"But—"

"No, Samad. It's too dangerous."

"I was hoping to stay out until Abeha's eggs hatch."

"So was I, but we just can't stay out here any longer."

He sighed. "It's going to be a very long winter."

Poor Samad; he hated Viento. Teller couldn't blame him. The barren, rocky island lived up to its windy name. There was grazing for sheep in the sheltered upland valleys, but most of the people on Viento were fisherman, who stayed in port during the turbulent storms of winter. She'd never wintered this far south before because of the harsh weather. But living on Viento had given them nearly three weeks more this fall, and she'd probably see Abeha at least two weeks sooner in the spring.

"Hey, Teller, look on the bright side. We can always get jobs nailing down sheep so they don't blow away."

Teller laughed, grateful for his company. He would make this long, cold, miserable winter less lonely.

"Gracias, mijito," Teller said.

"What for?" Samad asked.

"For putting up with a crabby old lady," she replied.

"Oh, I'm just putting up with you for the chance to stay on Viento. It's such a charming place, and the people are *so* outgoing!"

Teller laughed.

"I'm so glad to hear that, Samad. I was thinking of retiring there, but I wasn't sure you'd like it," she teased.

Samad looked horrified. "If that's the case, then maybe I should just jump overboard and end it all, now!"

"Not before you put on those storm lashings!" Teller scolded.

Samad looked up as the door flew open. Teller came in with an armload of damp peat, letting in several gallons of rain. He got up and helped her push the door shut, thinking for the thousandth time how much he hated Viento, with its endless wind and sideways rain. They'd been here for three months now, and it felt like forever.

"Are the sheep still nailed down?" Samad asked. The joke

was wearing thin by now, but there wasn't much else to laugh at. The wind seemed to have scoured all the humor out of the dour fisherfolk and the silent, stoic shepherds. Teller told the traditional tales, which were received with a grunt and a shrug of thanks. Samad's shorter, funny stories received only stares and silence, except for one or two of the youngest kids, who were cuffed into a decent and respectful reticence by their elders.

"A harsel came into port today," Teller mentioned as she knelt near the hearth with her armload of peat bricks.

Infected by the islanders' taciturnity, Samad raised his eyebrows in a wordless question.

"He came by to let me know that Abeha's eggs have hatched. The hatchlings are thriving. Abeha's keeping her weight up." Teller started stacking the peat next to the fireplace, careful to arrange the damp peat in a crisscross fashion so that air could circulate between the bricks and dry them.

"Good," Samad replied.

"The ice is starting to break up, farther south," Teller added, propping several bricks up close to the fire to dry. "The harsels will be heading north soon. They'll start arriving in a couple of weeks. Our stay in Purgatory is nearly at an end."

"I'm looking forward to seeing Abeha even more than I'm looking forward to leaving," Samad said.

Teller nodded, then looked into the fire for a long moment, a brick of peat in one hand.

"You've never seen a female harsel give birth, have you?"

It was a rhetorical question, and Samad didn't even bother to shake his head.

"I've seen it. Too many times." She glanced up at him, her eyes full of old pain. "It's hell, Samad. It's a long, slow, ugly decline. The harsels try to make it seem noble with lots of sad songs of sacrifice, but it's a horrible way to die." She sighed. "We'll be getting off this awful goddamned island, but things aren't going to improve much." She was silent for a long while, considering. "Samad, I want you to promise you'll let me know if it gets to be too much for you. I'll find you someplace to stay until it's over."

"I promised Abeha—" Samad began.

"I know what you promised her, Samad, but Abeha's not human. She doesn't understand when she's asking too much of a child."

Abeha wasn't the only one who asked too much of him, Samad thought, remembering some of the grim nights Teller had spent drinking this winter.

He met Teller's eyes, his gaze unwavering. "I need to be there as much as you do," he told her. "Even if it is unpleasant and ugly. I watched the drugs take my mother, and that was bad, too. If I can do that, I can watch Abeha's death as well."

Teller smoothed her hands down the thighs of her drying trousers and shook her head.

"You were too young to have any choice with your mother, Samad. But you have one with Abeha. You can leave if it gets too bad. I'll understand, and I'll make sure that Abeha does, too. Or you can stay all the way through to the grim and bloody end if you want to. But I want you to know that you have the freedom to choose."

"I understand," Samad said. "I'll stay."

"As you wish," Teller said. "Now that's settled, how are you doing on those math problems I gave you the other day?"

Abeha arrived at Viento about three weeks later. From a distance, the huge harsel looked pretty much the same, but as she glided up to the dock, Teller saw that Abeha was riding lower in the water than when they'd last seen her. The harsel was already drawing on her fat stores in order to secrete food for the thousands of hatchlings in her hold.

Teller stepped onto the harsel's back. Last fall, Abeha's skin had been stretched tight over a hard layer of thick fat. Now the harsel's skin gave slightly as she walked on it, another sign of Abeha's diminishing stores of fat. Teller tried not to let her grief show on her face or in her thoughts.

"MY LITTLE HARLINGS ARE DOING WELL IN THERE," Abeha announced proudly. "I CAN FEEL THEM WRIGGLING. THEY TICKLE."

Teller, too horrified to speak aloud or inwardly, said nothing.

"I'M NOT IN PAIN," Abeha reassured her. "AND MY FAT STORES ARE HOLDING WELL. I SHOULD BE ABLE TO LAST FIVE OR SIX MONTHS MORE, IF THE FEEDING IS GOOD."

"Oh, Abeha, we have so little time!" Teller finally managed.

"WE HAVE ALL THE NOW THERE IS."

"It's still not enough." Teller lamented, tears coursing down her cheeks.

"I KNOW, BUT IT IS WHAT WE HAVE," Abeha said gently.

Teller nodded through her tears. She knelt on the harsel's broad back and wept until the knot inside her was gone. In its place was a still, bottomless pool of unending sadness. Abeha took in Teller's grief and shared her own sadness at leaving this beautiful, living world for the cold unknown of death.

"Oh Abeha, I've missed you so much." Teller said when she could speak again.

"AND I HAVE MISSED YOU," Abeha replied. "MY OTHER HALF."

"Yes," Teller said. "As you are mine."

They were silent for a long while, sharing their happiness

at being together, trying to stay in the present, with no thought for the future.

"HOW IS SAMAD?" Abeha asked at last.

"Good. He misses you, too. He's been waiting until we're ready for him to join us."

"COME ON OVER, SAMAD," Abeha said. "I WANT TO FEEL YOUR FEET ON MY BACK. I'VE MISSED YOU SO MUCH!"

Teller and Abeha shared a flash of amusement at the boy's eagerness as Samad ran down the dock and leaped onto Abeha's back. With a pang, Teller remembered that he was only eleven years old. They had loaded so much onto his shoulders in the past year.

"Hello Abeha!" he called, coming forward to embrace the harsel's mast. "I missed you. It's been a long winter. And there's been nothing to do but study," he complained.

"AND DID YOU LEARN MUCH?" Abeha asked, amused.

Samad shrugged. "I guess. Nothing very interesting, except for some new stories."

"He learned a lot!" Teller protested.

"OF COURSE HE DID. I CAN TELL," Abeha soothed. "HE FEELS EVEN SMARTER THAN WHEN I LEFT."

"Really?" Samad said. "I feel smart?"

"MOST OF THE TIME YOU DO," Abeha said, gently amused. "ARE YOU READY TO LEAVE THIS FASCINATING IS-LAND?" she inquired.

"Absolutely!" Samad said eagerly.

"We need a few hours to get some fresh provisions and make our farewells. But the *Esmeralda* is ready to go," Teller replied. "We could be ready to leave by the evening tide if we hurry. I don't want to keep you from the grazing grounds for too long," Teller said.

"IT'S ALL RIGHT, TELLER," Abeha said. "ONE DAY SPENT NOT EATING WON'T MAKE MUCH DIFFERENCE IN THE LONG RUN."

"Perhaps," Teller replied, looking grim. "But it might mean another day or two of life for you. We should get busy."

They squared accounts with their landlord, said a brief good-bye to the host of the local taverna, and hurried to buy their supplies. The *Esmeralda* set sail as the red glow of the sunset faded from the sky. As they sailed away, Samad looked back at Viento. A scattered handful of waxy yellow lantern lights gleamed against the island's black bulk.

"God, I'm glad to leave!" Samad said. "That must be the most godforsaken place on the planet!"

"Oh no," Teller said. "There are worse places, and I've spent longer in some of them than we have here on Viento."

"How did you manage?" Samad asked.

"Just like I'm doing now," Teller said. "One day at a time, one foot in front of the other, until it's all over with." Teller glanced over at Abeha sailing just off their starboard bow, her sail silhouetted against the dying sunset. "I wish I was as good at it as I used to be," she said thoughtfully.

"You need some food," Samad declared and went below to make dinner.

The gathering night plucked at Teller's resolve as she tried to fend off the looming, dark cloud of grief that was a constant presence in her life now.

"One day at a time. One foot in front of the other, until it's all done," she muttered to herself as she adjusted the helm slightly to keep on course.

As the year slid slowly from winter to spring, Teller and Samad followed Abeha and her escorts as they moved northward. They followed an erratic course toward the equator, moving from one rich bloom of plankton to the next. Abeha ate almost continually now, but that only slowed the loss of her reserves as she secreted food for the growing harlings inside her. Teller spent every minute she could spare on the harsel's back. By late spring she had given up even the pretense of teaching Samad.

They were nearing the tropics now, and the fat was melting from Abeha's bones like wax near a flame.

"What happens when you run out of food to feed the harlings?" Samad asked Abeha, as she crisscrossed a patch of plankton.

"THEN THEY EAT THEIR WAY OUT," Abeha told him.

"But why?" Samad asked, appalled. "Can't you just open your hold and let the harlings go?"

"NO I CAN'T, SAMAD. THE OPENING TO MY HOLD HAS FUSED SHUT. MY BODY WILL BE MY LAST GIFT TO THE CHILDREN WHO WILL CARRY MY MEMORIES," Abeha said.

"Won't it hurt?"

"YES, IT WILL. BUT THE OTHER HARSELS WILL HELP DROWN THE PAIN WITH THEIR MINDSONGS."

"Are you afraid?"

"SOMETIMES, YES. BUT MY MOTHER MADE THE SAME SACRIFICE FOR ME, AND HER MOTHER FOR HER, AND SO ON AS FAR BACK AS HARSEL MEMORY REACHES. IT IS A SACRIFICE THAT IS PART OF WHO WE ARE."

"I wish things were different."

"I'VE LIVED A VERY LONG, RICH LIFE. MY MEMORIES WILL BE CELEBRATED BY MANY GENERATIONS OF HARSELS. MY ONLY REGRET IS THE GRIEF I AM CAUSING TELLER. BUT HER LOVE FOR YOU MAKES ME FEEL BETTER ABOUT MY DEATH. I WILL NOT BE LEAVING HER ALL ALONE."

"She says that you ask too much of me."

"AH, BUT I KNOW THAT YOU ARE STRONG ENOUGH TO DO WHAT I ASK. I KNOW THAT YOU WILL NOT LET HER DIE."

"I won't," Samad agreed, remembering his mother, lying cold and dead in her bed. He wouldn't let Teller die. This time he was going to fight death and win. But even in the fierce heat of his determination there was a cold seed of fear in his heart at the immensity of the burden he had promised to carry for Abeha.

"THEN I AM NOT AFRAID OF DEATH," Abeha told him.

Another month passed. By the beginning of summer, every one of the massive bones of Abeha's skull, backbone, and ribs were visible under her skin. Teller could hardly bear to look at her. But the harsel's mental voice was as strong as ever. If she closed her eyes, Teller could pretend that Abeha was the same as always.

"IT WON'T BE MORE THAN TWO OR THREE WEEKS NOW." Abeha confided to Samad. That night, as Teller slept, Samad radioed the Guild with a message for Florio, asking him to come.

Word also spread among the hars. Abeha's escort grew to several hundred harsels. The hars believed in mourning their dead while they still lived, that they might know how well loved they were. Their sad songs of mourning reverberated through Teller's mind until she thought she was going to go mad. Then she would sail out of range of the hars' elegiac singing and stand on the bow, looking back at the sails on the horizon.

Three weeks later, Samad woke Teller. "It's Abeha. Her sail—it doesn't work anymore!"

Teller pushed past Samad and hurried to the deck. Abeha's magnificent purple sail trailed in the water like the broken wing of a drowned bird.

"Abeha!" Teller shrieked. "No!"

"IT WON'T BE LONG NOW, A FEW DAYS, NO MORE. IT DOESN'T HURT," Abeha reassured her, "I'M JUST VERY . . . TIRED."

Teller turned her head away. "I'm tired, too, Abeha. I wish I could just—"

"REMEMBER THE BOY, TELLER. SAMAD NEEDS YOU. AND MY CHILDREN WILL NEED YOU, TOO. YOU MUST BE STRONG."

"No, Abeha. You ask too much, I—"

"I'M NOT ASKING, TELLER. THERE ARE THINGS YOU *MUST* DO WHEN I AM GONE. LET SAMAD HELP. HE CAN DO MORE THAN YOU REALIZE."

"Abeha, no! He's only a child."

"YOU UNDERESTIMATE HIM. THERE IS SUCH FIERCENESS AND STRENGTH IN HIS LOVE FOR YOU."

Teller shook her head, so full of grief that she could not speak, even inwardly. Abeha cradled Teller in her mind, accepting the grief and sharing her own sadness with Teller. There really was nothing more to say, nothing more to do. There was only the waiting and the sharing left.

The next day a mixed fleet of harsels and man-made boats arrived, carrying grim-faced har captains and subdued fishermen. One of the fishing boats pulled up alongside the *Esmeralda*. Florio was aboard. Samad closed his eyes and breathed a quiet prayer of gratitude.

"*Yasou!*" Florio called in greeting. "I thought I'd come and see if there was anything I could do. I brought a few friends with me, and some nets to help catch the harlings before they get eaten. I—"

Florio stopped speaking, and a look of shock came over his face. Teller had emerged from the main cabin. Samad looked at her and realized how much she had changed in the last couple of months. She had lost weight. Her face looked gaunt, and her hair straggled every which way like a crazy woman's. He looked back down at the deck, suddenly ashamed. He had been so caught up with Abeha's health that he had forgotten to look after Teller.

"*Yasou,* Florio, come aboard," Teller said.

Florio handed over a couple of net bags full of food. There was fresh bread, a foam container of eggs, and a roast chicken. Samad's stomach growled, and he realized that Teller was not the only neglected one. He was suddenly conscious of the tangled state of his own hair. When had he last combed it?

"I brought some supplies," Florio offered. "There's lunch in here, too. The boy looks hungry, Teller. He needs feeding."

"Goddammit, Florio! The last thing I need is a lecture on nutrition! Abeha's dying!"

"I know, *aghapitee.* I've seen her. How long?"

"Her bones have softened. She can't feed herself anymore. It's a matter of days, now."

"How can I help?" Florio asked.

Teller shook her head and turned away. "There's nothing anyone can do, Florio."

"There is something that you can do to help Abeha, Teller."

"What?"

"She needs you to be strong. Eat. Both of you," he commanded, glancing meaningfully at Samad. "You cannot help Abeha and her children if you are starving yourselves."

"HE'S RIGHT." Abeha said. "EAT, PLEASE. I NEED YOU TO BE STRONG TO PROTECT MY HARLINGS."

Florio bent over and took a cloth-wrapped jar out of one of the bags he carried. "Avgolemono. Your first course."

The soup was warm and filling. Samad sat back from his empty bowl feeling more alert and aware than he had in days. He glanced over at Teller, whose bowl was still half full.

"Come on, Teller. You need it as much as I do," Samad urged.

Grudgingly, Teller began to eat. Samad glanced at Flo-

rio, who winked at him. Samad felt an immense wave of relief wash over him. He didn't have to go through this
alone.

Florio fixed their meals and helped coax Teller into eating them. Teller started combing her hair again, and she
looked a little less crazy. Samad felt as if an enormous
weight had been lifted off of his shoulders.

"TELLER, IT'S BEGUN."

Teller's eyes snapped open in the darkness, then closed
again briefly.

"I'm coming," she said and slid from her bunk. She
dressed, climbed into the *Esmeralda*'s inflatable raft, and
rowed toward Abeha.

The other harsels had drawn close to Abeha when the
pain first began. Teller could hear their plaintive, high-
pitched songs of comfort. The circle of attendants parted to
let her row in. Teller removed her shoes and climbed onto
Abeha's back. Her stomach churned with nausea as her feet
sank into Abeha's spongy flesh with a soft squelching noise.
Teller walked carefully over to the harsel's dorsal fin, which
sagged over to one side, the bones too soft now to hold it
upright.

"I'm here, Abeha."

"THANK YOU."

"Does it hurt?"

"YES. BUT THAT DOESN'T MATTER. I NEED YOU TO RE-
MEMBER WITH ME AS MY CHILDREN BEGIN TO EMERGE, SO
THAT THEY WILL KNOW YOU AND REMEMBER YOU."

"Yes, Abeha," Teller said obediently.

"PERHAPS ONE DAY A CHILD OF MINE WILL COME TO
YOU AND TAKE THE PLACE THAT MY DEATH LEAVES OPEN."

Teller's heart squeezed. The thought of partnering with
one of the greedy morsels that were eating their way out of

Abeha's body made her feel ill. But she hid that thought, replying only, "Perhaps."

"MY CHILDREN WILL NOT ALWAYS BE MINDLESS ANIMALS,
TELLER. PROMISE ME THAT IF ONE OF MY CHILDREN SEEKS
YOU OUT, THAT YOU WILL MAKE HIM FEEL WELCOME."

"I-I'll try, Abeha," she faltered.

"THANK YOU, IT EASES MY HEART TO KNOW THIS,"
Abeha replied. "LET US REMEMBER WHAT WE CAN, BEFORE
IT'S TOO LATE."

And together they dove deep into the well of their memories, from their first unlikely meeting, to their years spent
exploring Thalassa together.

Abeha's memories twined with Teller's, memories of lifting Teller from the water, carrying the shuttle, and the
months spent converting one of the Jump ship's lifeboats
into a suitable crew pod. How clean and simple it had been,
with only the harsels for company. There were memories of
perfect blue-water sailing, just her and Abeha alone on the
endless sea. There were islands explored and storms weathered, and Abeha's wonder of learning about life on land.
There were the other harsels, some curious, some startled,
and still others scandalized by their partnership. But as they
came to know Teller better, the other harsels began to trust
her, especially after she spent long hours cleaning their bottoms and holds of parasites and seaweed.

Then there was the excitement of seeing the winged silver needle bearing the first colonists. Abeha had shared
Teller's first exultation, and then her turmoil and fear at the
prospect of seeing other humans. Instead of announcing herself openly, Teller had put on her last set of good clothing
and slipped into the crowd of people emerging from the second ship down.

The colonists were too busy to question her origin. Vol-
unteering to be on the exploration crew, she had "discov-

ered" the orchards she had planted. When the company of the colonists became overwhelming, Teller would slip away with Abeha for a couple of weeks of companionable solitude.

Abeha remembered carrying supplies on Teller's anonymous rescue missions as the Pilot. Teller had helped many desperate colonists through a hard winter with gifts of food and supplies from her own surpluses. Sometimes she only left a note, pointing out an overlooked source of food, shelter, or fuel, or perhaps an essential tool bartered from some other, luckier homestead. It pleased her to provide this help anonymously, signing her notes only as "The Pilot." Gratitude only made Teller feel awkward. She and Abeha had both reveled in the secrecy of it all.

In a few years, other colonists began copying her good deeds, so that the Pilot appeared to be everywhere at once. When charitable organizations named after the Pilot began to flourish, Teller decided that her work as the Pilot was finished. She settled down among the taciturn Corsicans who colonized the island of Bonifacio. It was there that she met and married Stephano. His silence absorbed her secrets like a sponge; heard, acknowledged, accepted, and then held close. The Corsicans were good at secrets, and the tight-knit community of Bonifacio accepted her without comment, grateful for her knowledge and expertise.

Their memories wove gradually from the past to the present. Through centuries of partnership, of seeing ephemeral generations of humans come and go. The Har-Human Compact. The slow, steady growth of har-human partnerships and how they opened up new out-islands to settlers. There were Teller's keenly painful memories of the death of her family, and Abeha's memories of her slow, wordless healing.

There was the creation of the Storytellers' Guild, and how it grew and changed the world yet again. Of stories found, recorded, and shared.

Decades together became centuries of sharing. Over the last century there arose between them an increasing tension over Abeha's need to mate, and Teller's fear of losing her. And finally, they shared their memories of meeting Samad and the last three years, so rich with love and sorrow. Such long, long lives, so completely woven together, so full, so loving, so rich a tapestry of memories. They unrolled it for each other and admired what they had shared.

The sun was fully up when they emerged from their entwined memories into the bright, painful present.

"YOU MUST GO NOW," Abeha said. "THE HARLINGS WILL BEGIN TO EMERGE SOON, AND STAYING WILL BE DANGEROUS. AND THE OTHER HARSELS WISH TO SING THEIR OWN MEMORY SONGS BEFORE IT IS TOO LATE."

"Please, Abeha, don't make me live on alone! Let me die with you," Teller pleaded.

"NO," Abeha told her. "YOU MUST LIVE, OR MY DEATH WILL BE IN VAIN. YOU MUST CARRY ON MY MEMORIES AMONG THE HUMANS. WITHOUT YOU, THERE IS NO REMEMBERING."

"Abeha!" Teller cried in anguish.

"I WILL NOT LET YOU DIE! GO! PLEASE!" For the first time, Teller could feel the pain Abeha was in, and how much her control cost.

Teller got up slowly, sadly. "I love you, Abeha."

"I KNOW. I LOVE YOU, TOO." There was a surge of love, sadness, and regret from the harsel.

Stepping into the little gray rubber boat was the hardest thing Teller had ever done. Teller could feel Abeha watching her, feel the harsel's love and concern as she sat down and started to row jerkily away, blinded by tears. She bumped into something hard, a boat. Dimly, Teller heard Samad and Florio calling to her, felt them lift her up out of the boat. Teller sat in the bow of the sailboat watching the brilliant tropical sunlight flare and die on the water. Something essential had broken inside. She would never move again.

Samad had been afraid since the moment when he woke up and found Teller's bunk empty. He had watched Teller sit on Abeha's broad back for three hours, and had almost managed to convince himself that everything was all right. But when Teller woke from her communion and lurched like a broken toy toward the raft, he suddenly *knew*. He called urgently to Florio as Teller began to row mechanically, without looking where she was going. They maneuvered the *Esmeralda* to intercept her and hauled her aboard. Now Teller huddled motionless on the deck of the boat. The harsels ranged around Abeha had begun singing with a desperate new intensity.

Now what? Samad wondered. He looked over at Florio, who shrugged helplessly.

Samad sat down beside her. "Teller! Teller! It's Samad. Come on Teller, wake up!"

Teller blinked as he passed his hand in front of her eyes. Other than that, there was no response. Her skin was icy cold.

Florio knelt beside Teller and wrapped a blanket around her.

"Come on, *aghapitee*. Wake up. We need you." He saw Samad glance at the blanket. "Shock. She's in shock. Lay her back on the deck. Raise her feet up a bit," Florio commanded. "I'll get her something warm to drink. Once we rouse her, we'll need to keep her too busy to think."

He returned a few minutes later, stirring something into a glass of warm water. He made Teller drink it all, a couple of sips at a time. A few minutes after she drained the glass, she began to move.

"Wake up, *aghapitee*. Abeha needs you."

Teller opened her eyes. "What?" she inquired.

"The harlings are emerging, Teller. You have to tell us what to do. We need you to help us save Abeha's children," Florio urged.

Florio's pleading seemed to wake her from her trance. Teller pushed herself up. "Bring the boat closer in. Is the tank ready? And the nets?"

"Can you get the nets out? Samad will start the water in the holding tank," Florio said. "I'll take us in closer to Abeha."

"Tell the other boats to get ready," Teller told him.

Samad ran back to the stern and turned on the pump. There was a low, smooth throbbing, and then seawater surged into the hundred-gallon holding tank mounted on the deck just aft of the helm. The *Esmeralda* settled a little by the stern as the tank filled.

Florio skillfully maneuvered the boat until it was only a few meters away from Abeha. Something squirmed under Abeha's skin. Samad swallowed hard, nauseated by the sight. Then there was a bright flower of blood. A slender shape, silvery gray under a slick coating of bright red blood, writhed up out of the wound and slid into the water. Immediately one of the harsels surged forward, its mouth gaping wide, and scooped up the harling.

"Once the young emerge into seawater, they stop eating. The harsel attendants take the harlings into their mouths to protect them from predators," Teller explained. "Later, the harlings are transferred to another harsel's hold. They'll live in the hold for a year or more, only coming out to feed. We help the harsels by catching the ones they miss."

"Emergence is the most dangerous time for harlings. All the blood in the water draws predators from miles away," Teller continued. "We're here to rescue the harlings and try to drive off the predators. We'll try to catch as many harlings as possible. When it's all over, we'll transfer them to the harsels. A good crew can sometimes save a hundred harlings."

More harlings squirmed out from Abeha's body. Blood oozed from the wounds left by the harlings, staining the water red. Samad looked over at Teller, who stood frozen near the railing, several long-handled scoop nets in her arms. Samad realized that she had forgotten them. He took the nets from Teller.

"What do I do with these?" he prompted, holding up one of the nets.

Teller blinked and came back to herself. "You stand in the stern next to the tank. Watch for harlings, scoop them up like this," she moved the net in a long, smooth arc through the water, lifting it with a quick flick of her wrist. "Then put them in the holding tank. You need to work fast. Be careful. Don't lean over too far. There will be hungry manaos in the water, and some tibiria as well. They're after Abeha, but they'd be just as happy to take a bite out of you if you fell in."

"Teller!" Florio called, holding up the microphone on the comm unit. "Ibrahim isn't sure about the nets. Come talk to him."

By now the harlings were coming out two or three at a time. The attendant harsels were scooping them up as quickly as they could. The water around Abeha was stained with swirls of red. Samad saw a thin silver shape slip between two harsels and scooped with his net.

"I got one!" he called. He drew in the net and looked at the slim, wriggling shape caught in the fine mesh. "That is, I think I've got one. Is this a harsel?" It was bigger than he'd expected, nearly half a meter long and silvery gray, more like an eel than a harsel with its mouthful of razor-sharp teeth. Its eyes were huge and round, and there was no sign of a sail, only a strange, bony fin on its back.

Teller peered into the net. "That's a harling, all right. It's big! Abeha's offspring should do well! Go put it in the tank."

"Manao!" someone shouted. Samad saw a dark, slender shadow cutting through the water toward the knot of harsels. He heard and felt the harsels' alarm. One of the harsels patrolling outside the ring of attendants folded its sail and dove toward the dark shadow of the predator. Samad saw the two shadows merge as the harsel rammed the manao, which swam away. But more shadows were approaching. A fisherman with a harpoon got one, but another slipped past two harsels, only to be rammed by a third just outside the ring of attendants.

"Samad!" Florio called. "Keep your eyes on the harlings! Let the others worry about the manaos."

Dutifully, Samad returned to watching the water for harlings. They were emerging thick and fast now. He saw a tight cluster of several harlings circling in confusion. He netted two, but the others scattered. Samad quickly dumped the baby harsels into the holding tank and turned to scoop up more. Teller was netting and dumping harlings with a fierce concentration. Soon he was dipping and running and dipping again so quickly that he had no time to watch for predators in the swiftly reddening water.

"SAMAD?" Abeha said as he dumped another toothy, squirming harling back in the tank.

Samad stopped and straightened in surprise. "Abeha? Is that you?"

"NOT FOR MUCH LONGER. I WANTED TO SAY GOOD-BYE. THANK YOU FOR SAVING MY YOUNG, AND FOR LOOKING AFTER TELLER." Abeha's voice sounded faint and distant.

"AND THANK YOU FOR LETTING ME BE ONE OF YOUR PAR-
ENTS. IT WAS A RARE GIFT TO WATCH YOU GROW UP."

"Abeha!" Samad called. "I love you!"

"I KNOW. AND I LOVE YOU. WE WILL REMEMBER YOU,
SAMAD. WE WILL AL—"

Just then a swift-moving shadow slipped through the attendants and hurtled toward the dying harsel. The manao
bit into Abeha's side, twisting and shaking its head to tear
off a hunk of flesh.

Abeha's control slipped, and Samad screamed as Abeha's
pain and fear jolted through his body like a bolt of lightning. "My harlings!" he screamed, Abeha's thoughts emerging from his mouth.

Then one of the fishermen drove a barbed harpoon deep
into the back of the manao's head, and the predator's thrash-
ing was stilled.

Abeha's presence slipped away from him. Samad saw
Teller straighten as though listening and knew Abeha was
saying a final farewell to Teller.

"TELLER." The harsel's voice sounded strained and distant. She was fading fast.

"Yes, Abeha. I'm here."

"TAKE CARE OF MY CHILDREN. THEY WILL BE YOURS AS I
WAS YOURS. WE WILL REMEMBER YOU. WE WILL REMEMBER
YOU, WE WILL REMEM . . ."

Then there was nothing but a sense of loving presence
that slowly faded, finally winking out. The attendant
harsels keened and boomed in mourning, sounding like
slow sirens and heavy doors shutting on echoing emptiness.

She was gone. Abeha was gone. Teller reached for that
place where she had sensed Abeha, even when half a world
separated them. There was nothing there.

"Abeha!" Teller keened. "No-o-o-o!"

A black shadow broke through the cordon of harsels and

arced smoothly toward Abeha's enormous corpse. Then another, and another. The other harsels moved to stop them,
but they were too late, and there were too many blood-
maddened predators. Several of the fishermen frantically
beat at the manaos with harpoons and boat hooks, while
Abeha's corpse wept silver harlings. Other sailors redoubled
their efforts at scooping harlings out of the water.

Teller looked down at Abeha's corpse. She felt numb,
empty.

First Samad, then Florio tried to comfort her. She
shrugged them away.

"Save the harlings," she commanded, as more manaos
found their way through the cordon of harsels. "That's what
Abeha would want."

They picked up their hand nets and bent to scoop up the
long, silvery fish. Teller watched the manaos approach
Abeha's corpse, take a lunging bite, then with a twisting
shake, tear off great chunks of her flesh.

Teller put one leg over the railing, looking into the
churning, bloodstained water. Abeha's body was beginning
to sink. It was time to finish it. Teller started to lift her
other leg over the rail, and was stopped with an abrupt jerk.

"No!" Samad shouted, his arms wrapped around her
chest. "Florio! Help me!" he cried as Teller tried to writhe
out of his grasp. The boy clung to her with amazing
strength.

"Let me go!" she cried, as Florio arrived. "I want to go
with her!"

"Stop struggling, Teller! Do you want to take Samad
with you?"

Florio's words sank in, and she let them help her back
over the railing. Suddenly she twisted out of their grasp and
made another lunge for the side, but this time Florio
caught her. The two of them carried her downstairs, strug-

gling all the way. Samad held her down as Florio opened the
first aid kit.

"No!" she cried as Florio approached with a hypo.

"I'm sorry, Teller," Florio said, as he stuck the needle in
her arm.

There was a painful poke, then a spreading chill up her
arm. Florio smoothed her hair as the drug took effect. She
tried to jerk away from his touch, but her neck had turned
to rubber, and her chin barely twitched. Behind Florio,
Samad's face was pale and drawn with worry and fear. Her
anger was a huge, expanding balloon that slipped out of her
grasp and floated away. She felt a pang of loss. Then a sodden blanket of sleep smothered her pain.

CHAPTER 10

THE EARLY-MORNING LIGHT FELL SOFTLY
on Teller's sleeping face, casting the gaunt hollows under
her cheekbones into shadow. Over the last few weeks, Teller
had wasted away alarmingly. Samad's lips tightened as he
remembered the betrayed look in her eyes when Florio had
first sedated her. The trip back to Nueva Ebiza had been
grim. They'd had to keep Teller drugged and restrained the
whole way. The Guild and the har captains' Trading Al-
liance had done what they could, but without Teller's coop-
eration, there was little that anyone could do to help.

"Take me home," Teller had told them. Samad had been
startled. Until she had mentioned it, he hadn't known that
Teller *had* a home.

So they had taken her back to her house on Bonifacio Island. The house was a broad-beamed gray farmhouse set on
a hill overlooking a small, sheltered bay with a view across
to Sartene Island. The house guarded an orchard of gnarled

and ancient fruit trees. The orchard looked as if the pioneers might have planted it. When they got there, Teller stopped at a cluster of low, rounded boulders just off of the driveway from the house. She sat on one of the boulders, shrugging herself deeper into her enormous black mourning shawl.

"I'm back," she announced to no one in particular. Then she turned to Samad. "When I die, bury me here," she told him.

Samad realized that they were standing in an old pioneer graveyard. The boulders were headstones, their inscriptions almost obliterated by time and lichens. Teller had been speaking to the dead buried under those stones. She sat for a while longer, clearly remembering another time, and then slowly, slowly got up. Leaning on Florio's arm, she walked back down to the silent, deserted farmhouse.

Florio and Samad settled her comfortably on the porch and started airing out the musty old house. They were just getting ready to start cleaning up when a group of women appeared, their heads covered with black shawls. They went straight to Teller, who was sitting on the porch in a high-backed old chair made of bent branches.

To Samad's amazement, each woman, from rose-cheeked girl to ancient crone, set their baskets aside and knelt before Teller, asking for something in the impenetrable Corsican dialect still spoken in this archipelago. As naturally as though she'd been doing it all her life, Teller had set her hands on each of their black-veiled heads and murmured a formal blessing over them. Then the women had transformed themselves from mystic sybils to housewives in the shake of a dust rag. To Teller's evident amusement, the women briskly invaded the house. They shooed Florio and Samad outside and took over the task of making the house habitable, leaving Florio and Samad to sit next to Teller on the front-porch.

"Relatives," Teller had said with a fond smile. "I come from a very large and very old family."

The women left as suddenly and silently as they had come, leaving behind an immaculate house. The sweet smell of beeswax, lemon, and flowers had banished the scent of dust and mildew. The worn plank floors and old wooden furniture gleamed. A pot of lamb stew steamed quietly on the back of the wood-fired stove. Lamps were trimmed and filled with oil, and three places were laid at the newly polished table.

Teller had glanced at Samad's and Florio's stunned faces and laughed. Then she sat down and ate a hearty meal of stew and fresh bread and butter. It was the last meal of any substance she had eaten.

That had been nearly two weeks ago. Since then, Samad and Florio had coaxed and sometimes bullied her into eating a few swallows of soup or applesauce, but it wasn't enough. Day by agonizing day, her flesh drew tighter around her increasingly prominent bones.

Samad looked out the window at the brightening morning, steeling himself for another day spent fighting off Teller's death. He was losing. Everyone around him seemed to have accepted the inevitability of Teller's death, even Florio. Once word spread that Teller was home, a steady trickle of visitors began arriving. Teller greeted them with dignity, sitting in state upon her bed like a dying queen. After seeing her, Teller's visitors spoke in hushed and solemn tones to Samad and Florio, thanking them for taking care of Teller. Samad had lost count of the people who had made quiet offers to look after him when Teller died. He had swallowed his anger and thanked them gravely, for they had come to help, and sometimes they managed to coax Teller into eating a few bites while they were visiting.

There was a touch on his arm. Samad jumped, startled.

He had been so lost in memories that he had forgotten the real Teller lying there.

"Good morning, Samad," Teller said. "Could you help me up?"

And so the morning began. After helping her freshen up, Teller asked him for some water with a little lemon in it. Samad surreptitiously added half a spoonful of honey and a few drops of vitamins. He put a bowl of similarly fortified applesauce on the tray and carried it over to Teller in bed.

She reached for the water.

"No!" Samad said holding it out of her reach. "Not until you've eaten the applesauce."

Teller looked up at him, her eyes blazing mutinously. "Goddamn it, Samad. Give me the water."

"No," Samad repeated. "I promised Abeha I'd keep you alive." His voice shook with a sudden surge of anger, frustration, and grief.

"Well then. I'll just die of thirst instead of starving. It's faster, I hear."

"But not nearly as pleasant. Come on, Teller, just a couple of bites, and then you can have a sip of water," he coaxed. "It'll soothe your dry throat."

"Why can't you just let me die in peace?" she complained.

"Because I don't want to be an orphan again," he shot back angrily.

"That's bullshit, and you know it," Teller replied. "I've had dozens of people offer to look after you when I die."

"I don't want them," Samad said. "I want you. Maybe I'll just go back to Melilla. Or Nueva Ebiza. I hear there's a demand for boy whores there. I can make good money doing that."

"Stop it, Samad," Teller snapped. "Leave me alone!"

"Eat your applesauce, Teller," Samad cooed maliciously, "and you can have your sweet, cool, lovely water."

"Fuck you!"

"You're not strong enough for that, Teller," Samad pointed out. "Eat your applesauce, and then you can do whatever you want to me."

"Go away and leave me in peace, you sadistic little bastard!" Teller snarled.

"That's enough, both of you," Florio said from the doorway. "Samad, go take a walk. Teller, you eat a couple of bites of applesauce so Samad will stop pestering you."

His anger still simmering hotly, Samad shouldered his way past Florio and left them to argue over the applesauce. He walked up the hill to the little graveyard with its age-worn headstones. He sat on one of the cool, mossy boulders, shoulders slumped, shame flooding him as his anger cooled.

He hadn't meant to speak like that to Teller. His anger and resentment had just popped out, like pus from a squeezed abscess. He should go in and apologize, but he still couldn't face her.

So Samad sat there, looking out over the hills. The grassy slopes were dotted with low shrubs, natives like the aromatic dalmana, and the cinnamon-leaved ansinia, mingling with thyme, lavender, and rosemary, from some long-lost herb garden. The Terran escapees had flourished here on the dry, stony hills. The morning sun was already drying the dew, and soon a rich, spicy, wild fragrance would rise from the shrubs. He heard the whistle of a greenlark rising high into the bright blue sky, beckoning him into the wild, rolling hills. It had been a long time since he had gone exploring. He glanced back at the house guiltily, then got up. He filled a waterskin with sweet, cold water from the old pitcher pump. Then he fetched a leaf-wrapped lump of cheese from its niche in the coolness of the springhouse, and headed for the wide, sunny hills.

•   •   •

Teller watched Samad storm out the door.

"He's a stubborn, scrappy little bastard," she acknowledged with a rueful, admiring smile.

"He's so much like you it scares me," Florio told her. "He has your self-destructive streak."

"Me? Self-destructive? Given how long I've lived, I hardly think that's fair."

Florio shrugged. "I heard what he said about going to Nueva Ebiza."

"Quite a threat, wasn't it?" Teller said.

"I think he meant it," Florio replied. "I wish you'd stop torturing him, Teller. If you're going to die, why don't you just slit your wrists and get it over with?"

"That's a hell of a thing to say, Florio!"

"It's how I feel. Samad is turning himself inside out to save you, Teller, or hadn't you noticed?"

"I have," Teller replied with a tired sigh. "I keep hoping he'll stop."

"He's as stubborn as you are, old woman."

"But I have more experience," Teller replied.

"And he's too young to know when to back down. Offhand, you're about even, but he has one advantage that you don't."

"What's that?" Teller asked.

"He has more to lose. He's already lost one mother. He's not about to lose another."

Teller looked away.

"He needs you, Teller. If you die now, I truly believe your death will kill him. It might take years, and he'll probably drag a few people down with him, but if you die now, you'll kill some essential part of him."

"You think I have a choice?" Teller said, but her eyes didn't meet his.

"If you really wanted to die, you'd be dead by now," Florio said. "What's stopping you?"

"I can't live without Abeha!" Teller said.

"You've managed it for nearly a month," Florio told her.

"It's not like I've had a choice!" Teller shot back.

"Maybe not on the boat, and not in Nueva Ebiza, but you could have done yourself in anytime over the last ten days with that knife you have hidden between the mattress and the headboard."

Teller's hand stole guiltily to the side of the bed before she could stop herself.

"It's still there," Florio told her. "What's stopping you?"

Teller licked her lips nervously. "Courage. I don't have the nerve to use a knife. I've tried." She pulled back her sleeves and held out her arms. Florio could see a network of fine cuts on her tanned wrists. "I can't do it, Florio, and God knows I've tried."

Florio gathered her hands in his and kissed the red lines on her wrists. "*Aghapitee,* I think some part of you isn't ready to die yet. That's why you can't do it."

"No, Florio, please. I—"

Florio shook his head. "You don't need to argue with me about it, Teller. You need to look inside yourself. Eat a little applesauce, *aghapitee.* It'll help you think more clearly."

"*Aghapitos,* I—"

"Eat," he said, thrusting the bowl into her hands. He took the knife from under the bed and placed it on her lap. "Or use the knife. Personally, I'd rather you ate a little bit. I promised Samad that you would." He kissed her forehead with a gentle fondness and went outside.

Teller looked from the bowl of food to the knife gleaming on the blanket. She picked up the knife and turned it, watching the light shine on its finely honed edge. She laid the edge along her inner arm and drew another fine, red line. Blood beaded up on the edges of the cut. She put the knife against her arm again, and tried to push harder, but her throat locked up in sudden panic, and she hurled the knife across the room. It clattered and spun on the wood floor and came to rest in a shaft of light pouring through one of the front windows, where it gleamed mockingly up at her.

"Damn!" she swore, and and started to weep.

When she was through with tears, Teller picked up the bowl of lukewarm applesauce and began eating.

Samad walked over the hills until he reached the coast road. A little farther along was a point where the cliffs of twisted yellow stone rose from the choppy turquoise sea. He hiked along the cliff, watching the birds hover and dive out over the suck and swell of the waves. At the crest of the cliff, a long, narrow promontory called the Giant's Nose thrust out over the ocean. The rock was dotted with nesting seabirds, and a cloud of them soared and called overhead.

Samad stepped carefully between the bird nests, heading for the point of the Giant's Nose. He sat at the very tip of the promontory, his feet dangling over fifty meters of nothing, his hair swirling in the steady updraft. He looked down at the surging water. Around him seabirds wheeled and called, brilliantly white against the cerulean sky and the blue, wave-flecked sea. Off on the horizon, where the sea darkened to azure, he could see the sails of three harsels moving south.

He thought about Teller, wondering how she could want to die so much. He also thought of his mother and her death. In his memory, Teller and his mother blended together, alike in so many ways. He couldn't recall the sound of his mother's voice. In his memory it sounded just like Teller's. And like his mother, Teller was plagued by a death wish.

Thinking about the vast emptiness that lay before him

when Teller died, he looked down at the surging water below him and understood a little of what Teller must be feeling now, shorn of Abeha's presence. A couple of tears forced themselves out of his eyes. He could feel as she felt, but he could not follow her any farther. He had to leave before Teller's death wish carried him over a cliff as well. He pushed himself back from the edge. Then he stood, shouldered his waterskin, and headed back to the house.

What he would do and where he would go when he left, he did not know. He only knew that he must go, before his love for Teller overwhelmed his will to live. He was abandoning his promise to Abeha, but until Teller stopped wanting to die, nothing he tried would make any difference.

Samad paused and looked back out to sea. "I'm sorry, Abeha," he murmured. "I've done everything I could, but I can't make her want to live."

Teller was asleep again when he reached the house. Samad could hear Florio's snores issuing from the upstairs loft where he slept. Teller's face was dim in the fading light. She looked younger and more relaxed than she had this morning. He bent forward to look at her, suddenly frightened that she had died while he was out. She stirred slightly in her sleep, and he relaxed.

He tiptoed to the kitchen. The ancient tile cookstove was cold. He filled the firebox with tinder and kindling and lit it. Soup would be easy and quick tonight. He would try to get a few spoonfuls down Teller before he told her of his decision. It would cushion her against the shock.

The soup was getting hot when he heard Teller stirring.

"What's for dinner?" she called. "I'm hungry."

The spoon clattered on the stovetop as Samad turned. "What?"

"I said I'm hungry, Samad. What does a girl have to do to get some food around here?"

"Uh," Samad managed, unable to believe what he was hearing.

"I thought you were trying to starve yourself to death," he said when he recovered a bit from his surprise.

"I changed my mind. Is that soup?"

"Yes. Yes it is. Here." He carefully ladled soup into a small bowl. "It's hot, be careful."

Teller cradled the bowl in her hands, smelling the soup. She blew on it, and took a small sip. "It's good."

"Thank you," Samad said, blinking back tears. He felt as though his world had been turned upside down, shaken, and then turned right side up again. He sat and watched her drink every drop of the soup in her bowl.

"You should eat, too, Samad," she said. "You're too thin."

Samad smiled. "You're a fine one to talk."

Teller glanced down at the coverlet. "I know." She looked back at him, her face solemn. "Samad, I put you through hell. I'm so sorry."

Samad shrugged. There was a long silence.

"I went out to the Giant's Nose," he said at last. "And I sat and thought about how I'd feel if you died. I knew why you wanted to kill yourself." He was silent again for a long time, then said. "There's an empty place in my head where Abeha used to be. I miss her so much."

Teller nodded, her eyes swimming. "I know," she whispered. "I know." She looked out the window at the gathering twilight. There was nothing more either of them could say.

"Well," she said, breaking the somber silence. "Could you get me a little more soup, Samad?"

He nodded, and the two of them sat in the gathering darkness, eating soup and not talking.

Samad and Florio took turns feeding Teller small meals every couple of hours around the clock for the next two weeks. Teller recovered quickly. After a week she was able to sit up. By the end of the next week, she could move around the house, first with help, and then by herself. After another week she started making short trips outside. Her gaunt frame began to look less skeletal, and her strength began returning.

When Teller was well along the road to recovery, Florio decided it was time to gather up the scattered threads of his own life. Teller and Samad accompanied Florio as far as the road.

Florio put his hands on Samad's shoulders and gave him a friendly squeeze. "Take care of her, and take care of yourself, too."

"Don't worry, I won't let her push me around too much," Samad replied with a mischievous grin.

"Good! Good!" Florio embraced Samad briefly, then turned to Teller.

"Good-bye, *aghapitee*," Florio said, embracing her. "I'm glad that this wasn't our final farewell."

Teller looked down, embarrassed. "I'm sorry, *aghapitos*. I was—"

Florio lifted her chin so that her eyes met his. "No. Don't apologize. I understand. You lost the center of your life. Now you're rebuilding it, and that isn't easy. But I wouldn't leave you now if you weren't well on your way." He glanced past her at Samad and smiled. "Good luck, *aghapitee*. I hope we'll see each other soon." He kissed her forehead tenderly and then gave her a lingering kiss on the mouth.

"You'd better go before I drag you back to the house for some more of that," Teller teased.

"But you taught me to always leave them wanting more, teacher," Florio protested with a teasing grin. He gave her one last quick kiss, settled his pack, and started off.

Teller and Samad stood watching him walk away. Just

before the first bend in the road, Florio turned and waved one last time. Teller waved back, and stood with her arms wrapped around her as Florio's path took him out of sight.

"Well," Teller said, breaking the silence. "Let's head back." Samad held out his arm, and she took it. By the time they were halfway up the hill, she was panting and out of breath.

"Let's rest for a bit," Samad suggested. He helped her into the old graveyard.

"I hate getting tired so easily," Teller grumbled.

"You're getting better," Samad reminded her. "Last week you couldn't have made it half this far."

Teller nodded. "But I feel like an old lady, and I hate that."

"Let's sit down on that log," Samad said. "You can tell me a story. I've missed hearing them."

Teller looked grim. "I've neglected your education," she apologized. She eased herself down onto one of the smooth boulders that served as grave markers and was silent for a while.

"I never told you what happened to the Pilot after she left her family, have I?" Teller said.

Samad shook his head. "I thought that was the end of the Cycle."

"Actually, the official end of the cycle is after she rescues that family over on Sartene Island. That's where the manuscript in the Guild archives ends. No, this is an unofficial story, something that I never tell to an audience. It's not in the archives. You'll know how I know it after I tell you the story, but you can't tell anyone. Do you want to hear it?"

Samad nodded. "Yes, please, sera," he said, slipping easily back into the role of pupil.

"After losing almost all of her family, the Pilot lived with the harsels far out among the Western Isles, living on fish

and old caches of stored food. She listened to the harsels'
deep-toned memory songs; letting them fill the empty
spaces in her heart. Freed from the weight of human needs,
the tide of her grief slowly ebbed. One day, she realized that
she had not seen another human being for nearly two years.
She pushed the thought away, but it kept returning.

"It was her harsel who finally took matters in hand. They
were near an inhabited archipelago, and one night while the
Pilot slept, the har sailed into the nearest harbor. The Pilot
awoke to find herself and the harsel surrounded by boats at
anchor.

"'As long as we're here, you might as well go in and
have a bite to eat at the local taverna,' her harsel suggested
innocently.

"The Pilot spluttered angrily at her harsel, who ignored
her as placidly as a cat. When the Pilot's angry tirade ran
down, the harsel politely pointed out that she did need
some new gear, and this was a good chance to get some."

Samad smiled at this. Teller paused and raised an inquiring eyebrow.

"They sound like you and Abeha," he said. He looked
down and then up again, and Teller could see that he was
worried that he had hurt her. "I'm sorry—" he began.

Teller laid a gentle hand on Samad's arm. "Abeha's always in our thoughts these days. We might as well talk
about him."

"Him?"

"I know that for the harsels, the honorable dead are all female, but I'm not a harsel," Teller said. "Abeha was male for
most of his life, and that's how I remember him."

Samad nodded. "What happened next?"

"Well, the Pilot stormed off angrily into town and returned several days later, looking less tattered and very satisfied. She had forgotten how much she enjoyed fresh bread,

cheese, coffee, and beer. And she'd managed to take several hot baths. Her satchel bulged with produce and cheese. She had also bought new clothes and some sturdy foul-weather gear.

"When the fresh food ran out, she stopped in at another harbor and bought more. Slowly they made their way north again. Half a year passed like that, and then one day she woke to find that they were lying just off Bonifacio Island. As the Pilot saw the familiar silhouette of the island on the horizon, her breath caught in her throat. Should she go back? She had left her daughter alone with a family and a farm to run, leaving no word of where she was going, or why. What kind of welcome would she have if she returned?

" 'There's no way to know without trying,' her harsel told her. 'Go, see for yourself.'

"And so that night the Pilot and her harsel slipped into the sheltered bay near her farm. The Pilot rowed ashore in her little gray rowboat. Moving silently, she approached close enough to see the farmhouse, but not so close as to wake any sleeping dogs. She could see sheep lying in the fold, like gray humps of fluff, and remembered that it was shearing season. The farm looked well-tended and prosperous. Clearly the family had got on well without her. She slipped around the house and through the orchard to the little family graveyard. She sat there and watched while Amphitrite rose out of the ocean. It lit the rounded boulders that served as gravestones, and she saw that the names of everyone in the family who had died in the plague were there. She got up and found the boulder with her husband's name on it. Kneeling before it, the Pilot kissed her finger and then ran her fingers over her husband's name. She looked more closely, but her own name was not there.

"A stick snapped, and the Pilot whirled around, ready to flee like a frightened animal.

" 'For nearly three years I've wondered whether I should put your name on that boulder next to his, Mama.'

" 'Barbara!'

" 'I've missed you,' the Pilot's daughter said. 'Every night for a year the children asked me where *Nonna* was.' She came closer, and the Pilot was shocked to see how much her daughter had aged. 'Finally, I couldn't stand it anymore, and I told them to stop asking. Still, I see them wondering where you are, every time they come up here.' The moonlight gleamed off of the tears in her daughter's eyes.

" 'I'm sorry, Barbara. I couldn't stay. The memories were too strong. I was drowning in them.'

" 'Where have you been?'

" 'With the harsel. He sends his love.'

"Barbara smiled. 'Give him mine in return.'

" 'Has it been hard?'

"The Pilot's daughter looked away, shrugging, and then smiled fleetingly. 'Of course. But the girls helped, and the neighbors, when they could. The first year or two was hard on everyone, after the plague. One of the young dogs got out one night and chased the sheep into the ocean, where they drowned. We lost half the flock. But we got in a champion merino ram three years ago, and the flock is coming back.'

" 'Have you . . . Have you remarried, or found someone?'

"Barbara shook her head. 'Too busy. And the plague hit the men harder than the women. So there's no one to spare.'

" 'I remember,' the Pilot replied, her eyes hooded. 'I remember.'

" 'The children have grown. Stephano looks more like his father every day.'

" 'He must be nearly grown.'

"Barbara nodded. 'He turned fourteen two months ago.

When the others are all grown, I'll turn the farm over to him.'

" 'What will you do then?' the Pilot asked.

" 'Travel. I want to see Thalassa before I die. Will Abeha take me?'

Samad jumped as though stung, and opened his mouth to ask a question. Teller held up a hand, and he subsided. He would have to wait and see.

" 'I think so, but you'll have to ask him,' the Pilot said. 'Do you want to travel alone, or would you like to travel with me?'

" 'A little of both, I think,' Barbara said. 'Oh, Mother, it's so good to see you again!'

"They embraced.

" 'How long can you stay?'

" 'Till after the shearing,' the Pilot offered.

" 'We could use the help. The children will be glad to see you.'

"After the shearing, and another quiet month with her family, the Pilot began visiting other islands, other settlements, paying attention to how things were changing. What she saw troubled her deeply. Everywhere the colonists' grandchildren were forgetting their history. They were forgetting their parents' and grandparents' pride in their newly colonized world, and were striving to be as much as possible like the people they saw on the Tri-V programs exported from the Central Worlds.

"The Pilot remembered her years among the harsels. Some of their memory songs were several millennia old, ancient even by the long-lived standards of the harsels. The people of Thalassa were already forgetting themselves and their past. She was watching a generation of Thalassans growing up without any traditions.

"The Pilot pondered the problem as she traveled. Then one night she was caught by a sudden blizzard in the Gavadhos Range, and sheltered in an isolated farmhouse. The farmhouse was filled with a big family. Grandparents, parents, and almost a dozen children of all ages sat around the fire, telling stories about the settling of Thalassa, and ancient stories from Earth, too. She stayed at the farmhouse until the passes were clear, helping with the chores during the day and sharing stories at night.

"She left the farmhouse behind but never forgot her visit there. She kept remembering the storytellers' firelit faces, and the rapt faces of the listening children. That farmhouse was a place where history lived through the stories that the elders told.

"And so the Pilot began traveling all over Thalassa, stopping in farmhouses and inns, asking for stories, and telling them in return. And when her children were grown, Barbara de Benedetti joined her mother, telling stories to remind Thalassans of who they were. Eventually, Barbara de Benedetti formed the Storytellers' Guild. The Pilot traveled everywhere, collecting stories and bringing them back to the Guild House. As the years passed, the Pilot acquired a nickname. People began to call her Teller, after the stories she told."

"But that's your name!" Samad exclaimed. "Did you name yourself after her? Was Abeha the Pilot's harsel?"

Teller nodded. "But, you see, I'm the Pilot. I did all those things in the Pilot Cycle. That's why I tell those stories so well."

Samad looked at her, frightened. "That can't be! The Pilot lived centuries ago. She must have been dead for a long, long time. Nobody lives that long."

Teller shook her head. "That's my daughter Fiorenza's

headstone you're sitting on, Samad. Fiorenza died in the epidemic. I'm sitting on my husband Stephano's headstone." She looked down, smoothing the worn stone with one weathered hand. "All these years, these centuries, and I still miss him." She looked back up at Samad. "I was waiting until our children were married, and then I was going to take him to Hanuman for a rejuve treatment. It was only going to be another year or two." She bowed her head sadly.

"But nobody lives five hundred years, not even with rejuve! And how could you afford such a thing?"

"I was a Jump pilot, Samad," Teller replied. "Back then, pilots were much rarer. They were trying all kinds of crazy things to keep our Talent from burning out. They gave me rejuve. Lots of rejuve. Maybe it worked, because I had a very long career. I was sixty when I was marooned in this system, but my body looked like a twenty-year-old's. I still looked like that when the first colonists arrived. That was why no one recognized me. I don't know why I've lived so much longer than anyone else, Samad. The doctors say that my body has a freak reaction to the stuff. And I've kept it up. Every century or so I go back and get another treatment." She shrugged. "It's worked so far. Despite my best efforts, I've even managed to outlive Abeha," she said with a resigned smile.

"Teller, you've been under such a strain—" Samad soothed. "Let me help you back to the house. I think you need to rest a bit."

"You don't believe me. I know it's hard to accept, but I can prove it. Follow me."

Samad followed Teller up around the shoulder of the hill. It was a steep climb, and Teller paused to rest several times on the way. They passed through the ancient orchard and into a patch of brushy woods. A stone outcrop rose out of the ground. Teller stopped again to catch her breath. Then she pushed through the brush toward the ridge of stone, swearing as the twigs caught in her clothes and hair.

"Here, let me," Samad offered, and began pushing aside the brush while Teller guided him. Suddenly he saw a dark gap in the yellow stone.

"There!" Teller said excitedly. "In there!" They forced their way past the last few shrubs and stooped under the low brow of rock covering the opening. Inside was a dry, empty chamber, big as a large living room, but bare and empty except for the skeleton of a long-dead nicino and a pile of loose rubble lying along one wall. Samad looked around at the empty cave, feeling worried and confused. Had grief and starvation unhinged Teller's mind?

But Teller was scrabbling at the pile of rubble.

"Help me move these rocks, Samad!" she called.

Samad helped her move aside the loose stones. The corner of a small, gray plasteel switch box appeared. Teller lifted away the last few stones covering the lid.

When the box was uncovered, Teller flipped up the lid, revealing a keypad. She tapped in a code, and a green light went on. With a rumble of hidden machinery and the rattle of falling rocks, part of the cave wall slid back, revealing a short passageway and a door sealed by a palm lock. Teller set her hand against the sensor, and the palm lock opened with a heavy clunk. A light came on in the chamber behind the door as Teller opened it.

Teller looked at Samad and smiled. "Welcome to my secret laboratory," she joked.

Samad stepped through the doorway and found himself in a large, high-ceilinged cave. The walls of the cave were lined with shelves filled with books and an amazing array of artifacts. There were odd bits of machinery, tools, mineral specimens, and preserved plants and animals, some so wholly alien that Samad wasn't sure what they were.

"You like it?" Teller asked.

"I—it's amazing!"

Teller shrugged, but there was a pleased smile on her face. She went over to the shelves and pulled down a large, thick tome. She opened it and paged through it until she found the picture she wanted.

"Here. Look at this."

Samad took the book. The photo was eerily familiar. He'd seen an almost identical picture reprinted in several different books on Thalassan history. There were the same three members of the Founding Families, posed in front of a newly built cabin, but in this picture there was a fourth person. The hairs on the back of his neck prickled. Samad looked closer, unable to believe his eyes. It was Teller, her face a bit weathered but still youthful. In one hand she held a shovel; in the other she held a fruit tree, its roots wrapped in a burlap ball. The poses of the other three Founders were just different enough from the ones in his history book to convince him that the picture was not a fake.

He paged back through the album and stopped at a picture of Teller, looking considerably less weather-beaten than she had in the Founders' picture. She was sitting on a rock in front of a row of newly planted fruit trees. On a ridge above the new trees sat a small space shuttle, and in the far distance loomed the unmistakable shape of Pilot's Peak, the highest point on Pilot's Island.

"I took that picture with a remote camera. It was my first orchard," Teller told him. "I was all alone, and desperate for something to do. So I broke into the agricultural shipment on board my Jump freighter and started playing with the germ plasm bank. I wasn't much of a gardener back then,"

she admitted. "I thought fruit trees would be easy to grow."
She grinned ruefully. "I had a *lot* to learn. But some of the
trees made it, despite my help."

Samad touched the picture lightly with one marveling
finger. It was real. He flipped farther back through the
book, almost to the beginning, stopping at a picture of a
group of young men and women, dressed in severe black
uniforms, a gleaming starburst emblem arced over each of
their hearts.

He glanced up at Teller, lifting an inquiring eyebrow.

"My graduating class at the Pilot's Academy," Teller said.
"Can you find me?"

Samad studied the faces in the picture. He glanced up at
Teller and then back at the photograph. There were half a
dozen women, but one stood out. She stood a little off to the
side, a familiar, ironic smile on her mouth, her eyebrows
dark and a little too heavy, her nose long and distinctive,
even in youth. She looked impossibly young, but no one else
in the picture could possibly be her.

"There?" he asked.

She glanced at him sidelong and nodded. "You're pretty
good at faces. Sometimes I have trouble recognizing myself
in that picture." She shook her head. "It's hard to believe
that I was ever really that young." She touched the picture
reminiscently. "I guess it all started there. Once I became a
Jump pilot, everything else was inevitable." She looked into
the distance of memory. "Though if I hadn't lost my Talent
when and where I did, I'd probably have died."

"Why?" Samad asked.

"Pilots usually die within a few years of losing their abil-
ity to Jump through hyperspace," she said. "If it hadn't been
for Abeha, I'd have killed myself, too. But somehow Abeha
kept me from missing my Talent. Now he's gone." Her eyes

started to fill with tears. She wiped them away, closed the photo album, and put it back on the shelf.

Samad felt suddenly awkward and uncertain. He thought he had understood Teller, but now—

"You really are the Pilot," he whispered in amazement. "It really is you in all those pictures."

Teller nodded. "You're the only other person who's ever seen this place," she told him.

"You haven't even shown this to Florio?"

Teller shook her head. "Florio knows that I've had rejuve, and that's a big enough secret. If he knew that I was really the Pilot, and if he saw some of the things here, then sooner or later, he'd feel obliged to tell someone in the Guild. I built this after Barbara died. I wanted a place where my memories would be safe."

"But—if you didn't show it to Florio, why are you showing it to me? I'm just a kid."

"Florio is a Guild member, first, last, and always." She reached out and pulled gently at one of Samad's black curls, letting it stretch out, and pull back between her fingers. "But you're my son. If I hadn't known that already, I'd know it after these last few months, Samad. Everyone else gave up on me. You hung on and refused to let me die."

Teller swept him up in her embrace. Samad clung to her, tears pushing behind closed lids.

"Thank you for trusting me, Mother," he said.

Teller pulled back far enough to meet his gaze. "That's the first time you've ever called me your mother, Samad."

Samad, shrugged, embarrassed, and looked away. Teller hugged him again.

"Thank you, Son," Teller whispered into his black curls, tears pricking her eyelids. "Thank you."

CHAPTER 11

TELLER TIPTOED INTO SAMAD'S ROOM AND stood for a moment, smiling down at her lanky, handsome, sixteen-year-old son. How had he grown so big so quickly, she wondered? Already he was the youngest Master Storyteller the Guild had ever had. She reached down and lightly stroked his sleep-tousled black curls. He stirred sleepily.

"Samad, Samad. Wake up, it's time for you to get ready to go to the theater. José's going to be here in a few minutes."

Samad groaned and rolled over, clutching his pillow. He lay like that for a minute; then, just as Teller was going to say something to rouse him again, he inhaled, stretched, and yawned.

"All right, all right," he said. "I'm up."

"Are you sure you need to go to the theater this early?" Teller asked him when he emerged from his room, fully dressed and ready to go. "Your performance won't be for another three hours, and they did all the sound and lighting checks this morning."

Samad shrugged. "I've never performed in the Grande before," he said. "It's such a prestigious venue. I want to make sure that I'm familiar with it."

"You'll be fine, Samad. You know the story and tell it well. I don't want you to wear yourself out before you go on."

"I'll be fine," Samad told her. "I'm just worried about the arrangements José made."

"He did a fine job, Samad. You're worrying too much."

"I know. But I can't help it. And I might as well do my worrying at the theater as around here, where I'll drive you nuts."

Teller smiled; he was right. But she still worried, as any parent of a sixteen-year-old would do. But mostly she worried because he gave her so little cause to worry. He seemed so mature, so self-contained, so obedient and dutiful. What would happen if he really decided to cut loose and rebel?

There was a knock at the door. It must be José. She opened the door and welcomed him in.

"Samad's just finishing his packing, José. He'll be out in a couple of minutes."

At the sound of voices, Samad looked up. "I'm almost ready. I was just double-checking my costume for tonight."

"You'll be fine, Samad," Teller said.

José smiled. "He just wants everything to be perfect."

"I know, I know," Teller told him, rolling her eyes.

Samad emerged from his room with his costume in a garment bag and a satchel full of makeup and other supplies in the other hand.

"Okay, I'm ready to go," Samad announced.

"One moment, *mijo,*" Teller said. "I have a present for you." She handed him a small box. He opened it and lifted out a pendant of cream-colored stone on an expensive silver chain. The smooth, fine-grained stone was carved into the shape of a weathered column, with the faces of a man and a woman carved on opposite sides. It was a replica of the monument erected over the graves of Roxane and Paoli, whose story he was to tell tonight.

"Teller, it's perfect. Thank you! It'll be perfect with my costume tonight."

Teller smiled. "I'm glad you like it, Samad. I'll see you tonight, just before the show?"

Samad nodded.

"Buenas suerte, mijo," she said, "and please, don't forget to eat a little something before you go onstage."

Samad gave her a hug and bent down to kiss her forehead. "I will, *mi madre.* I will."

Then he and José headed out the door. Teller heard their feet clumping downstairs and sighed. Samad still seemed so young. Too young to be a Master Storyteller with students of his own. But he was. José was only six months younger than Samad, and Teller wondered how Samad could maintain authority over the other boy. But José seemed willing and eager to be Samad's pupil, and he was learning a great deal from Samad. She shook her head. She worried too much.

Samad followed his student José into the darkened theater, carrying his costume over one shoulder.

"The dressing rooms are down this corridor," José said.

As part of José's training, Samad had put him in charge of handling the details with the theater manager. They walked down the carpeted hallway until they came to a featureless door.

"Here, the theater manager said it would be unlocked." José tried the knob, and then they went through the door and into a backstage like any one of the many backstages

Samad had been in: worn, dingy, utilitarian, dimly lit, and oddly spooky.

Samad felt a rush of arousal at being alone with José in this darkened theater. Quickly, Samad suppressed his desire. He didn't want to be like the predators the other beggar children had whispered about in the streets, who did unspeakable things to boys in the dark. He would not do such a thing, no matter how his desire tugged and whispered at him. He had chosen to teach José because he had wanted to put José out of reach of physical temptation.

But despite the change in their relative status, he still desired José. If only he were not so handsome! Such eyes! Such hands! At night Samad fought to keep from thinking about his handsome student, and always failed. If only José were not so eager to please, if only José wasn't standing so near him in the darkened theater!

José opened the door to the dressing room and turned on the lights. Samad set his satchel on the dressing room table, feeling a wave of relief wash over him as the bright lights chased his predatory yearnings back into the shadows, where they lingered, waiting for another opportunity to tempt him.

"Thank you, José," Samad said. "Why don't you go and get us some coffee while I get ready."

"Are you sure there's nothing I can do for you here?" José asked.

"No, José. Thank you." Was he being too curt? Had José sounded hurt?

"All right, then. I'll go get the coffee."

José left, and Samad closed his eyes tightly in despair. He should find José another teacher. But José was a good student, and Samad could find no plausible excuse to send the boy away. He sighed and wondered if Teller had ever felt like this when Florio was her student. He wished he could ask her, but he was afraid of what she might think. Besides, this was his problem. It was his job to find a solution.

Turning his mind away from his troubles, Samad walked out onto the stage, pacing off his blocking and rehearsing the key moments in the story. When some of the other performers arrived, he greeted them and returned to his dressing room. He put on his costume and regarded himself critically in the mirror. He looked good. The tunic emphasized his slenderness and made him look taller. He had let his hair grow a bit longer, and it fell in dark, curly waves to just past his jawbone, framing his face and giving him a sense of mystery and romance.

The costume's long, flowing lines and flaring, archaic sleeves evoked an earlier, more turbulent and romantic period in Thalassan history, the time of Roxana and Paoli, the story he was to tell tonight. That had been the time of the vendetta, the evil eye, and the mystical dream-hunting *mazzeri*.

He had heard the story first from an old *voceratrice* on Bonifacio Island, late one night as the flickering fire in her hearth died down to embers. When he expressed an interest in performing the tale, Teller had shown him other versions of the story in the Guild archives. Tonight, he would be premiering his own version of this ancient tragedy of forbidden love. He would take all the hidden desire that smoldered for José and pour it into the story before it drove him mad.

Samad got out his makeup case and began working on his face, darkening the hollows of his eyes and shading his cheeks so that he would look gaunt, mysterious, and tragic onstage. He was pacing back and forth in his dressing room, muttering parts of the story to himself, when José returned with the coffee. "You look marvelous!" José declared. "Just a minute, let me get those loose threads off of your tunic."

José delicately brushed a few loose threads from his clothing. Samad felt himself responding to the touch of his student's hands and stepped away.

"It's all right, José. They aren't going to see a few specks of lint, even in the first row." He picked up the pendant and put it on. "Do you think Teller will be pleased?"

"Of course I am," Teller said, standing in the open doorway. "But you know that already, *mijo.*"

"Hello, Teller!" Samad said. He gave her a hug and kissed her cheek, grateful for her presence.

"They're going to start in a few minutes. I just came by to bring you a little supper and wish you luck with your performance," she said. "I'm looking forward to your new story."

"But Roxana and Paoli isn't a new story, Teller," Samad protested.

Teller smiled. "In your hands it will be."

Embarrassed, Samad looked away. When he looked back, Teller was gone, leaving only a couple of containers of stew on his dressing table.

His restless, seeking fingers stroked the smooth, fine-grained stone his pendant was carved from. Caressing the stone seemed to ease the tension within him. He glanced at himself in the mirror. The pendant was the perfect touch with his costume.

José looked at it. "You're lucky to have such a mother," he said wistfully.

Samad nodded. "I know."

Just then, the stage manager stuck his head in. "Five minutes to curtain, Ser Bernardia. You'll be on in forty-five minutes."

José handed Samad a container of stew. Samad carefully swathed himself in napkins to protect his costume and ate. The hot stew settled his stomach, made him feel less like he was going to fly away at the slightest breath of wind. He heard the applause and the music as the show began. He would be on last, which gave him even more time to fret.

"I think I'll go watch the show," Samad said, feeling suddenly nervous. He always felt this way before presenting a new story, and this was such a prestigious venue, especially for someone as young as he was. Even off-worlders came to the Grande.

He watched the comedy and the dances. Tonight, a troupe of traditional Arabic dancers from Sursur were performing, and he watched the women and especially the men writhe sensuously onstage, until at last he had to look away.

Then it was his turn. Samad took his place behind the closed curtain. He could hear the murmuring audience on the other side and felt a rush of doubts. What if he forgot the story? What if no one liked it? He closed his eyes, breathing deep and slow into his belly, stroking the smooth stone pendant, until he felt centered and confident again. Then he nodded to the stage manager, and the curtains parted with a smooth sweep of fabric.

The applause swelled as he stepped forward into the bright spotlight. As his eyes adjusted to the glare, he could see Teller sitting off to one side. He smiled at her, and his fingers brushed the pendant in a quick gesture of thanks. He saw her nod in response. Then he turned to smile at the entire audience, bowing as their applause swelled again. He stepped another pace forward and drew himself up. The applause died away into silent anticipation. He waited another beat and then began.

"Roxana and Paoli should never have met, and meeting,

should never have fallen in love. But meet they did, and fall in love they did. Here is their story. . . ."

Teller watched Samad enthrall the audience with the romance of Roxana and Paoli. Over the centuries following the lovers' deaths, she had seen and heard Thalassa's most poignant and well-known love story hundreds of times. She had seen it performed in almost every conceivable manner, from plain storytelling to high opera.

Samad's simple rendition of this classic tale was one of the finest versions she had ever seen. He set the air afire with the exquisite torture of the lovers' forbidden yearning. His mobile hands shaped houses and people and emotions on the empty air. Samad's deep-set eyes glowed like embers as he wound the tension between the two lovers tighter and tighter. She heard the audience sigh as one when the lovers finally kissed. In the hands of a lesser performer, the telling would have seemed mawkish and extreme, but Samad infused the story with a passion that surprised Teller with its intensity.

Looking across the first few rows, Teller saw tears glistening in the eyes of even the most hardened critics, as Samad brought the story to its compelling, tragic conclusion. The silence was broken only by the soft sounds of weeping as he described how the lovers' deaths had ended the cycle of vendettas that had afflicted the Corsican Archipelago for generations.

After Samad was done, the audience sat in a gathering silence, too overwhelmed to respond. Then all of a sudden they burst into applause, slowly at first, then faster and faster as they released their pent-up emotions in wild acclaim. Girls tossed flowers onto the stage. Samad picked up the flowers and bowed deeply and gracefully in acknowledgment. When the applause diminished, he made one last sweeping bow and exited the stage.

A group of girls were waiting at the stage door when he emerged with José. Samad shrugged the girls' adulation off like water and hurried to meet Teller, waiting at the mouth of the alley. José followed close behind, with barely a glance at the crowd of admiring girls.

Teller snorted and shook her head. There he was, the most talented storyteller of his generation, handsome as any off-world Tri-V star, with girls following after him like a line of male tala after a female in season, and he seemed completely oblivious to the opposite sex. Teller shook her head. He was sixteen. Adolescent hormones should be running riot throughout his body right now, and he didn't even notice the girls.

Ah well, Teller told herself. *It's not like he's had much of a chance. We've been traveling so much.* And Samad wasn't really the type to have a girl on every island. He was too serious, too intent on his storytelling. But when she looked at José's face, shining with admiration for his teacher, another, more complex possibility crossed her mind.

She pushed the thought out of her mind. Samad was still young. He would figure it out. They always did.

Samad came up and kissed her once on each cheek. He looked at her. "How did I do?" he asked, a hint of anxiety appearing in his eyes.

"You know very well how you did, Samad. Why do you even bother to ask me?" she chided him affectionately.

Samad shrugged. "You make it real," he told her. "I'm not sure until you tell me."

"Well then, *mijo,* you were fabulous. As always."

"Can José join us for dinner, Teller?"

"If you don't mind dining with an old lady like me, José."

"What old lady? I see only you, beautiful señora," José said gallantly.

"Ah, José," Teller said. "You're wasted on me. You should go talk to those pretty girls over there." She gestured with her chin at the crowd of disappointed girls standing in the alley.

"But I only have eyes for you," José said, clasping his hands to his breast theatrically. He glanced at Samad as he said this. Teller's suspicions flared. Whatever Samad was growing into, she had no doubts about José's preferences.

"José, you are an outrageous flirt and a heartbreaker," Teller scolded. "You may join us for dinner." It would be wise to keep an eye on this one, she thought. It wouldn't do to have Samad's reputation as a teacher tarnished by an overly affectionate protégé.

They went to Carlucci's, a small, very old restaurant in a quietly exclusive quarter of the city. Teller looked around at the warm, wood-paneled room, remembering the place when it was new. That had been nearly ninety years ago. She had known the owner then, a young widow named Maria Carlucci, who was working as a chef at one of the out-worlder hotels. She had been struggling to find capital to start her own restaurant. Through intermediaries, Teller had quietly arranged a loan at an outrageously low interest rate. The Carlucci family had created and maintained a wonderful, intimate restaurant that had lasted several generations. Whenever the restaurant was in trouble, Teller found a way to help out. Sometimes it was something as simple as sending them a good chef or headwaiter, occasionally another small loan. In return, Teller had a tiny island of continuity that had lasted over the years.

Teller needed such familiar places even more since Abeha's death. *How I miss you, Abeha,* she thought to herself. She smiled, remembering sitting on the harsel's broad back, the wind in her hair, the sun on her back, and Abeha savoring the glorious day in his own familiarly alien way.

". . . Isn't that right, Teller?" Samad was saying.

"What?" Teller blinked, startled out of her reverie. "I'm sorry, Samad. What were you saying?"

"We were trying to remember which island the story of Roxana and Paoli originally came from. José insists it's from Ventiseri, and I say it was Filitosa."

Teller paused, trying to remember. For a long, frightening moment, the memory simply would not come, and then she remembered the funeral cortege, the grieving, weathered faces of the farmers and herders following the two coffins past a row of rough stone columns carved with austere faces. The rest sprang instantly to her mind. "It was Filitosa. But Roxana was from Ventiseri, so it's easy to be confused."

Teller sat back, feeling immensely relieved to have answered the question. She should have known it immediately. One of Roxana's cousins had married her grandson. She had felt the impact of the two young lovers' deaths on the islands, so heavily embroiled in vendetta. The tragedy had brought peace, but at a dreadfully high price. She had ensured that peace by making sure that the story had been told throughout the Corsican Archipelago. The story had been popular, and other storytellers had carried it all over Thalassa.

"What a tragedy it was," she murmured, remembering.

"But beautiful, and so romantic," José sighed. To Teller, he seemed impossibly young in that moment. She pressed her lips together and said nothing, letting the rest of the dinner pass uneventfully.

That night, Teller paused as she was brushing her hair, and regarded her reflection in the mirror. An old woman looked back at her. Her skin had grown thin and papery; her hair was growing in completely white now. Thinking back, she'd been feeling tired, and her joints had begun to ache over the past year. But she'd been too busy to notice.

Her rejuve was wearing off. It was time to go off-world and get another treatment. She set the brush down on the counter thoughtfully. At least this would help separate Samad and José. Visiting the Central Worlds required at least six months, two months there and back, and at least two months for the treatments. And as long as they were going, it would be nice to do some sightseeing afterward. By the time they returned, José would be well-established with a new teacher.

She picked up her hairbrush again and began to brush her hair thoughtfully, remembering how good the last rejuve had made her look and feel. Perhaps she could have a discreet off-world affair when she had her new, young body. And she wanted Samad to get a rejuve baseline done. He was too young for it now, but in another decade he would be a prime candidate, and having a youthful baseline made a big difference in how well the rejuve worked.

But what if this rejuve didn't work? Teller set down the brush and stared at her reflection. At her age, rejuvenation was far from a certainty.

Well, there was no way to find out except by trying. Teller tried to push the possibility of rejuve failure out of her mind as she braided her hair.

In bed, waiting for sleep, her mind reached back, remembering family, friends, and lovers, all dead now. Through the decades and centuries of her life she had watched them all grow old and die. Abeha had been her constant companion. Now he was gone, too. She remembered Samad, burning with intensity up onstage tonight. Her son. She wanted him to remain that young and vital forever. With rejuve, he would. And she would have someone who would not leave her behind.

•   •   •

Samad picked up his backpack and followed Teller down the ramp of the shuttle and into the spaceport. He stopped at the bottom of the ramp and took a deep breath of the alien air of Hanuman. It smelled sweet and clean after the recycled air of the ships and the stations, but there was a metallic, industrial tang to it. As they walked toward the baggage station, he tried hard not to gape at the fortune in metal that surrounded these people. There were shiny metal panels on the walls of the corridors. In the lobby of the spaceport, there was a huge bronze statue of a shuttle taking flight. On metal-poor Thalassa, a bronze statue that large would have been immensly valuable, but here, people walked past the statue with hardly a glance.

They had cleared customs and quarantine when they arrived at the port satellite. All they needed to do was get their luggage and take a jitney into the city of Bindara. It was warm and humid as they stood at the jitney rank. The air smelled of oil and rubber. There was a fitful breeze, and it felt like it was about to rain.

The jitney arrived. It was brightly painted with stylized flowers and birds.

"Hotel Li Salle please," Teller told the driver as he took their bags and stowed them in the back of the vehicle.

"Yes, madame," the driver replied crisply. His accent was nasal and harsh. He put the jitney into gear with a jerk and hurled the car into the midst of the traffic speeding by.

To Samad, everything in Bindara had a metallic sheen. Tall buildings of glass and steel towered like faceted metal cliffs over the streets. The streets were filled with crowds of people. Cars and trucks raced everywhere, honking their horns. Even the big city bustle of Nueva Ebiza seemed sleepy beside the Bindaran traffic.

The jitney pulled up in front of a gleaming hotel.

"The Li Salle!" the driver announced.

Two men in bright red coats with stiff, high collars of some shiny black material stepped up to help Teller down from the jitney. Samad reached for his suitcase.

"Allow me, monsieur," one of the uniformed men said, deftly taking the suitcase from him before he could protest.

"Teller, why can't we carry our own suitcases?" he whispered as they followed the red-coated retainers and their luggage through doors held open by still more servants.

Teller smiled. "It's a very good hotel, Samad. They're famous for their excellent service. Just relax and try to enjoy it."

By then they were in the lobby, and Samad stopped dead, astonished by the magnificence surrounding them. Metal, glass, marble, and wood gleamed under tasteful lighting. Deep carpets with elaborate patterns and rich colors covered the floors. Everything seemed to quietly murmur the hotel's luxurious expense.

"Teller, we can't be staying *here!*" he whispered. "It must cost a fortune!"

Teller turned, her smile widening. "It does. It's all right, Samad. We can afford it."

"But—" Samad protested.

"I'll explain it to you later, Samad. In the room," Teller told him. From her tone, Samad knew better than to talk about it any further.

At last the platoon of porters, greeters, servers, and room fluffers had all performed their duties and been thanked, tipped, and seen to the door. Teller kicked off her shoes and settled into a deep chair with a glass of champagne and a sybaritic sigh. Samad prowled the room restlessly, examining the suite and its elaborately luxurious fittings.

"Hey, Teller, there's two toilets in here! One's kind of funny looking. Is it for aliens?"

Teller hauled herself out of the comfortable chair and peered over his shoulder.

"That's a bidet, Samad," Teller said, and then she told him what it was for.

"Oh," Samad said, emerging from the bathroom considerably subdued.

Teller hid her amusement. "Stop prowling around like a caged tiger and come sit down and drink your champagne. It's the real thing, and it's absolutely lovely."

Samad settled himself self-consciously into one of the chairs. He jumped as the cushions oozed into a more comfortable position.

"Teller, this chair's moving! And it's *way* too friendly!"

"It's all right, Samad, that's a formchair. They're supposed to do that. Just relax and let it make you comfortable. Here, try some of this," she said, handing him a delicate crystal flute of a clear, golden champagne. Tiny bubbles rose to the surface. He sipped at it cautiously. Behind its initial astringency, a wealth of complex flavors blossomed.

"It's good," he admitted and took another sip.

Teller beamed. "Every few decades, I like to take a year off and come to the Central Worlds and wallow in luxury for a while. I figure I deserve it."

"You said you were going to explain about the money."

Teller nodded. "I was working my way up to it. You remember I was a Jump pilot, once, a long time ago."

"Of course, you were the Pilot," Samad agreed.

"Yes, well, on Thalassa, I'm the Pilot. But out here, in the wider universe, I'm just another pilot. Pilots are very well paid, and once they burn out, they receive a lavish lifetime pension. I spent most of my piloting career out in space, so my salary just piled up in the bank. And then when I was marooned on Thalassa, I couldn't spend anything. After the colony was up and running, I went back to the Central Worlds, proved who I was, and collected my back pension. After I invested my pension, I was downright wealthy.

She took a sip of champagne and smiled smugly. "The Pilots Union is *still* paying me my pension."

"After five hundred years?" Samad said, his dark eyebrows raised in surprise.

Teller shook her head. "It's only been four hundred and some. But it's a lifetime pension, and it does pile up. You've heard of the Thalassan Land Trust?"

Samad nodded. It was Thalassa's biggest conservation organization; they owned millions of acres and took care of millions more.

"That's me." She named half a dozen of Thalassa's largest companies, as well as several more that he had never heard of. "I'm a majority owner of all of them, mostly through holding companies and a number of different aliases, which change over time. I've also invested in hundreds of major Galactic companies."

"How much money do you have?" Samad asked.

Teller shrugged. "I don't know, exactly. That's one of the things I'll find out in the next few days. I'll be meeting with my financial people and getting current reports. As my heir, I'd like you to come with me."

"Your heir!" Samad said, incredulous. "But Teller, you'll outlive me by several lifetimes!"

Teller shook her head. "Not if you get the rejuve treatment, too," she said. "Samad, even with the rejuve, I could get hit by lightning, or fall off a mountain, or drown. I've been very lucky for a very long time, but no one lives forever. I need an heir, and you're the most logical choice."

"But—" Samad began and then stopped. He felt dizzy and disoriented by so many changes.

Teller touched his arm. "I'm sorry, Samad. I've hit you

with too many things in too short a time. Go unpack, lie down for a bit if you need to. When you feel a little better, we can explore the city. We'll go shopping and get some local clothes so we don't look quite so much like tourists."

Samad started to leave, then paused in the doorway. "Teller? You're not—you aren't planning on killing yourself, are you?"

Teller shook her head. "Of course not! Would I be spending a fortune on a rejuve treatment if I were? I'm just planning ahead. I'd rather pass on what I've built to you. I want someone to carry on what I've started."

"I'm just glad that you're not planning on dying anytime soon, Teller." Samad said and went into his room to unpack.

That evening, dressed in the latest Bindaran fashions, they dined at one of the most exclusive restaurants in the city. The restaurant was set in a huge glass teardrop suspended from one of the city's jeweled, gleaming towers. From their table they had a commanding view of the spaceport and the wide, dark bay. The sky overhead looked into the heart of the Galactic core, and the haze of brilliant stars shone so brightly that it was possible to read by their light. They ate exotic dishes imported from a dozen worlds and drank wines that tasted like floral-scented sunlight.

"Teller, how come you don't live like this all the time?"

Teller set down her glass and looked thoughtful. "What would people back on Thalassa say about me if I did?"

Samad rolled his eyes expressively.

"Exactly," Teller said. "Besides, if I lived like this all the time, I'd get bored with it. And I'd be the size of a house. But if it's a rare treat, I savor it when it comes around." She took a last sip of the incredible wine. "Still, I wouldn't mind drinking this more often. I wonder if we could grow these grapes on Thalassa." She asked the wine steward for the empty bottle. "I know someone who can pass the word to the Thalassan agricultural development office. It's a long shot, but we really could help our wine exports if we could pull it off."

The bottle, discreetly wrapped in a monogrammed linen napkin, arrived along with the check. Samad glanced at the check, and his eyes widened in shock. Their dinner had cost half a year's wages for a Thalassan shepherd.

Teller saw his shocked expression. "It's all right, Samad," she told him. "We can afford it."

"But it's so much money!" he blurted. "Couldn't we help someone with it instead?"

"Samad, do you remember Agnese and her mother?"

He nodded.

"You remember that her mother was left some money by a long-lost great-aunt that she didn't know she had?"

He nodded again.

"There wasn't any aunt, Samad. That was me. I arranged it. Agnese's mother doesn't know. She thinks it really was her great-aunt. But it was enough money for her to build a new life on another island. I was sorry that you had to lose your friend, but I could see what living there was doing to her. I help when I can, Samad, which isn't as often as I'd like. Money isn't the solution to every problem. Sometimes it's as simple as the right word in the right ear. There's a lot of good that can be done simply by listening for trouble and finding a way to help. The Guild does a lot of that. You and I aren't the only storytellers who help people out and report trouble back to the Guild House. The Guild is continuing and expanding on what the Pilot did. Do you remember the tsunami that hit the Kerkenah Archipelago two years ago?"

Samad nodded. "We went there with Hannah, Fatima, Juan, and Miguel to help out. Oh," he said, as he realized that they had all been Guild members, except for Miguel and Fatima, who were still apprentices. "But it was the har captains who brought in all the food and tents and stuff," he added, and then another realization struck him.

"The har captains: Do you help there, too?"

Teller shook her head. "The har captains are financially pretty self-sufficient. But the Pilot inspired a lot of people to step in and lend a hand. They set up a transport network for disaster relief supplies without any help from me. But I did help start the harsel hospitals. Those hospitals have rescued thousands of harsels. A lot more of them live to become mothers now." She looked away, out at the brilliant view, her expression somber and preoccupied. She was remembering Abeha's death again, Samad realized, and cursed himself inwardly for reminding her of it.

"I'm not sure that we're doing the harsels any favors by healing them so that they can die as mothers, but they think so," Teller added after a long silence.

The check paid, they rose from the table. "Shall we walk back to the hotel?" Samad suggested. Perhaps the walk would distract her from Abeha.

Teller shook her head. "We should take a taxi. The streets here can be dangerous at night."

"Dangerous?" Samad said.

"This isn't Thalassa, Samad," Teller pointed out. "There's real poverty, and real crime here."

"And there isn't on Thalassa?" Samad demanded.

"Not like here. This city has nearly as many people as all of Thalassa. We're strangers. We don't know which neighborhoods are safe and which ones are dangerous. We could get killed simply for being outworlders in some parts of this city. I didn't get to be five hundred years old by taking silly chances for no reason. Besides, I'm tired. It's been a long day."

They rode back through the glittering streets in silence.

Samad looked moodily out the windows at the alien city passing by. There was a whole world to explore, and they were going home to their hotel.

When they got back to the room, Teller went to bed almost immediately, but Samad felt restless. He stared out at the brilliantly lit city streets, itching to explore them, despite Teller's warnings. Teller had already been everywhere and done everything. But this was his first time on another world. He wanted to have some adventures, too. He scooped his wallet and room card off the coffee table, grabbed his jacket, and headed for the door.

Samad walked down the busy street that the bellhop had directed him to. A group of gaudily dressed women stood on a corner.

"Hey handsome, you busy tonight?" one of them asked.

"Not particularly," Samad said. "You?"

"Not as busy as I want to be," she said with a knowing look at the other women. "Want to have a good time?"

Samad shrugged, aware that he was missing something and unwilling to commit himself until he understood the situation a bit better.

"You could have a really good time with two of us if you've got the money," another woman volunteered.

Samad finally understood. These were hetaerae, only much more forthright than the discreet women of Thalassa. He blushed deeply red. But moved by a sudden impulse, blurted, "I-I'm sorry, I like men."

He fell silent, amazed at himself for saying it out loud. It felt somehow safer to speak such secrets here, a thousand light years from home.

"Well then you're in the wrong neighborhood!" the second hetaera said.

"Oh," he said. Then, made suddenly bold by the same impulse that had driven him to blurt out his hidden truth, asked, "Where's the right neighborhood?"

"That depends," the hetaera said. "You buyin' or looking for free sex?"

Samad blushed darkly. "Uhm, free, I guess. Is it hard to find?"

The women standing around listening to this conversation erupted in raucous laughter.

"Look in a mirror, *manis,*" one of them remarked. "They'd pay *you!*"

Samad's blush darkened, but inwardly he was reassured and a bit flattered.

"Go on over to the corner of *Bebas* and *Sepuluh* Streets. There's a bar there called Denys' Place. Go in there and ask around for Miss Corazón. Tell her that Sumalee said to take good care of you."

"A-all right." Samad stammered. Why was he being sent to a woman, when he was interested in men? Never mind, it was the next step on his journey. He turned to go, but remembering his manners amid his eagerness, he paused and looked back. "Thank you!" he called, and then ran off to the nearest taxi rank.

"Why do all the good-looking ones like men?" one of the women complained as Samad climbed into a cab.

"S'a damned shame," another one agreed. "Hope he knows what he's getting into."

"He'll learn," said the one who had directed him to the bar. "He'll learn."

Denys' Place was dark and elegant. He caught the faint, subdued gleam of polished wood and the aqueous shine of mirrors made of rippled glass. There was the smell of sweat and some kind of exotic dreamsmoke in the air. The music

was loud and slow, horns and drums peaking and fading
like warm, lapping water. The bar was full of men. Samad
was struck by how ordinary most of them seemed, chatting
in groups around small, high-topped tables. There were a
few women in the bar. They were tall and elaborately
dressed in shimmering gowns, clearly posing for effect. He
wasn't really sure what he had expected, really. A seedy bar
full of furtive, solitary men in baggy coats taking a break
from preying on children, perhaps. The thought seemed so
outrageous in this setting that his lips quirked in a sudden
grin. Then, in a corner, he saw two men kissing each other
with a passionate, focused intensity. His breath caught for a
moment, then quickened. He had found what he was looking for.

He stepped up to the bar. The bartender wore a very
short kiltlike skirt and sheer stockings of some glittering,
figured fabric. Tiny green gems glittered in the young man's
bright copper hair. The bartender's skin was pale as ivory
and gleamed as though coated with oil. Samad stared at him
in awe. He had never seen a man like this on Thalassa.

"Can I get you something?" the beautiful bartender
asked him with a sultry pout.

"Do you have Thalassan pear cider?" he asked hopefully.

"No," the bartender said. "I'm afraid not."

"A beer then. Whatever's on tap." The bartender drew
him a beer.

"Is there a Miss Corazón here?" he asked as he paid for
the beer. "I was told to ask for her."

"Over there," the bartender said, pointing to a corner lit
by one dim spot. A tall woman sat there, alone on a stool,
watching the crowd with tired, worldly eyes. As he
watched, a man came up and said something to her. She
laughed, patted him on the cheek, and ran one hand slowly
up the inside of his leg. Samad blushed.

"Go ahead," the bartender urged. "She won't bite—at least not *too* hard." He smiled and added, "She'll *like* you," in an insinuating voice.

Samad took a sip of his beer, gathered his courage, and walked over to introduce himself to Miss Corazón.

"Good evening, young man," she said, in a deep, velvety voice. Sitting on her barstool, Miss Corazón was almost as tall as he was. She looked incredibly elegant in a long, high-necked gown that glittered in the dim light of the bar. Her dress was slit almost up to the hip, revealing a long, smooth expanse of leg. "Where did the strong west wind blow *you* in from?"

"Thalassa," he said simply. "I'm here with my mother."

"How charming," she replied, chilling perceptibly. "And did you bring Mother with you tonight?"

"She's asleep. I met a woman named Sumalee over in the Market, and she said I should talk to you."

Miss Corazón took out a cigarette and carefully placed it in a long, jeweled holder. She held it up, eyebrows lifted questioningly, and he realized, after a long moment, that she was waiting for him to light it. He patted his pockets and blushed.

"I'm sorry," he said. "I don't have a lighter."

Miss Corazón arched one thinly plucked eyebrow. For a moment, Samad thought she was insulted. But then she laughed lightly. "You *are* a charming young thing." She reached into her gold purse, pulled out a lighter, and handed it to him. Her jaded eyes studied his face as he fumbled to light her cigarette. Then she took a puff and blew out the smoke with airy experience.

"And what did this Sumalee want you to talk to me about?"

Samad shrugged. "I-I'm not sure," he said. "I told her I was interested in men, and she sent me to you. I think she was a hetaera. Um, you call them prostitutes, here. She said to tell you to take good care of me."

"Oh. *That* Sumalee. I see."

"But why did she send me to you, when I was interested in sex with men?"

Miss Corazón stared at him for a long moment, clearly startled, and then laughed, a surprisingly deep-throated, chesty laugh, almost, he thought, a man's laugh.

"My dear young man," she said. "As far as I'm concerned, the pronoun *she* is a courtesy title. I'm a man. In drag. Dressed like a woman," she explained with a hint of asperity.

"Oh," Samad said again, noticing a certain heaviness along the jawline, and the size of the knuckles on her beautifully manicured hands. "We don't have that sort of thing on Thalassa."

"You poor thing! What a very dreary place it must be."

"No, actually, it's beautiful. I love it there." He remembered sailing through the Bonifacio Strait, with towering cliffs of twisted golden rock rising out of the startling turquoise water, a cloud of white seabirds calling overhead, and he was suddenly, powerfully homesick.

"But now you're here. For how long?" Miss Corazón asked.

"A couple of months."

"And you're sightseeing?"

"I guess. I've never been in a place like this. There's nothing like it on Thalassa."

"I'm sure there is, dear. You just haven't found it yet. Now, let me introduce you around."

Corazón took him over and introduced him to the men in the bar. They welcomed him with sultry looks and flirtations, and soon he was the center of a laughing, talkative group, telling stories about Thalassa and eagerly listening to their gossip to learn as much as he could about the new world he found himself in. He felt simultaneously keyed up and oddly at ease. For once he was being completely himself. Then one of the handsome, laughing men put his hand on Samad's knee and slid it slowly higher, his eyes lingering on Samad's face. Samad felt his heart begin pounding.

"So, are you going to talk all night long, or do you want to do something more?" the man asked him in a low, urgent voice.

"Sure," Samad said, his groin suddenly tight. "Let's go."

As they left, Samad looked over at Miss Corazón, who was now sitting on the bouncer's lap. She glanced up at him, smiled a slow, sexy smile, and fluttered a long-nailed hand at him in farewell.

Samad followed the man out of the bar and into the sultry, humid night. The man led him into a warren of darker streets. Once off the main street, the man slipped an arm around Samad's waist. As the night grew darker around them, they stopped, kissed, and then continued on to the man's apartment, where all of Samad's forbidden desires were finally realized, several times over.

The light leaking past the drawn shades had grown watery and pale when his lover finally fell asleep. Glancing at the clock, Samad realized that Teller would be waking in another couple of hours. She would worry if he wasn't there, and there would be questions that he wasn't ready to answer. He slipped out of the bed, dressed, and found his way back to a main street, where he was able to get a taxi back to the hotel. Halfway home, he realized that he'd never learned the name of the man he'd slept with, and he laughed out loud.

During the next two weeks, Samad returned to the bar as often as he could get away. The rest of the time he spent with Teller. They toured the city, shopped, and met with Teller's investment managers. He tried to be interested in the details of her financial empire, but his heart and mind weren't in it. His real life was at night, in the bars and in bed with the men he met in Denys' Place or one of the other bars he learned about as he slept around.

Then Samad found Teller waiting for him in the living room when he came in one night.

"The night doorman says that you've been going out late and coming home early. Would you mind telling me where you have been going? I'm responsible for your health and well-being, and I need to know where you're going," she said.

"I was out," Samad told her, playing for time.

"I was aware of that, Samad," Teller replied. "But that was not what I asked you. Where did you go when you went out?"

"I've just been exploring the city," he said. "I'm fine."

"Please, Samad," Teller said. "Don't go out alone. It's a strange city. All kinds of things could happen to you."

They already have, Samad thought, *and they were a lot of fun.*

"Teller, I've been out there, and I'm fine. Really."

"Where did you go? What did you see? Do you have any stories to tell?"

Samad looked down and shook his head. "Not really. I just went places and saw stuff."

Teller arched an ironic eyebrow. "That doesn't sound like the Samad I know. Usually I can't get you to stop telling me stories about what you've seen. Are you afraid I'll be mad at you? Are you in some kind of trouble? Is it a girl?"

"Damn it, Teller, I'm not a child anymore!" Samad lashed out at her. "It's my own damned business where I go and what I do."

Teller's face became expressionless. "Yes, I suppose it is, Samad. But it's been my business to keep you safe for the last eight years, and it's a hard habit to break." She laid a gentle hand on his arm. "If you ever need help from me, Samad, all you have to do is ask."

"Thanks, Teller," he said. "But I'm fine, really."

"The rejuve clinic called," Teller said, changing the subject. "One of their clients had to change their appointment. They have an opening the day after tomorrow. I'd like to leave tomorrow, so that I have an extra day to settle in before my treatment starts. It would give me a chance to get the treatment over with."

"Oh," said Samad, trying to hide his disappointment. "How far away is the clinic?"

"Just a couple of hours by 'thopter," Teller said. "You'll like it there, it's green and unspoiled and private. It reminds me a little of some of the islands in the Dellys chain."

"Yeah," Samad said, trying hard to summon up some enthusiasm for leaving behind this incredible new banquet of sex, after years of secret longing. "It'll be great."

"Better get some sleep, Samad. You sound tired, and we're going to have to get up early tomorrow to pack."

CHAPTER 12

THE REJUVE CLINIC LOOKED FAMILIAR. *OF course it does. They understand what it's like,* Teller thought to herself. The directors took great pains to ensure that the rejuve clinic was an island of reassuring continuity in an ever-changing universe. Even the paintings on the walls looked exactly the same as they had on her last visit, fifty years ago. They'd looked just the same the first time she'd visited the clinic three and a half centuries ago.

The clinic staff even looked familiar, though many of them were not rejuved. They were all tall, blond, and tan, with the same professional, welcoming smiles. Even the rejuved staff seemed to glow with healthy youthfulness.

The clinic director met her at the door and escorted her through a phalanx of applauding clinic staff and flashing cameras.

She had never had this kind of welcome before. "Why all the fuss?" she asked the director.

"You're the oldest living patient in our files, Sera Bernardia. There are very few people who've lived as long as you have."

"I see," she said. She was tempted to ask just how much older the oldest person alive was, but refused to yield to the impulse. "I must be good advertising then. I don't suppose I'd qualify for a discount?" she inquired with an ironic lift of one eyebrow.

The clinic director paused noticeably. "I'm afraid that isn't our policy here, Sera Bernardia. You must understand that the older the patient, the more difficult the rejuvenation becomes. For a person of your exalted age, the difficulty and the cost are . . ." He spread his hands.

"Considerable?" Teller supplied.

"Exactly. I will be meeting with you to discuss your treatment after you and your companion are settled."

"Samad is my adopted son. I was hoping that we could begin the preliminaries for his future rejuvenation."

"I see. That will require a full gene scan, and ah, some blood tests."

"I believe that there is enough in my account to cover such things," Teller assured him. "And I have also purchased a full rejuvenation policy for him, so that when the time comes, the funds will be assured."

"We will be privileged to provide whatever services Ser Bernardia would require."

"Thank you," Teller said.

The director lifted a hand to cover his right ear, listening intently to his internal phone. "I'll be right there," he said, replying to the person on the phone. "Forgive me sera, ser, but there is something I must attend to. My staff will see to your every comfort, and I will meet with you later this afternoon to discuss your treatment."

They were ushered into their suite, which transformed

the sterility of a medical clinic into a monastic, Zen-like elegance.

"Well, that was a graceful preliminary to letting me down easily," Teller remarked when they were finally alone in their suite.

"What do you mean?" Samad asked, a note of concern in his voice.

"They give me a similar speech every time I come here, a polite little lecture about how the treatment may not work this time." She shrugged. "It always has before."

"Are you worried?" Samad asked.

Teller frowned. "I always am, and then everything turns out all right. The director was just preparing the ground for his usual little speech."

"What about me?" he asked. "What are they going to do to me?"

"They'll just draw a little blood, Samad, and scrape the inside of your cheek for some cells."

"The gene scan, what's that for?"

"They're looking for any genetic defects that might affect your longevity. If they turn up anything, they'll want you to stay long enough to repair them."

"I-it won't tell me anything about my family, will it? I mean—" he began.

"It's all right, Samad. I understand your need to know. By itself the gene scan will tell us nothing." She scowled. "We'd have to go to the Pilots Union for that information, since both of your parents were pilots. They'd have any next of kin on file."

"You don't sound happy about that," Samad observed.

"The Pilots Union always seems to get their kilo of flesh," she said. "I don't trust them. But knowing more about your parents is important."

"Thank you, Teller."

She shrugged and smiled. "I expect that the Union will try to get their cut, but I know the kind of tricks they pull. I'll make sure that they don't try anything with you." She sat down on the bed. "Time for this old lady to get a nap," Teller said crisply. "You should go and get settled in your room."

"All right then," Samad said, "Let me know if you need anything."

"I know." She took Samad's hand in hers and gave it a brief, reassuring squeeze. "I'll be fine. Thank you, Samad." He slipped out, taking care to close the heavy door as silently as possible.

Teller smiled at Samad's care in closing the door. He needn't have bothered. Everything in this expensive mausoleum of a place was carefully engineered to be expensively unobtrusive. It was impossible to slam the doors here. She lay back on the bed and closed her eyes, glad to be alone. She had lied to Samad. She was very afraid. Her last rejuvenation had not lasted nearly as long as previous treatments. And Abeha's death and her subsequent starvation had both taken their physical toll. Had she waited too long this time?

Raising Samad had brought her closer to people again, especially after Abeha's death. She liked her life. It was not the life she had with Abeha, but it was still a life filled with love and things to do. She didn't want to die.

Tears of self-pity threatened to well behind her eyelids. *Well, waiting won't make this any better,* she told herself with asperity. She sat up and blinked to clear her eyes, then reached for the phone and called the front desk.

"Yes, this is Ariane Bernardia, could you please tell the director that I'm ready to meet with him? Thank you."

Teller surfaced from the light doze that always followed the rejuvenation treatments. She stretched, seeking what she in-

wardly referred to as "that golden feeling." It was a sense of
well being and pleasant warmth, like spring sunshine on her
back, only all throughout her body. But this time she felt
only a very faint glow.

Perhaps, she told herself, fighting back a rising panic,
*perhaps I'm remembering that feeling to be stronger than it actu-
ally was.*

Teller held that thought firmly in her mind and let it lull
her back to sleep.

The director sat, poised and confident in his too-familiar
office.

"It's not working, is it?" Teller stated.

The director held out his hands helplessly. "To be honest,
Sera Bernardia, you're responding to the treatments,
but . . ." His hands flew wide, like two startled birds.
"You're not responding well enough."

"I see," Teller said. "How long do I have?"

"Perhaps another dozen years in good health; then, with
good geriatric care . . ." His hands flew wide again. ". . . perhaps another five or even ten years."

"And my mind?"

The director looked less poised. "Good geriatric care
takes into account the wishes of the patient. It is possible to
manage your care so that your body accompanies your mind
into death."

"But how long do I have as an alert, aware, mentally
present person?" she persisted.

"Perhaps fourteen or fifteen years, maybe a year or two
more than that if you're lucky. A great deal depends on the
patient's attitude. Many of our patients become severely de-
pressed when they discover that the treatment has failed to
take." He looked sad. "I'm afraid that they squander the few
remaining years they have left in regrets and recrimina-

tions." He paused. "We have grief counseling available, if you would like it."

Teller just shook her head. So little time left.

"If you are willing to stay for another week, there are several other treatments that will help keep you physically sound for as long as possible."

Teller nodded. She wanted her last years to be good ones. "Thank you, I would appreciate that, Director."

The director stood, "Sera Bernardia, I hope you will allow me to express my sincere and profound sadness at your bad news. I was a resident here when I first met you, a hundred and fifty years ago. You taught me a great deal then. I had hoped that the treatment would work, despite my doubts."

"Thank you," Teller said, touched by his words. "I appreciate all you've done for me over the years."

Teller went back to her room and sat down. She closed her eyes and rubbed her face with her hands, waiting for whatever feelings would come. But there was nothing there. She felt oddly numb. She got up and looked out the window at the manicured gardens.

"Well," she said to herself, "so I'm coming to the end of it all at last." She felt only a vague sadness at the thought. But there was so much to do in the decade she had left. Who would take care of Thalassa and her people? Who would look after the Guild and the harsels when she was gone? If only Samad were a few years older, she thought, with a twinge of guilt. He was too young. She didn't want to load such a burden on his young shoulders. But there really was no one else. There were some who loved the harsels, others who carried Thalassa's history in their heads, and still others who worked on behalf of Thalassa itself. But no one else balanced those three drives as equally as Samad did. Ever since she had recovered from Abeha's death, she had been preparing Samad to be her heir, but she hadn't expected to have to turn it all over to him so soon. Ten years was too short a time for him to learn everything he needed to know. If only she had another fifty years.

Well, you don't have fifty years. You're going to have to do it in fifteen, she told herself. And that meant a lot of hard work and careful planning. She sighed, feeling the weight of all she had to do. This would probably be the last real vacation she would ever have.

There was a tentative knock at the door. It was Samad, clutching a sheet of paper in one hand.

"The Union has sent me the results of my gene scan," he said.

He handed her the sheet of paper. She read it.

"According to our records," the paper said. "Your mother was Ruth Anne di Bernardi. Your most probable father, based on genetics and location at the time of conception, was Charles Helmison. We regret to inform you that both of your parents are deceased. Your parents were both reared in the Arthur Robinson crèche on Oda. They have no known relatives."

"Oh, Samad, I'm so sorry," Teller said. "This must be very hard news."

He shrugged. "At least I know who my parents were," he told Teller. "The rest doesn't matter much. I have you."

Teller smiled and tugged lightly at one of his curls. "And I have you. But it's not exactly true that you have no known relatives. Your mother was a di Bernardi. The di Bernardi line was descended from a genetic sample the Union took from me. Even though I never knew your mother or your father, you and I are related."

"Really?" Samad said, brightening.

Teller nodded. "It's a distant relationship. We're probably fifteen or sixteen generations removed from each other.

But Samad, it doesn't really matter to me. You couldn't be more my son if I had carried you inside me. But if it comforts you to know that you have relatives, you do."

"Does that mean that I'm related to all the other di Bernardi pilots?"

Teller was silent for a long time. "Yes. But there's a difference between sharing genes and being family. You and I are a family. We've been through so much together. The other di Bernardi pilots are all crèche-raised. The only thing you share with them is some DNA. They don't understand family the way you and I do. There are no mothers or fathers in crèches, only caretakers."

"It sounds awful."

Teller nodded. "If I'd known what they were going to do, I would never have let them use my genes. But I was young and foolish then. I was proud to be the progenitrix of a line of pilots. Although it hasn't been all bad. I have at least one descendant who I'm very proud of." She smiled at him, her eyes hazed with tears. "You've been such a gift to me, Samad."

They embraced, and then Teller remembered her own bad news. "Sit down, Samad. I have something else to tell you."

Samad listened to her with all the attention of a trained storyteller. His hand stole into hers when he realized what she was saying.

"Teller, I wish I could give you some of my years."

"No!" Teller said. "Never say that! I've had more than my share of life. It's just that there's so much I'll have to leave behind."

"Teller, fifteen years is a long time," Samad said. "Who knows what will happen between then and now. Maybe they'll even find another way to extend your rejuve."

Teller smiled at Samad. For him, fifteen years was a long

time. Perhaps she should think of it that way, too. A lot could happen in fifteen years.

"Good morning, Ser Bernardia. May we please speak to you?"

Samad gestured his visitors into the room. He recognized their uniforms from the pictures he had seen in Teller's album. They were from the Pilots Union. One was a gray-haired older man with a deeply lined face. The other was a startlingly beautiful young woman.

"Please sit down," Samad said, wondering why they were here.

"Thank you, Ser Bernardia," the older man said. "I am Patrick Turner, and this is my assistant, Trinh di Bernardi. As you know, the Union recently reviewed your gene scan."

"Yes," Samad confirmed. Had the Union made some kind of mistake?

"Your genetic markers indicate that you have the potential to be a very strong Talent," Turner told him.

"Talent?" Samad asked. "What kind of Talent?"

"You could be a Jump pilot. Possibly one of our best," Turner explained.

"We're here to invite you to be tested to confirm that Talent," di Bernardi added.

Turner took a neat dossier out of his briefcase. "The universe could be yours, young man."

"It's been wonderful for me!" di Bernardi added, her eyes shining. "There's nothing like Jump Space."

"You're a pilot?" Samad asked.

"For the last five years," di Bernardi replied. "I've been to more than thirty systems, all the way round known space. I'm on my five-year service leave now, but I can hardly wait to get back into space!"

"What's it like to Jump?" he asked. He never could get

Teller to talk about her years as a Jump pilot. At last, he had someone who could answer his questions.

"I—it's hard to describe," she said. "It's like a dream. It seems to last forever and no time at all. You're everywhere and nowhere, all at once. And then you're out of the Jump, and feeling . . ." She shook her head and looked at him, her eyes wide and dark. "I really can't describe it to you. But it's the most wonderful feeling in the world." She smiled like an eager child. "You should come and be tested. There are so few lucky enough to be blessed with true Talent."

"The testing is free. You're under absolutely no obligation," Turner told him. "It would be a shame to waste this chance." He held out the sheaf of documents, "Here—"

There was a knock on the door, and then Teller walked in.

"Samad, I—" she began and then stopped, taking in the Union uniforms of Samad's visitors. Her expression became grim and angry.

"Get out," she told di Bernardi and Turner, her voice flat and very hard. "You have no right to contact my son without my permission."

"Teller—" Samad began.

"Your son has a right to decide for himself what he wants to do with his life," di Bernardi said, her eyes flashing. "You have no right to keep him from us."

"I'm his mother," Teller shot back. "And I was a pilot, too. Don't you dare lecture me about rights! I've known what it's like to burn out, and I don't want Samad to have to go through that."

Teller took the sheaf of documents that Turner had given Samad and tore them up.

"Teller!" Samad said, horrified at her behavior.

"Now go!" she ordered the recruiters. "Go! And don't contact my son again, or I will have you up on charges."

"It's my life, Teller!" Samad protested.

"It's your life when you're twenty, Samad," she replied.

Turner and di Bernardi picked up their briefcases. "Our offer remains open, Samad," Turner said. "I hope you will consider it when you are free to do so."

"*Out!*" Teller shouted, pointing at the door. Her face was purple with fury. Samad had never seen her this angry before. It frightened him. "Get out!"

"Teller," Samad said, taking her arm in an attempt to calm her. She was quivering with rage. Turner and di Bernardi left as quickly as their pride would permit.

"Teller, calm down," Samad said. He was furious at Teller's abrupt and peremptory interference, but knew better than to show it now. "It's all right. They're gone now."

Teller shook her hair back from her face. She still looked furious. "I forbid you to have anything to do with the Pilots Union."

Stung by Teller's high-handedness, Samad lost his temper. "It's my life, Teller. I do get to make some choices for myself!"

"I forbid you to throw your life away," Teller insisted. "Not now, not ever. You're my son, and I won't let those Union bastards near you!"

Samad stared back at her defiantly. If he wanted to become a Jump pilot, there was nothing she could do to stop him.

A boy in every port, some dark, tempted portion of his psyche whispered. *The stars! The stars would be yours, not just tiny, backwater Thalassa. You could be free! Really free!*

"Teller, I'm goddamned tired of being your good little boy!" he shouted. "It's time to let me grow up and make my own fucking mistakes!" He yanked the door open and tried to slam it behind him as he left. The door whispered shut on the silence surrounding Teller.

• • •

Teller stared out the window, her rage dying to ashes and
fear. She had forgotten how angry she still was at the Pilots
Union. But when she saw them trying to steal her son, her
centuries-old resentment of them had exploded into new life.

Had her rage driven Samad away from her forever? She
hoped not. She needed him, needed someone to care for her
as she declined, and more than that, she needed him to carry
on her legacy. She thought of all she had done on Thalassa.
She had planted orchards and bred livestock to feed the first
arrivals. By helping those in need, she had started a legend
that had helped inspire her people to generosity. With the
harsels she had founded the Compact that bound har and
human together in a partnership that helped both species.

And she and Barbara had created the Storytellers Guild,
which had taught Thalassans to be proud of who they were.
The Guild also acted as her eyes and ears, keeping her ap-
prised of the world's troubles, both large and small. All that
had been left for her to do in the last few centuries had been
to fend off outworld interests seeking to exploit Thalassa's
rich oceans and its lovely, fertile islands. Lately, she hadn't
even had to do much of that. Thalassa was considered a
backwater, where off-world businesses did not prosper. Perhaps once or twice a decade, she had needed to intervene to
prevent off-world exploitation.

But what would happen when she was gone? Much of
what she had fostered would remain for a few generations,
but sooner or later, a crisis would come. And when it did,
who would be able to take the long view needed to guide
Thalassa through it? Who would look after the harsels?
Who would keep the planet's myriad islands from being de-
spoiled? Who would maintain her legacy?

It must be Samad. And now the Pilots Union was trying
to steal his heart with dreams of freedom and adventure.
But the freedom they offered was only a tempting illusion.

The reality behind the illusion was the intense craving for Jump Space, which grew and grew until all you lived for was the next Jump. The Union would use Samad up, steal his soul, and when his Talent was gone, they would spit him out. Their fat pension was no fair payment for what burnout did to your soul.

Her eyes grew sad and dark as she remembered those long days and longer nights when she was the only human on all of Thalassa. If it hadn't been for Abeha, whose mind-songs had soothed the pain and filled the hole left by her Talent, she would have taken her own life.

Even so, there had been times when she had taken out her knife and watched the light run down its sharp, silver edge. But she had never been able to use it to end her urgent longing for Jump Space.

Teller shook her head. It was dangerous to remember such things. But she would not let Samad become prey to that suicidal craving. If only Abeha were here. He could have talked some sense into Samad.

For a moment, her longing for Abeha was as keen as her old craving for Jump Space had ever been. She rested her forehead against the cool glass of the window, tears filling her eyes. *I miss you, old soul,* she told Abeha in her thoughts.

Abeha would have known what Samad wanted, would have felt beneath the surface impulses to the deeper need, and found some way to resolve it. She wondered what Abeha would have advised her to do? Abeha would never have let Samad's silent secrecy last so long. Abeha would have asked Samad to trust him, to tell him what was wrong. But after her towering, imperious rage, would Samad trust her enough to unburden himself to her?

Samad strode determinedly down the hall of the clinic and out into the garden, seeking a place where he could be alone with his anger and frustration. Damn Teller! How dare she order him about? It was his future, his life. He would spend it as he chose. And if he chose to be a pilot, then Teller was just going to have to get used to the idea.

He found a quiet spot, hidden by the arching branches of a weeping tree with slender, dark purple leaves. He lay back; looking up at the tiny bits of sky that showed through the tree's leafy canopy. He squinted until the spangles of sunlight blurred and became stars in a dark purple sky. He imagined himself in a pilot's chair, looking out at those stars, visiting alien worlds, and exploring unknown planets. Maybe, like Teller, he could find a world that would be his and his alone to explore. How he envied her those years alone on Thalassa. She had seen it all first. Thalassa was hers in a way that no other human could claim.

The sun was low in the sky, and it was getting cool when he finally came inside. Teller was waiting for him in the darkened living room of their suite. The freedom of his day-dreams slipped out of his grasp like a handful of seawater.

She stood as he came in. "Samad, I spoke harshly to you this morning, and I am sorry," she said, stiffly formal. "I thought it might do us a bit of good to get out of this mau-soleum for an evening. There's a nice restaurant in the vil-lage. Would you like to go out for dinner?"

Samad nodded acknowledgment of her invitation. Her anger this morning had frightened him. "I'd like that," he said. It would be good to get away from the clinic for a while.

The restaurant was small, and the food was good. There was a large tree rising in the middle of the dining room, up through the roof, sheltering the building under its wide branches. Small, brightly colored lizards inhabited the tree, scuttling nimbly up and down the trunk. Flyers fluttered their leathery wings in the branches. The restaurant's slatted shutters of dark wood gave the place a feeling of screened-in intimacy. As night drew on, the flyers rustled and cheeped among the tree branches, occasionally settling to the ground to pick up a fragment of bread dropped or tossed to them by the diners. Lizards scuttled along the walls and ceilings, catching bugs drawn by the candles on the tables.

Teller kept up an amiable flow of innocuous small talk and reminiscences. She looked more alert and younger, but underneath that was a sense of fragility he had not seen before, as if her new youthfulness was only a brittle shell. Occasionally she looked off into the distance, her face closed and sad, and he knew she was fretting over the failure of her rejuve.

He felt a pang of guilt. The failure of the rejuvenation treatments was a death sentence for Teller. She had given him so much, everything except life itself. How could he abandon her to die alone? But the Pilots Union had offered him the stars. And he wanted them very much. He felt torn apart by his desire for freedom and his debt to Teller. But would Teller even want him for a son if she knew that he desired men rather than women?

"Samad?" Teller asked, laying a hand on his arm.

"I'm sorry, what did you say?" Samad said, shaken out of his reverie.

"I was just saying that we don't seem to be communicating like we used to," Teller said. She sounded faintly amused.

Samad looked down, embarrassed by the truth. "I guess you're right, Teller," he admitted.

"So, what's keeping us from talking?" she asked.

Samad looked down at the polished wood floor of the restaurant and shrugged.

"Please, Samad, whatever it is isn't as important as you are to me."

He looked up at her, a long, serious, searching look. He took a deep breath, then looked away. He was so afraid that she would hate him for what he was.

"You promise you won't be angry again?" he said. He was afraid to ask her not to disown him.

"I promise," she said. She gripped his hands, which were knotted together so tightly that his knuckles were white. "You're my son, Samad. Talk to me. Please."

"I—" he began, but his throat was dry. He took a sip of water. "I like men, not women. As lovers, I mean."

Teller's firm grip never wavered; her olive eyes never left his. "Yes," she said. "I was beginning to think so, too. I just didn't know if you knew it yet."

"You knew?" he asked incredulously.

Teller shrugged. "No. I suspected. Was that where you were going, those nights in Bindara?"

He nodded, not quite able to believe how easily she was accepting this. "Are you angry?" he asked. "That I'm—"

Teller laughed, "Lord no, Samad. Why would I be?"

"Well, it's just that no one on Thalassa is . . ." He groped for words. "Like me," he finished.

"Of course there are, Samad. What about Isidro and Demitrios? And there's Juana and Esther. And—"

"Isidro and Demitrios? They're lovers?"

"Why do you think they always convoy together? I thought you knew."

Samad shook his head.

"There are a lot of people like you on Thalassa, Samad. I'll make sure you meet them when we get home."

"You're not disappointed? I mean, there aren't likely to be any grandchildren."

Teller laughed, loud and long, harder than he'd heard her laugh in a long while. People at nearby tables stared at them. "Oh, Samad. I think I've got descendents enough," she said, wiping tears of laughter from her eyes. "It really is all right. I don't mind. In some ways, it will be easier for you. You won't have to watch your children grow old. I offered rejuve to Barbara, and she refused it." Teller shook her head, eyes darkening. Samad could see her slipping back into the dark mood that had dominated her thoughts ever since she had learned that the rejuve had failed.

"Hey," Samad said, deliberately interrupting her reverie, "the night is young, and we've escaped from the mausoleum. Let's go dancing!"

Teller smiled at him. "What a great idea! It's been ages since I've done that!"

Teller's treatments ended two days later, and they flew back to Bindara. There was a message from the Pilots Union waiting on his console at the hotel, inviting Samad to visit their testing facility. He furtively memorized their address and comm code and then erased the message before Teller saw it.

Teller kept him so busy with business meetings, shopping, and touring that it was a week before Samad was able to visit the Union's testing facility. The facility was elegant and expensive; something about it made Samad want to whisper so that he wouldn't disturb the quiet there. Turner ushered Samad into a well-appointed office. There was a tall console made of dark wood, with a panel of instruments. A pair of deferential technicians fitted a spiderweb of sensors over Samad's head and down his spine, dabbing anesthetic gel on each tiny lead. Despite the anesthetic, there was a prickling as the tiny sensors buried themselves in his skin. He flinched and shivered as they attached themselves to his nerves.

After ten minutes, one of the technicians nodded to Turner. He turned a knob on one of the instruments and clicked a few buttons on his keypad.

"Watch the red light, Ser Bernardia," Turner said.

The red light danced and flickered for a moment or two, and then settled into a steady pulsing as it swung back and forth across the screen. The sensors seemed to generate a pleasant glow of warmth, and there was a steady humming that made him feel relaxed and a little drowsy. The red light receded into a dream of shifting lights and colors that felt timeless and very good in a way he couldn't quite find words for. It reminded him vaguely of the harsel's mindsongs.

Then, suddenly, he was back in the testing facility, feeling disoriented and a little odd and disjointed. There was a tingle singing through his nerves. Turner handed him a drink. The tart, sweet liquid helped settle him back into reality. He glanced over at the technicians, who were examining the printout with muffled excitement.

"Well, Samad," Turner said, "how was your first taste of Jump Space?"

"Was that what it was? I thought that it would be more . . ." He paused, shrugging. "Intense, I guess."

"That was only a test, Samad. Real Jump Space is much more intense than that. Or so I'm told." One of the technicians handed Turner the printout. His face became carefully expressionless as he read it.

"You're not a Pilot?" Samad asked when Turner looked up from his test results.

Turner shook his head. "I only have a tiny bit of Talent. Enough to help set up the machines. But you . . ." He paused. "Your tests are very promising."

"I see," Samad said. He felt a rising excitement. "So you think I could become a pilot?"

"Absolutely. If your Academy scores are as high as your test scores, you would have your choice of missions. You could go anywhere in known space that you want," Turner assured him. "If you'll step this way, we have some informational tapes for you."

He was ushered into a hushed, darkened room and shown several enthusiastic tapes of the brilliant future he had as a Jump pilot and the training he would receive. Then Turner showed Samad into a brightly lit office.

"Well, Samad, are you excited?"

"Yes," Samad admitted.

Turner laid a brightly printed folder in front of him and opened it. "You've seen what we have to offer you. Do you think you'd like to become a pilot, Samad? Do you want the stars?"

Samad nodded, but inwardly, his gut roiled with guilt.

"Well, then, all you need to do is sign some forms, and we'll get you enrolled in a pretraining course. The physical shouldn't be any problem for a healthy young man like you." He slid a pen over to Samad.

Samad took the first form out and started to read it, his mind whirling with excitement. Turner sat beside him, watching his face intently.

"What about the guardianship issue? Legally, I'm still a minor," Samad asked, when he was finished reading the document. "My mother would never sign this. She doesn't want me to become a pilot."

Turner shrugged. "Our lawyers can find a way around it. It would be a shame for a brilliant career like yours to be blighted by a bitter old woman."

Samad remembered Teller's face, contorted with anger, and nodded. But thinking of Teller reminded him of all she had been through since they left Thalassa. She needed him. How could he leave her now? And yet, he had only to sign the documents, and his life would be his own. He picked up the pen, and then set it down again, still uncertain. Teller was old. Her life was nearly over. He wiped his palms on his pants and looked up at Turner.

"How old are your recruits?" Samad asked.

"Well, we prefer younger recruits," Turner told him. "We find that they adapt better to the training and the rigors of interstellar travel. But people in their thirties and even their forties have become pilots, and, with rejuve, had long and productive careers. However, the sooner you start, the sooner you'll be a Jump pilot. And the training will be much easier for you now."

"I see," Samad said. "In that case, I think I'll wait."

"What! Why?" Turner said, suddenly a little frantic. "You could start tomorrow!"

"I have some obligations at home," Samad said. "May I take these documents with me?"

"B-but you're turning down the opportunity of a life-time!" Turner stammered.

"Only for a while," Samad said. He tucked the folder under his arm and tried to walk calmly out the door. He didn't want Turner to know how very much he wanted to sign those documents. He was terrified that the man would say something that would change his mind. But he owed Teller, and he always paid his debts.

"Samad! Wait!" he heard Turner call as the door swung closed. Samad glanced at his chrono. Teller would be expecting him home soon. Walking out of the recruiting office had been hard, but the more he thought about it, the better he felt. The stars were not going anywhere. Much as he wanted his own life, he could wait until Teller was gone. He owed her his life for that long. But when that debt had been paid, his life would be his own. Someday he would come back. Someday he, too, would have the stars.

CHAPTER 13

SAMAD STEPPED OFF THE SPACE SHUTTLE
into Thalassa's spaceport. It was much smaller than the
spaceport on Bindara or any of the half-dozen other worlds
they had visited on the way home. The people passing
through the port seemed sparse and a little lost, even in that
small immensity. Now that he had seen other worlds, he
knew just how much of a backwater Thalassa was.

Still, it was good to be home again. From the moment he
arrived, everything—the just-right gravity; the smells of
falafel, olive oil, and the nearby ocean; the kiss of the wind
on his face; and the polyglot ring of Thalassa's blend of languages—embraced him and welcomed him home. A tension that he hadn't known he felt slid from him. His face
was stretched into an idiot's happy grin. Home.

"Glad to be back?" Teller asked, with a fond smile.

He nodded. "I didn't know how much I missed Thalassa

until we landed. It's like slipping into a favorite pair of old shoes."

"I know," Teller said. "It's like that for me, too. Let's drop our luggage at the Guild House and go over to Carlucci's to welcome our stomachs home."

"That sounds great," he said. "I'm starving!"

The next few weeks were an idyll of nostalgia and familiarity that all but erased his nascent desire to be a pilot. In between visits with old friends and familiar places, Teller took him to some of the better bars and coffee shops that catered to *omophilos* of both sexes. He was amazed at how many there were, and the welcome they extended to Teller and him. Clearly Teller was as quietly respected here as she was everywhere else on Thalassa.

While he appreciated Teller's kindness in introducing him to the other *omophilos*, he resented the number of older men who clearly considered it their duty to keep an eye on him for Teller. He remembered the forbidden excitement of his secret expeditions to the Bindaran bars. Looking for lovers with an audience of concerned parental figures watching over him took the spice out of it all.

In addition to introducing him to Nueva Ebiza's *omophilos* community, Teller was busy catching up on all that had happened in their absence, reading back newspapers, meeting people, and listening. To his surprise, she took him along to the meetings and frequently asked his opinion on the discussions. Before the meetings, she was careful to explain who they were talking to, and why these people were important, and what the purpose of the meeting was. After the meetings, she would quiz him about what he had learned and ask if he had any suggestions. It was rather like being an apprentice all over again, but what he was learning was so interesting that he did not mind.

One evening, they were having a relaxing supper at a

restaurant in the Old Harbor after a long afternoon of meetings.

"I was rather pleased that we managed to keep Cabrillo reined in over the mining question." Teller was saying. "Mining's one of the hardest things to keep in check. Metal's in such short supply, even with the asteroid mining. I expect you'll have your hands full when you take over from me."

"What do you mean, take over from you?" he demanded.

"Samad, I've got maybe a dozen good years left. Someone needs to take over from me when I can't look after things anymore."

"But why me?" he asked.

"Because I trust you to do a good job. No one else knows my mind like you do. In many ways, I've been training you for this since the day I decided to adopt you."

"Damn it, Teller, you could at least have *asked* me before you decided what I was going to do with the rest of my life!" He threw his napkin on the table and stalked out angrily.

Samad walked down the waterfront, away from the popular night spots and into the working part of the port, deserted now that the workers were off shift. His anger cooled enough for him to think, but he was still furious at Teller for planning his future so callously. He leaned against a stack of empty shipping containers, feeling the rough wood catch on his shoulders. Perhaps he should go now, contact the Pilots Union, sign their paperwork, and leave Thalassa forever.

He looked out across the graveled expanse of the shipping yard, across the dark, shining water that surged quietly in a gentle swell, to the lights of Nueva Ebiza, glistening like an overturned tray of jewels. A flock of night-flying kaala-oo birds flew by overhead, heading out to sea to fish. The sound of their wings was like rustling grass. He took a deep breath. Under the smell of oil, wet wood, and dry gravel, there was the scent of the sea, salty and familiar. Samad felt a lurch of sadness. It would be hard to leave again so soon. But living here meant being caged by Teller's plans and expectations.

He heard footsteps on the dry gravel and looked up. A man was walking toward him; the collar of his dark wool fisherman's coat was turned up high against his face. Under his open coat he was shirtless.

"Hey," said the man. "You here for some fun?" As he came closer, Samad could see that a small bead of bright steel pierced one nipple. There was a tiny bead of gold dangling from an earring, nearly hidden under the russet gleam of his hair. He was not poor, despite his shabby sandals and rough clothes.

"Depends," Samad said carefully. "What kind of fun?"

"Just guys, together. You know what kind of fun I'm talking about," he said with a sidelong look that was both flirtatious and challenging.

Samad nodded, his breathing suddenly coming faster.

The man came closer. "I was going to leave, but then I saw you, and suddenly I wasn't tired anymore." He stopped so close to Samad that he could smell the man's sweat and the familiar, musky scent of sex. "So. You interested?"

Samad lifted his chin and leaned forward just a little. The man slid one hand behind Samad's head and drew him closer. They kissed. The man trailed one finger down Samad's chest, then cupped the urgent bulge in Samad's groin.

"You're interested," the man confirmed with an eager grin. "Come on."

Samad followed the man into a narrow maze of shipping containers. Then, suddenly, there was a gap in the rows of containers, and there, revealed by the fugitive moonlight were more than a dozen men, some watching, others having sex. Men appeared and vanished into the stacks of shipping containers. They skirted the opening and walked into another passageway. Samad could hear the soft sounds of flesh sliding against flesh and urgent cries of release or excitement.

Then they were in a dark cul de sac, and the man knelt in front of Samad. It was so dark that Samad could only just make out the faint gleam of the man's reddish hair as the stranger took Samad's cock in his mouth. Samad lifted his head and stared up at the moon. He felt wild and free again, out from under Teller's well-meaning thumb. Samad gave himself up to the simplicity of sensation.

Samad stayed until the sky grayed toward dawn and the other men scattered. He walked along the deserted waterfront. The moon Amphitrite setting behind Mount Eularia looked pale and spent in the coming dawn. He was tired and sore, but his anger had vanished in satiation. He was too tired to think anymore. All he wanted was sleep. He would worry about Teller after he woke up.

Teller cracked the door to Samad's room and peered inside. He was still asleep, which was no surprise. The gray light of dawn had been shining around the edges of the curtains when she finally heard him come in. She had been awake for several hours, worrying over his angry refusal of all she had offered him. If only she had not sprung it on him so abruptly. She cursed herself for her blunder. It was not how she had planned to tell him. But there was no taking back her mistake now. It would be best not to mention it for a while. She would wait until Samad came forward with some questions.

Teller eased Samad's door shut again and tiptoed down to breakfast. Her business in Nueva Ebiza was nearly done. In a few more days, they would resume their usual peripatetic routine. Once they were traveling again, she would have to find ways to show him that no one else on Thalassa had the training and preparation needed to keep their world green and peaceful.

Samad woke in the late afternoon, feeling sore but pleased with himself after last night's adventure. At last he had found a place where he could escape Teller's all-encompassing oversight. He got out of bed and stretched luxuriously. He had no idea what to do about Teller's expectations for him. They were impossible to live up to. He hoped that she would soon realize it and leave him alone. But he wasn't ready to leave Thalassa yet. For the time being, he would leave things as they were. There would be time for him to realize his own dreams later.

The issue of whether Samad would take up Teller's mantle loomed silently between them for almost a year. Neither of them wanted to acknowledge its existence. Life was much the same as it had always been. But now Teller included him in meetings with an amazing assortment of people: everyone from important public officials and wealthy merchants to fishwives and members of the Beggars' Guild.

"Teller, why are there beggars on Thalassa?" Samad asked one afternoon after leaving a meeting with the head of the Beggars' Guild about how the drought had affected their guild members in the Solegiatta Archipelago.

Teller looked out across the hills to the deep blue sea and shook her head. "I tried for centuries to eliminate poverty, Samad. But you can't completely eradicate poverty without taking away people's freedom to make bad choices as well as good ones. At least no one starves on Thalassa, unless they're too stubborn to accept help."

She sighed. "I'm not God, Samad. I can't control what choices people make. I have done my best to help genera-

tions of good-hearted, compassionate people provide help
for anyone who needs it. If you are hungry, there is food; if
you are naked, there are clothes; if you need shelter, there are
places to take you in. If you're crazy, or poor, or escaping a
bad marriage, there is help. And even that doesn't always
work. I thought that everything was finally working well,
and then I met a child who was hungry, cold, and had no
one to take care of him."

"Me?" Samad asked.

Teller nodded. "So I took you in, but I also started working with the Guild and others to help all the other lost children. We found homes for many of them. And best of all, we
were able to keep others from getting lost. Every few years,
I find a crack where people fall through. And I do what I can
to make sure that it's filled. But new cracks are always opening up. And sometimes there just aren't any solutions. People choose to drink, take drugs, gamble, whatever. And even
if I did have some magic wand that I could wave to make
them stop, I wouldn't. People have a right to make bad
choices as well as good ones, Samad. If that choice was taken
away from them, then this wouldn't be a world I could live
on. I stopped trying to construct a utopia a long, long time
ago. I've just tried to help make Thalassa a world where it
was easy to live a happy life."

"And what makes you think that I'm qualified to fill
your place?" Samad challenged her.

Teller gave him a long, level look. Samad realized that he
was as tall as she was now, maybe even a centimeter or two
taller.

"I've known people twice your age with less than half
your judgment. You listen well, you're compassionate, but
you also see people clearly as they are. You've traveled with
me all over Thalassa. We've seen most of the major inhabited islands on the planet, and many of the minor ones as

well. We've visited hundreds of uninhabited islands. You've seen Thalassa in her wild state, like it was before humans came here. In another ten years, you'll know this world better than all but the oldest and best-traveled storytellers. And lastly, the harsels think you can do it."

"They do?"

Teller nodded. "The harsels' Council of Memory has approved you."

"How long have you been planning this?"

"Ever since you became the youngest Master in the history of the Guild. But I thought I'd have decades, maybe even a century or more to train you. I thought—" She paused. "I thought a lot of things," she finished bleakly.

"Teller, what if—what if something happens to me? Then who would you train to take over for you?"

Teller looked away again. She was silent for a long time. "There isn't anybody else, Samad."

"There has to be. What about Florio?"

"He can't hear the harsels."

"What about Senior Captain Marquez? He's head of the Har Captains' Guild."

Teller shook her head somberly. "He's a merchant at heart. He'd be so interested in prosperity that he'd make Thalassa grow too fast."

"Thalassa's growing?"

"Very slowly, perhaps a quarter of a percent per year. Most of it's due to population growth." She shook her head. "In another four centuries, Thalassans are going to have to start having fewer children." Teller put her hand on Samad's shoulder. "All of the other people I've considered have biases and ties to one group or another. You're young enough not to have to unlearn such things. Trust me, Samad, I've looked for many years for an heir, and you really are the best person for the job." She shook her head. "I wish Abeha were still alive. He could make you understand."

"But he wouldn't try to make me want to do something I didn't want to do," Samad said gently. "I need to be free to make choices you don't like."

Teller looked away, but Samad could see tears welling against her eyelashes. "I need you, Samad."

"I know, and I will be here for you as long as you live. But . . ." He paused, choosing his words carefully. "I want my own life, Teller. You're asking me to take over your life. I can't. I won't."

"But what about Thalassa?" Teller asked.

"Other worlds manage without someone like you. Thalassa will have to manage also."

"Other worlds manage, but not very well," Teller shot back. "Our crime rate is low, maybe one or two murders and a dozen serious crimes of violence a year, on a planet with a population of two million people. Most other planets measure their murder rates in the thousands. We have poverty and poor people, yes, but they have food, and clothing, and usually a warm place to sleep. Other worlds?" She shrugged and looked away. "Perhaps we should have spent more time visiting slums when we were off world. I've spent my whole life working to make Thalassa a good place to live."

"I want my own life, Teller," Samad insisted. "Not yours."

"I know you do, but at least help me while I'm alive."

"I've already said I would," Samad told her.

"But I was talking about Thalassa," she said. "As I age, it's going to be hard for me to keep up with it all. I'll need your help there as well. Please, Samad, there isn't anyone else I trust to do it."

"All right, Teller," Samad said grudgingly. "I'll do it," he said. "But I'm not agreeing to anything more than that."

"I understand, Samad. And I'm grateful to you for what help you've offered."

And so Teller started sending him on errands, carrying messages to this person or that one. Or he carried money or goods where they were needed. Sometimes he was only sent to listen and remember someone's story. A great many of his errands involved the harsels, and these he did gladly. He had sorely missed the company of the great sailing fish. It had been years since Abeha's death, but the company of harsels gave Teller such pain that she rarely sailed on them, preferring to travel on the more expensive human-built sailboats and steamers. So Samad found himself in charge of any problems involving harsels, and any problems that involved traveling via harsel. To his surprise, the harsels were eager to carry him and always told him that Abeha was alive in their memories.

Samad learned quickly. He had to. Many of the errands Teller sent him on were important, if not to the world as a whole, at least to the people involved. As time passed, his responsibilities increased. He spent most of a year working as the aide to a member of the Thalassan assembly, learning the ropes of Thalassan politics from the inside. His Guild-trained memory served him well here. He could repeat long speeches verbatim. He learned to spot treacherous loopholes and irregularities in a piece of proposed legislation.

And he found himself at college, pushed into an accelerated and demanding course of study. Teller had taught him more than he realized. He did very well at school. His grades were good, and he graduated with honors and a sound foundation of useful knowledge.

But as busy as Teller kept him, he still had time to slip out and find the dark places where other men congregated for sex. And sometimes, late at night, he would lie awake and imagine himself riding through Jump Space to a world he had never seen before, free and untethered from the needs of an importunate planet.

Teller closed her 300-year-old diary and turned off the computer. She pushed her chair back from her desk and stood, shrugging her stiff shoulders and massaging her lower back. She had done enough work for today. Samad would be sailing into Bonifacio harbor by the afternoon tide, and she wanted to get the house ready for him.

Teller closed the door to her hidden archives, activated all the palm locks and security codes, and heaped a pile of stones over the keypad box. Stepping back, she frowned at the concealed door, looking for signs of use. Teller picked up a couple of crushed blades of grass that she had tracked into the cave, and then surveyed it all one more time. With a curt nod and a grunt of satisfaction, she headed down the hill.

Teller was grateful to see the house. Her knees were acting up again. For a moment, she pondered the problem of what to do when she couldn't make the trip up the hill anymore, and then pushed it away in annoyance. Hopefully she would be done sorting her archives before then. As she rounded the corner of the house, she saw someone sitting on the front porch. She paused, peering into the shadowy porch, trying to see who it was.

"Hey Teller, it's me," Samad called. "The harsel got in early, and I thought I'd come straight up here and surprise you."

She relaxed when she recognized Samad's voice. "Well then, help me up the stairs, *querido,* and tell me how things are going. I don't get nearly enough gossip up here."

He came down the stairs and gave her his strong right arm to lean on. She needed it more than she would have liked to admit after her long walk. "Ay, you're as handsome as ever, *mijito!* To think of all the women's hearts you've broken."

"Me?" he inquired with a grin. This was an old joke between them. "How would a man of my tastes manage such a thing?"

"By being a man of your tastes, my dear."

"But think of all the men I'm making happy!"

"Ah, you troublemaker!" she scolded. "Come here and give me a hug."

"So," she said, as they went inside, "do you have any new lovers I should know about?"

Samad shrugged. "Maybe. There's Max. We've been going out for a while now, but I don't think it's going to last. I travel too much. He's already started to complain about it. Besides, I'm not ready to settle down yet. Is there anything to eat? I'm hungry."

"There's some nice lamb stew." Teller shook her head. "I wish you'd find a serious lover, Samad. It bothers me that you're so alone."

"It will happen when it's time for it to happen. Stop worrying about me. I'm happy the way I am," Samad reassured her.

"If you say so," Teller said dubiously. Privately, she doubted that, but there was no point in arguing over it. "Sit down and tell me all about what's going on in the world."

Over a bowl of stew that had been simmering on the back of the stove, Teller listened hungrily as he brought her up to date. She was getting lonely up here on her hillside. It was time for her to travel a bit and visit old friends while she still could. She smiled, thinking of Florio, grown broader and fatter and sessile now that he was on the Guild's High Council. It was a good place for him, but perhaps he could do with a bit of a trip as well.

"So what do you think I should do about Cooper Mining and the Islas Verdes?"

"What?" Teller said. "I'm sorry, I was thinking of something else."

Samad looked at her. Was he wondering if she was starting to get senile? It was a question she asked herself a great deal, too, especially when she got caught in the maze of her own memories. Working in the archives only made the problem worse, but there was so much she needed to do.

"I'm fine, Samad," she told him. "I was just thinking of Florio. How is he?"

"Fat and happy, last time I saw him. He and Juana are very happy."

"Oh," Teller said. She had forgotten about Florio's recent marriage. Perhaps she really was getting senile. Or perhaps her wounded vanity had pushed it out of her mind. "I'm glad to hear that, Samad," she said.

"You are?" he asked. "I thought you weren't very happy about Florio's marriage."

Teller shrugged and looked away, "Maybe if I say it often enough, I'll come to believe it."

Samad smiled at her wry comment. "So how are you, really?" he inquired.

"I think I'm spending too much time cooped up with old memories," she admitted. "It's time to give the archives a rest and do a little traveling."

"Where would you like to go?"

She looked past Samad's shoulder, out the window, and past the long, grassy slopes, out at the beckoning azure sea. "I don't know, really. Just away somewhere. It would be good to see old friends again, and maybe even someplace new, someplace I've never been before."

"Is there somewhere you've never been on Thalassa?"

"Samad, there are nearly three million islands on this planet. I haven't managed to set foot on even a tenth of them."

"Yeah, but Teller, you know as well as I do that more than half of those islands are just dots and rocks barely above high tide."

"There are still plenty of sizable islands I've never been to. I've only seen one or two islands in the Sporades chain, and I've never been to the Malagas at all."

"All right then, I'll see what I can do. There's a flyer now to Cabra. We could fly there and then charter a boat and tour the Malagas in style."

"That would be lovely." She glanced down at her legs. "But my knees are starting to trouble me. I don't know how much walking we can do on this trip."

"We'll work something out."

"Maybe some sort of sedan chair, carried by big, strong, handsome men. We can share the big, strong, handsome men," she said with a wicked grin and a lift of one eyebrow.

"Teller!" Samad said, pretending to be shocked.

"Now, dear, don't carry on like that. I know I taught you to share your toys. And they can't *all* be gay, can they?"

"I suppose not," Samad said, heaving a heavy sigh of mock regret. Then he caught her eye and the two of them collapsed in giggles.

Samad watched Teller stumping up the hill to her archives. Teller had always looked old, but until now, she had never *seemed* old. Teller was becoming more lost in her own memories, more absentminded. She moved stiffly now, pushing herself out of chairs when she got up. And sometimes, when Teller was very tired, her hands had a slight tremor.

But most of the time, Teller was her old self: funny, sardonic, and deeply engaged with the world around her. The first draft of her memoir was vivid and compelling, even in its unpolished state, and the archives were beautifully organized. But Teller was lonely, and she was having trouble getting around. He needed to spend more time with her. He decided to encourage more old friends to visit.

But first, they would take a trip. He smiled reminiscently. Traveling with Teller. It would be like old times for him as well. He wasn't even thirty yet, but he felt much, much older. Teller had warned him that the job would take over his life if he let it. But it wasn't until he had boarded the harsel for Bonifacio that he realized how true her warning was. He had felt the surge of the swell rising and falling under the harsel and the wind teasing dark tendrils of his hair, and he realized how small and gray his life had become.

He was spending entirely too much time in his office lately. Teller had managed Thalassa while traveling as an itinerant storyteller. She had no office, and her comm was set to refuse incoming calls. He would have to ask her how she did it. It would make his job so much easier.

"You're doing too much, Samad," she told him as they waited for the ferry. "Sitting still, you're a target for everyone who wants their problems solved by someone else. I moved around, looking for the hidden troubles, the ones that nobody had noticed yet, and the ones that nobody wanted to see. Sometimes the problems were small, a farmer unable to get his crops in because his wife was sick and needed tending. Or it might be the beginnings of a drought on one island, where getting help early would make the difference between a bad year and famine. But always, always, I would try to make sure that there were people ready to fix a problem the next time it came up. That way I wasn't always having to rush back to fix something I fixed a decade ago."

"But you can't be everywhere at once," Samad pointed out.

"No, but the Guild is. I let them do most of the heavy lifting, and only stepped in when I was needed."

"But how could they find you?" he asked.

"They didn't. I found them. I checked in every few weeks."

"Every few weeks!" Samad said, alarmed. "But what if something big came up?"

"Samad, I've never run the planet, I've only been its fairy godmother. There were plenty of other people who could respond to a real disaster without my help. Besides, if a problem was big enough, I'd hear about it anyway. And by checking in infrequently, I'd make sure that the smaller problems got solved by someone else. I'll wager that most of the problems you left behind are going to work themselves out before you get back."

"But there'll be another bunch waiting for me," Samad told her.

"Of course there will be. You've given them a bench to sit on," she observed.

"But how can I turn away from people who need help?"

"You know, when you were young, I used to watch you struggle to do something. I just ached to help you, but you were so proud and so determined to do things yourself. It was the hardest thing in the world to watch you struggle and fail and struggle and fail, but usually you succeeded if I gave you enough time and a bit of encouragement. And by struggling and failing a few times, you learned patience. You need to give the people of Thalassa the chance to learn things the hard way, too, Samad."

"You could have told me that sooner," Samad complained.

Teller looked at him and raised an eyebrow. He knew that look well. There was something he hadn't figured out.

"Oh," he said, and blushed. He realized that she was still letting him learn the hard way.

Teller smiled. "You're doing a fine job, Samad. I'm proud of you."

"I suppose. But I still feel like I've got a lot to learn," he said with a rueful sigh.

"So do I, *mijo*. So do I," Teller replied with a wry smile. "Come on. They're lowering the gangplank, let's go aboard. I'm really looking forward to this cruise, Samad. Thanks so much for arranging it!"

"*De nada, Mamacita,*" Samad said with a fond smile. "It was my pleasure."

Samad watched Teller's face as she slept on the flight back from Cabra to Nueva Ebiza. It had been a good trip. He had enjoyed himself, and so had Teller. They had swung through the Sporades and the Malaga chain, visiting dozens of islands that Teller had never seen before. Despite her aching knees, her eyes were as keen and astute as ever. She had stumped eagerly up and down and around each island, noting the differences and the similarities between the flora and fauna of these remote archipelagos and those of more familiar islands. She listened to the residents' stories about the islands and told a few stories herself. She did all of this at a pace that exhausted him. Yet she showed no signs of weariness until they returned to their inn at Cabra. Then she fell asleep as soon as she climbed into bed and slept the clock around.

She was still the Teller he knew and loved, but it was costing her a great deal to stay that way. She needed someone to help out with the chores. Someone to talk to. Someone to be there if there was an emergency. But Teller regarded her privacy very highly, especially now that she was working so hard on her archives.

He looked out the window of the flyer at the broad, wrinkled expanse of dark blue ocean far below. A small fleet of harsels sailed east toward the Malaga Archipelago, their sails tiny dots in the immensity of the sunlit ocean below.

Teller needed him. No one else would do. He sighed inwardly. He would miss his comfortable life in Nueva Ebiza. Living at Teller's place in Bonifacio meant leaving behind all the comforts of the city: the food, the gossip, and the men. But Teller was worth it.

But who was going to look after her when he had to travel somewhere to put out a fire?

Perhaps he could find some eager young Journeymen storytellers to look after her. And perhaps, just perhaps, one of them might learn enough to take over from him after Teller died. He closed his eyes, sinking into the comfortable, familiar daydream of sitting in a pilot's Jump seat, preparing for a Jump. Just a flick of a few switches, a sudden surge of acceleration, and all his problems would be left behind. . . .

Teller sat alone on her porch, watching the path that led to the house from the road. Samad had been due for several days now, and she was beginning to worry. There had been no major storms, but perhaps some other emergency had arisen that had delayed him.

Teller shook her head, wishing that she could be more help to Samad. But these days, she was barely able to advise. She was so out of touch with current events. It was easier to sit and let herself be waited on by the tribe of eager young apprentices who came and went like flocks of sparrows, picking up the crumbs of stories as they passed through. She still had her stories and an eager audience to listen to them, renewed every few months with fresh ears. But even that was starting to slip away.

Three months ago, she had forgotten the ending of the story about the wise man's donkey attending classes at the University of Chelm. The apprentices sat looking sidelong

at each other as she groped for the ending. At last one of the
Journeymen whispered a prompt in her ear, and the story
sprang back into clear focus. But it had been a bad moment.
She hadn't forgotten the ending to a story since . . . She
couldn't remember when she'd ever forgotten a story. And it
had started happening more and more often. She didn't
mind the everyday memory lapses, forgetting names, or
what day of the week it was. But her stories were her life,
and she was losing them. It was more than she could bear.

The director of the rejuve clinic had talked about manag-
ing her medicines so that her body accompanied her mind
into death. All her preparations for her death had been made
a long time ago. Her estate was prepared, her memoir was as
polished as she could make it, and her archives were all organized and ready for strangers to see. She was ready. It was
time to stop taking the medications that propped up her
failing body. She would speak to Samad about it as soon as
they had a quiet moment together.

She wondered, for perhaps the millionth time, what
Samad would decide to do with his life when he was free of
her. She had made other plans if he chose to walk away from
Thalassa, while still secretly hoping that he would continue
her work. Even vastly expanded Guilds could not do the job
a tenth as capably as Samad. But she saw the longing on his
face whenever he looked up at the night sky.

Teller felt a flicker of her old rage. If only the Pilots
Union had not tried to recruit Samad! But she was too old,
too tired to stay angry for long. She had done her best to
convince Samad to stay and look after Thalassa, but it was
not a job that could be done with an unwilling heart.

If only he weren't so damned good at looking after things.
She had done very little these past few years, nor had she
needed to, and frankly, she had been glad to let him assume
the responsibilities she had shouldered for so very long. She

was so tired and so alone. Abeha was gone, but not forgotten, not yet, at any rate. She missed the harsel and his gentle presence so much. She closed her eyes, and remembered. . . .

"Hey Teller, wake up."

Teller struggled up from a dream of sailing on Abeha's back, blinking and confused. She wasn't on board the harsel; she was here in Bonifacio. Abeha was dead. So were Stephano and the children. Her closed eyes tightened momentarily in pain as she felt the weight of her years. So many people gone, leaving her behind. It was time for her to follow.

"Teller, wake up."

Samad's insistent voice pulled her up out of the last shreds of past dreaming, into the waking present. She still had Samad. He was her last gift to the future, she thought with a smile.

"*Mijo,* you're finally here," she said, looking up at him. "I was getting worried."

"We were windbound coming out of Valldemosa. The harsel had to scull out, half the time against the tide. Then the winds were against us most of the way."

"It sounds like a trying voyage."

"Especially for the harsel. Pakiki tried to talk me into going somewhere else. But when I told him I was visiting you, he strained his sail to get me here. His mother was Wailana, and he says that her memories of you are good ones."

Teller nodded, "And I remember her well, too. Wailana was a sweet, graceful har, small, but fast on a reach. I'm pleased that her line has continued. There was concern that, because she was so small, her young would not survive." Teller felt a twinge of regret at yet another reminder of the centuries of dead friends that trailed in the wake of her memory.

"How are you, Teller?" Samad asked.

Teller shrugged and looked down at the worn floorboards of the ancient house's front porch. "I feel old," she said at last. "Old and tired. My memory's going. And what good is a storyteller who forgets her stories?"

"Everyone forgets once in a while."

"It's not that kind of forgetting, Samad." She looked at him, her faded olive eyes meeting his youthful hazel ones. "I've had all the years the doctors promised, and one or two more besides. I don't think the drugs can prop me up much longer. Nor do I want them to. I don't want to watch my mind go. This last year's been bad enough."

"Teller, I—"

Teller laid her hand on Samad's arm to stop him, "No, *querido,* don't argue with me, please. You saved my life once before. Not this time. I've had half a millenium, and that's enough. It's time to stop the drugs and let nature take its course."

He looked at her, steadily and long. She met his gaze and reached out to touch his cheek. "Please, Samad," she whispered, feeling the tears welling. "Let me go."

"All right," Samad said. "But please wait a few more days. You may be ready for this, but I'm not."

"For a few days, Samad, but no more than that. You won't be losing me right away. It'll take several months for my body to wind down." She smiled. "I don't think this old heart will stop beating very easily. It's too used to ticking along."

"I hope so," Samad said. "It will be like having my heart torn out of my chest when you die."

Teller gave him a piercing look. "But when I am gone, you will be free to live your own life instead of mine."

He looked out across the hills to the sea. "I don't want your death to be the price I have to pay for my freedom."

"Then you should go now. Before I die."

"No," Samad said, shaking his head. "I can't—"

Just then a laughing group of apprentices came up the path from the garden, interrupting their conversation.

The apprentices, perhaps a bit guilty at leaving Teller unattended on the porch, became extremely attentive. It was two more days before Samad and Teller had a quiet moment together.

Finally, Teller sent the apprentices off on errands. "It'll give me some time to catch up with Samad," she said a little pointedly as she sent them off.

"Help me out onto the porch," she said. "It's too nice a day to sit inside."

Taking her arm, Samad helped Teller into her favorite chair and sat beside her. For a while they just sat there quietly, enjoying the beautiful summer afternoon, watching the swift, brilliant sunnu birds speeding after insects, sometimes skimming within inches of their heads as they swept under the overhang of the porch. The iridescent green patches on their backs blazed brilliantly as the birds emerged into the afternoon sunlight.

"It's a beautiful old world," Teller said after a long silence. "I'm going to hate to leave it."

"All the color will go out of the world when you're gone," Samad said, his voice husky with grief.

"Perhaps for a while, *querido,* but I have watched countless people die, and countless more live on. For almost all of the survivors, the color comes back eventually. Perhaps it is muted and more somber in tone, but they do recover. I confess I'm more curious than afraid. I have seen so many people die, leaving me behind. I wonder where they go and what happens. Perhaps nothing at all, perhaps there is some sort of afterlife. For myself, I think I'd prefer to be reincarnated as a harsel. Their souls are so full of joy."

"Teller please, I—" Samad began, feeling tears threaten.

"It's not a tragedy, Samad. I've lived a good life, and an exceptionally long one. I feel a bit of regret and some sadness at leaving this world behind, but I can hardly say that I've been cheated. Besides, I've a bit of time left. Don't bury me just yet."

Samad nodded but didn't speak. Teller could see tears gathering in his eyes.

"You know what I'd really like to do?" Teller said.

"What?" Samad replied.

"Go up to the cave one last time, and sit in my old crew pod. Can you help me up there?"

Samad put his arm under Teller's shoulders, and helped her walk slowly up the hill. They stopped to rest every dozen steps or so. What had once been a fifteen-minute walk took them nearly an hour and a half, but they made it. The door opened at the touch of her palm on the lock. With Samad supporting her, Teller walked to the smallest of Abeha's old crew pods. Samad opened the hatch for her and helped her in.

The pod's lights came on as they entered. Teller smiled. "I'm glad I kept the batteries up on this lifeboat," she said.

"This was a lifeboat?" Samad asked.

Teller nodded, then eased herself into what would have been the pilot's chair. The ancient upholstery crackled and crumbled as she sat down on it, but she paid it no heed. It was old, too.

"Yes, this was Abeha's first crew pod. I brought down one of the starship's lifeboats and adapted it to fit Abeha's hold. It didn't take much to make it work, just a thick layer of soft foam insulation to cushion the sides. I made do with the space-based air system, though it left a lot to be desired. Nowadays the crew pods are much better designed. But this one was the very first pod, and it did its job well enough."

Samad looked around the tiny cramped space, barely four

meters long by three meters wide, and a little more than two meters tall. "I'm amazed you didn't go crazy in here."

Teller shrugged. "I was a Jump pilot, Samad. I was used to living in small, cramped spaces. In some ways living in this pod was much easier. I could go out onto Abeha's back whenever the weather cooperated. And there were always new islands to explore when I couldn't stand it anymore. Besides, I had Abeha's company, which made it all worthwhile. Life was hard but never boring."

Teller closed her eyes, clearly lost in her memories. Samad perched on the edge of the tiny galley table waiting for her to return to the present.

At last she opened her eyes. "Be a dear, Samad, and go get the photo album, the first one."

He went to the shelves and brought it back. He carefully settled the heavy volume in her lap. She opened the album, not to the early pictures of Thalassa, as he had expected, but to the pictures of herself as a young pilot.

She shook her head. "I had the universe by the tail back then," she reminisced with a wistful smile. "I was young and Talented, and by God I knew everything there was to know about being a Jump pilot. Which meant that I knew everything important there was to know about everything. I visited every inhabited world during my career. Leave regulations being what they were, I had a couple of weeks to see the sights, if there were any to be seen. You can cram a hell of a lot of sightseeing into two weeks. Most of the other pilots thought I was crazy, spending all that time sightseeing on a dirtball, but it was what I liked doing. I used to have a huge picture file of all the places I'd been to, but I erased every last copy in a fit of depression. I've regretted it ever since. But my remorse over that loss led to all of this," she waved, her gesture taking in the archive that filled the huge cavern.

"I had an incredible time while my Talent lasted, Samad.
And my Talent lasted much, much longer than most of the
other Jump pilots of my time. But when it ended . . ." She
shook her head. "It really was like all the color was gone out
of the world, and the flavor, and the music as well. If it
hadn't been for Abeha—" Teller shook her head, her eyes
hooded. "It was years before my life got back into some kind
of balance. And I was lucky. I've searched all the Pilots
Union archives I could get into, and I talked to others with
access to the restricted archives. As far as I know, I'm the
only Pilot ever to live more than ten years beyond the loss of
their Talent. That fat pension they offer is a joke. Since pilots die only a few years after burnout, the Union actually
makes money on it. That's why I've taken such pleasure in
collecting my pension all these years. I don't need their
blood money, but I enjoy milking them of every penny they
owe me."

She looked at him, her eyes returning from the distant
past to the present. "I know you want to be a pilot, Samad. I
understand better than you do why it calls to you so. But
promise me one thing. Before you accept the Union's offer,
go talk to some ex-pilots. There's probably one or two in the
bars around the spaceport, poor souls."

Samad looked down, deeply ashamed. All these years
Teller had known his secret desire.

"I didn't want you to know," he said. "I didn't want to
hurt you."

"It's all right, Samad," Teller soothed. "I understand, and
I appreciate the kindness you were trying to show me."

"Thank you," Samad said when he could speak again.
"I'm sorry."

Teller shrugged. "Nobody said that life is fair. I've lived a
long and mostly fortunate life. I'm sorry that you don't want
to take over from me. But it is your life, Samad. You have to

live it for yourself. Just promise me that you'll talk to an ex-pilot before you go. Please, Samad. It's important. I can't rest easy until you promise me that." Her hand gripped his arm, and her eyes focused with burning intensity upon his face.

"All right, Teller," Samad said gently. "I will. I promise."

Teller searched his face a moment or two longer. "Thank you, Samad. Let me rest here for a few minutes, and then we can start back." Her eyes slid shut, and she lay back against the ancient upholstery. Her breathing became deep and even, and then a small snore rattled in her nose. Samad smiled. She was asleep.

Two days later, Teller stopped the geriatric drugs. For a few days nothing happened; then she began sleeping a lot more. When she was awake she seemed distant and distracted much of the time, as though she'd let some essential part of herself slip from her grasp.

Samad watched with a growing sense of pain and help-lessness. A logical part of his mind knew that Teller had lived a long, full life and was ready to die. But the boy who still needed her overwhelmed his logical mind. He waited on Teller as attentively and anxiously as he had during their first months together. They sat on the porch, looking out over the rolling hills and the ocean, and watched the birds sweep and glide, making the air joyous with their flight and their song. Sitting there on the porch, it seemed somehow impossible that Teller should be slipping away from him while the world was in the full flood tide of summer.

Word of her slow dying spread. During the rest of the summer, visitors came to the little house in a respectful trickle. Only a very few of the visitors roused Teller from her absent graciousness, and those were old, old friends. Large fleets of harsels assembled in the channel offshore. Once,

Samad and the apprentices carried her down to the beach to hear their singing. Supported by Samad and one of the apprentices, she waded into the warm, calm water. They held her up as the harsels sang their farewells. She closed her eyes and listened, her seamed and ancient face alight with joy. Then suddenly her eyes widened in shock, and she clutched Samad's arm tightly.

"It's Abeha, Samad! Abeha's out there. I can hear him!"

"Teller, it can't be! Abeha's dead! We saw her die!" Samad told her.

"But I hear him!" she insisted "Abeha!"

She tried to struggle free of their grasp.

"Take her out of the water!" Samad shouted at the frightened huddle of apprentices. "Take her!"

She struggled as the apprentices carried her back to shore. Once they put her in the litter, she seemed to remember where she was. Samad waded back out in the water and looked at the now-silent fleet of harsels. He reached outward, searching with his mind. He had heard that fleeting voice, too. It had sounded hauntingly similar to Abeha's. But it was gone now. He wasn't even sure it had been real.

Teller wept quietly all the way home.

Florio arrived a week later. He came slowly up the path, dressed in black as always, his bright cloak draped over one arm. Teller watched him come, her faded eyes squinting against the glare, her face giving away nothing. Florio came up to the front steps and stood looking at Teller for a long moment. There was a liberal salting of gray in his hair, and he had grown much wider and softer about the middle.

"Hello, *aghapitos,*" Teller said at last. "I hoped you'd come."

"I'm here, *aghapitee,*" Florio said.

"And Juana?" Teller asked a little coldly.

"She's home with the children," Florio told her. "I came alone."

"I see," Teller said. "Thank you."

"Of course," Florio replied.

"Samad, could you ask the apprentices to bring us some lemonade and a cool, damp towel? Florio must be very hot and thirsty from his long walk."

"Of course," Samad said and headed inside, grateful to escape the building tension on the porch.

Teller had never really forgiven Florio for marrying, but Samad knew how much Florio had longed for a family, something Teller could never give him. He took his time with the lemonade, leaving the two of them alone for as long as he could manage. When he came out, Florio was kneeling before Teller, his head in her lap, weeping. Teller was stroking his head. She looked up at Samad and held a finger to her lips. Samad set the tray down and slipped quietly back inside.

Florio stayed the night. He seemed subdued and quiet. After Teller went to bed, Florio and Samad sat on the porch watching Thetis, the smaller moon, rise over the orchard. Nightflicks whizzed past in search of flying insects.

"I thought I was over her, Samad," Florio said. "I knew she had lived a long time, but she never really seemed *old* before. Seeing her like this, it—" He shook his head and took a deep pull from a bottle of the potent local cider. "How can you stand it?" he asked.

"She's my mother, Florio. Maybe that makes it easier to accept. But it's just as hard as losing Abeha. Worse, in some ways. When Teller goes, it'll be my last link with Abeha. With Thalassa, too, I guess." He looked up at the rising moon and sighed.

"You're still determined to become a pilot?" Florio asked.

"It's been my dream for a long time. I've only waited because of Teller."

Florio took another pull of his cider. "God, I'll miss you, Samad."

"But you have Juana and the kids," Samad reminded him.

"I do indeed. Some days it's all that keeps me anchored to this world," he confessed. "I envy you a bit. You'll get to see so much. Bring some of it back here to share with the rest of us." Florio got up a little unsteadily. "I'm starting to feel that wicked cider of yours. Time for me to turn in. Good night, Samad."

Florio left shortly after breakfast, walking down the long drive. Teller and Samad sat on the porch and watched until he was out of sight.

"Well, that's another thread cut," was all Teller said. But Samad could see the sheen of unshed tears in her eyes.

The late-summer heat was broken by a sudden thunderstorm. The weather turned cool and cloudy, and then the fall rains began in earnest. One of the apprentices came down with a cold after a trip to the village. Despite all their care, Teller caught it as well. It rapidly developed into pneumonia. She refused all treatment except some mild pain medication and a little supplementary oxygen to make her more comfortable.

"I appreciate your concern, but it's time for me to go," she said in response to the doctor's suggestions. "I'm in no pain and that's the important thing. Samad, come sit by me for a while."

He sat in the familiar chair by her bed.

"It won't be long now, Samad," she told him and paused to get her breath back. "Pneumonia's gentle and not too uncomfortable." Another pause for breath. "At least so far." She looked up at him. Her expressive eyes looked tired, her face seemed haggard. Her lips were tinged with blue. "We've already said it all. Several times."

Samad nodded. *"Sí, mi madre.* But I still love you."

Teller smiled, a radiant, room-lighting smile. "I know. And I love you." She drew another breath. "Don't waste time grieving for me." Breath. "The world—" A pause, searching for words and breath together. "The universe is too beautiful. Life is too short. Even mine."

He nodded, stroking her hand, trying not to cry. She lifted her hand and put her fingers to his cheeks and gently thumbed the tears away.

"You won't forget what you promised? About talking to the pilots?"

Samad shook his head. "Of course not."

"Thank you, *mijito.* Thank you for everything."

Samad nodded and squeezed her hand. He wanted desperately to say something, anything, but there were no words for how much he was feeling.

Teller looked at him and put her fingers to his lips. "I know," she said. "I know."

They sat together in silence, holding hands for a long while. Eventually Samad realized that she was asleep. He tiptoed out.

Later that day Teller's fever rose. She slipped in and out of consciousness. There was one moment when she awoke, looked at him with deep, knowing lucidity and said, "Tell Abeha to remember me with love. I'm sorry I couldn't wait for him."

"I will," Samad reassured her, hair prickling on the back of his neck. "It's all right, Teller, I'll tell Abeha for you." He smoothed her anxious forehead. "Sleep now, *Mamacita.* I'll be here if you need me."

"Thank you, *mijito,*" she said and slid into unconsciousness again.

Samad sat beside her all that day and the next as Teller's life slowly ebbed. The apprentices slipped in and out bringing food, water, and whatever comfort they could. By the evening of the second day, she was deep in a coma, her breathing wet and labored. Samad sat beside her bed, keeping vigil. Sometime late in the night he fell asleep. He awoke in a gray, watery dawn, aware that something had changed. He looked at Teller and realized that she had stopped breathing. He put his head to her chest, listening for a heartbeat, felt at her throat for a pulse, and found only cooling stillness.

He sat staring at Teller's bony, worn-out corpse, feeling oddly light and unreal. It was finally here, the moment he had both dreaded and looked forward to. He was finally free. And he was utterly alone.

CHAPTER 14

THE FUNERAL AND THE VERY FEW LOOSE ends that Teller left behind after her death were all taken care of. Samad checked the dark, silent farmhouse one more time to make sure that everything was turned off and safely stowed. Then he hefted his pack onto his back. He closed and locked the door behind him. After hanging the key on a hook by the door, he started down the slope. The Guild would take over and maintain the house as a retreat for storytellers. Thirty years from now, someone would "discover" Teller's archives. By then, Samad supposed he would be long gone. He draped his brightly colored storyteller's cloak over his shoulders to keep off the light autumn drizzle, picked up his staff, and walked down the porch steps.

He walked quickly from the house, shoulders hunched into the load of his pack. He did not look back. He wanted to remember the house as it was when Teller was alive, not as the darkened, desolate place it seemed now. He strode down the long, half-overgrown track leading away from the house and onto the road that led to Bonifacio's small harbor. From there, he would take a ship to Nueva Ebiza. And then he would deal with his last promise to Teller. But for now his life would consist of one step in front of the other. He felt empty as an old, weathered, burlap sack hanging on a fence line, the sort of thing shepherds hung up during lambing season and then forgot. He smiled. That's what he was, and that's what he wanted to be: forgotten, even by himself.

A small, prim black-and-white nameplate over the doorbell welcomed the visitor to Our Lady of Perpetual Devotion Mission, run by Father Russell. Samad hesitated a moment, his finger wavering over the doorbell. This promise was the last thing that tied him to Teller, and he was oddly reluctant to free himself. He smoothed his hair back nervously, then rang the bell.

A fine-boned woman in her late forties answered the door. "Can I help you?"

"Is Father Russell here?"

"I'm Father Russell," she told him with a wide, distinctly unclerical grin. "How may I help you?"

"It's kind of an odd request, ah, Father."

"We get those from time to time here," she said. "Why don't you come into my office and we'll talk about it over some coffee. We make good coffee. It seems to attract lost souls."

Father Russell ushered him into a comfortably shabby room lined with bookshelves overflowing with well-thumbed books. She motioned him into a battered leather armchair beside a small table set with a chessboard. A wimpled novice in a snow-white habit brought in a small tray with coffee and a plate of ginger cookies. Samad glanced at the novice, and then looked again.

"You look familiar——" Samad began.

"Perhaps it was in my former life," the nun replied in a husky contralto. "I'm Sister Valencia now." There was a note of finality in that statement that invited Samad to rein in his curiosity. But he remembered where he had seen Sister Valencia before. She had been in one of the *omophilos* cruising grounds near the port, wearing only a leather harness and metal jewelry in improbable places. And Sister Reynolds had been most unquestionably male.

"Thank you, Sister Valencia," Father Russell said, fixing Samad with a quelling look that reminded him painfully of Teller, though this slender, birdlike woman was nothing at all like her.

Sister Valencia left the room, closing the door.

"I'm sorry. I think I met Sister Valencia under rather different circumstances," Samad began. "I hadn't realized how liberal the Catholic Church had become."

"We're not quite *that* liberal. But I thought that Sister Valencia should be given a chance to sort out . . ." she paused, hovering over the pronoun, ". . . his vocation," she finally finished. "It's not like the other sisters' chastity is in any danger, is it?" she confided, pouring coffee. "I've, ah, sent word of my spiritual dilemma to the Mother Church in Rome. Unfortunately, it wound up going by slow freight. Hopefully, Sister Valencia will have worked out her vocation one way or another by the time my letter reaches Rome."

"It should be interesting," Samad remarked dryly.

"What was it you said you wanted, Mr.——?"

"Bernardia. Abd-al Samad Bernardia. Call me Samad," he told her. "The Storytellers' Guild gave me your name."

"Ah yes, the Guild said you might contact me."

"Do you still work with retired Jump pilots?"

"Among other people in need, yes." Father Russell admitted warily. "But Jump pilots are a special case." She looked distant and very sad for a moment. "They have such physical riches and such empty souls," she murmured. Then, returning to the present: "Why are you interested in retired Jump pilots?"

"I want to become a pilot, but I promised my mother that I'd talk to some retired pilots before I committed myself. She died about a month ago."

"I'm very sorry to hear that Samad."

Samad shrugged, not really wanting to talk about Teller yet.

"You know, not everyone can be a Jump pilot," Russell began carefully.

"I've been tested," Samad assured her. "I'm Talented."

"I see," she began. "And you're sure this is what you want?"

Samad shrugged, then nodded. "All I need to do is talk to a couple of retired pilots to fulfill my promise, and then I can go start my training."

"Well then," she said, activating her comp unit.

Samad waited while she frowned severely at the screen and tapped some keys. "Aha!" she said, at last. "Here we are." She flipped the screen so that he could see it. There was a long list of names. Beside all but three the word *deceased* blinked in red letters.

"We don't have very many pilots in our active lists at the moment, Samad. Usually we don't release names like this, but the Guild has assured me of your discretion. And who knows? Perhaps you'll distract them from their self-destruction for a bit." She tapped another key, and the printer hummed. She pulled the sheet from the printer. "One of the things I like about Thalassa is that you still use paper. Everyone else prints out on plastic, and I hate the slick feel of it." She looked up at him, her blue eyes serious. "Don't expect too much when you visit these pilots. They're drunk or drugged most of the time. I'd appreciate it if you could make a point of visiting Eric Kellen. We haven't heard from him for some time, and I'm a bit worried that he's joined the deceased list. We can't do much for the pilots, but we try to keep them alive as long as we can. Where there's life, there's always the possibility of redemption."

"Thank you, Father Russell. It'll be my pleasure to find him for you."

"I doubt it," she said flatly, "but thank you for the trouble you're taking. The Guild said you were extremely trustworthy, or I wouldn't have given you those names. I hope you won't violate that trust by taking advantage of those poor souls."

Eric Kellen was passed out drunk in his apartment. Flies swarmed on the rotting food and dirty dishes in the sink. Samad opened all the windows to air the apartment, then cleaned the unconscious Kellen up with the skill he'd gained from nursing Teller. The mattress was beyond saving, so Samad eased the man onto the couch, its filthiness covered with the only clean sheet Samad could find. Kellen barely stirred as Samad laid him back down.

His patient taken care of, Samad tackled the kitchen. He cleared out the rotting food and washed the dishes. He was finishing up the counters when Kellen awoke.

"Who the hell are you?" Kellen said groggily.

"Father Russell sent me to check up on you. She was worried."

Kellen sat up slowly and looked around the apartment, his face pale and haggard. "Since when do the Jesuits provide maid service?"

Samad shrugged. "It needed doing, so I did it."

"And who was the drunk in *your* family," he asked cynically.

Samad stared at him for a long moment, too shocked to speak. "My mother. She was a pilot, too. I found her body after she overdosed. I was six years old."

Kellen scrubbed irritably at his face, covered with several days of graying stubble, and looked ruefully up at Samad, standing in the door of the kitchen. "Ah, hell. I'm sorry. I'm just an old drunk shooting off my mouth. You shouldn't pay any attention to me."

Samad shrugged.

"Look, let me buy you breakfast," Kellen offered. "'S the least I can do. Give me a few minutes to get cleaned up and woken up some more."

He staggered into the bathroom. Samad heard retching sounds, then the sound of the shower running for a very long time, and finally a shaver. Then Kellen emerged wrapped in a torn and battered-looking bathrobe, and vanished into the bedroom. He reappeared dressed in wrinkled but serviceable clothes. By then, Samad had made some coffee.

"Thanks, son," Kellen said as he took the steaming cup that Samad held out. "A couple of liters of this stuff, and I'll be nearly human again. C'mon, let's go get some breakfast. There's a café at the end of the street that makes really good cinnamon rolls."

"So what was it like, being a pilot?" Samad asked as the waitress poured their coffee.

"Mostly it's a job, like driving a jitney. Go here. Load this. Check that. Make sure life support is running. But then you'd Jump and that—" He shook his head, and his grim, pasty face was suddenly illuminated by a smile as beautiful as it was unexpected. "It was like . . . like . . ." He shook his head. "It was wonderful, more wonderful than you can imagine. But after the Jump, you forgot everything except how wonderful it was, and all you wanted was to Jump again." He shook his head. "I shaved my leave time, traded ships, bribed people, anything to get back into Jump Space as quickly as possible." His smile vanished as suddenly as it had come, and his face seemed to crumple like wet paper. "But never again. My Talent's gone. Crapped out. I barely made it back alive. I wish to hell I hadn't." He looked at Samad. "That's why I drink. To remember how good it felt to Jump. Or maybe it's to forget how good it was."

"But you're killing yourself," Samad pointed out.

"Hell, kid, we're all dying one day at a time. Besides, what the hell else am I going to do with my life?"

"You could do what other people do with their lives. You could savor good food. Read a book or two. Plant something and watch it grow. Make friends. Fall in love. Raise children."

"Or drink," Kellen said. He signaled the waitress for the check, slapped a bill on the table for at least twice the amount of the tab, and stood. "Don't try saving me, Samad. It's my life, and I don't want to be saved." With that, Kellen turned and left the restaurant.

Samad stared after him, feeling lost. Eric Kellen wasn't at all what he had expected. He had expected moroseness, or drunken maudlin ravings, not this clear, cold self-knowledge. It chilled him. Was this his future? And if it was, did he still want the freedom of the stars so much? Was there anything he could do to help Kellen? Perhaps, if he could find a way to help Kellen and the others, he might find a way to avoid their fate.

"Actually, he's doing better than I expected," Father Russell told him when Samad reported back on Kellen's condition.

"Isn't there anything that can be done to help him and the others?" Samad asked. The other pilots had been much worse than Kellen. One had attacked him in a blind rage.

Fortunately, he had been drunk and easy to dodge. The other pilot had been dying of an overdose when Samad found her. She'd cursed at him when she woke up in the hospital, still alive. He shuddered, remembering his birth mother's cold, unresponsive corpse.

Father Russell spread her hands skyward in beseeching helplessness. "If there is, I don't know it. I'm good at my vocation, Samad. I've helped hundreds of people: drunks, addicts, runaways, the insane, and the just plain lost, but pilots—" She shook her head. "Pilots are different. They've crossed some kind of event horizon, and there's no pulling them back. There's something missing in their heads, and they drink and drug themselves to kill the pain of that. I've tried everything I can think of to save them, but it's as though part of them is already gone and the rest is eager to follow. No one really understands why burned-out pilots have such a strong death wish."

"Isn't anyone doing anything about it?" Samad asked.

Father Russell shrugged. "Many people have tried, but nothing works. People have to *want* to live before you can help them. And pilots—" She spread her hands again. "It's like they have a hole in their soul, Samad. Something about losing their Talent changes them. I don't know whether it's a physical change or a spiritual one. But it's real, and it's deadly, and as far as I know, every single burned-out pilot has that same desire to die." She held up one pale, delicate forefinger. "Candle. Moth," she said as her other hand fluttered toward her upheld finger, touched the tip, and fell away again to lie limp on her desk. "Every single one."

"Not all of them. I know one who lived a long, full life afterward. She overcame that urge to die." He remembered Teller after Abeha's death. "Most of the time," he added.

"Either she was made of steel, or she stumbled onto something that saved her. If you can figure out what it was,

Samad, and can make it work for the others . . . Go ahead and try, son. Go ahead and try. I think I can trust you not to cause them any further harm."

"Thank you, Father Russell. I'll do my best."

Samad walked along the waterfront, watching the boats and harsels loading and unloading, and turning the problem of the pilots over in his mind. Teller had somehow avoided the other pilots' grim fate. But he could not strand the ex-pilots on deserted planets, and he could not give them Abeha to keep them company.

But there were other harsels. Perhaps a harsel's presence could help the other pilots the way Abeha had helped Teller. It might not work, but it was worth a try. He strode with sudden purpose down the long floating pier where the harsels docked.

Eric stood with him on the long wharf, blinking in the bright morning sun like a freed prisoner. "God only knows why I let you coax me out here at this god-awful hour of the morning. Hell, the sun isn't even properly up in the sky yet," he said, squinting up at the late morning sun. "And all this just to ride on the back of a goddamned fish. I'll say this, Samad, you sure are a persistent bastard."

Samad lifted one eyebrow in sarcastic inquiry, but he was pleased that Eric had shown up. It had taken a month of nagging and pleading to get him to agree to this trip. He hadn't really expected him to come.

Just then, the harsel surfaced, snapping its sail open in a bright explosion of spray. A few drops landed on Samad and Eric.

"And I'm wet, on top of everything else," Eric muttered sourly.

"I RATHER LIKE IT WET," the surfacing harsel remarked.

Eric jumped and looked around. Samad smiled innocently. "Something the matter, Eric?" he asked.

"Just thought I heard someone say something," he
grunted with a suspicious glance at the approaching harsel.

Samad looked from the harsel to Eric and back again,
startled but relieved. Eric had heard the harsel. That was an
excellent sign. It meant that there was hope after all.

Just then, their har captain came striding down the dock.
"I'm Jahan Billacois, partner to Elawe. I understand we'll be
taking you to Formentera Island. Are you all ready to go?"

Samad saw Kellen looking at Jahan, with her thick braid
of dark hair and long, slanted, flashing eyes. "Maybe it
won't be such a bad trip after all," he murmured to Samad,
as the har captain stepped aboard the harsel. "The scenery
just got a hell of a lot better."

"She's married," Samad murmured reprovingly. "Behave
yourself." He wanted Eric's mind focused outward, on the
harsels, not on Jahan, who was beautiful and very, very single.

"Hell!" Eric complained. "The booze on this island
you're taking me to had better be worth the trip."

Samad saw Jahan watching them. Eric noticed, too, and
smiled at her. She tossed her braid disdainfully over one
shoulder and stepped onto the harsel.

Samad had lured Eric on this trip with tales of the fabled
wineries over on Formentera, a three-day trip by harsel.
"Don't worry, Eric, it's worth the trip." It was, too. But
Samad was hoping that the harsels would distract him from
the wineries.

"We're ready," Samad told her.

"Good. We should be on our way before the tide turns."

The harsel opened his hold. Jahan showed them where to
stow their gear in the crew pod's guest cabin and then went
back up onto the harsel's back.

"Whenever you're ready, Elawe," Jahan said.

The harsel sculled once, twice, three times, with his powerful tail, driving them away from the dock. Then his sail shifted and tightened, filling with wind, and they were under way.

"Jahan, would you introduce us to your harsel?" Samad asked.

"Can he talk to them?" she said, gesturing at Eric with a toss of her head.

"I think he can hear Elawe when he talks to him."

"I see," Jahan said, sounding a little less condescending. "Elawe, allow me to introduce Samad to you."

"GREETINGS, SAMAD. THE HARSELS REMEMBER YOU. IT IS AN HONOR TO TRAVEL WITH YOU."

"Thank you, Elawe," Samad said inwardly, moved by the harsel's words. As far as the harsels were concerned, a person was not truly dead until she was forgotten. For the harsels, Teller was still alive. Samad felt the sudden pricking of tears. "And may I introduce you to my friend Eric," he said aloud.

"GREETINGS, ERIC."

Eric had been watching this exchange with puzzlement. He jumped as though stuck with a pin. "What the hell was that?" he asked.

"That was Elawe," Samad explained. "The harsel that's carrying us."

"They talk?" Eric asked.

"To those who have the gift of hearing them," Jahan said. "Not many can." She looked at Eric with a little less disdain.

"H-how do I talk back?" he asked. He looked shaken but excited, too.

"You can just say something out loud while holding him in your mind. It takes a little practice before you can speak silently to a harsel," Samad said.

"Hello, Great One," Eric said.

The harsel gonged laughter. "MY NAME IS ELAWE, ERIC."

"It—he talked back!" Eric said. Jahan glanced at Samad, clearly wondering what was going on.

"Just wait and see," Samad whispered to her before she could speak.

"OF COURSE," Elawe said. "YOU SPOKE TO ME, DIDN'T YOU?"

"I—you—" Eric stammered. "How do you *do* that?"

"DO WHAT?" Elawe inquired.

"Talk. No, I mean—talk like *that?* In my head," He glanced at Jahan and Samad.

"I'M A HARSEL, ERIC. IT'S HOW WE TALK."

"You mean," Eric breathed, his face shining now, "there are others like you?"

Laughter gonged through their minds. "OF COURSE. SEVERAL LARGE OCEANS FULL," Elawe told Eric.

Jahan gave Samad a questioning look. He drew her aft, giving Eric privacy. "I was hoping he'd bond with a wild harsel," he told the har captain.

"I see," she said, looking at Eric speculatively. "Do you think he could become a har captain?" Samad could hear the doubt in her voice.

"I don't know. This is the first time I've tried anything like this. He's an ex-pilot, and I was hoping that it would help him."

"You think he's another Pilot?" she asked incredulously.

"No, but I think the hars can help him," he told her.

Jahan looked again at Eric with a frown on her face.

"The Pilot was the only Jump pilot who didn't kill herself," Samad explained. "Maybe it was because of her harsel."

"The Pilot is a legend," Jahan said.

"And Pilot's Island?" Samad replied, unwilling to reveal Teller's secret.

"No one ever found the Pilot," Jahan pointed out. "Perhaps she killed herself like all the other pilots did."

"The harsels don't think so."

Jahan looked at him dubiously.

"It's true," Samad said. "Abeha told me so." Telling the truth about the Pilot was like sailing into the wind's eye. He could come only so close and no farther. "The harsels still remember the Pilot. Ask Elawe," he said, hoping that the harsel would finally be willing to reveal their closely-held secret.

Jahan's eyes unfocussed as she spoke inwardly to Elawe.

"IT'S OKAY?" Elawe asked him.

"Yes," Samad replied. He sensed Elawe mind-speaking to Jahan.

Jahan's eyes opened wide in shock. "He says you're right. He told me that the Pilot is real, and that she still lives in their memories!" Jahan looked at Eric, who was seated near the mast, watching the channel markers. "But ex-Jump pilots are not exactly reliable, Samad. What if Eric hurts the harsel he bonds with?"

"I think we should let the harsels decide," Samad told her. "They see what we can only guess at."

Jahan looked at Eric, who was seated near the base of Elawe's mast, gazing up in wonder at the curve of the harsel's sail. "Very well," she said. "We will leave it up to the harsels." Her broad face took on the absorbed look of someone speaking inwardly for a moment.

"Elawe agrees. If he judges that Eric is worthy, he will approach some of the wild harsels and see if any of them would like a partner."

Samad nodded. "Thank you, Jahan." And inwardly, "Thank you, Elawe."

"IT'S AN INTERESTING PROJECT, SAMAD. I'M GLAD TO BE ABLE TO HELP," the har replied. "BESIDES, I LIKE ERIC."

It was as much as he could hope for. Everything now depended on Eric. The rest of the day was smooth, sweet sailing across the Strait, with Nueva Ebiza dwindling behind them. Eric sat near the mast looking out over the water and communing with the harsel, his face alight with wonder.

"He certainly likes Elawe well enough," Jahan said. There was a sharp note in her voice.

"Are you jealous?" Samad asked.

Jahan shrugged. "I'm used to getting a little more attention from men."

"Some of that may be my fault," Samad confessed. "I told him you were married."

"Why the hell did you do that?" she asked.

"He needs to focus on the harsel, Jahan. He's no good to anyone the way he is. If the harsel can pull him out of his decline, then maybe he'll be worth something to somebody." He shrugged, embarrassed. "And I didn't think you'd be interested."

"Did I say I was interested?" Jahan inquired.

"No, you didn't."

"Well then," Jahan concluded and turned back to watch Eric at the mast.

Samad turned away to hide his smile. For someone who wasn't interested, she certainly was spending a lot of time looking at Eric.

The next morning dawned fair and clear, with a stiff wind whipping up whitecaps. Jahan made breakfast. Eric ate with a good appetite, alert and almost chatty. His eyes seemed clearer today, too.

"Can I get you anything to drink?" Samad asked him.

"No thanks, Samad. This orange juice is just fine."

"All right," Samad said. He hadn't seen Eric drink anything stronger than orange juice the whole time they'd been on board. And judging by his alert interest in the world, he hadn't been drinking on the sly. But Samad was afraid that asking him outright would upset Eric's fragile new balance. Still, the signs were promising.

"HIS BODY WANTS A DRINK, BUT HIS MIND DOES NOT." Elawe told him. "SO FAR HE'S FIGHTING THE DESIRE, BUT HE NEEDS A HARSEL OF HIS OWN SOON."

"Any luck in finding one?" Samad asked inwardly.

"I AM CALLING AND LOOKING. I WILL LET YOU KNOW WHEN I FIND THEM."

About an hour after breakfast, Elawe suddenly fell off to leeward. Jahan sat up and looked around.

"THERE'S A FLEET OF WILD HARSELS JUST OVER THE HORIZON," Elawe announced. "I THOUGHT ERIC MIGHT LIKE TO SEE THEM."

"SEVERAL OF THE YOUNGER ONES ARE CONSIDERING PARTNERING WITH A HUMAN," the harsel told Jahan and Samad privately.

Eric went forward and searched the horizon intently, heedless of the spray that dashed over him as the harsel breasted the white-capped waves. Sensing Eric's eager curiosity, Elawe trimmed his sail, heeling over as he sped through the water.

It had been a long time since Samad had ridden the back of a fast-sailing harsel. He had forgotten the exhilaration of it. He felt a pang of longing for Abeha. He missed her so much.

"HER MEMORIES LIVE ON," Elawe reminded him.

"Look! There they are!" Eric cried. And in the distance Samad could see a cluster of sails, dark against the light sky.

The harsels came about, clearly intending to cross their course. Jahan handed Samad her binoculars, and he surveyed the fleet as it approached. It was a large fleet of twenty-eight, no, twenty-nine sail of harsels. It was a créche fleet. More than half of the approaching harsels were youngsters from several different breeding seasons. They ranged in size from two to eight meters long. The smaller harlings were escorted by four or five young adults.

As they approached, two or three of the harlings, curious about Elawe and his passengers, sailed out from the shelter of their escort. Immediately two of the escort tacked sharply, herding the harlings back into the shelter of their elders. Elawe headed up into the wind and slowed to a slow cruise, while he introduced himself and explained their mission.

A young harsel broke off from the fleet and circled them curiously. He was a trim harsel, about a dozen meters long, with a very white sail. The young harsel was just one season older than Abeha's offspring. Seeing the harlings made Samad wonder if any of Abeha's children had survived.

The young harsel probed his mind.

"I AM HAU'OLI. ARE YOU THE ONE WHO IS SEEKING A PARTNER?" the har asked, its voice subdued with nervousness.

"No, the one you seek is up there," Samad said looking at Eric, standing just forward of the mast. "But he does not yet know that he is seeking a partner."

"THANK YOU." The young harsel paused. "YOU KNEW ABEHA BUT WERE NOT HER PARTNER."

Samad inclined his head in assent.

"ABEHA'S MEMORIES ARE ALIVE WITH US. SHE SENDS YOU GREETINGS."

Samad felt his stomach lurch with a mingling of cold surprise and illogical hope. He still found it hard to accept the harsel's belief in the real presence of memories. "Thank you," he managed. "I carry Abeha's memories in my heart." It was the polite formula the harsel used when speaking of the dead.

"AND SHE HOLDS TELLER'S MEMORY IN HERS," Hau'oli told him.

Samad was relieved when the wild harsel's mind shifted

its focus to speak to Eric. Eric's face lit up as Hau'oli spoke to him. Jahan glanced at Samad, her face carefully neutral.

There was a long, hanging moment as Eric and the wild harsel probed each other. The lapping of the waves and the wind in the harsels' sails seemed suddenly very loud.

"Hau'oli wants me to ride on his back!" Eric called excitedly. "Is it all right?"

"Of course it is!" Jahan called. "It's a great honor to be invited to ride on a wild harsel."

"Go ahead, Eric. We can wait."

The circling harsel respectfully approached Elawe from the leeward side. Elawe slackened his sail and graciously invited the young harsel to approach. When they were alongside, Eric stepped onto Hau'oli's back, his face radiant with happiness. The younger harsel sculled away from Elawe, then tightened its sail and shot off on a tight-hauled beam reach, clearly elated to have coaxed Eric aboard.

"What do you think?" Jahan asked Samad. "Will they partner?"

"I thought we were letting the harsel decide," Samad teased. "But I hope so." He looked at Hau'oli, pleased and hopeful for Eric, but also a little sad. He missed Abeha so much. There was a large, unacknowledged hole in his heart that he had been stepping around for the better part of two decades. He had hidden his own grief in order to spare Teller from further pain. He sighed, feeling suddenly torn in two. He couldn't be both a Jump pilot and a har captain. And he had clung to being a Jump pilot for so long.

"Let's go below," Jahan said. "I'll make some lunch. Eric will be hungry when they get back."

Eric was hungry, sunburned, and ecstatic.

"Hau'oli, and I, we're—" Eric began, and then stopped, searching for a word to describe their relationship.

"Partners," Jahan suggested. "You've bonded, haven't you?"

Eric nodded, his face glowing with happiness and a touch of sunburn.

"Congratulations, Eric, what are your plans?" she asked gently.

Eric looked overwhelmed by his good fortune. "I—we— I don't know," he floundered.

"What you need first is a crew pod," Jahan suggested. "I know several good outfitters, some of them offer financing, if you don't have the money. A pod can cost quite a bit."

"No, no, money's not a problem. I have a good pension. It's just that this is so sudden."

"Did you have other plans?" Samad asked him.

"Of course not," Eric said. "It's just that it'll take some getting used to. And . . ." He hesitated. "I want a drink. I'm afraid—" He shook his head. "I'm a used-up old drunk. I'm worried that I'll let Hau'oli down."

"You've managed to go without a drink for nearly two days already," Samad pointed out. "And you know that Father Russell will be happy to help you when you need it."

Eric shrugged. He looked at Jahan. "Do you think I can do it? Do you think I could be a good partner to Hau'oli?"

"Hau'oli chose you, and harsels see what we can only guess at," Jahan reassured him. Her gaze flicked momentarily to Samad, acknowledging his words.

"But what if—"

"One day at a time, Eric," Samad said. "Take it one day at a time for now. Why don't you and Hau'oli cruise with us back to Nueva Ebiza, and see how it feels. You two need time together. And maybe Jahan can show you how to clean the parasites off of the inside of Hau'oli's hold."

"I'd be glad to let you demonstrate on me," Elawe volunteered.

"Oh you! I just cleaned your hold out," Jahan scolded
fondly.

"YES, BUT THERE'S THIS NEW SPOT UP FORWARD, ON
THE STARBOARD SIDE. IT *ITCHES*."

"All right Elawe, we'll see to it. But Hau'oli needs cleaning a lot more than you do."

Elawe grudgingly acknowledged this and subsided into
silence again.

During the rest of the trip, Eric quizzed Jahan closely on
what he would need to equip a crew pod.

Samad, worn out by Eric's persistent questioning, and
saddened by the ex-pilot's happy mood, slipped out of the
pod, and up onto the harsel's back. The two moons were
slivered crescents, looking like barely open eyes. The stars
hung bright and illusively close, as though he could almost
reach up and touch them. He looked up at the dark, familiar
immensity of the Thalassan night sky and sighed.

"YOU'RE LONELY, SAMAD," Elawe said. "WHY?"

Samad nodded. "I miss Teller," he said inwardly. "And
Abeha. It's not the same for humans. We don't remember
people the way that you do. When someone is dead, to us
they're gone forever."

"POOR SAMAD. I WISH I HAD KNOWN ABEHA AND
TELLER, SO THAT I COULD REMEMBER THEM FOR YOU. I
SAW ABEHA ONCE, BUT I WAS TOO YOUNG AND SHY TO
SPEAK TO HER. I'M AFRAID THAT I DO NOT HOLD THEIR
MEMORIES. BUT IF YOU SEEK AMONG THE HARSELS, YOU
WILL FIND ABEHA AND TELLER BOTH. I AM SURE OF IT."

"My heart isn't ready yet, Elawe," Samad told him. He
was too afraid that Abeha and Teller's memories might tie
him to Thalassa when he was on the brink of leaving.

"THEY WILL BE THERE WHEN YOU ARE READY," Elawe
reassured him.

"Thank you," Samad told the harsel.

He sat down, leaning against the harsel's mast, letting Elawe's presence rest in the back of his mind. At last he woke from a light doze. By now Eric and Jahan were almost certainly asleep.

"Good night, Elawe," Samad said, as he rose to go below to his bunk.

"GOOD NIGHT, SAMAD. MAY YOU SAIL AT PEACE THROUGH YOUR DREAMS."

When they landed at the harsel pier in Nueva Ebiza's harbor, Samad bid good-bye to Jahan and Eric. They were so preoccupied with their plans for outfitting Hau'oli's new crew pod that they hardly noticed his departure. Already the two har captains were well on their way to becoming a self-contained unit. He was sure they would somehow work out the little white lie he had told about Jahan's being married.

He wandered aimlessly through the gathering twilight, turning over the last few days' events in his mind. Teller would be proud of the way he had transformed Eric's life. He had done very well. So why did his victory make him feel so sad and empty?

He looked up, and there, glowing in the darkness was the sign for Father Russell's mission. Samad quirked one eyebrow and laughed. His subconscious must have been guiding his feet. He stepped up and rang the bell. Sister Valencia answered the door.

"Good evening, Sister, is Father Russell available?" Samad asked.

"She's celebrating Mass in the chapel. You're welcome to join us."

Samad followed Sister Valencia down a long hall and into a small, simply appointed chapel. Father Russell was saying Mass for a congregation of about two dozen people. Many of them had the weathered look of longtime alcoholics.

Father Russell seemed larger up at the altar. All her fine-boned, intense energy was focused on celebrating Mass. He watched as the congregation filed up for communion. As she finished with the last communicant, Father Russell glanced up and saw him. She nodded acknowledgment. When the Mass was finished, Sister Valencia came up to him.

"Father Russell said that she would be happy to see you in her office in a few minutes."

"Thank you, Sister. I'd appreciate a few minutes of her time."

The nun nodded. "Please come this way." Sister Valencia showed Samad into Father Russell's comfortably shabby office. She returned a few minutes later with a pot of coffee and plate of ginger cookies.

Father Russell came in about fifteen minutes later. "I'm terribly sorry to keep you waiting, but my parishioners—"

"It's all right," Samad assured her. "I understand. I appreciate you taking the time to talk to me, Father."

"How's Eric? Did you get him out on a harsel?" she asked, pouring coffee for herself and Samad.

"Yes, I did."

"Well? How did it go?"

"He's bonded with a wild har, and it looks like he may have acquired a lover in the process. He didn't drink a drop during the whole trip, either."

"Samad, that's wonderful! I'm so pleased. Congratulations on your good work." She held up her coffee cup in a toast of acknowledgment.

Samad lifted his cup in response, but his smile failed him.

"You don't seem nearly as pleased about it as I thought you'd be, Samad."

He nodded. "I'm glad for him, but . . ." Samad shrugged and looked away.

"What's the matter?"

"I think maybe I feel a little left behind," Samad told her. "My adopted mother was a har captain. Her harsel died when I was about twelve. I hadn't realized how much I missed Abeha until this trip. Now Eric's gotten what he wants and I—" He paused. "I guess I don't know what I want, Father."

Father Russell set down her coffee cup and regarded Samad intently. "If you could have anything in the world that you wanted, Samad, anything at all, no matter how crazy, what would it be?"

"I want Abeha and Teller alive again. But that's impossible, no matter what the harsels think."

"And what do the harsels think?" Father Russell asked.

"They believe that as long as they remember someone, that person isn't really dead. But I was there. I saw Abeha die. I *felt* her die."

"Maybe the harsels are right," Father Russell speculated. "Maybe Abeha's spirit lives on in some form. It doesn't seem impossible to me. If humans have souls, why not harsels?"

"I'd like that to be true, Father. But I'm afraid that I just can't believe it."

"How long has it been since your mother died?"

"About two and a half months now."

"You've just lost the only family you had, Samad. It's perfectly normal that you should feel a little lost right now. Did you ever think that you might be missing Abeha more because of your mother's death?"

"I suppose," he admitted. "But it isn't just grieving. I don't know what to do with the rest of my life. I thought I did, but now?" Samad shrugged. "The decision isn't as simple or straightforward as I'd like."

"Would it help to talk about it?"

Samad smiled and shook his head. "It's kind of a long, strange story."

Father Russell met Samad's eyes with her intent, birdlike

gaze. "I've got as long as it takes, Samad. And it wouldn't be the first strange story I've heard. I'll ask Sister Valencia for some fresh coffee."

"Well," Samad began, after Sister Valencia had brought the coffee and left. "It all started with the Pilot. . . ."

"And so here I am, trying to decide what to do. Should I stay here and fill Teller's shoes, or should I leave and become a Jump pilot? I can't decide."

Father Russell rubbed her temples with her fine-boned hands, then peered up at him with an aggrieved expression on her face. "Hang on a minute, Samad. I need to catch up here. Let me see if I understand you correctly. You claim that you were adopted by a woman who was the legendary figure known as the Pilot, and that she left you in charge of the planet?"

"Not exactly," Samad replied. "She left the planet in my care. I don't run things; I'm just supposed to help people and try to protect Thalassa. Except that I can't decide whether I really want to stay here and continue doing that or become a Jump pilot. Look, I know it sounds far-fetched, and I don't have a shred of proof with me, but just for the sake of argument could we assume that what I'm saying is true? I mean if harsels have souls, why couldn't the Pilot be real?"

Father Russell stared at him for a moment, blinking, then nodded. "All right, Samad."

"Thank you."

"So you're trying to decide whether to stay here and take care of the planet, or go off and become a Jump pilot."

"Yes, Father," Samad agreed. "That's what I have to decide."

"So basically this is a choice between responsibility and freedom," Father Russell stated. She looked a little relieved to have finally reached the familiar ground of a moral dilemma.

Samad nodded grudgingly.

"I can't decide for you, Samad. The burden of this choice is yours. But if you can do for even one other person what you appear to have done for Eric, then your duty is clear. You should stay here."

"But I've spent most of my life being Teller's dutiful son. I'm sick and tired of duty, Father."

"So am I sometimes, Samad. Some days, I want to kick over all the neatly stacked boxes of my life, put on a hot red dress, and go out and raise some serious hell. But I took a vow to help people, and to follow the teachings of God and the Catholic Church. And my duty to God keeps me here in this mission, ministering to drunks and the poor, even when I'm so bored and frustrated and lonely I could go nuts."

"What do you do then?"

"I pray, and I talk to other priests, or I lock myself in my office and scream and throw things."

"You do?" Samad said, glancing around the room for signs of damage.

"Not very often, and only as a last resort." She grinned. "Under this cassock, I'm a human being, too. Duty isn't easy or fun. And some days it feels utterly pointless. But occasionally, everything comes together, and you're blessed with an understanding of why you've made the sacrifices that duty and responsibility require. But first you have to choose to take up that duty, and then, every day, you need to reconsecrate yourself to it." She laid a gentle hand on Samad's arm. "Not everyone can do that, Samad. I would understand if you took the easier path. But it would break my heart to see you wind up like Eric."

"But Eric's better now, Father."

"Perhaps, but I've watched addicts recover, and it takes a

long time. Eric's made the choice to quit killing himself,
but every day he will have to wake up and make that choice
again. It's just like a religious vow in that sense. Not everyone can stick to it. In six months, a year, or maybe in ten
years, he'll be recovered. But now . . ." She shook her head.
"Now he'll need help to stay on the path he's chosen."

Samad looked at her. "Father, I can't help him with that.
It hurts too much, watching him and Hau'oli together. I
miss that life so much."

"I wasn't asking you to, Samad. That's my job and the
job of the others here at the mission. You set Eric's feet on a
new path, and that's enough. Now, it's time for you to decide what you want to do with your life. But Samad, you've
seen Eric and the others. You know what will happen to you
when your Talent goes."

"Yes, Father. I know. But I *want* to go so much!"

"I've given you my advice, Samad. But it's your life. Your
soul. You must choose your own path."

He thanked her and got up to go. Father Russell laid her
hand on his arm again. "Samad, promise me one thing, will
you? Come and tell me what your choice is when you've
made it."

Samad hesitated for a moment, then met her clear, direct
gaze. "All right, Father, I will."

So Samad went wandering. He caught a ride on a fishing
boat to the Islas di Fascino and wandered the grassy hills of
the islands, pondering his dilemma. Three months passed,
and he was no closer to a decision than ever, and the weather
was turning colder. He had reached the Isla di Sogno, the
northernmost of the Islas di Fascino. It was inhabited by a
handful of shepherds and a great many sheep. A gale blew
up as he was crossing the high pass between Mount Pensiero
and Mount Memoria. He trudged on through the biting

wind and the horizontal sleet, hoping that the storm would abate as he descended. He was chilled through and the setting sun was only a bright spot on the murky horizon, when a flicker of light drew his eye. The light vanished after a moment or two, but Samad kept heading toward the hill where he'd seen the light, stumbling in the gathering dusk. Then he heard the baaing of sheep. As he drew closer, he could make out a low mound, with smoke rising from a rough stone chimney. It was a shepherd's hut dug into the side of the hill. The flicker of light must have been firelight shining out of the hut's briefly open door. The sheep were penned for the night in a stone-fenced corral in the shelter of a long, knife-sharp ridge of stone.

He staggered through the door, clumsy and stupid with cold, and promptly fell on the rough stone steps that led up to the raised floor of packed dirt. The shepherd's shaggy dog barked wildly at Samad. The surprised herder shouted at his dog to be quiet as he helped Samad up the steps and over to the fire.

The shepherd settled Samad near the fire and pushed a cup of hot coffee into Samad's trembling hands.

"This is dangerous country to be walking alone in at this time of year," the shepherd chided. "You're lucky you found me. There's no other shelter for miles." Samad nodded and sipped at the coffee. It was almost too hot to drink, but the warmth was intensely welcome.

Dinner was warm, salty sheep's cheese, garlic wrapped in leaves and roasted in the ashes, olives, and coarse, sour bread, augmented by two tins of oily braefish and a skin of wine from Samad's pack.

Andros, the shepherd, had grinned happily at the wine, and after the food was gone, they sat in front of the fire passing the wineskin between them.

"So," Andros said, "What brings you tramping through

this godforsaken part of the world at this wretched time of the year?"

Samad took another swig of the wine, wiped his mouth, and belched, happy to be warm and alive. He could feel the wine working in him. He had nearly died out there tonight. "I can't make up my mind," he said. "So I decided to go wandering and see if that helped. So far, it hasn't." Samad sighed and ran his fingers through his hair. He was so tired of wrestling with his choice.

"Couldn't you make up your mind someplace warmer?" the shepherd asked.

"This was where I wound up," Samad confessed. "I don't know why I kept heading north, but I did, and here I am."

"So what is it that troubles you so?" Andros inquired.

"I'm at a crossroads in my life, and I can't decide which road to take. I've been thinking it over for months now, and I'm no closer to a decision. I've never felt this stuck between two choices before."

The shepherd drank from the wineskin and then fumbled in the pocket of his worn and sweat-soiled vest. He brought out an ancient copper coin and held it up to the firelight. The Greek writing was barely discernable on its face.

"This came with my ancestors when they left Earth," Andros told him. "It belonged to my father, and his father before him, and on back to before the beginning of Thalassa. Whenever my father was troubled by a hard choice, he would flip this coin." He pressed the coin into Samad's hand. "Let the coin decide for you," he urged.

"But what if I don't like what the coin chooses?" Samad asked. He'd struggled so long with this decision that the idea sounded tempting.

"My father always claimed that he knew when the coin had made the wrong choice," the shepherd told him. "You don't have to abide by the coin's choice. But if you let the coin choose, at least you'll no longer be stuck at the crossroads."

Samad turned the coin in his hand, examining its worn surface. At least he'd no longer be stuck. It seemed so easy. He took a long pull from the wineskin and then tossed the coin in the air. "Heads I go, tails I stay!" he called as the coin flipped over and over in the air. He felt suddenly light and heady now that the decision was out of his control.

The coin landed. Andros and Samad leaned forward to look at it. The worn profile of Athena's head gazed serenely toward the fire. It was heads. He was going to the stars. He felt a great wash of relief at having the decision over and done with. It was followed by a deep and profound sadness at leaving Thalassa. But at least he had made his choice. Freedom had won out over responsibility.

Samad thanked Andros and handed his father's coin back to him. He was leaving Thalassa. Memories flooded over him: blue water, rock-girt green islands, the harsels' sails in the distance, friends, lovers, Teller, and Abeha. He would be leaving it all behind him. And yet, remembering, he realized that he wasn't ready to leave. He needed to say good-bye. He would spend one last sweet, long season on Thalassa, visiting all the places he had loved as a child. And then, having made a proper farewell to the world that gave him birth, he would head for the stars.

Once again, Samad stood at the door to the mission. Once again, he rang the bell. This time Father Russell answered the door herself. Her face broke into a wide, expansive grin, with an unclerical hint of mischief in it.

"Samad! What a pleasure to see you! Please, come on in."

"Where's Sister Valencia?" Samad asked.

"Sister Reynolds is Brother Reynolds now. He has been

accepted as a postulant monk at the Sergeian Order. It's an order of gay and lesbian nuns and monks on the frontier world of Espíritu Santo." Her grin widened. "The universe is a strange and wonderful place. I had no idea there was such an order. He's very happy there, but I do miss those ginger cookies he used to bake.

"So, how are you, Samad?" she asked when they were settled in her office. "You look wonderful."

"I've been traveling around Thalassa, Father. It was my farewell trip. I've come to say good-bye. I'm leaving in two days' time for the Pilots Academy."

Father Russell looked down for a moment and then back up at him. Her eyes were very sad. "I'm sorry to hear that, Samad. We will miss you. Have you seen Eric since you got in?"

"No, Father, I haven't."

"You should go and say good-bye to him and Jahan. He'd like that. They're living down near the harbor these days."

"They're still together?"

Father Russell nodded. "They're getting married next spring. They were hoping to invite you to the wedding."

"That's wonderful news, Father," Samad said. "I'm sorry that I can't be here for their wedding. But I'd like to visit them before I go."

"I know they'd appreciate the chance to thank you for all you've done for them," Father Russell told him. "They're in port right now. They're berthed in the Old Harbor." She scribbled their address on a piece of paper. Then the priest looked at him, her intense gaze seeming to see into the deepest recesses of his heart. "Samad, are you absolutely sure that you want to become a Jump pilot?" she asked.

"It's going to be hard to leave Thalassa, Father," Samad admitted, "but this is a dream that I've had for a long time."

"Well then, may God keep you on your journey, and bring you back safe to your friends here on Thalassa when your travels are ended. *Vaya con Dios,* Samad," Father Russell said, making the sign of the cross over him. Her face was solemn and intent as she blessed him in farewell.

"*Gracias para vuestro benedicion, Padre.*"

Father Russell showed him to the door. "Samad, if there's ever anything that I can do to help you, please let me know."

"Thank you, Father, I will."

"Good luck, Samad."

It took Samad a moment to recognize Eric. His formerly pasty skin was deeply tanned, and there was a settled, content look in his eyes. He was busy repairing an oxygen extractor.

"Hello, Eric."

Eric's face lit up when he saw Samad. He set aside the extractor he was repairing. "Samad! It's you! We've been hoping you'd turn up! How are you?"

"I'm doing well," he said. "And you?"

Eric spread his arms. "Wonderful! Jahan and I are getting married next spring. I'd like you to be our best man," he said. His tanned face flushed with embarrassment and pleasure. "We tried to reach you, but Father Russell didn't know where you were."

"I'm sorry, Eric," Samad said. "I've been traveling."

"No, no, Samad, it's all right. It's just that so much has happened over the last eight months! Father Russell, Jahan, and I have introduced three other ex-pilots to the harsels."

"And what happened?"

"Two of them have healed themselves and are becoming har captains. The other—" Eric's face sagged back into the lines that Samad remembered from before, and he shook his head sadly. "She could hear the harsels, but they couldn't reach her. She was too far gone." There was deep pain in his eyes as he looked up at Samad. "But we've saved two, and we're hoping to save more." His eyes looked less haunted as he said this.

"You'll bankrupt the Pilots Union," Samad joked.

"Damn," Eric said with an edged grin. "I'd just hate that." Eric sobered again. "Seriously, Samad, I've been wanting to thank you for giving me my life back."

Samad shrugged. "You've done all the hard work. I just gave you the nudge that got you started."

"But without that nudge, Samad—" Eric shook his head again. "Without you, I'd be dead, or worse, still stuck in that living hell. Please, say you'll be my best man. Jahan and I, we owe it all to you."

"Eric, I—" Samad began. "I'd be honored. But I can't. I'm on my way up and out, to start my pilot training. The shuttle leaves the day after tomorrow."

Eric's face grew serious and very sad. For a moment, Samad saw the shadow of the man he had first met, the lost Eric, whom he had guided into a new life as a har captain. "Oh, Samad, no," he pleaded. "Don't do it. Please. You don't know what it's like, to lose everything like that. I'm better now, but the longing never quite goes away. There are still some very dark nights, even with Jahan, Hau'oli, and Elawe."

Samad took a breath. "I understand, Eric, but I've held onto this dream for so long. It's something I need to do."

"I'm sorry if that's so, Samad. There's so much you can do here. But promise me one thing." Eric's face was intent. "Promise me that when your Talent burns out, you make your way from wherever you wind up back to Thalassa, and let us help you heal. I owe you too much to let that debt go unpaid."

Samad remembered Eric's face, just after he had bonded

with Hau'oli, lit from within with joy. "I will come back, Eric. I promise. I will return."

Eric clasped Samad's hands in his work-roughened ones. "Thank you Samad. We'll be waiting for you."

"Good-bye, Eric, and thank you."

"Farewell, Samad. We will carry your memories in our hearts," Eric said, but his face looked like he was leaving the new grave of a dear friend.

Samad strode back up the long, floating dock. It seemed longer walking away than it had when he had come. Perhaps it was the ebbing tide lowering the floating dock. But more likely it was his heavy heart.

Samad spent the next day visiting all the places he loved in Nueva Ebiza, old inns where he and Teller had stayed, parks where they'd told stories, and stopped just outside the old Grande Teatro, closed now for renovations, remembering how he had performed Roxana and Paoli, remembering José. How different life had been then. It seemed so much simpler now, looking back. He raised a pint of cider in a couple of his favorite *omophilos* bars, remembering José. How he had longed for his student, and how deeply ashamed he had been. If he had never gone to Bindara, what would he be like now?

Then Samad spent an hour in the Museum of the Storytellers' Guild, reviewing the public history of Thalassa, and remembering Thalassa's secret history, locked away in Teller's archives. He smiled, holding his invisible memories of Teller to himself and trying not to feel the pain of leaving. He would carry Thalassa in his heart. No matter where in the Galaxy he went, these ties of love and longing would go with him.

He had one last quiet dinner alone with his memories at Carlucci's, Teller's favorite restaurant. The maître d' and the waiters greeted him by name. He was seated at a small table in a private corner near the front window, where he could see both the street outside and the restaurant in a single, sweeping glance. The waiters retreated, giving him his privacy, but his wineglass was never empty, and his food came quietly and swiftly, served with warm, welcoming smiles. It was an odd, professional kind of love, born of many years of meals that they had served him and Teller. Sitting there, he remembered all the times they had eaten here over the years, for celebrations, birthdays, or just because Teller needed a familiar place. He lifted his glass of ruby red wine in a silent toast to Teller.

God, I miss you so much, Teller! he thought to himself. *I wish I could be two people. One to stay here, and one to go off to the stars.* But neither self would be happy with their fate, he realized with a wry smile. Each of his separate selves would have wanted the life of the other.

Ser Carlucci, the great-grandson of the original owner, came by as he was finishing up his dessert.

"Ser Bernardia, your dinner is on us tonight," he told Samad. "It's our way of thanking Teller for the handsome bequest that she left us. Her bequest has enabled us to send my son and my daughter to the finest cooking school in the Central Worlds."

Samad smiled, deeply touched. "Thank you very much for this exquisite meal, Ser Carlucci. And good luck to your children. They've had such excellent training from their parents that they may be able to teach their teachers a thing or two. You've certainly taught me to appreciate fine food. Every other restaurant I visit has to measure up to your standards. But most do not."

"Thank you, Ser Bernardia," Carlucci said with a proud smile. "It's been a great pleasure to have you come here over the years. We hope we'll continue to see you often."

Samad opened his mouth to tell Carlucci that he was leaving Thalassa, but he couldn't quite bring himself to say the words aloud here in this beloved restaurant. No, it would be better to just vanish, and let this tie wane with the passing years. Besides, someday he would return. Perhaps in a few years, in the full glory of his piloting career, or perhaps not until his Talent was gone. But tonight, he wanted to leave his tie to this place intact, to pretend that he could come back and everything would be the same as it had ever been.

Samad walked back alone through the rain-washed streets and climbed the worn steps to his room. He packed everything but the clothes he would be wearing the next day, and went to bed.

He woke from an incredibly vivid dream. In the dream, Abeha was gliding noiselessly away from him. Samad ran as fast as he could along the breakwater, calling to Abeha, pleading with her to come back. But the huge harsel continued to sail away across the mirror-still water, into the gray mist. He felt as though his soul was being torn from his body, and he was helpless to stop it.

Samad lay there, blinking up at the ceiling as the dream faded. Then he remembered. He was leaving Thalassa today. His dream lingered in his mind as he got up and showered, shaved, and dressed. Then he packed a few remaining items into his satchel and checked out of his room. The dream haunted him as he ate a quick, cold breakfast in the inn's parlor, looking out at the fine drizzle falling outside. The dream still clung to him as the bus to the spaceport pulled up to the curb.

He found a seat among all the other early-morning travelers headed for the port. He was leaving Thalassa. The bus's windshield wipers seemed to echo his thoughts, whispering, "Leaving, leaving, leaving," with each squeaky swipe of their blades. He felt as desolate as the chilly rain. In the back of his mind, Abeha continued to sail farther and farther away.

Then they were at the spaceport. Samad pulled out his ticket and joined the line at the check-in desk. Somewhere in the back of his mind Abeha had paused, waiting for him. It was only a leftover shred of dream, but it felt oddly real. He tried to push the image away. He was going to be a Jump pilot, like his mother, like his father, like Teller. It was his destiny to follow where they had gone. An image of Teller, drugged and helpless with grief after Abeha's death, came to him. He saw his birth mother, dead and cold in her bed. And he remembered Eric Kellen, passed out amid his own filth. *No!* he thought. *Not like that! I won't be like that! I want my own life!*

"Ser! Ser! It's your turn!" Samad came back to himself with a start. It was his turn to step up to the check-in desk.

Samad set the ticket in its brightly colored folder on the desk. The world seemed to be moving in slow motion. There was a roaring in his ears.

The desk clerk looked up at him. "Yes, ser. How may I help you?"

"I—I, uh . . ." Samad cleared his throat. "I want to turn this ticket in. I'm not going."

Suddenly the roaring went away, and the world resumed its normal pace. The old shepherd had been right. If he didn't like the choice the coin gave him, he could always change his mind. He could be just as free here on Thalassa as he could be in space.

"But this is a Pilots Union ticket, ser," the blond, off-world woman behind the desk said, studying the folder. "We can't pay you anything for it. The money goes back to the Union."

"I know," Samad said. "I don't want any money. I just want to tell you that I'm not going." In his mind's eye, Samad saw Abeha turn and glide back toward him as the mist dissolved into bright morning sunlight, and a flight of greenthrushes spiraled into the heavens with wild, piping cries of joy.

He stepped away from the desk.

"Ser! Wait! You need to fill out this form!" the desk clerk called.

He ignored her and walked out of the spaceport into the soft drizzle falling from the skies of Thalassa. He reached the sidewalk and hailed a taxi.

"Where to, ser?" the driver asked.

"Our Lady of Perpetual Devotion Mission," Samad said. "It's not far."

CHAPTER 15

"AND SO THE PILOT CLIMBED ABOARD HER harsel and sailed away. No one knows where she went after that. The fate of the Pilot remains a mystery," Samad concluded. As always, when he told of the Pilot's disappearance, he felt a twinge of guilt. But it was not yet time to reveal Teller's secret.

The audience applauded. One by one, they paused to put a button, a coin, or some other small gift into his bowl. Samad thanked his listeners and chatted with those who had questions. When the last listener had filed away, a har captain approached him, a hesitant expression on his weathered face.

"Are you Teller Samad?"

"Yes I am," Samad acknowledged.

"My name is Spiros Anatolios. There's a harsel who wants to see you."

"What does he want?" Samad asked."

"I don't know. They only ask for you to come as soon as you can."

"Is it an emergency? I'll need a few minutes to pack my bag."

The har captain shook his head. "Wouldn't do any good with the tide like it is. Could you come to the har dock half an hour before the tide turns tomorrow morning?"

"I'll be there," Samad assured him. "Should I bring anything? A harsel med kit?"

The har captain shook his head. "Just yourself."

Samad lay awake long into the night, puzzling and worrying over the fragment of information Spiros had given him. What could this harsel want from him? Was there some kind of trouble? He had heard no rumors of any problems. He tossed and turned for a while before falling into an uneasy slumber filled with dream-memories of Abeha and Teller.

Despite his sleepless night, Samad woke well before sunrise. He was waiting on the dock with a satchel of provisions long before the appointed time. Spiros and his harsel glided smoothly up to the pier about an hour before they were due to meet. The har captain accepted Samad's gift of provisions with a pleased grunt of thanks. He stowed Samad's gift, invited him on board, and then strode up the dock carrying two large empty shopping baskets.

Spiros's harsel, Kupohu, greeted Samad with quiet respect.

"Why have I been sent for?" Samad inwardly asked the harsel.

"YOU WILL SEE," Kupohu replied. The harsel radiated excitement and anticipation, but there was a thread of concern underneath his eagerness.

"Very well then, go ahead and be mysterious," Samad told him.

The harsel gonged a slow, deep chime of laughter. A little while later, Spiros returned, his baskets laden with supplies. Kupohu sculled away from the dock, set his sail to the wind, and they were on their way.

They sailed steadily westward for three days. The next morning, Samad saw Saint Sophia's Rocks on the horizon. The Rocks rose from the midst of an upwelling of nutrient-rich seawater that supported a rich bloom of plankton. The ocean around the rocks was alive with millions of fish. Seabirds nested on the rocks, and the air was full of birds, wheeling and diving. Every so often, Samad could see a patch of water churned into tiny wavelets that flashed silver as bigger fish fed on the enormous schools of braefish. Huge fleets of harsels were feeding in the distance.

As they neared the feeding grounds, Kupohu began calling to the other harsels. At last there was a faint reply. The haunting familiarity of that distant harsel's presence brought Samad to his feet. He reached out with his mind, searching, as Kupohu veered toward a fleet of harsels.

"SAMAD? IS THAT YOU, SAMAD?"

"Abeha?" Samad was simultaneously hopeful and terrified. "No! It can't be! You're dead!"

There was a brief chime of laughter from the surrounding harsels. Samad realized that he was the center of a still pool of focused awareness. In that stillness, a young harsel, not quite ten meters long, sailed out of the group. He looked exactly like a miniature version of Abeha. He still bore the fading markings of a juvenile.

"MY NAME IS AWILI," the small har told Samad. "ABEHA WAS MY MOTHER. I CARRY HER VOICE, HER MEMORIES."

"But, how—" Samad began.

"ALL HARSELS CARRY SOME OF THEIR MOTHER'S MEMORIES, ENOUGH TO SPEAK AND SING. SOME CARRY MORE, STORIES, FRAGMENTS OF THE PAST. BUT IN EACH GENERATION, THERE ARE A FEW HARSELS THAT CARRY ALL THEIR MOTHER'S MEMORIES. WE ARE THE KAHIKO, THOSE WHO REMEMBER."

"But why didn't Abeha or Teller tell me about the Kahiko?" Samad asked.

"BECAUSE KAHIKO ARE EXTREMELY RARE. WE EMERGE VERY LATE FROM OUR MOTHERS, AND ARE OFTEN LOST. I WAS LUCKY TO LIVE. ABEHA DIDN'T WANT YOU TO GET YOUR HOPES UP AND THEN BE DISAPPOINTED. AND TELLER ONLY WANTED ABEHA. SHE WASN'T WILLING TO ACCEPT A KAHIKO."

"But why are you coming to me?"

"ABEHA STILL CARRIES YOU IN HER HEART. SHE LOVES YOU VERY MUCH. AND YOU LOVED HER SO INTENSELY IN RETURN. THERE WAS SUCH FIRE IN YOUR HEART. I CAME TO SEE IF IT WAS STILL THERE." Awili hesitated, his presence roiling with dissonant fear and plaintive longing. "I WANT TO BE YOUR PARTNER, IF YOU WILL HAVE ME," the harsel told him.

Samad was stunned. He had thought about seeking a harsel to partner, but just hadn't felt ready. Abeha still dominated his thoughts, and he had feared that his longing for Abeha would sour another partnership. Now, here was Awili, looking and sounding so much like Abeha. He claimed to remember everything that Abeha remembered. It was tempting, very tempting.

"I need to know you better, before I can decide," Samad replied. "May I come aboard?"

Awili glided alongside Kupohu. "BE WELCOME, SAMAD," he said formally. Samad could feel the young harsel's excitement, and he felt his own heart beating faster in response.

"Thank you, Awili," he said, stepping onto the harsel's back. Awili drew his sail in, catching the stiff breeze and bearing away from the crowd of watching harsels. He was much faster than Abeha, and more maneuverable.

"ABEHA WAS THIS FAST AND NIMBLE WHEN SHE WAS MY

AGE," the young harsel explained. "AND I REMEMBER EVERY-
THING ABEHA KNEW ABOUT SAILING."

When the sails of the har fleet had dwindled to white
flecks on the horizon, Awili turned into the wind and folded
his sail. He arched out of the water, opening his ballast
chamber. Samad could feel the small harsel bobbing on the
waves. There was an enormous silence, broken only by the
hush of the wind and the occasional splash as a fish jumped.

"PLEASE BE WELCOME IN MY HOLD," Awili invited shyly.
"YOU WISHED TO KNOW ME BETTER."

Samad nodded and swung down into the harsel's hold.
The familiar smell of the harsel surrounded him, and he
heard the muffled beating of the harsel's hearts. Awili was
still very young. Even a small crew pod would be a tight fit.

"ONLY AT FIRST," Awili reassured him. "I'M GROWING AS
FAST AS I CAN. IN A LITTLE WHILE, ANOTHER YEAR OR
TWO—"

"I know," Samad soothed, touched by the har's eagerness
to please. "It's all right, Awili, it doesn't matter."

He splashed through the ankle-deep water, running his
hands along the smooth, damp wall of Awili's hold, auto-
matically checking the harsel's condition as Teller had
taught him. There were some weeds and barnacles, but only
a few parasites. Overall the young har's hold was very clean.
Then Samad reached the forward wall. The three-beat
rhythm of Awili's hearts was much louder here. He could
feel the young harsel's anxiety.

He leaned against the forward end of Awili's hold. The
har's slick, resilient flesh was cool under his touch. Samad
closed his eyes and opened his mind.

"I'm here," Samad said inwardly. Then, guessing at the
source of the harsel's fear, he said. "But if we partner, Awili,
I will be partnering with you, not your memories."

"THANK YOU," Awili said with a gentle chord of relief.

Then Samad felt Awili's presence roll over him like a wave. He yielded to it, letting Awili wash over and through him like clean, cold saltwater. Though Awili sounded much like his mother, their presences felt very different. Underneath the young harsel's shyness there was a joy and a sense of playfulness. Even after he had come to love Abeha, Samad had always been a bit awed by the huge har's majestic presence. He realized now how that awe had distanced him from Abeha. But he felt no such distance from Awili. He liked the young harsel very much.

"YOU FEEL DIFFERENT FROM ABEHA'S MEMORIES OF YOU. THERE'S MORE CONTROL. YOU COULD GET SO ANGRY, SO QUICKLY. IT FRIGHTENED ME," the harsel confessed.

"I have grown."

"YES HE HAS," a familiar voice said from within Awili.

"Abeha! Is that really you?"

"AWILI CARRIES ME INSIDE HIM," Abeha explained. "I LIVE IN HIS MEMORIES."

"But you sound alive! How can that be?"

Abeha laughed. "WHO ARE WE, IF NOT OUR MEMORIES? BUT THERE IS SOMEONE ELSE WHO WISHES TO SPEAK TO YOU."

"Hello, mijo. I have missed you."

There was a long moment of pure emotion, too intense for speech or even thought. Then he hesitated; this was not the Teller he remembered. This Teller felt younger and much more wounded than he expected.

"I'm only what Abeha remembers of me. I remember nothing after her death."

Samad felt sorrow cut through him like a knife. This Teller had never fought her way through suicidal grief. Or decided to keep on living. This Teller had never trusted him with the fact that she was the Pilot. Or shown him her secret archives. She had never heard Samad call her Mother, or helped him grow from apprentice to master. She had never seen him perform Roxana and Paoli, or any of his other masterworks. She had never known or accepted the fact that he loved men.

But this Teller had also missed the failure of her rejuve. She had not been hurt by his desire to become a Jump pilot. She had missed the slow, painful decline of the last decade of her life. She had not had to endure her memory loss or the slow choking of the pneumonia that finally took her. Perhaps she had been more fortunate than the real Teller had been.

"No, Samad," Teller replied with a deep sadness. "*I would have lived through so much more than those miseries if I could have seen you grow into the fine man you've become. But it isn't all bad. You can experience my memories directly. You could see Thalassa as it was before colonization. Would you like that?*"

"Yes, I would," Samad said.

"*Here you are!*"

And suddenly he was in the midst of Teller's memories. Her childhood and her piloting career were a blurry montage of emotions. But Teller's memories became suddenly sharper when a huge creature lifted her out of the depths where she was drowning, back into the air. Samad felt Teller's terror and her anguish at not being able to die. He felt the deep wound that the loss of her Talent had left in her spirit. Then he shared her dawning wonder at the harsel. He experienced her early years of discovery, seeing a new world for the first time. He shared her joy and fear at the arrival of the human colonists, then watched as she joined them.

Centuries passed, months and years both bright and dark. He saw Thalassa grow and change through her eyes. There were the years of struggle, as the colony gained its first foothold, and Teller's delight in performing her anonymous good deeds. Then her years with her husband Stephano, watching their children grow and start families of their own.

Then came the shattering loss of her family and the solitary years of grieving that followed. Samad shared her reunion with Barbara and her grandchildren and watched as she and her daughter founded the Guild. The memories scrolled past, joys and sorrows, change and stability.

Then Teller unfolded her memories of him, first as a wary, painfully scrawny runaway, then as the determined child who clung to her like a burr, refusing to accept any other parents. How he had blossomed when Teller finally accepted him. He experienced her yearning to do well as a parent. He felt her shame when she leaned on him for support and the times she spent trying to drown her misery in alcohol. Remembering, Samad felt Teller's pain, and his own as well.

But he also felt how very much Teller loved him. And all the memories associated with that. There was the pleasure of seeing his face light up when he learned something new, and her pride in his skill. And her gratitude for the quiet way he had of helping her during her rough times. But many of Teller's most powerful memories were very simple. Watching him read, his head bent over a book. And the sight of him sleeping. He had looked so young and vulnerable then. It was not at all how he remembered himself.

"Of course not. This is how I remember you. But now it's Abeha's turn. I will be here whenever you need me, Samad."

And then Teller faded away, and he was reliving Abeha's memories. He shared Abeha's memories of being a harling, and then an adult. He experienced her training as a mindsinger. Then he felt the shock of the shuttle landing, and shared her wonder at encountering Teller's alien mind. He saw Teller's wondrous awareness begin to dim as she drowned. Abeha's immense curiosity would not let Teller extinguish herself. The harsel used every shred of her skills as a mindsinger to rebuild Teller's will to live, in order to preserve this alien creature's strange insights.

Abeha's curiosity about Teller quickly flowered into a partnership of profound depth and intensity. It was a partnership that grew and changed over the centuries, each learning from the other.

But as she grew older, Abeha's desire to become a mother became very strong. She had held back on her desire out of love for Teller, but soon she would have to act. It was then that Samad came into their lives. At first, Abeha only wanted Samad because she thought that it might help Teller accept Abeha's need to become female, but as time passed, Abeha came to love Samad deeply. It pained the harsel deeply to cause Samad pain, but she could not wait any longer to pass along her memories.

Samad shared Abeha's mating, and felt her pride at the huge clutch of harlings growing inside her. He felt Abeha's growing weakness as her body destroyed itself in order to feed her increasingly hungry brood. The harsel's memories of her last days were indistinct, seen through a haze of pain and mindsong. Samad felt her final agony from a merciful distance. Then her memories came to an end, and there was only silence.

But out of that silence, a bright thread of melody wound through Abeha's body, aware, but unsentient. It fought its way through Abeha's dying brain, eating as it went, driven by its appetite and its need to escape. It became trapped inside the dome of its mother's skull, but it continued to eat and tunnel through its mother's flesh, until finally it emerged into the clean darkness of the ocean, its belly distended painfully from all it had eaten. Then it rested, drifting silent and unnoticed in the darkness of the deep. At least it sensed a pull, a calling. It began to swim upward toward the light that filtered dimly from above. The journey was long, and it had to dodge the dark shadows of predators many times. At last the tired harling reached the surface and the safe shelter of an adult's hold.

Samad felt the harling grow from awareness into consciousness. With consciousness came memories. At first
they were merely memories of surviving the hazards that
every harling had to face. Then Awili remembered mind-
speech, and remembering, began to speak to the harsels
around him. After that, Abeha's memories began to unfold
more and more rapidly.

When the multitude of memories of his mother, Teller, and
Samad grew too overwhelming for the harling to bear, the
mindsingers taught him to separate himself from the vivid,
powerful memories that dwelt inside him. Driven by Abeha's
memories, Awili yearned to meet Teller and Samad. He joined
the fleet that sang farewell to Teller. He reached out to Teller,
and was shocked at how different she was from the Teller who
dwelt in his memory. And the real Teller heard him and
thought he was Abeha. Awili still cringed from that memory.

"It's all right," Samad told him. "She was upset at first,
but once she was home, and had a good night's sleep, she
seemed happy to have heard Abeha's voice once more."

"THANK YOU," Awili told him. "WHEN SHE DIED I—"

And Samad was plunged back into Awili's memories. He
saw how Awili grieved with Abeha, after Teller died. Then
word came that Samad was planning on leaving Thalassa,
and Awili had grown frantic with worry. It was then that
Awili realized that he wanted to be Samad's partner.

A surge of guilt distanced Samad from the flow of Awili's
memories.

"If I had known you were waiting for me—" Samad began.

"NO. I DID NOT WANT TO TIE YOU HERE AGAINST YOUR
WILL," Awili told him. "AND THEN, AFTER YOU DECIDED
TO STAY, I WAS STILL TOO YOUNG. AND I WAS AFRAID THAT
IT WAS ABEHA YOU WANTED, NOT ME." Awili hesitated.
"SO, DO YOU WANT TO BE MY PARTNER?" the young har
asked in a small, frightened voice.

Samad felt a rush of love and tenderness at the young har's question. Awili felt so young and alone. He was reminded of his own youth, before Teller and Abeha. And Samad could feel how well the two of them fit together. Awili was the piece his life was missing.

"If you still want me," Samad replied.

The harsel's joyful exultation rang through Samad's mind like a thousand pealing bells. Samad's heart soared. Together they plunged into a giddy gyre of excitement.

Awili and he were partners now, harsel and captain. The legacy of Teller and Abeha had been passed to the two of them to carry.

"Come on, let's get back. Spiros must be getting worried," Samad said. "We'll need to go to Nueva Ebiza and get a crew pod."

Samad tried to restrain his anxiety as the fitting crew lowered Awili's new crew pod into his hold for the first time.

"Easy now. Gently," he called. "Keep your hold open wide, Awili."

"I'M ALL RIGHT, SAMAD," Awili reassured him. "ABEHA SAYS THEY'RE DOING FINE."

"I know, I know," Samad told him, "But I can't help worrying. I'd never forgive myself if you were hurt."

"This is the best fitting crew in Nueva Ebiza," Jahan reminded him. "They know what they're doing."

Eric smiled. "I was just as worried when they fitted Hau'oli's pod."

"Well, I'm praying as fast as I can," Father Russell remarked. "So I think we've got the situation covered from every possible angle."

"The pod's in place now," the foreman announced to the visible relief of everyone assembled on the dock. "We just have to make a few more adjustments. Ser Bernardia, could you ask Awili how the pod feels?"

"HEAVY, BUT COMFORTABLE," Awili told him. "ABEHA SAYS THE FIT IS GOOD, BUT IT'S A LITTLE TO THE LEFT AND ASTERN OF THE BEST BALANCE POINT."

Samad relayed these instructions to the fitting crew. He peered into Awili's hold anxiously as the crew made the last few adjustments.

"THERE!" Awili announced. He waited until the crew was out, and then closed his walls around the pod. Then he sculled away from the dock, sailing back and forth for a few minutes, testing the fit.

"IT FEELS MUCH BETTER NOW," Awili said when he returned to the dock. "ABEHA SAYS THAT IT'S AN EXCELLENT FIT."

Samad relayed this information to the fitting crew.

"Well then, we're done," the foreman said, as his crew began gathering up their tools. "Congratulations, Captain Bernardia. All you need is some gear and provisions, and then you'll be ready to sail."

"Everything I need is right here," Samad said, nodding at several large hampers full of food, clothing, and gear. "It'll only take a few minutes to load it all."

"Then let's get started," Eric said. "I know how eager you and Awili must be to get under way."

Father Russell and Eric handed down the hampers while Jahan and Samad found places to stow everything.

"There you go, Samad," Jahan said, when they had finished stowing the hampers of gear. "You're all ready to go! Congratulations," she added, giving him a quick hug. "I'm so happy for you and Awili!"

"Good luck, Samad!" Eric said, shaking his hand.

"Here," Father Russell said, handing him a hand-carved

plastic container. "Some ginger cookies. Brother Valencia finally took pity on me and sent the recipe."

Then the priest drew herself up, just as Teller used to do before beginning a story. "With your permission, Samad, I'd like to bless you and Awili."

Samad nodded. "That would be very kind, Father Russell."

"May God protect this harsel and all those who sail with him," she intoned, making the sign of the cross and sprinkling a bit of holy water over Awili's back. "Amen!"

Samad smiled and thanked Father Russell for the blessing, and the others for their help. After another round of fond good-byes, Samad's friends climbed onto the dock.

"All right, Awili, we're ready to go," Samad said inwardly.

The harsel glided away from the dock, caught the wind, and headed out of the harbor. Samad waved at his friends until the dock was lost to view. Away from the land, the breeze was stronger now, blowing little whitecaps onto the waves. It was a perfect day for sailing.

"Where are we going?" Awili asked.

"Melilla's a good place for beginnings, and we can be there by tomorrow morning. I think I'll find a spot in the market, and tell the Pilot's Cycle. I've got a couple of new stories to add to it."

"They'd better be good ones," Teller cautioned tartly.

Abeha gonged amusement at her remark. *"OF COURSE THEY'LL BE GOOD, TELLER! THIS IS SAMAD!"* she chided gently, and then the two of them faded back into the depths of Awili's memory.

Awili tightened his sail until he was racing through the whitecaps, throwing up a fine sheet of spray.

"MELILLA IT IS!" he sang, and the two of them raced through the choppy water, bound for Melilla with a cargo of memories.